'Skelton writes grittily authentic crime novels'
The Times

'Atmospheric . . . with an ironic sense of humour'
Sunday Times

'*A Rattle of Bones* is an intriguing Highland mystery
peopled with quirky characters and peppered with wit'
Times Crime Club Pick of the Week

'A page-turning novel in a fine series'
Scotland on Sunday

'An intricately plotted thriller . . . lyrical and thoughtful'
The Library Journal (US)

'Exquisite language, credible characters
and unrelenting suspense'
Publishers Weekly (US)

'Dark humour, a fast pace and gritty plot'
LoveReading

'Highland history and dark humour . . . drips with tension'
Press and Journal

'Skelton's talent is casting his descriptive eyes on the familiar
and rendering truthful characters with a believable backstory'
The Scotsman

A note on the author

Douglas Skelton was born in Glasgow. He has been a bank clerk, tax officer, taxi driver (for two days), wine waiter (for two hours), journalist and investigator. He has written several true crime and Scottish criminal history books but now concentrates on fiction. *Thunder Bay* (longlisted for the McIlvanney Prize), *The Blood Is Still*, *A Rattle of Bones* (also longlisted for the McIlvanney Prize), *Where Demons Hide*, *Children of the Mist* and *The Hollow Mountain* are the first six novels in the bestselling Rebecca Connolly thriller series.

THE HOLLOW MOUNTAIN

A REBECCA CONNOLLY THRILLER

Douglas Skelton

First published in Great Britain in 2024 by
Polygon, an imprint of Birlinn Ltd

Birlinn Ltd
West Newington House
10 Newington Road
Edinburgh
EH9 1QS

www.polygonbooks.co.uk

1

ISBN 978 1 84697 663 6
eBook ISBN 978 1 78885 684 3

British Library Cataloguing-in-Publication Data
A catalogue record for this book is available
on request from the British Library.

Typeset by Biblichor Ltd, Scotland

For Sarah, who not only reads them, but sells them.

Prologue

Murder on the Mountain:
The Personal Testimony of Alice Larkin, regarding the
events of 1964 in and around the Cruachan project

I'm writing this because it's time the truth was told and, frankly, I'm the only one who *can* write it. Or who *will*, I suppose. Very few remain who can remember the events of sixty years ago, and nobody is willing to speak out.

What occurred that summer has never been spoken about in any great detail since. There is a mention here and there – a single line in a report, no more than a paragraph in the books I have read about the Cruachan project. But nobody has expanded on it, not even me.

Until now.

What follows is the truth, at least the truth as I see it. You will make your own inquiries and decide how much of my truth is fact and how much is opinion or faded memory.

As I will have already explained to you, my story will be delivered to you in instalments. I wish you to read these words and then make your own minds up as to who you need to speak to. Further pages will be released as you relay your findings to me. That is the way I wish to go forward with this, and there will be no negotiation. As you know, there are no ground rules to uncovering facts. You turn over every stone along the way and hope to find something wriggling in the glare of the sun. But that is my ground rule. This testimony will be released gradually, and you will watch the events unfold again in these printed pages and glean from it, and whatever else other witnesses might reveal, what you will.

But two unambiguous facts remain:

Murder was committed.

And I know who was responsible.

The former I believe will become clear to you as you go along. The latter I will reveal in the closing pages. Nobody else knows what those last few pages contain, for I have kept their contents to myself.

My late husband, Dennis, was fond of an American television show called *Mission: Impossible*. They have made films from it more lately, I understand. Personally I found the series tedious, but a phrase from it has entered the public consciousness:

'Your mission, should you choose to accept it . . .'

You can choose to hand these first few pages back to me and walk away from this, and there will be no harm done. However, I don't think you will. I have been, in my professional life, an astute judge of character. In my personal life, less so. I judge you both to possess that one thing good reporters must have – curiosity. The need to know.

So, Elspeth McTaggart, Rebecca Connolly, your mission, should you choose to accept it, is to follow the facts and reach a conclusion.

2

1

The sun shone from a clear blue sky and that meant it was time for the young men of Glasgow to follow the tradition of 'taps aff'. The divesting of upper garments was called for whenever there was the slightest blink of sunshine, but this was a full-on solar stare and so those tops were tossed aside with the abandon of a Chippendale who loved his work.

Rebecca Connolly emerged from Queen Street station into the sunlight and was immediately greeted by the sight of three such individuals, their chests bared, their football tops either carried or tied around their waists to flap at their skinny-jeaned legs like loincloths. She wouldn't have minded if they had bodies like Ryan Gosling, but one was lean to the point of emaciation, while another looked as if he had imbibed somewhat too freely on cans of Tennent's lager – one of which he carried in his hand. The third had possibilities, but he would need to commit to more exercise than bending his own elbow. Their skin was pale but in fairness it was still the early summer following a particularly dull winter and spring, so if she was charitable, she might tend to think that the pallor would be burned away by exposure to the old ultra-violet. She suspected, however, that no amount of potentially harmful rays could relieve the unbearable whiteness of their being.

They barely looked at her as she wheeled her suitcase to the edge of the kerb. They were deep in conversation, a fragment of which seemed to relate to a political scandal, which surprised her as she really thought they would be talking football, or sex, or football and sex. She realised she was guilty of profiling, and that annoyed her. The fact that they didn't give her an appraising glance was something of a relief, and perhaps showed that there was some progress being made in the modern male. Unless they had somehow engineered to disguise it. As she crossed the road, she pursed her lips, conscious that once again she was being judgemental where no such judgement was needed. Was that a sign she was getting older, she wondered. After all, she could see thirty on the horizon.

The sight of the three young men *sans* upper garments was certainly a sign that some things in her home city never changed – unlike the railway terminus she had just left, which boasted a shiny new concourse, trendy coffee counters and a general feeling that it had been dragged kicking and screaming into a bright new age of transport. It all looked clean and tidy and, well, spruce, which was a word she never would have thought applied to a station in Glasgow. But spruce it was, and she was strangely proud.

That feeling of unexpected orderliness extended to George Square itself, which stretched to her left. It still had its statues and benches, but such immaculacy seemed somehow alien to her, although if she searched her memory, she really couldn't recall it ever being particularly cluttered, unless there had been a demonstration, an Old Firm fixture or, in the case of the movie *World War Z*, which used the square as a filming location, an outbreak of zombies. The grand edifice of the City Chambers still loomed at the far end, granite hard like the city around it, the classical frontage screaming of the city's Victorian prosperity. The road at the western end was now pedestrianised, or it was as far as pedestrians could walk before they were brought to a halt by tables and chairs set out by one of the large pubs that had been hewn out of a former bank headquarters.

The external seating area was already busy with patrons keen to enjoy the summer for however long it lasted – Glaswegians seeing summer as something to be grabbed with both hands and held down, for it could be as fleet of foot as Usain Bolt in a hurry. Her mouth was shaped for a coffee, and perhaps a scone, and she would have enjoyed the opportunity to take a moment to watch the foot traffic because it had been – she made a quick mental calculation – two years since she had last visited Glasgow. Guilt washed over her with the sun. Two years, good God. She had felt the city pull at her while she was in Inverness, but she had never made the journey back. Things just got in the way. Life. Work. Love. All that jazz.

Her phone rang so she stopped, propped her suitcase up on its wheels and fumbled in her jacket pocket. She thumbed the screen to answer it. 'Hi,' she said.

'You landed in the metropolis?' Stephen's voice, calling from Inverness.

'Train just got in, heading to meet Elspeth.'

'I thought it was tomorrow you were being interviewed?'

Rebecca was in Glasgow to be interviewed for the first of two documentaries based on Elspeth McTaggart's books about cases on which she had worked. 'I am, but Elspeth messaged and asked me to meet her this afternoon. Something about a story.'

'You're supposed to be on a break.' Stephen's voice was even, but she knew there was a note of caution there somewhere. 'Taking time to see your mum.'

She held the phone with one hand and trundled her case behind. 'And I will see my mum, but Elspeth is my boss and when the person who transfers money into my bank account every month wants to meet, I'm duty-bound to agree. I'll head home afterwards.'

5

She heard him laugh. Or growl. It was difficult to tell with the rush and roar of the city around her. 'What's the story, Balamory?' he asked.

'She didn't say. Just that she wanted me to meet someone in a Princes Square café.'

She heard a wince in Stephen's voice. 'Ouch, I hope she's paying, Princes Square ain't cheap.'

'If she doesn't, I may have to wash their dishes for a week. They . . .' She stopped talking and pursed her lips. 'Aw, that's a shame.'

'What's a shame?'

'The Duke of Wellington is still coneless.'

She stopped before turning into Royal Exchange Square to stare at the bronze statue of the Duke of Wellington astride his horse, which was unadorned by its customary traffic cone. Some writer had posted on Twitter about it the day before and she had half-expected the unofficial headgear to have been replaced overnight, but there he was, still bareheaded. Even the horse seemed perplexed by the turn of events.

'You Glaswegians and that traffic cone. I'll never understand the affection for it.'

'It's a tradition.'

For as long as she could remember there had been a traffic cone on the Iron Duke's head, occasionally with one on his steed's for good measure. At times the colours of the cones would change, during the Scottish independence referendum, for instance, or in support of Ukraine when Russia invaded. Seeing it in this condition was, to her eye, all kinds of wrong. She knew there were people who saw the cone as something akin to vandalism, but she didn't. For her it was an example of the Glasgow she loved – cheeky, even cocky, unabashed and showing a lack of deference.

'How are things in the Sneck?' she asked. 'How was court?'

6

'Inverness is sunny and warm. Court was dull and boring.'

'You didn't get to be Atticus Finch, then?'

Amazingly Stephen had never read *To Kill a Mockingbird* when she met him. That should have been sufficient for Rebecca to end the relationship right there, but she had set about educating him instead, not only ensuring he read Harper Lee's book, but also watching the film with him. Luckily for him, he loved them both. Gregory Peck always reminded Rebecca of her father, not because he looked like the actor but because she saw John Connolly as being as wise and as caring as Atticus Finch.

'Not today,' Stephen said. He never talked about his day in court. It used to bother her, but not so much now. 'Will you still be back in time for the dinner at the weekend?'

It was his parents' wedding anniversary and a family dinner had been arranged at a luxury country house hotel overlooking Loch Ness. Rebecca wasn't particularly looking forward to it, but she would attend. She had learned that give and take was the name of the game in relationships.

'Of course I'll be there,' she said. 'I'm looking forward to it.'

Little lies were also part of the game.

He laughed, also playing along. 'Yes, sure.'

Stephen knew she didn't particularly relish the idea of the gathering, not because she didn't like his family but because she was uncomfortable with anything remotely formal. She was a jeans-and-comfy-shoes kinda girl, and for this event she would have to smarten up.

She turned into Buchanan Street now, the foot traffic increasing in the busy pedestrian retail area. She skirted round a crowd clustered in front of a street magician doing something wondrous with cards. From somewhere further down came the skirl of the pipes and the beat of a drum. 'I'm almost there, can we talk later?'

He said of course and the call ended. She put her phone back in her pocket and weaved between the shoppers towards the iron canopy over the entrance of the Princes Square shopping centre.

If the traffic cone headgear was an illustration of Glasgow's cheeky side, then Buchanan Street – known as the Style Mile – and Princes Square were prime examples of its constant reach for upward mobility. It had ever been a thrusting city, a scrappy urchin determined to make something of itself, keen to cast off – or, at best, ignore – its grubby past. Rebecca had met people who had either never visited the city, or who had spent little time there, but who believed the image of violence and deprivation. Both existed, of course, but just as the new look Queen Street station was bright and shiny, so was this street and the adjacent mall, situated in an enclosed Victorian square. Here were designer stores, top-class restaurants, coffee shops and even a boutique cinema, whatever the hell that was. Rebecca had never visited it, so thought that it was some sort of arthouse venue, but she passed a poster of attractions and saw that it was running the mainstream flicks of the day, including one where a Hollywood star wanders through the cast shooting dozens of people in the head with some ease because every other person with a gun is a lousy shot. Rebecca decided she'd give that one a miss. She'd had enough of real-life gunfire, thank you very much.

A series of wood-panelled escalators criss-crossed the interior of the shopping centre like classy kisses on a page and Rebecca found Elspeth already in situ in a café on the next floor, her canes propped against the table, a large cup of tea already half-finished. Her close-cropped hair was dyed a red so bright that it seemed like a warning. Diminutive of stature if not girth, she needed to lose a little weight, for in the time Rebecca had known her she had ballooned, perhaps thanks

8

to lack of exercise after damaging her hip in a fall a few years before. The knee on her other leg also gave her trouble, which was why she needed two canes to get around. Elspeth knew she should get both attended to, but she harboured a mortal fear of surgery and would brook no suggestion of going under the knife. There was no sign of Julie, her partner, which didn't surprise Rebecca one bit. Julie was no lover of cities and would have chosen to remain behind in their home in Drumnadrochit, on the shores of Loch Ness, tending to their own café-cum-bookshop in a converted barn.

Elspeth's fingers drummed on the tabletop, a sign that she craved a cigarette but knew she couldn't fire up here, a legislative restriction that did not sit well with her. Rebecca had endured many a diatribe about the draconian anti-smoking laws in this country and the way they seemed to be intent on choking the life out of any kind of pleasure. As Rebecca stepped off the escalator and waved, she knew the first words out of Elspeth's mouth would be a rant.

'I'm beginning to wonder if there's any point in getting myself out from under the eagle eye if I can't spark up a Woodbine when I want,' she said. Julie was doing her level best to curtail her partner's nicotine habit but, like stemming the tide of idiocy on social media, it was a losing battle.

'Hello, boss, and nice to see you, too,' Rebecca said, sitting down and tucking her suitcase out of the way of passers-by. 'I had a lovely journey, thanks very much for asking.'

Elspeth briefly nodded a hello. It was grudging but it was something.

'And can you still get Woodbines?' Rebecca asked, trying to figure out if there was table service.

'Turn of phrase,' Elspeth said. 'Don't get literal on me. I'm an artist, darling.'

She waved with practised ease at a dark-haired and impeccably tanned young woman who made a simple white blouse

9

and black skirt look like they were the epitome of high fashion.

'I'll have another of these,' Elspeth said to the waitress, indicating her cup, because she could drink enough tea to refloat the *Titanic*.

'For sure,' the young woman said before turning to Rebecca. 'Can I get you something?'

Her accent was American, or perhaps Canadian, or even affected, Rebecca couldn't tell. Maybe she should get her to say a sentence with the word 'about' in it. If it came out *aboot*, then she was Canadian. Or she could be Scottish. Damn it, there was a flaw in her thinking.

'I'll have a white coffee,' Rebecca said.

'For sure. Is that a latte, a cortado, a mocha, a café au lait or an Americano with milk?'

Rebecca sighed inwardly as the young woman outlined the choices. Her friends mocked her impatience with the growth of coffee variations, which she deemed pretentious and merely a means of gouging more cash out of her pocket. She had been brought up in a house where coffee was spooned from a jar and the only choice you had was whether to drink it or not. However, it was not this woman's fault.

'An Americano with milk,' she said. 'And a scone, if you have them.'

The woman smiled, showing teeth on which Elton John could have rattled out a tune. 'We sure do. Is that a fruit scone, plain scone, cheese scone?' She pronounced it to rhyme with 'own'. Rebecca's preferred pronunciation sounded like 'on'.

'Fruit,' she said.

'With butter, butter and jam or cream and jam?'

Dear God, Rebecca thought. 'Just butter,' she said, hoping that there wasn't a choice between butter, it-calls-itself-butter-but-it-really-isn't or something veggie that pretends to be butter but is really butter-adjacent.

But the waitress simply flashed her luminescent ivories again. 'For sure. Be right back, folks.'

Rebecca decided to divert Elspeth from her hankering for carcinogenic vessels. 'So, who am I meeting?'

'An old pal from the dailies,' Elspeth said. 'He's retired now.'

'And why am I meeting him?'

'He has a story we can work on.'

'We?' Rebecca smiled, knowing she would do the bulk of, if not all, the work.

Elspeth grimaced. 'There you are, being literal again.'

'What's the story?'

'He didn't say.'

'A bit mysterious, is he?'

'Old school, likes the face to face.'

Rebecca bit back a suggestive retort. Given the surroundings, it felt out of place. 'So, who are *we* meeting?'

Elspeth's lips twitched in what was her approximation of a fond smile. 'An old friend called Forbes MacKay.'

'His name is Forbes?'

'Yes.' Elspeth's eyes narrowed at the little smile flitting across Rebecca's lips. 'Is there something wrong with that?'

Rebecca shook her head and didn't tell her that the name had conjured up someone in tweeds with his trousers tucked into long socks. Probably carrying a shooting stick. And wearing a deerstalker. 'What kind of journalist was he?'

'He was an editor kind of journalist.'

'He was your boss?'

'He was everyone's boss. He was well respected and even loved.'

'Unusual for a boss,' Rebecca said.

'Hey,' Elspeth objected.

'Present company excepted, of course,' Rebecca said, laughing as she watched the dark-haired waitress making her way towards them carrying a tray.

They fell silent as the cups were set before them, and a plate with two wrapped pats of butter and a scone big enough to be hurled at a besieged castle wall.

'There you go,' the waitress said. 'Is there anything else I can get for you today?'

'No, that's fine,' Rebecca said. 'Thank you.'

'For sure.'

She headed away in search of fresh victims to irradiate with her smile.

'Canadian or American, you think?' Rebecca asked.

Elspeth drained her first cup. 'Norwegian.'

Rebecca tilted her head. 'Really?'

'Yup.'

'How do you work that out?'

'It's obvious to anyone who has an ear for dialects and who can detect the influences of language and culture in slight hitches in pronunciation. If you listen carefully, you can hear the song of the fjords in her voice.'

'The song of the fjords?'

'That's right.'

'The influences of language and culture?'

'Correct.'

Rebecca opened one of the butter packs. 'You asked her where she was from, didn't you?'

'Just before you arrived.'

Rebecca felt a broad smile spread. She enjoyed her interactions with friends such as Elspeth. There were others: Chaz Wymark and his husband, Alan; Val Roach, a Detective Chief Inspector in Inverness; even Bill Sawyer, a former Detective Sergeant. The bond with those last two had taken a little while to develop, but it was there, and she was thankful. She was grateful for all her friends because she knew she had a tendency towards the melancholy, and they often seemed to conspire to drag her out of it. And now there was Stephen

Jordan, a solicitor in Inverness. Her boyfriend. She winced inwardly as that word came into her mind. She was nearing thirty, for God's sake. Women nearing thirty don't have boyfriends. They have ... what? 'Significant other' was so nineties. 'Partner' was too touchy-feely, and Rebecca didn't do touchy-feely. They were dating. They were lovers – boy, were they lovers. But no matter what she came up with, it all seemed lame.

'So, have you popped the question yet?'

Startled from her brief deliberation on the correct way to describe her relationship, Rebecca gave her boss a quizzical look. Elspeth smiled knowingly. 'You had that faraway look in your eye that you take on when you think about him.'

Rebecca frowned. 'I have never had a faraway look in my eye.'

'Please, you were over that heart-shaped bridge and gambolling in the sunlit uplands with the cherubs and the unicorns.'

Rebecca pulled a disbelieving face. 'Aye, that'll be right.'

'So, have you?'

The first butter pat had barely covered the scone, so Rebecca opened another. She knew what Elspeth meant, but she decided to be obtuse. Faraway look, her arse. 'Have I what?'

'Popped the question?'

'No. What makes you think I'm going to do anything like that?'

'You told Val Roach you were going to do it.'

Rebecca was momentarily thrown, then she recalled making a somewhat rash comment a few months earlier in the aftermath of a stressful time. 'I inferred I might do it. I didn't say for certain.'

Elspeth stirred some sugar into her second tea. 'Just get it done, girl.'

Rebecca smeared the butter on the scone. 'I'm not sure I'm ready to be married.'

13

'Nobody is ever ready to be married. It just happens.'

It was time to turn the tables. 'Then why don't you marry Julie? You've been with her far longer than I've been seeing Stephen.'

'We're too long in the tooth for such things. We don't need a bit of paper to support our relationship.'

'But I do?'

'Marriage is something everyone should experience at least once. Twice, at a push, but three times is more likely a triumph of hope over experience.'

'How do you know if you're making the right choice first time round?'

Elspeth studied her intently, and Rebecca realised that she had asked the question seriously. 'You don't, that's the thing. You can go out with someone for years, marry them and then discover they are not the person you thought they were, or that you're not the person you thought *you* were. Look at me, I didn't realise I wasn't into men until I'd been married for years.'

Elspeth had been with her ex-husband for a decade before it occurred to her that she preferred sleeping with women. A period of sexual abandon had ended when she settled down the Julie, who was ten years younger and strong-willed enough to keep her under control. Elspeth's former husband had been unhappy with the marriage, too, because he preferred women to be at home waiting for him with his pipe and slippers while overlooking his string of infidelities. Elspeth could do the latter, but she wasn't a pipe-and-slippers kinda woman. She wanted to continue with her career. She had spent some time in daily newspapers, even a stint on what they used to call Fleet Street, but eventually took the job of editor at the *Highland Chronicle*, based in her hometown of Inverness.

'Life is all about leaps of faith, Becks,' Elspeth continued. 'Sometimes you just have to risk it.' She sipped her tea and stole a piece of Rebecca's scone from her plate. 'Anyway, as the saying goes, you have to get married. You can't go through life just enjoying yourself.'

Rebecca smiled but felt suddenly uncomfortable at the direction the conversation had taken. She loved Elspeth and all her friends to bits, but she had never fully embraced the idea of sharing personal thoughts. She had indeed suggested to Val Roach that she might ask Stephen to marry her, but it had been off-the-cuff. At the time, Rebecca herself was unsure if she had been serious. She remained unsure. She had feelings for the man, that much was certain, but were they strong enough to merit a commitment? And did he have strong enough feelings for her? Life could be very difficult to understand. Love, damn near impossible.

Time to change the subject. 'Was I early, or is this old boss of yours late?'

'Forbes works to his own clock, always has.'

'That must have been difficult, come deadline.'

'Professionally he was right on the button, but personally, time for him is an abstract concept. He'll be here, don't worry.' She looked towards the escalator, where a tall, slim man wearing absolutely no trace of tweed had just appeared. 'In fact, here he is now.'

Forbes MacKay must have been in his late sixties at least, given he had been Elspeth's boss and she was no spring chicken – though her exact age was the kind of secret that was normally protected by armed guards, attack dogs, piranha fish and possibly a curse, for good measure. However, the tall, trim man who strode towards them with a wide and genuine smile might have passed for ten years younger. His grey hair displayed no sign of thinning at all, his skin was so smooth she suspected the involvement of Botox, and he was elegantly dressed in casual clothes that he very likely bought from the kind of designer stores that demand a credit reference just to window-shop.

'Elspeth,' he said and leaned down to kiss a cheek that she had already raised to him. She returned the favour. Rebecca was, frankly, gobsmacked. She had never seen Elspeth do the cheek-kissing thing and wasn't sure if she should look away, for the sake of decency. Forbes turned to Rebecca and for a moment she feared he might want to do the same to her, but he held out a hand. 'And you'll be Rebecca.'

'"I'd better be, I've got her bank cards in my bag,"' she said, quoting a line she'd read in a book. His grip was firm but not a test of strength.

He smiled. 'I'm Forbes MacKay.'

She certainly hoped so, otherwise Elspeth had allowed a complete stranger to kiss her. She was finding that kiss difficult to get past, to be honest.

He pulled up a chair and caught the eye of Miss Norway 2021. 'Can I get you ladies anything?'

'We're fine thanks, Forbes,' Elspeth said before Rebecca had the chance.

He looked at the half-eaten scone on in front of her and said to the waitress, 'I'll have a latte, please, and a scone with jam and cream.'

'For sure,' the waitress said and moved away.

He settled back and smiled at Elspeth. 'God, Elspeth, it's good to see you. You're looking well.'

'I'm a decrepit old hag, and you know it. I've got a dodgy hip and a buggered knee, I eat too much and smoke too much and I drink too much of this stuff' – she pointed at her tea – 'and more besides. I look like shit and feel like it half the time, but life goes on. You, though, look as good as ever. You got a portrait in the attic or something?'

'I live a pure and unsullied life, as you know.'

'Forbes MacKay, you've been sullied more often than I've had hot dinners, and I've had way too many of them. What's your secret?'

He laughed. 'Retirement and a good hydration regime.'

'You don't miss the job?'

'Hell no! It was changing before I took my pension, and none of it was for the better. God knows chasing circulation was hard enough in our day, but now it's like trying to catch a moonbeam in a jar. You know it's there somewhere, but you just can't get a hold of it. People would rather get their news from online sites that speak to their own prejudices. It's easier for them to handle than true objective reporting.'

'We weren't always objective, it has to be said. Depending on whoever owned us at the time, there were stories that leaned heavily in one direction or another.'

'Yes, but back then we fought them, and the NUJ fought them, but these online sites don't even make a pretence at fair reporting. The same can be said for certain titles, too.' His eyes flicked towards Rebecca. 'Sorry, Rebecca, this must be dull for a young person, talking about the way things were.'

'No, I understand. I saw it in the weeklies.'

'You worked with Elspeth on the *Highland Chronicle*, right?'

'Yes, but she jumped ship and left me alone to watch the bosses race to the bottom.'

'I saw the writing on the wall,' Elspeth said, 'and knew the future was not for me.'

'They were interested only in sensation, not real news,' Rebecca explained. 'I remember one editor telling me to go out and find a paedophile story that week. Go find one. It wasn't news, it was pandering, and any attempt to properly reflect life in the area was ditched in favour of headlines. I didn't sign on for that kind of journalism.'

This interested him. 'What kind of journalism did you sign on for?'

'I want to report the news, without fear or favour. To use the cliché, I want to comfort the afflicted and afflict the comfortable, not support special interests or parrot political mantras. Obviously we have to cover the nuts and bolts, the court reports, the human interest—'

Elspeth snorted. She hated human interest.

'—and I've learned that there has to be an element of commercial realism. Elspeth has bills to pay and my salary to cover, after all. But now and again we get to do a story that speaks to injustice, that deals with an issue at its heart. What's the phrase? "The news is something that someone somewhere doesn't want printed. All else is just advertising."' She felt a bashful smile coming. 'Sorry, I'm ranting.'

Forbes smiled. 'No, you have passion, and that's a rare thing in journalists today. Too many want to merely report on sport or celebrities or get into PR.' He turned to Elspeth. 'You taught her well.'

Elspeth shrugged. 'Not my doing, she dropped fully formed into my newsroom. All I did was smooth off some rough edges.'

Forbes looked across the table to Rebecca again. 'So, where did you develop this zeal?'

Rebecca had only just met this man, but she felt he understood her. 'My father.'

'He was a journalist?'

'No, a police officer. A DCI.'

One eyebrow raised. 'In Inverness?'

She shook her head slightly. 'Glasgow.'

'Retired now?'

Elspeth shifted in her seat as Rebecca paused, just slightly, and swallowed. 'No, he died. Cancer. A few years ago.'

The humour in Forbes's eyes faded. 'I am so sorry, Rebecca.'

She raised a hand in a gesture that conveyed it was fine but looked away to study the other patrons walking, talking, browsing on the different levels, moving up and down those aesthetically pleasing escalators, as if she thought she might see John Connolly standing among them, smiling at her. But she didn't. She used to see him and hear him, even though she knew he wasn't really there. She hadn't seen him for some time, or heard his voice. It wasn't fine, but that sense of loss was part of her now.

'So, Forbes,' Elspeth said, moving the conversation along, 'what's this story you want to talk about?'

Forbes gave his perimeter a quick recce, then edged his chair closer to the table and hunched forward, his voice dropping to just above a whisper. 'I take it you've heard of Alice Larkin?'

Elspeth tilted her head, a sign that she was already intrigued. 'Of course I've heard of Alice Larkin.'

Rebecca asked, 'Who's Alice Larkin?'

Her boss's lips thinned, then she tutted. 'Young folk nowadays, don't know anything beyond Take That and the Cardassians.'

'Take That, really?' Rebecca laughed. 'And it's Kardashians. Cardassians were aliens on *Star Trek*.'

'Although used more extensively in *Deep Space Nine*, to be precise,' said Forbes, then shrugged when Elspeth frowned in his direction. 'What can I say? I'm a Trekker.'

Elspeth's eyes rolled slightly, then she explained to Rebecca. 'Alice Larkin was a bloody legend in the industry. Began as a reporter on a weekly, moved to the dailies in the late sixties, then became a presenter on *Reporting Scotland* on the telly. She helped pave the way for the likes of you and me. I'm surprised you haven't heard of her.'

Rebecca had felt some memory stirring. Nevertheless, she smiled. 'Sorry, my head's too full of nineties pop music and aliens on social media.'

Elspeth snorted again. She liked to snort. 'So, what about Alice Larkin?'

'She's a cousin of mine,' Forbes replied, then amended. 'Well, by marriage. She married Dennis Holmes in the early seventies.'

'Dennis Holmes QC?' Rebecca asked.

Elspeth's eyes narrowed. 'You've heard of him, but not Alice Larkin?'

'My dad spoke about Dennis Holmes – said he was the Rottweiler of the criminal courts and he could make even the hardest cop or crook weep.'

'He was fierce, certainly,' Forbes said, 'and unremitting when it came to anyone lying to him in the box.'

Elspeth said, 'You kept this family connection quiet.'

'I wanted to make my way without any hint of nepotism. A breath of a family connection to Alice Larkin and you know what would be said, that I only got where I did because of her.'

Elspeth accepted that. 'Okay, so what is it you want from us?'

'She wants to meet you.'

'She's still alive?'

Forbes's face turned serious. 'Yes, though she's in her eighties and doesn't get around much.'

'So, what does she want to see us about?'

'She has read your books, Elspeth, and some of your stories, Rebecca.'

Elspeth had written two books on cases that had involved them both: one about a murdered man whose body was found on the battlefield of Culloden in full period Highland dress and a claymore through his chest; the other on a miscarriage of justice concerning the death of a lawyer and political spin doctor. She was now working on a third about the curious death of a woman on the island of Stoirm. For all three books, Rebecca had done most of the legwork, but Elspeth had gathered further information and pieced it all together into highly readable works of non-fiction. Both published works were being prepared as TV documentaries for Netflix.

'Alice Larkin has read my books?' Elspeth's voice was awed. Rebecca had never seen Elspeth awed before. If she kept a diary, she would have noted it immediately.

'She's a fan of your work,' Forbes said, and Rebecca smiled as Elspeth's jaw dropped further. 'She wants to talk to both of you about a story.'

Rebecca grew more interested. 'What story?'

'What do you know about the Hollow Mountain?'

'Ben Cruachan, over in Argyll?' Rebecca asked.

'Yes.'

'I visited it once with my mum and dad, years ago. It's part of the hydroelectric network, right? They carved this massive power station out of the centre, like something from a James Bond film.'

'That's right. Back in the early sixties it was a huge project for Scotland, and Alice was in the middle of it. She worked for the *Argyll Sentinel* at the time, just starting out in news-papers.'

Elspeth had picked up her jaw and self-respect from the floor. 'I think there have been books and documentaries about the Cruachan project already, Forbes, you must know that.'

He nodded. 'And so does Alice.'

'So, what does she want to talk to us about?'

'I want to let her fill you in, Elspeth. But take my word for it that it's right up your street.'

'In what way?'

He smiled. 'Because it's about a murder.'

2

When documentary makers, even those from Glasgow, made something about Glasgow's history, they never showed places like Milngavie. They wanted the mean streets, the slums, the violence, the gangs – not neat streets, neat houses and neat cars. Rebecca had been brought up in a semi-detached villa set back from a quiet road by a mature garden skirted by a high hedge. It was as far away from blades, bottles and bullets as you can possibly get without actually disconnecting the TV.

As she climbed out of a taxi and wheeled her suitcase up the gravel driveway, noting the lawn needed to be cut, she was suddenly transported back to her teenage years, coming home from school and trudging up that same driveway, her thoughts on homework, friends and boys. Not necessarily in that order. She still expected to see her father's face at the window, depending on what shift he was on. He had been based in Stewart Street in the centre of the city and if he was home when she arrived, he would always, in his words, put his finger to the kettle and butter a fruit scone or a pancake, or even gingerbread.

But there would be no face at the window today, for John Connolly was gone.

She used her key to open the front door and caught the aroma of home baking hanging in the air like a sweet memory. Good old mum, she thought.

'In here, Becks,' her mother's voice reached her from the kitchen at the end of the hallway. Rebecca left her case at the foot of the stairs and followed the delicious smell to the back of the house, where Sandra Connolly was pulling a tray of freshly baked scones from the oven. Rebecca smiled. It was good to be home.

Her mother placed the tray on the dining table and opened her arms for a hug. Rebecca obliged, even though she was not by nature a hugger, something she had inherited from her father. Sandra, however, was always open for an embrace, and both Rebecca and her father learned to accommodate her.

'You've lost weight,' Sandra said as she stepped back and gave her daughter her customary survey. 'It suits you.'

'Are you saying I was fat before?'

Her mother's lips twitched. 'Pleasantly plump, perhaps.'

'Alliteration aside, I'm not sure that's as complimentary as you think it is.'

The smile broke out. 'I'm teasing. You were fine. I'm just saying that you're looking well.'

Rebecca knew her mother was having fun. The one thing she had never been was overweight. 'Thank you, and so are you.'

It was true. For a time after her husband had died, Sandra Connolly had looked . . . slumped, was the only way Rebecca could describe it. It wasn't that she walked around like a half-shut knife, she just appeared to be weighed down. His death had affected them both, but grief, as they say, was a process, and Sandra had managed to come out of it far faster than Rebecca, although her mother had never known the true extent of her daughter's mourning. She knew nothing of the visions of her father perched on the edge of her bed in the night, or the conversations she had with him. Or rather, with herself, for Rebecca was hard-headed enough to know that these were no visitations from beyond the veil. These

23

apparitions were extensions of her own consciousness, her own reasoning powers, manifesting a man she both loved and respected.

But there were other times, flickers of something beyond reality, that she could not quite explain so readily. She had never told her mother about those, either. There were many things Sandra didn't know because Rebecca had never told her, might never tell her.

Now, however, the only word to describe her mother was radiant. Her eyes sparkled in a way Rebecca hadn't seen since her father died. Her hair was immaculate: the grey that had crept across the auburn Rebecca had inherited was now concealed under a professional dye job. She had also somehow managed to contrive the lifting of years from her face – exactly how, Rebecca could not say. Or was it that her smile was now easier than it had been before?

'You look great, Mum, what's the secret?'

That smile faltered a little as Sandra's gaze slipped away. 'I'll get some tea going and we can have a scone. You still eating scones? Or is that how you've managed to shed some pounds?'

'Had one this afternoon, in fact, when I met Elspeth in town.' She breathed in the warm, cosy smell of fresh baking. 'But it wouldn't be anywhere near as good as yours.'

'Damn right,' said Sandra as she turned towards the kettle. 'Sit yourself down, help yourself – there's butter and jam on the table there – and we'll have a catch-up.'

Rebecca did as she was told but watched her mother intently as she filled the kettle. She knew an evasion when she saw it and had sensed one when she'd asked what Sandra's secret was.

Alice Larkin lay in her bed, her phone clutched to her chest, a smile playing on her lips as she looked vacantly towards the large flat-screen TV on the wall, aware of the lights of the quiz show flitting across it but not really taking it in. The sound was muted because she found the stupidity of many of the contestants excessively irritating, but the early evening news would be on in a few minutes so there was no point in switching channels. She watched the news every day, sometimes leaving the TV on the news channel for hours on end, often with the sound muted as she read, occasionally flicking her eyes towards the ticker tape headlines at the bottom of the screen. Old habits die hard, she thought. So do old reporters. She was eighty-five now and her body was failing her, but her mind was sharp. Perhaps not as sharp as she once was, but she was far from being a doddery old fool. Dennis had lost his faculties towards the end, which was dreadful to witness. He'd had such a fine mind, not a bad body either in his day, and she had enjoyed both. She'd loved him for both. He had died two years before and she missed him every day.

The news she'd received by text was most welcome. Forbes had done as she had asked, had hooked those women. They would visit later that evening, with him.

Her eyes strayed to the bedside table and the thin pile of pages there. It was time for it all to come out. Those pages were only the beginning, a teaser, just enough to finally land them. She had dictated the bulk of it into a small voice recorder, to be transcribed, but had typed the final few pages herself. It hadn't been easy sitting in this damn bed. Forbes had suggested using a laptop, but she much preferred a desktop. She was unable now to reach the office on the top floor of the home she had shared with Dennis, so the old electric portable typewriter had been unearthed and, my God, that took her back. She had only a handful of pages to type, but it took her three days.

She used to be such a swift typist, but arthritis had taken its toll on her joints, and she was reduced to stabbing at the keys with only her two index fingers. She had seen many old hacks back in the day battering out their news reports in that way, often with a cigarette wedged between their fingers like some sort of growth, but she had been trained to touch type, so when she made the transition to the daily paper she was often called upon to input other people's stories as they dictated over the phone with deadlines looming. She didn't mind doing it at first, but eventually she realised that some of the men were treating her like a secretary and she didn't like that.

She remembered one hardened journalist taking extreme umbrage when she refused to take a story down the line. She could hear boozy voices in the background and realised he was in the pub. She referred him to a copy taker, saying she had stories of her own to write. He made some disparaging comment about the women's pages having to wait, this was real news, but she cut him off before he could continue. She had never allowed herself to provide copy for the women's pages, point blank refused to be pigeon-holed as a lifestyle reporter, and what was more he knew it. Naturally he complained to the news editor about her attitude, but she didn't care. The news editor, himself an old-fashioned reporter who enjoyed a dram and a fag and chewing the fat with the boys, suggested that she tread more carefully around the more experienced journos. She knew he was struggling to be diplomatic, wording his lecture as delicately as he possibly could, given that he was more used to barking out orders and insults, but it wasn't out of deference to her gender. Normally he didn't care whose feelings he hurt – he was an equal opportunities offender who would terrorise men or women, and his caustic remarks were known to leave scars. No, he was slightly – only slightly – more deferential towards her because of her father, and for that reason she could very easily have simply told him to fuck off right to his face and would have got away with it, but that wasn't her way. Instead, she remained calm. She apologised for any upset caused and told him that she was willing to help when she could – when a reporter was unable to return to the office in time and a copy taker wasn't available, she had happily taken stories over the phone – but she would not be treated like an office junior simply because someone couldn't be arsed leaving the pub. Nothing more was said after that, and the reporter in question never again asked her to take his copy, though he did often mutter disparaging things under his breath – that, if it could be bottled, would go well with ice and soda.

She had many stories to tell of the old days in print journalism and then broadcast news – of stories told and untold, of sexual discrimination, predation, infatuation and fornication. She was unlikely to do so now. The only story she wanted to tell was the one that began on that thin bundle of pages on the bedside table. The rest of the pages were tucked away in a drawer and would be produced over time. Not too much time, though.

No, those stories about the days of print and TV would never be told now.

This one, the one about the hollow mountain and the men who worked it, would be the last story she'd ever tell.

Rebecca lay on the bed of her old room, staring at the wall opposite. There used to be a poster of Robbie Williams up there, but the space was now taken up by a large, framed print of a shepherd tending his flock on a snowy field at sunset. Or maybe it was sunrise. Without a compass, or a sign saying, *This Way is West*, there was no way of knowing. She had a feeling she had seen that field in Perthshire earlier in the year but could not be certain whether it was actually a Highland scene. Neither did her mum, who said she bought it because she liked the colours and the atmosphere. Rebecca understood. Despite the fact that it was a winter setting, there was a warmth to it, the shepherd and his dog little more than spectral figures in the background, the sheep in the foreground, the sky shades of pastel behind the dark, skeletal trees. There was something deeply restful about it.

Or were they ghosts of a shepherd and dog past, still standing sentinel over their charges?

She took a deep breath, let it out, and let her eyes drop to the laptop open beside her, the screen having gone to sleep. She knew if she activated it once again, she would see the article she had half-read about Ben Cruachan, the Hollow Mountain. Her mind was more intent on what her mother had told her over tea and scones. To be truthful, she was having trouble processing it and didn't really know why.

She had known her mother was building up to something but, as usual, she'd filled the conversation with small talk.

'How's work?'

'It's fine, Mum, always busy.'

'Is Elspeth well?'

'Yes, but still having trouble walking.'

'She should get that seen to.'

'Yes, she should.'

'Are you being interviewed together?'

'I don't know. I'll find out tomorrow, I suppose.'

'And Stephen, how is he?'

'He's doing well. Very busy. Crime never sleeps.'

'You should hang on to him, he's a good man.'

Rebecca didn't say anything further on that subject for fear that Sandra might also urge her to propose to him. After all, it was she who had told her many times that if a woman wanted something she should go out and get it, don't wait for a man to make a move.

The small talk exhausted, there then followed a silence before Rebecca saw her mother reach a decision. Whatever it was she had avoided saying earlier, she was going to say now. Rebecca had seen that look before, when her mother had told her that her father was dying. John Connolly, a strong man, a brave man, a man who had delivered more than his fair share of bad news in his professional life, could not bring himself to tell his own daughter that the cancer treatment hadn't worked and he had perhaps months to live. So, Sandra Connolly had sat Rebecca down at that same kitchen table, took her hand in hers and gently relayed the news. Rebecca wept, then ran into the sitting room where her father waited and threw herself in his arms, held him tighter than she had ever held him before. Neither of them was a hugger, but they clutched one another as their separate tears became one. In the end it wasn't months but weeks before John Connolly was gone.

This time, Sandra hadn't taken her by the hand, but all the same Rebecca steeled herself for bad news.

But it wasn't bad. Not really.

Sandra Connolly took a deep breath. 'I've been seeing someone.'

Rebecca blinked a couple of times. She was relieved it wasn't something about her mum's health but remained unsettled. 'Seeing someone, as in . . . ?'

Sandra's lips compressed. 'Don't be obtuse, Becks, it ill becomes you. You know what I mean.'

Feeling slightly shamed, Rebecca forced a smile. 'So, who is he?'

'His name is James. James Wilton. He's a chartered surveyor.'

'And how did you meet him?'

'At a party.'

'Whose party?'

A slight smile from Sandra. 'Your Auntie Ginny.'

Ginny Reynolds, not actually related, but an old school friend of Sandra's who Rebecca always called auntie. She conjured up the image of a woman with a perma-tan, thick brown hair and a tendency to call her three ex-husbands 'Losers One, Two and Three'. So much for hope over experience. 'How does she know him?'

The smile began to grow. 'She's a surveyor, too, remember.'

Rebecca remembered. 'How old is he?'

'Two years older than me.'

That made him fifty-seven, maybe fifty-eight, depending on how flexible her mother was regarding her own age. She was fifty-five but had a birthday in three weeks. 'What is he? Divorced? Widowed?'

'Divorced.'

'Any kids?'

The laugh that had been building in her mother's throat finally broke free. 'Good God, Becks, do you want to get a spotlight out and shine it on me? This is like being on *Mastermind*.'

Rebecca had to laugh, too. 'Sorry.'

'If this is how you interview people, then I have to say, it's somewhat daunting. I half-expected you to produce an old phone book.'

Rebecca frowned. 'Why a phone book?'

'It could be used a cosh and didn't leave marks. You needed the old, heavy ones, not the flimsy things you get these days.'

'How on earth do you know about that?'

Sandra gave her a look that told Rebecca it was obvious. 'I read books. I watch telly. And I was married to a police officer. Not that your dad ever used one in that way, but he had heard of it.'

Mention of her father brought Rebecca back to the subject in hand. 'Sorry about the interrogation. It's just that I'm a little surprised.'

'Why?'

Rebecca opened her mouth, made a little noise in her throat, then closed it again. Sandra understood.

'Because of Dad, right?'

Rebecca didn't answer but for some reason she felt tears burn.

Then Sandra did take her hand. 'I get it, Becks, I really do. But, you know, I think he wouldn't want me to be alone.'

'You're not alone.'

'Becks, you're in Inverness or poking around a story somewhere up north. I haven't seen you for yonks ...' She held up her hand when she saw Rebecca about to defend herself. 'I know, I know – you're busy, you have your life, you have your work. I get that, I really do, and I'm not criticising. But I want a life, too. To be honest, I think I've grieved enough – there comes a point when it has to stop. And your dad would be the first one to say that. Remember what he would tell you? About life?'

John Connolly had told her many things, but she knew instantly the particular nugget to which her mother referred. 'You have to look ahead, not back, because you might miss something good.'

Sandra nodded, licked her lips. 'I've never told you this before, but your dad told me just before he passed that he knew I would meet someone else. He said I would know when the time was right.'

'And now the time is right?'

'I don't know, but I'm willing to take the chance. That's another thing you dad used to say, wasn't it? Always be ready to take a chance. This won't cost me anything. James is a decent man. Hard-working, caring. I like him.'

Her mother's words echoed what Elspeth had said earlier.

'Do you love him?' The words came out in a whisper, as if Rebecca was wary of breathing life into them.

31

'It's too early to say. But we get on well and I want to take this chance. Can you understand that?'

Rebecca didn't know what to say because she wasn't sure if she understood or not. Her mother had every right to be with someone new if she wanted. She had every right to take the chance on happiness. She had every right not to be alone.

And yet . . . Rebecca felt uncomfortable with the idea of her being with another man who was not John Connolly.

Later, she wandered into the sitting room. It hadn't changed very much since that night she had rushed into her father's arms, but it was different. There was a new settee, but his armchair, his favourite, remained because her mother couldn't bring herself to get rid of it. Rebecca eased herself into it, tucked her legs under her, rested her head on its high, soft back and breathed in, hoping to catch the ghost of his after-shave, to feel his arms around her again, to hear his voice telling her that this was all fine, that life goes on. But she smelled nothing, felt nothing, heard nothing.

3

The light was beginning to fade when Forbes turned off Hyndland Road into Westbourne Road. Up ahead, Rebecca could see the mature trees that marked the edge of the gardens. She had been to Westbourne Gardens once before but had never stepped inside one of the terraced houses that lined it. She had been out with friends – she must have been in her late teens at the time – and one of them was dropping something off at the home of a relative, and they had waited in the car while he did so. She had admired the architecture of the blonde sandstone buildings even then.

Lights shone above the doorways and from the windows of the terraces ringing the neat triangular garden area that gave the off-kilter square its name. The scrupulously tended lawns looked as if someone had got down on their hands and knees to trim each blade individually with nail clippers; the mature hardwoods at the edges were stately, the wooden benches and picnic tables in impeccable repair. All were enclosed within a green chain-link and post fence. The buildings themselves were four storeys, including the attic rooms and basements, which faced onto wells separating them from the pavement. Stone steps crossed these sunken areas to link the walkway with the front doors.

There was a feeling here of respectability, of comfort. And not just financially – these elegant homes, whose external and internal lamps beckoned in the twilight, looked downright cosy and safe. But if there was one thing Rebecca had learned in her almost three decades of life, it was that safety was tenuous. Tragedy can occur to anyone, anywhere, and death was the great leveller. Your bank balance didn't matter, your politics didn't matter, your religion didn't matter, for when the Reaper came calling, he didn't give a damn. It was your time and that was it. You could be walking along a street, you could be having breakfast, you could be making love, you could be making plans for the future, but in an instant none of it mattered because all of it was gone. A breath is taken. Then no more. A heart beats. Then it stops.

This very area, she knew, had been the scene of tragedy back in the 1950s. Her father had told her about it, for although he hadn't been born then – and indeed, wasn't even from Glasgow originally, but the island of Stoirm off the west coast of Scotland – he had made it his business to understand the past of his adopted city, especially its criminal history. He had related the story of an ostensibly decent young man who had embezzled money from the bank in which he worked but, when accosted by two police officers, pulled two guns and started blasting. He killed one officer and seriously wounded the other and was chased into a lane running behind part of Westbourne Gardens, where he put one of those guns to his head and pulled the trigger.

The telling of that story marked the moment when she first truly realised that her father could leave for work one morning and simply not return. Just like that poor police officer seventy years before, John Connolly could be simply going about his business, an otherwise uneventful day, and he could meet someone with a shadow in his heart. In the end, though, it wasn't a criminal's bullet or blade that took John Connolly but something far more insidious.

That memory made her think about her mother. Rebecca continued to struggle with the concept of her dating, but she pushed the thought from her mind. This was work and she had to focus.

They climbed the steps from the pavement to the door, Elspeth doing so with some difficulty but waving away any assistance. The door was opened by a woman who was blonde and big and broad and looked as if she knitted sweaters out of steel wool. Her massive jaw reminded Rebecca of Desperate Dan in a comic she read as a child, even though he was dark-haired. She wondered if the woman ate a cow pie for lunch every day. Her smile was genuine, though.

'Mr Forbes, sir, come away in. Her ladyship is expecting you,' she said, her accent vaguely Highland. Or Irish. Or Norwegian. Rebecca wasn't doing too well these days with accents.

'Thank you, Orla,' Forbes said as they crossed the threshold. Irish, then, Rebecca decided as she looked around her. Other houses had hallways, but this was a foyer. An ornate occasional table of some kind of dark wood supported a three-way chrome table lamp with a silk shade. Above it, a mirror hung on the wall, its frame made of what looked like real silver, or perhaps just chrome buffed up to a high standard. Orla certainly looked as if she could bring a shine to concrete without breaking sweat. A staircase ran up one wall while a corridor stretched off to the rear of the house. There was no way of telling how far back it went. The walls were cream, or some fancy name for it, the paint skilfully applied – unlike Rebecca's flat in Inverness, which she decorated herself, and the evidence lay in the smears on the skirting boards and over the light switch fittings. The dark wooden skirting boards here were devoid of such smudges. The floorboards visible around the series of plush rugs were so highly polished that the mirror seemed surplus to requirements. Rebecca's childhood home in Milngavie was no hovel, by any means, and her mother certainly kept it tidy, but this place looked as if a team of professionals had been in with a steam cleaner. Rebecca felt as if she was contaminating it by simply standing there. She wondered if she should take off her shoes.

Orla nodded to Elspeth and then Rebecca. 'You'll be Ms McTaggart and Rebecca.'

Rebecca wasn't a Ms, then. She was unsure if she should be insulted but, to be honest, she really didn't care enough. 'Rebecca' was fine with her.

'Her ladyship said to show you right up as soon as you arrive.' Orla smiled. 'I'll bring up some refreshments. Would it be tea, coffee or perhaps something a little stronger? The sun has sunk over the yardarm, after all.'

'Tea for me, Orla,' said Forbes. 'I'm the designated driver.'

'I'll have a gin and tonic, if you have it,' Elspeth said.

'Do you have a malt whisky?' Rebecca asked, prompting a surprised look from her boss. Rebecca gave her a little shrug. She felt the need for something with a bit of tang about it tonight.

'We do. What's your fancy, pet – Glenmorangie or Talisker? And we have a fine Springbank, if that's to your taste?'

Rebecca had never sampled the expensive malt distilled in Campbeltown – frankly, it was out of her price range – but she'd once interviewed a crime writer who recommended it. Of course, he was extremely successful and wouldn't think twice about the cost, but she was on a budget.

What the hell, she thought. 'Springbank, please. With ice and a dash of soda.'

A slight frown creased Orla's brow, as if in disapproval of ice and soda being added, but she said nothing. Rebecca didn't care. After all, Orla wasn't drinking it. To his credit, Forbes hid a smile, but Elspeth shook her head.

'I'll show you upstairs and bring you the drinks presently,' Orla said, already heading up the stairs. Forbes followed, while this time Elspeth, obviously having learned her lesson with the short flight of steps out front, grabbed Rebecca's arm for support.

'You don't put ice and soda in a Springbank malt,' Elspeth whispered when she judged Orla to be far enough away not to overhear.

'Is it a law?'

'Bloody well should be,' Elspeth said, her face tight with the effort of the climb. She looked up to see how far they had to go and blinked. 'If I'd known we were going to be ascending the north face of the Eiger I'd've brought some crampons, a rope and a Sherpa guide.'

'Sherpa guides are in the Himalayas.'

'He might have emigrated.'

Orla looked over her shoulder towards them. She had obviously overheard them, for she gave them an apologetic smile. 'We tried to get her ladyship to base herself in one of the downstairs rooms, but she wanted her own bedroom. She can be as stubborn as a mule, can her ladyship, isn't that right, Mr Forbes?'

Forbes allowed himself a slight laugh. 'Stubborn doesn't even begin to cover it, Orla. Alice can be single-minded to the point of obsession.'

Elspeth grunted. 'Sounds like someone I know,' she said, shooting a quick glance at Rebecca.

At the top of the stairs, they were led along a corridor where Orla knocked on a door and waited for permission to enter. Rebecca didn't hear anyone speak, but Orla opened the door and ushered them inside. 'Your guests are here, your ladyship.'

The bedroom seemed, to Rebecca, as big as her flat in Inverness. She almost expected there to be clouds forming in the high ceilings. A plush three-seater settee piled with thick throw cushions was positioned under the double windows, the drapes open to allow the evening's soft light through.

A large, dark wardrobe of some considerable vintage stood against the wall to the left, and Rebecca thought if she opened it she might find the entrance to Narnia. Alice Larkin lay in the centre of a king-sized bed, expertly propped up on an array of pillows and covered by a duvet thick enough to be used as soundproofing.

Earlier, Rebecca had found images of Alice on the internet, and she had been a striking woman back in the day. Her hair had been dark and full, occasionally piled in a beehive or cut in a short style that had been modish in the sixties, but now it was thinning to the extent that her scalp shone through, though it was still tied neatly back. Her face had narrowed, too, her cheeks sunken, the skin grey and corrugated with wrinkles. Her eyes, though, remained sharp and alert and they watched Orla move to the beside and begin to rearrange the pillows.

'They're fine, don't fuss.' Alice's voice was ragged with age but still strong.

Orla ignored her and tilted her forward while she puffed up the pillow at her back. Alice allowed it but repeated, 'I said they're fine.'

'They are not fine,' Orla said, easing her back into position. 'You'd be falling over in the middle of the conversation, is that what you want now? How undignified would that be, I ask you.'

Alice's eyes twinkled. 'How undignified would it be if I fired you right here and now, in front of my guests?'

Orla laughed. 'That'll be the day. I'm the only one with the patience to put up with you, as well you know.' She moved back to the door. 'I'll be back presently with some drinks and nibbles. Is there anything I can bring you?'

'Yes,' said Alice, 'a little respect.'

Orla laughed again as she left the room. 'Well, you never can tell what might happen some day.'

She winked at Rebecca and closed the door behind her. On the bed, a little smile played on Alice's lips. 'I don't know what I'm going to do with that girl.'

Girl, Rebecca thought. Orla was easily in her mid-forties.

Forbes perched on the edge of the bed. 'You'd be lost without her, and you know it.'

'I do know it, but the problem is that she also knows it, and that gives her an arrogance above her station.' Her eyes flicked now to Elspeth and Rebecca, taking them both in. 'I've read your books, Elspeth. I may call you Elspeth?'

Elspeth nodded. 'Of course.'

'I like your work. You have a flair for finding the colour in a story that is often missing in such accounts. Very nice work, indeed.'

Elspeth had the grace to look embarrassed by the praise, but Rebecca knew that inside she was preening.

Alice's eyes flicked in Rebecca's direction. 'And you, Rebecca Connolly, did all the legwork. Good though the writing is, the books themselves wouldn't have worked without your input, am I right?'

'I tell Elspeth that all the time,' Rebecca said, nudging her boss with her elbow.

Alice looked at Elspeth again. 'You made that fact clear in the writing, Elspeth. That shows you have some professional honour. Speaks well of you.' She waved a skeletal hand speckled with liver spots towards the couch under the window. They sat down. 'That's why I requested that you both attend. I hope you don't mind.'

'Not at all,' said Elspeth as she made herself comfortable, obviously glad to be off her feet after the ascent of the Eiger. 'In fact, we're intrigued.'

'What did Forbes tell you?'

'Enough to intrigue us.'

Alice smiled. 'I instructed him to be enigmatic, but he knew to be so already. Curiosity is easily teased in true journalists, is it not? A word here, a line there, a question hanging over all, and we are hooked. It's like being addicted to a drug, this need to know, am I right? I assume that was why you both entered the profession.'

The question didn't require a reply, so neither of them provided one. Alice was satisfied. 'Too many young reporters now seem to have no curiosity, no ability to question. They accept things too readily, don't you find? They think providing an alternative statement from the other side is sufficient, so they fail to probe, to analyse, to sift through those statements and to press matters further. They don't understand that the quest for balance is not only about presenting two sides of an argument but also about questioning statements that are obviously bogus. I've seen too many politicians on the news being allowed to say things that are never questioned.'

'There are still young people who question,' Rebecca said, feeling the need to defend her generation.

Alice studied Rebecca closely. 'You are one such young person, true?'

Rebecca was tempted to point out she wasn't so young, but it would have been a waste of breath. 'I do what I can, but as I said to Forbes earlier, it has to be tempered with commercial responsibility.'

'But you are one who questions, correct?'

'She is,' Elspeth said. 'But Forbes said something about an unsolved—'

She broke off as the door swung open again and Orla returned with a tray.

'You can speak freely, Elspeth,' Alice said. 'Orla knows all about this little project.'

Orla handed Forbes his tea. A mug, Rebecca noted with some satisfaction. 'I've heard very little else for weeks. Her

40

ladyship here dictated her account and I had to type it up on the computer. If I hear about that damned mountain and those tunnel tigers again, it'll be too soon.'

'Tunnel tigers?' Elspeth asked, as she accepted the glass of gin and tonic.

'The men who blew their way through the rock of Cruachan to build the power station,' Rebecca explained, smiling her thanks to Orla as she handed her a solid crystal tumbler bearing a hefty measure of whisky and soda. By its colour, the drink was heavy with the former and light on the latter.

'You've done a little homework,' Alice said as she indicated that Orla should place her own mug of tea on the bedside table. Orla pushed bottles of pills and tubes of ointment aside to make space, being careful not to place the mug on a sheaf of papers.

'A quick internet search, nothing more,' Rebecca said, ignoring Elspeth's murmur of the word 'swot' as she sipped her gin.

'I'll leave you folks to it, then,' said Orla. 'If you need anything else, just press the button.' She indicated a device on the bedside table and then left.

'And she'll ignore it, if she feels like it,' Alice said.

'That's not true, as I'm sure you well know, Alice,' Forbes said.

She shrugged and addressed Elspeth. 'Will you agree to be part of my project, then?'

'To be honest, we're not really clear on what you want us to do,' said Elspeth.

'I want you to do what you do best. To tell a story. But first, to investigate. And provide an answer to a mystery.'

'Forbes mentioned a murder.'

'The murder that they say never was,' Alice corrected.

'Is that what you say?'

41

Alice sported a smile that was the epitome of enigmatic and pointed a bony finger towards the little bundle of pages on the table. 'Forbes, please hand these over.'

Forbes placed his own mug on the floor and rose to do as he was told. He separated the papers into two, handing one bundle to Elspeth, the other to Rebecca.

'A copy for each of you,' he explained.

Elspeth glanced at the pages as she flicked through with her thumb. 'You've written the story yourself?'

'I've written my version of it. We are all storytellers, are we not, in our own way? All good journalists are, even though the approaches to reporting and storytelling are different. In reporting we put it all up front, but storytelling is all tease, am I correct, Elspeth? But we still must carry our reader along. I know you were a decent journalist in your day – Forbes told me so – but, naturally, I've made inquiries of my own. Your books also show that you have a sense of drama, an ability to capture the readers' imagination and draw them into the story. That's what I have done with my pages, but even so, I would expect you to take them as the basis and make your own inquiries.'

Rebecca scanned her copy, saw the first was a title page:

Murder on the Mountain:
The Personal Testimony of Alice Larkin, regarding the events of 1964 in and around the Cruachan project

'You will receive further pages as time goes on,' Alice said.

Elspeth asked, 'Why not all at once?'

'To keep you interested. Don't be fooled, I am not handing you this story on a plate. I would expect you to follow up on what you read. I've not written your book for you – or even an article, if you can sell it. That's your job, and I wouldn't presume to tell you how to do it. You can read what I have written, decide who you would wish to speak to and write your own account. If you choose.'

Rebecca glanced at the first page, saw the year 1964. 'Finding people after all this time might not be easy.'

'Nothing worthwhile ever is. But I can assure you there is a story here.'

'A murder?'

'Yes.'

'One that they say never was. "They", I presume, being the police.'

'And others.'

'But you say there was.'

'I know there was.'

As she scanned the introductory page, Rebecca had to admit that her interest was piqued. She suspected Alice Larkin shared a flair for the dramatic with Elspeth, something Rebecca didn't possess. She was a straight gather-the-facts reporter and found it difficult to provide the colour Alice had mentioned.

'Do you accept his challenge?' Alice asked.

Rebecca looked up from the pages and met her steady gaze. 'You mention ground rules here, I see.'

'I do, just one. Do this the way I wish.'

'I also have ground rules—'

'Rebecca,' Elspeth began, a warning in that single word.

Rebecca ignored her. She had been sipping the whisky, and her assessment of the measure had been correct. Orla must have developed a twitch when pouring it because the spirit was taking possession of her tongue. Is that why they called it the demon drink? It didn't matter, she was going to say what she was going to say, irrespective of Alice's stature and advanced years.

'If we decide to accept this job, we'll play along with this dripped approach,' she said, raising the pages a little. 'We'll

43

follow up strands. We'll interview who we can. But we don't run with rumour and we don't run with gossip. Whatever the solution to this mystery is, if we find it, then it will be properly sourced and backed up by facts.'

Alice inclined her head in agreement.

'And if we discover that there really was no murder, that your memory is faulty, then we are free to say so. Elspeth says you're a legend in the industry – and, from what little I have read about you, it seems you are highly regarded. But that won't stop me from saying that you're wrong. It also won't stop me from telling you where to go if you try to control me, manipulate me or guide me down a path of your choosing. I choose my own paths. Agreed?'

Alice had listened to Rebecca's speech with some amusement. 'I would expect nothing less. And what you have just said confirms that I have chosen well. In telling this story, you may have to tread on some toes. I feel you are not averse to making people limp a little.'

4

I never fully understood why my father was against the Scottish hydro projects across the Highlands, and the Cruachan scheme above Loch Awe, in particular. Perhaps it was because the whole notion of creating unlimited power out of natural resources that were renewable, to use one of today's buzzwords, was the brainchild of a former Red Clydesider. Perhaps it was because it meant a horde of working-class men from all parts of the country, and even abroad, would flood into areas that he and people like him saw as their personal playgrounds. Those very powerful and entitled people felt discommoded in the process, for they believed the mountains and the corries were for their use. They refused to accept that the times they were a-changing, and they took to the pages of the *Times* and the *Telegraph*, as well as the corridors of power, to voice their displeasure. My father took to the pages of his own publications.

My father, Sir Broderick Larkin, was what they called a press baron back then. He was no Beaverbrook or Rother-mere, even though he had ambitions to rub shoulders with them and their like. He had been born to privilege: minor aristocracy who made their fortune in tea and cotton back in the day, and in the early sixties continued to keep his bank account fat and healthy. He took that fortune and diversified into print media, buying a string of weekly newspapers across Scotland, as well as a daily based in Glasgow, but he also had interests in independent television stations.

If commercial radio had existed, he would have bought into that, too. But in 1964 the only such media were pirate stations like Radio Caroline, broadcasting from international waters, much to the chagrin of the BBC and the Board of Trade, as it was called back then. I often wondered whether my father had some money invested in Caroline, or any of the others that subsequently sprang up. It would certainly appeal to him because he was very much in favour of anything that challenged the BBC, which he saw as a bunch of left-wing nutters out to undermine the establishment. Nobody dared start him on the NHS. He was very much the establishment. He had been a Tory MP for a time, serving a safe seat in the south of England, but he didn't like the idea of compromise, which is what politics is all about, or at least used to be. Now it appears to be grab what you can, while you can, and never apologise. He once told me that he had watched his ideals being diluted by half-measures and he couldn't accept that, so he held the seat for one term only and moved back into commerce.

It was another Conservative politician, Harold Macmillan, who said that Britain had never had it so good. Yes, he was speaking in 1957, but by the early 1960s it seemed to be true. By 1964, Britain was said to be swinging. The empire was contracting, but we were colonising the world of culture like never before. The Beatles had stormed the charts in the UK and were doing the same in the US. Mary Quant was revolutionising fashion. Vidal Sassoon was giving us the bob cut. James Bond was topping bestseller lists and box office charts. If the 1950s were grey and dull, then the 1960s were bright and garish.

As for me, I was twenty-four and proud of my beehive hair-do – but later, when Sassoon's bob grew in popularity, I had it all cut off. Got to say, I much preferred it shorter. I was among the first in Oban to have a Mary Quant black-and-white miniskirt. It drew some looks from some of the older men, women too, but I thought what the hell. I had a decent pair of legs and no compunction in showing them off. For many, what became known as the permissive society was more a concept than a reality – for instance, the contraceptive pill was only available to married women in the UK at that time. I'm not terribly certain the permissive society ever fully reached Scotland, not in the way it did in London, if you believed what was printed in the *Daily Mail* or saw on television and films. So, the sight of my knees and thighs strutting down Oban's Shore Street was a talking point. Not that anyone would say anything, of course, because I was Sir Broderick's daughter and, let's be honest, that meant I could have walked naked down the street and nobody would have done anything more than tut, or hope that I didn't catch my death of cold.

My family's influence in the West Highlands was second only to the Kirk then, and we were gaining fast on that top spot. My father did once raise the issue of me displaying my legs in such a brazen fashion, but when I made clear my intention to continue, he let it go. He always let it go with me. That song from a few years back, from that cartoon film, might have been his anthem had it been written back then. Being an only child, and with my mother dead, brought certain privileges. The fact is, he doted on me, and though I don't think I acted like a spoiled child – well, not all the time – I really was spoiled. Whatever I wanted, I got. An expensive doll. Clothes, records, whatever was new and trendy, you name it, if I wanted it, I got it.

He wanted to buy me an E-Type Jag, but I much preferred the Mini Cooper. I'd been enthralled when Pat Moss won the

Dutch Tulip Rally in one. Women were coming to the fore, and I idolised her. Men thought her brother Stirling was a sporting hero, but she was mine. The E-Type was a man's car, but the Mini Cooper was cooler. It was groovy. Do they still say groovy? I don't know and don't care. The Mini – the dress, the car – were both groovy, and I embraced them, and my father indulged me.

The one area in which he was strict with me was in who I dated. Even though I say it myself, I was a most attractive young woman. My mother had been beautiful, my father extremely handsome, and I had inherited their genes and bone structure. Coupled with my inheritance, I was quite a catch, even though Father had once said that if he couldn't take it with him, he wasn't going. He made it his habit to scrutinise any boy in whom I displayed an interest, more than once going to the length of hiring a private investigator to probe their backgrounds. He approved of very few of the young men I went out with and tried to dissuade me from seeing them, but I was very stubborn, even then.

The only one he had any time for, and in fact promoted most exhaustively as a suitable consort, was Lance Abercromby, who would one day become Lord Abercromby of Kindorres. He was a most attentive young man but had a temper on him that made Ebenezer Scrooge look like Gandhi. He was handsome enough, certainly, and charming most of the time but he had a nasty side that I found not just off-putting but slightly sinister. Then again, we all have a nasty side, do we not? Anyway, apart from his temper, which manifested in bouts of jealousy, there was no way I was going to marry a man whose given name was Lancelot, and that was that. I knew that the man I wanted would not be from Father's set but someone who had made something of himself by his own efforts and not simply by an accident of birth.

When I met Dennis – much later than the events I am out-lining here – I know that Father would not have been overly impressed. Had Dennis chosen to prosecute rather than defend, that might have made a difference, but he had also been born in a council house in Drumchapel. I feel sure that Father would have had to consult a street directory of Glasgow to find out exactly where Drumchapel was – and would be horrified when he did. The West End, where we made our home, would have been acceptable, but not that far north-west, and a council estate to boot.

However, Father had passed away by that time. A heart attack, completely out the blue. One day he was walking around, then suddenly down he went. Dead before he hit the ground, apparently. I still miss him, for despite his faults, he was my father. And we all have faults. A girl needs her father sometimes, and there were times in later life when I wished I still had him around to consult. I might not have followed his advice to the letter – in fact, being the stubborn besom that everyone knows I am, I probably wouldn't – but I would still have liked to discuss things with him. He knew his way around problems, my father.

Anyway, when I said I wanted to work in newspapers, he saw to it that it happened. At first, he thought it would be on the women's pages, what they later called the 'lifestyle' section, but I refused. Pat Moss was my sporting hero, and I looked up to other women who had achieved success in a man's world . . . Women who made their way in the world of print journalism, like Rachel Beer, who was the first female editor of the *Observer* back in the nineteenth century and later bought the *Sunday Times*. But I was particularly interested in Elizabeth Cochran, who you may not have heard of, but if I mention her pen-name Nellie Bly, it might ring a bell. She broke Jules Verne's fictional eighty-day around-the-world record by eight days, and she practically invented investigative

49

journalism by going undercover in a mental institution to expose conditions. This was in the late 1800s, so it was quite something. She was also the first woman to report from the war zone between Serbia and Austria during the First World War.

And there were other women, here and in the USA, who sparked the desire within me to be a real reporter, not just a glorified housewife. Helen Kirkpatrick, Martha Gellhorn, Lee Miller . . . the list goes on and on. Nowadays their names aren't terribly well known, but I worshipped them and wanted to be like them. Being who I was – with a father who could quite cheerfully ruin a rival to gain some sort of business or financial advantage and not lose a wink of sleep, yet indulged his daughter's every whim, even if it made him a figure of fun among other men – I had the means to follow in their footsteps.

So, when I told him I was not going to work on the women's pages, he agreed. I had wanted to go straight to the daily in Glasgow, but he wisely advised that I learn the ropes on the *Argyll Sentinel*, which was based in Oban but covered as far down as Campbeltown and up north to Morven and Ardnamurchan. I say 'advised', but I recall now that he was quite insistent upon it. And so, the *Sentinel* it was. It was an astute move on his part, but then my father was a very astute man. Spoiling me was one thing, allowing me to make a fool of myself, and by extension him, was not to be countenanced.

Unlike my role models, there were no wars for me to cover. Yes, there was trouble in Cyprus and the Aden Emergency kicked off, and British troops were despatched to corners of what was once the Empire, but not to my corner of West Scotland. I became disenchanted with the small stories I was required to follow – the lifeblood of a local newspaper they may be, but I wanted something bigger. And so my eyes turned to the Cruachan project. Father was against it, of course, but eventually he agreed. I suspect he rather hoped I would find something that would cast it in a poor light, but for my part, the entire project was fascinating.

Had that not been the case, I would never have met Gerry Rawlings . . .

5

Gerry Rawlings.

Rebecca was back in her old bed, lying on her stomach, the sheets of printed paper before her. She dragged her laptop closer and typed the name into an internet search. Nothing, not even links to social media sites, although there was a string of listings for a Jerry Rawlings, who was head of state in Ghana for a number of years. Rebecca was fairly certain it wasn't the same guy.

She tried the search term *Cruachan project murder*. Again, nothing apart from a one-line mention in an article about a book on the history of the project. No details, no other links.

The murder that never was, Alice had said. What the hell did that mean?

She rolled onto her back, propped her head up on her pillows and stared at the pastoral sunrise/sunset scene on the opposite wall. She could still feel the burn of the Springbank in her stomach, even felt a little drunk. While they had talked, Orla had returned with another, and she had felt behoven to finish it. That crime writer, whose name she couldn't quite recall, had said it had a peaty taste with a hint of the sea about it. She could detect the peat but hadn't heard any seagulls. He hadn't mentioned it would make her use the word 'behoven'. She wasn't a great drinker – just a gin, now and then – so wasn't accustomed to such good whisky, but she felt she could learn to love it. That wouldn't happen anytime soon, not on what Elspeth paid her.

Her laptop alerted her to a Skype call. She accepted it and was presented with a close-up of her boss's face. Rebecca heard the sound of a siren somewhere near Elspeth's city centre hotel.

'You got your window open?'

'No, I'm outside in the street,' Elspeth replied, holding up a cigarette in her hand. 'Having a smoke. Bloody no smoking regulations are draconian. I'd've popped out when we were in Westbourne Gardens, but I couldn't face those stairs again without an oxygen mask. And even Forbes has drunk the Kool-Aid.'

Forbes had denied her permission to smoke in the car, which had pissed Elspeth right off.

Elspeth took a drag as the siren faded. 'Have you read those pages?'

'I have,' said Rebecca. 'I felt behoven to do it right away.'

'They don't tell us much,' Elspeth opined. 'In fact, they tell us bugger all. And did you just use the word "behoven"?'

'Yes, it's a word I never thought I'd ever use, but turns out I can behove like an expert. As for Alice, she's telling a story.'

'Well, it's a pain in the arse. I wish she'd felt behoven to give us everything all at once.'

'I don't know, Elspeth, she's kind of hooked me. You told her we were intrigued, and I really am.'

Elspeth sucked in some more nicotine, held it for a moment then exhaled. 'So, you think we should accept this mission?'

'Doesn't do any harm to spend a few days on it, does it? We're here till the end of the week, anyway, and all we have to do is the TV stuff for the next two days.'

'I thought you were visiting your mum.'

'I *am* visiting my mum, but I'm capable of multi-tasking,' Rebecca said.

Elspeth paused, ostensibly to take another draw on her cigarette, but Rebecca realised her words had come out sharper than she meant them. She immediately wondered if she should apologise.

'Okay,' Elspeth said before Rebecca could reach a decision, 'do you want to tell me what's up?'

'There's nothing up.'

'Becks, darling, I read a lot of books and I can read you like one. You hit that whisky this evening like it was personal, and I can tell from your eyes and the slur in your voice that you're feeling the effects.'

'I am not slurring my words,' Rebecca slurred, then thought, oh shit, I am slurring! Her mum had given her a strange look when she returned home, the not-quite-disappointed-but-certainly-on-nodding-acquaintance-with-it look that Rebecca had seen so often in her teens. She always knew when Rebecca had been drinking, even when she had opted for vodka as a teenager because someone told her it had no odour. Her mum could smell it, though. It was like a bloody sixth sense. Just like she'd known, or seemed to know, when she'd had sex for the first time. It had been with a boy at university, and it hadn't been terribly satisfactory for either of them – they had both been too nervous – but when she came home afterwards, her mum gave her a similar knowing look, as if the very act of sexual congress had somehow resulted in some kind of sign on her forehead that said, *Virgin no more*.

Elspeth added, 'And you've been even more crabby than usual.'

'Pot and kettle there.'

Elspeth accepted that. 'I'm old and jaded and my knee and hip hurt, I'm allowed to be crabby. So, what's it all about?'

Rebecca grimaced but told her about her mum and her new beau. Christ, she really was drunk, she'd just thought of this guy whatsisname as her mum's 'beau'. That's both 'behoven' and 'beau' in a matter of minutes, she thought, and both begin with 'b'. The nineteenth century will be knocking on the door asking for its terminology back. Her mum said she'd been talking to . . . What the holy hell was his name again? Shit, it had been washed away by the booze. Anyway, she'd been talking to her beau, and he'd suggested they all have dinner the following night. Naturally, Rebecca had fixed a smile – the whisky had helped with that, even though she feared it might have been a touch lopsided – and agreed, but inside she felt something twist. What if she didn't like him? That would hurt her mum, and she didn't want to do that. Or worse, what if she liked him? That would betray her dad, and she didn't want to do that, either.

When Rebecca stopped speaking, Elspeth was silent for a moment as she fired up another cigarette, then said, 'Everyone has a right to be happy – your mum, too.'

'I know.'

'She's still a young woman.'

'Youngish.'

Elspeth gave her a warning look. 'She still has needs.'

Rebecca was horrified. 'Don't go there!'

'Right, because sex is just for young people. You didn't invent it, you know.'

'I know that.'

'So, you want her to take the veil, is that it?'

'No.'

'You want her to live the rest of her life alone?'

'No.'

'Then what is it?'

Rebecca couldn't answer because she didn't know why she had been so disturbed by this development.

'Don't be a brat, Becks,' Elspeth said. 'Let your mum have some fun. She deserves it.' She paused. 'Be happy for her.'

'I am happy for her,' Rebecca insisted.

'Tell your face that.'

Rebecca felt tears burn in her eyes and she didn't know why. The 'brat' comment hurt, but she couldn't deny that there was an element of that in her thinking and behaviour. She was being a brat. She was being unreasonable. She knew her mum had every right to happiness.

'Okay, I've nagged you enough for one night,' Elspeth said eventually. 'Why don't you get some rest. I'll let Forbes know we have chosen to accept the mission. I hope he doesn't self-destruct in five seconds.'

'Okay,' Rebecca said, still wondering if she should apologise.

There was another pause, filled by Elspeth stubbing her cigarette out on something out of shot. 'You're a bloody wee swot, you know that, right?'

No apology was necessary, Rebecca was relieved to note. 'It's been said before.'

'Showed me right up.'

'I'm the legwork girl, you're the talent.'

'You got that right, sister. Who do you think this Gerry Rawlings is?'

'I've just had a look online and found two things: bugger and all.'

'Yeah, me too.'

'Do you know anyone who would have worked a news desk back then?'

Elspeth's voice displayed mild outrage. 'Exactly how old do you think I am?'

Rebecca blew out her cheeks. 'I dunno. Pretty old.'

'Cheeky bugger,' Elspeth said. 'It's not the years, with me, it's the mileage.'

'Yeah, okay, Indiana Jones. You got your whip with you?'

'No, it's at home. Julie's oiling it up.'

Rebecca giggled a little too much, but it was just the tension escaping her body. Or the whisky. 'Too much information. Is there anyone you could maybe tap for info?'

Elspeth stubbed out her second cigarette. 'I'll think about it. It was sixty bloody years ago. Not everyone is as indestructible as Alice Larkin.'

'She looked pretty destructible to me.'

Elspeth didn't answer, but a slight sigh suggested she had noticed that, too. It's not easy seeing your heroes growing frail and fading. 'Okay, you do what you do, find out more about the project, because I get the feeling Alice won't be spending much time filling in the details. I'll message Forbes, see if he knows anyone who might still be around. He's been in the game longer than me. Don't be up reading all night – get some sleep, Becks. Big day tomorrow and you don't want dark circles under your eyes because these high-def cameras pick up everything. We can talk about the next step while we're waiting for the call into the studio. It's telly, so there will be a lot of sitting around while they faff around with lights and cameras.' Then she changed the subject suddenly. 'You spoken to Stephen tonight?'

'Yes, he phoned a wee while ago, just before he went to bed.'

'Aww, young love. Do you make kissy noises over the phone?'

'No,' Rebecca said. 'And don't start.'

Elspeth laughed and cut the connection, leaving Rebecca to stare at the screen for a few moments before looking down at the pages again. They hadn't even reached the meat of it yet, but the tingle at the nape of her neck told her there was something here. Despite her apparent negativity, she knew that Elspeth sensed it too, otherwise she would have already spiked the story. Or perhaps it was mere deference to a woman she revered, but Rebecca hoped not. Whatever the case, Alice

Larkin was right about the need to know being a drug – and Rebecca had already admitted to being hooked.

She hit a key on the laptop, pulled up the material on the Cruachan project, then dragged her notebook closer and picked up her pen.

Alice lay in the dark, staring at the ceiling where the shadows of the branches of the trees opposite, stirred by a slight breeze, beckoned to her as if inviting her to join them. She seldom slept with the drapes closed because she liked to awaken with the sunlight in the morning.

The house was silent. Orla had ensured she'd taken her medication then bade her goodnight. She'd be asleep by now, Alice reasoned. Alice herself didn't sleep much, even though she had pills to help, but they didn't do much except relax her a little. Too much going on in her mind. Dennis used to have the same problem: his mind was always restless and that communicated to his body. She would often awaken in the dead of night to find his side of the bed empty, and she would rise to find him in the lounge watching something awful on TV. She had mentioned *Mission: Impossible* in her short introduction to her memoir of the Cruachan murder – and there *was* a murder, she knew it – and it would often be that. He had bought boxsets of DVDs and she would find him in his favourite armchair, a glass of Springbank in his hand. Just the one glass, no more. Dennis was no drinker, but he liked the best. Sometimes she would sit with him and watch, never sniping – for she would not spoil his enjoyment – and even occasionally revelling in the show's ludicrous nature. Other times she would leave him where he was, knowing that he would eventually return to her side, kiss her on the forehead, then roll over and go back to sleep.

She had watched him gradually deteriorate, slowly lose everything that he was, and that had been painful for her. She had to admit, at least to herself, that when he passed it was something of a relief, probably for them both. She had been with him when he died, sitting reading at his side as he slept. He had woken with a start and for a brief moment, just a moment, she saw – thought she saw, was convinced she saw – the old Dennis looking back at her. The Dennis with the bright, inquisitive mind; the Dennis who had argued with judges, terrorised police officers, picked holes in the testimony of informants; the Dennis who was well aware that he defended, and cleared, the guilty, in the belief that he also saved the innocent. He had reached out and grasped her hand and smiled. And then with a little cough that became a sigh he was gone. She had held his hand for some time after that in the silence that death leaves in its wake, broken only by the ticking of the clock on the bedside table.

She would be with him soon, she knew it, for she felt the cold breath of the Reaper on her neck. He couldn't have her yet, though, for she had to see this through. She had a truth to reveal, a truth that she had guarded for too long. She had chosen her conduits to that revelation well, she believed. Before they left, Elspeth McTaggart had asked why she didn't simply approach a publisher with her account, but Alice knew that what she had written wasn't long enough. She had furnished the bones of the story, and now she needed the two journalists to supply the flesh. The truth was, she didn't have the time or even the stamina to attempt a full-length work. That damned Reaper lurked in the gathering shadows, waiting for his moment.

She was also well aware that she was yesterday's news: some old bat who once read the headlines on *Reporting Scotland* in the late sixties and seventies wasn't enough of a lure. Forbes had made a few discreet enquiries, but so few people remembered her now. That had hurt her vanity, certainly, but her reason had soothed it. Celebrity was a fickle lover and there was little point in mourning its loss. Thanks to the books, Elspeth McTaggart had something of a name now and the documentaries could only increase that. She and the Connolly girl were the right people for the job because Alice wanted someone who would not simply accept her word for what occurred, but who would look into it themselves. They might not find much after all this time, but they would at least try.

She closed her eyes, listened to a car cruise by on the road below, and thought of those days decades before. A lifetime ago. Writing it all down, even dictating it, had been a most rewarding experiment. The act of putting one word after another had brought everything flooding back. It had been a curious sensation, the remembrance of things believed lost, memories revived by the simple act of putting them into words. Good memories, bad memories, all combined to form a part of her life that for many years she had refused to consider, so intent was she on making a new life. Dennis used to say that memories, good and bad, make us what we are, and it was true. We are shaped by our experiences, and such remembrances are part of those experiences. She had been ordered to forget what she knew of those days, and she had obeyed. It was uncharacteristic of her to do so but she had complied, or at least given that impression. The appearance of burying the memories was forged out of self-preservation – and that of others. There was no need for such concerns now. Her days were almost done.

She closed her eyes. As she drifted off to sleep, she saw faces from the past, some clear, others blood-tinted.

Gerry Rawlings, smiling, as he often did.

Big 'Bronco' Lane, scowling as he often did.

Her father, telling her to forget it all.

Lance Abercromby, his face contorted by fury.

Dennis, who never knew what had occurred in her previous life.

A police officer who had suspected a truth that he never uncovered.

Ghosts of the past flitting across her eyelids like a slide-show. Ghosts that had to be laid to rest.

6

The production assistant was a burly young man sporting a
Peaky Blinders haircut, but he didn't have Cillian Murphy's
cheekbones to help pull it off. He wore a white T-shirt with
the sleeves cut off at the shoulders – all the better to show off
his well-developed biceps and triceps – and jeans so tight
that his legs and crotch were practically anatomical displays.
Rebecca hoped he didn't become aroused for any reason
because she was unsure the zip could take the strain. Or
perhaps she was being overly complimentary. He met her taxi
at the door of the disused warehouse on the banks of the
Clyde in Govan and told her he'd show her up to the green
room. He introduced himself as Tristan, his accent somewhere south of the Watford Gap, and suggested they take the
stairs, explaining that the lift was a little small and tempera-
mental. Rebecca was fine with that because she didn't want to
find herself in an enclosed space with his muscles and overly
stretched denim.

They only had to climb a couple of flights before Tristan
pushed open a heavy fire door into a large space that had, no
doubt, at some time been a hive of industry but was now a
vast empty area with only one corner near a large window
being used by the TV crew. Rebecca was surprised. She had
expected it to be just a camera person, a sound person and Leo
Cross, who would be conducting the interview, but there were
at least ten people laying cables, moving gear and doing

something vaguely technical with three cameras – two full-sized digital jobs and a smaller SLR. Netflix documentaries had budgets, it would appear.

'This is where we're shooting,' Tristan said, nodding towards the light being cast onto the exposed brick wall that was so authentic people would think it was fake. They were going for the impression of bars or vertical blinds, Rebecca wasn't sure which. 'We're just setting up, so you might have a bit of a wait.'

Rebecca said that was fine, she knew they were earlier than expected. She and Elspeth had arranged to meet here before the filming, to give them the chance to talk about Alice's story.

'The green room is this way,' Tristan said, already heading across the wide floor to another door. 'Your colleague is already here.'

Rebecca followed, searching for Leo among the people milling around, but she couldn't see him. Tristan held the door open for her and she edged past him, ensuring that she didn't brush against him lest it cause some kind of poppage. She smiled to herself, realising how conceited her thoughts were. She knew she was no gargoyle, but that didn't mean that the man would find her attractive. He might even be gay. That thought reminded her of a time once before when she had convinced herself that a young man had taken a fancy to her. Chaz had turned out to be gay and was now one of her best friends. He and his husband, Alan, would be in Glasgow soon because they were also going to contribute to the documentaries – and rightly so, for they had both played a role. Chaz, in fact, had been in at the kill of the Culloden case. Literally, as it turned out.

Elspeth was at a low table talking with Leo, who rose as Rebecca entered. He held out his hand and smiled a smile that would have had the Princes Square waitress suing her dentist.

Rebecca took it, grateful he hadn't moved in for a kiss. Leo was a telly person, after all, and even though he worked in factual programming, it was still showbiz, and showbiz folk could be very tactile. Rebecca didn't like that malarkey. She even felt exposed holding Stephen's hand in public.

She had only seen Leo before on screen, both in previous documentaries and in Zoom calls over the two years it had taken to develop and find a network for the shows. His flesh was tanned, not former US president orange but a delicate shading that was set off nicely by his pale blue shirt and black suit. Frankly, Leo Cross was quite possibly the most handsome man she had ever seen. He also smelled wonderful.

'Rebecca,' he said, genuine warmth in a voice familiar not just from their previous contact but also his voice-over work on documentaries and commercials. 'It's a pleasure to meet you in person.'

'You too, Leo,' she said. 'But I thought you'd be taller.'

He laughed. She wasn't being cheeky – he had once told her that people who had seen him on screen always thought he was taller. He wasn't vertically challenged in any way, but he wasn't going to be looking down when in conversation with Richard Osman anytime soon.

'Thanks, Tris,' he said to the young man in the doorway, 'I'll look after Elspeth and Rebecca for now.'

Tris nodded and vanished. Leo indicated that Rebecca should settle down at the table. 'Elspeth told me that you two want to chat about a new story, so I won't intrude. I've got to say, she's being very mysterious about it.'

'It's early days, Leo,' said Elspeth. 'It may not lead anywhere.'

'Fair enough. But if it does, I want first refusal for the rights.'

'We'll see,' said Elspeth. 'My agent would hamstring me if she thought I'd agreed anything without her input.'

Leo laughed. 'Yes, Jo is most formidable, and I for one would not like to get on her wrong side.'

'She's actually very lovely,' said Elspeth. Rebecca blinked. She had never heard Elspeth use the word 'lovely' before in relation to another human being. 'But her rage could knock the hard-on off a sailor. By the way, can I smoke in here?'

'Ah, sadly no,' said Leo.

'Why not?'

'All sorts of silly reasons. Health, safety. The law.'

Elspeth's lips tightened. 'Bloody stupid law.'

Rebecca guessed she wouldn't be hearing the word 'lovely' from Elspeth again that day.

'If you need to smoke, then you have to step outside, I'm afraid,' Leo said.

'That means another trip in that lift, which was like being hauled up by a rope.'

'Sorry, Elspeth.' Leo didn't sound the least bit sorry. 'Right,' he said, 'I'll get back out there.' He waved to a table against the wall. 'There's tea, coffee, juice, pastries, fruit, yoghurt. I'll send a runner out shortly for some breakfast rolls. She'll come in and take your order. It will be a little while before we're ready for you, so you have plenty of time to talk about this mysterious new project.'

He waited a moment, his eyebrows slightly elevated as if expecting Elspeth to crack and tell him what was brewing, but she simply stared back at him. He turned to Rebecca, curiosity in his eyes.

'Don't look at me,' she said, with a shrug. 'Elspeth's the boss.'

That smile broke out again. 'Tough room,' he said. 'I'll leave you to it.'

And then he was gone, leaving behind the after-glare of his teeth and the faint suggestion of cologne. Elspeth waited until the door closed behind him before she reached into the large canvas supermarket bag at her feet and fished out her cigarettes.

'They can sue me or cart me off in handcuffs, I don't care,' she said as she clicked her lighter, then delved again into the bag for Alice's pages. Rebecca set her laptop bag on the table and wandered over to the table. She wasn't hungry – her mum had ensured that she didn't leave the house without at least eating two boiled eggs and toast – but that wouldn't keep her hunger at bay for long. She rejected the treats on offer and decided to wait for a bacon roll. Maybe two. She poured a coffee, and a tea for Elspeth.

'Right,' said Elspeth, blowing smoke from the corner of her mouth, 'I told Forbes we're on the job and he, or probably Alice, had anticipated our request for a news person who was around at the time. We can meet them this evening, around six in the bar of my hotel. We'll be finished with this nonsense by then.'

Rebecca carried the mugs back, knowing that Elspeth didn't think of this as nonsense at all. She was pleased that her books were being turned into high-profile documentaries but would never admit it. The timing worked for Rebecca. She was to meet her mum and her new boyfriend at eight and, knowing her mother, that didn't mean drinks and chat – it meant sitting down with her napkin tucked in. She wasn't looking forward to it but she had to put a brave face on, for her mother's sake.

Elspeth looked at Alice's pages. 'So, tell me about this Hollow Mountain thing. And who was this guy Alice talks about, the one with the vision?'

'Tom Johnston,' Elspeth said, taking her notebook from her laptop case but feeling no need to look at it.

'And who was Tom Johnston?'

'A Scottish politician, a Red Clydesider.'

'I like him already.'

The Red Clydesiders were a group of fiery politicians from the Glasgow area who fought for social change after the First World War. They didn't quite call for revolution, but the government of the day feared it. After all, revolution had just torn apart the social fabric of Russia. They challenged the establishment of the day and that appealed to Elspeth, who could be equally challenging.

'He stood for Labour and won a seat in parliament and was so well respected that, come the second war, Winston Churchill invited him to join his coalition government as Scottish Secretary of State.'

'Churchill held out a hand to a Red Clydesider?' Elspeth asked. 'I thought he hated them? Did he not send in tanks or something to break up a rammy in George Square?'

She was talking about a rally in 1919 that became a battle between the workers and the police, sent in by the city authorities. 'No, there weren't any tanks. And no machine gun nests on rooftops, either, before you ask.'

'When did you become a student of labour history?'

'It was one of the sidetracks I took last night when I was looking up Tom Johnston. It seems Churchill respected him, but Johnston wasn't keen. He intended to leave politics, as he was sick of partisanship and wanted to write history books. Churchill urged Johnston to join him and help make history.'

'Sounds like old Winston. Did he?'

'Yes, and that was when he first formulated the idea of harnessing hydro power to generate electricity. He also, by the way, co-authored the White Paper that led to the formation of the NHS after the war.'

'God bless it,' said Elspeth, even though she refused to utilise it to fix her knee and hip.

'He thought hydro was a means of not only keeping the lights on in cities, but also bringing that light across the Highlands – some parts didn't even have mains electricity till the 1950s. He also saw it as a way of creating employment in the dark days after the war.'

'So, he's the father of the Cruachan project, right?'

'One of them, I suppose, especially as he later became a director of the Hydro Board. The Cruachan project itself didn't actually begin work until 1959 and ended in the mid-sixties. It was a massive undertaking to create a . . .' She looked at her notes '. . . reversible pump storage system that utilised water to generate power, the first of its kind in the world to be built on such a scale. It cost £24.5 million, maybe the equivalent of half a billion today.'

Elspeth snorted. 'We could crown two kings for that.'

Rebecca shrugged. She wasn't about to get into a discussion with Elspeth about the right or wrong of the monarchy and the cost of the 2023 coronation. That way lay madness. 'I told you I visited the Hollow Mountain, back when I was a teenager, but I didn't really pay that much attention. I'll need go back and have a look at it again because I didn't really grasp the scale of it.'

'Too busy dreaming about some boy band or other, I'll bet.'

'Something like that. I was a teenager, after all. Anyway, it was a huge scheme. Johnston knew it would create employment, but there simply wasn't enough manpower in the glens to meet the demand, so workers were drafted in from all over the country, thousands of them, attracted by the prospect of good money.'

'They paid well, did they?'

'They paid very well. And they had to be accommodated in hotels and guest houses. Some people rented out their homes. Sometimes the company itself bought property to house their top staff. But they also had to set up camps, rows and rows of Nissen huts. It was like the Wild West, on occasion. They blasted, drilled and shifted the heart out of the mountain, and the men who did the blasting were called "tunnel tigers". They earned the most money because it was dangerous work. But all the workers had money to throw away, really, although there were some who ensured that a portion of it was sent home. They worked hard during the week but, come the weekend, wanted to blow off steam. For many of them that meant drinking, gambling, womanising and fighting.'

Elspeth was scanning Alice's words as she listened. 'So, how big is this cavern in the Hollow Mountain?'

Rebecca glanced at her notes again, flipped a page. 'They took out 220,000 cubic metres of granite.'

Elspeth sighed. 'Yeah, like I know how big a pile 220,000 cubic metres is.'

'It's big enough to house a cathedral. I said it was like something out of a James Bond film, remember. Think about the interior of the volcano in *You Only Live Twice* and add a bit on.'

Elspeth visualised it and pursed her lips in a silent whistle.

'But they also carved out a warren of passageways, pipe-lines, aqueducts, generating stations and a dam, way up in the Pass of Brander. And some of the men didn't make it home. There were accidents, cave-ins, that sort of thing.'

'And a murder, if Alice Larkin is to be believed. Any ideas yet who it was?'

'I couldn't find anything.'

'And still no notion who this Gerry Rawlings is or was?'

'Nope. Did you ask Forbes, by any chance?'

'He had no comment to make at this time.'

'Does he know?'

'He has to, but he's not going to say. He's promised to bring the second instalment with him tonight, and we'll find out then. Bloody stupid way to go about things.'

Elspeth remained irritated by the way this was being handled, but Rebecca was enjoying it. So far, at least.

'So, what's the next step?'

'Get through this nonsense today, then talk to whoever Forbes brings tonight, read the next chapter and take it from there.'

'Okay.' Rebecca paused to think, then said, 'Who do you think she meant when she said we might need to tread on somebody's toes?'

'Could be anyone, although difficult to see after all this time who it might be. But remember the old industry saying: "The news is something that somebody, somewhere doesn't want printed . . ."'

'"Everything else is advertising",' Rebecca completed.

Jack Dredden was so lean he made a pencil look obese. His hair was also thin, but that didn't stop him from dyeing what there was crow black, and similarly his slim moustache. He had to be in his late eighties at least, but his face was almost wrinkle-free, just some lines above the nose and across his forehead. This was perhaps because his flesh, which was the colour of a page in an old paperback, seemed to be stretched tautly over his cheekbones, as though made of latex. Rebecca wondered if he'd had some work done at one time but discounted it. He obviously turned himself out well, but he didn't seem the type to go in for cosmetic surgery. He wore a blue three-piece suit that hung from his slender frame like his shoulders were a coat hanger, but Zorro could have used the crease in his trousers as a blade. A carefully folded white handkerchief square peeped from his breast pocket, and it matched a white shirt that gleamed like Leo Cross's teeth. His blue tie was expertly knotted and on the empty chair beside him sat a trilby with a feather. An actual trilby. Rebecca wondered if it had once carried a little card that said PRESS on it, and if he'd ever burst into a newsroom and yelled, 'Hold the front page.'

When Forbes said he'd get some drinks, Jack ordered a sparkling water, explaining that he hadn't had a drink in twenty years.

'I'd been bevvying since my teens, smoking fags, too,' he said in a gravelly voice that bore witness to the truth of his statement. 'Doctor said I should stop if I wanted to see seventy, and I gave it up that day, cleaned up my act. Stopped the booze, the fags, watched what I ate, even took up exercise. I saw seventy, then eighty and, by the grace of the big man upstairs, I'll see ninety. It wasn't easy, to be honest, but if I'd still been in the job full-time, it would've been nigh on fucking impossible . . . excuse me, ladies.'

He was excused. The word was hardly shocking to Rebecca and Elspeth. Jack had walked into the hotel like a man twenty years younger than he actually was, so was obviously still following the fitness regime.

He looked around the hotel lounge, taking in the black and chrome bar, the blue lighting and the glass and chrome tables, his eyes crinkling. 'Never liked these places, never feel comfortable. Gimme an old-fashioned pub, a man's pub – sorry, ladies, but that's the way of it. You could sit there all night and if you kept your ears open, you'd hear all sorts of things going down. The boozing was important back then, part of the job. In places like this, all you hear is the price of quinoa and how little Tarquin is having to acknowledge his disappointment over not making the fucking croquet team, excuse me.'

Forbes returned and set a bottle of sparkling water and a tall glass with ice in front of Jack, a gin and tonic for Elspeth and a Coke for Rebecca. She had learned her lesson the night before and wanted to have a clear head to meet her mum's new boyfriend later. The thought of it made her heart sink.

Jack picked up the bottle of water and stared at it as if it was something worthy of examination. 'Aye, there was a lot of boozing in the job in my day. You know the old cliché about reporters with a bottle of whisky in the bottom drawer? Well, there's a reason it's a fucking cliché, excuse me. There were nights when most of the news desk was rat-arsed by deadline. We used to have a right laugh.'

A hoarse chuckle rasped from his throat at the memory of those far-off days when the ability to hold your drink while all others were losing theirs meant you were a man, my son.

'The industry isn't the same now, is it? No bottles in the bottom drawer, no bevvying during work hours. It's all serious, head-down, you need a degree before you can get a job. See, if it had been like that back then I'd never even have got in the door. I was just a lad from Maryhill who joined the paper right from school. I never had a degree – I had my Scottish Leaving Certificate, but to be honest I wasn't much of a scholar. Learned on the job, from guys who knew what they were talking about, not some lecturer who's never known what it's like to be yelled at by a chief sub who wonders if you know how to spell your own name, or a news editor who wants someone to say exactly what he wants them to say and God help you if you don't get that exact fucking quote, excuse me. S'not like that now. Can't shout at anybody now, unless you want to be accused of bullying. And chief subs are gone, too. What are they now – "content editors", or some such? I mean, Jee-sus Che-rist. And fucking websites, excuse me. Not real reporting at all, neither it is. Glad I got out before all that shite kicked off.'

He paused to take a sip of the water and perhaps ease the stress on his vocal chords after delivering his speech. Rebecca decided this was a man who had grown used to talking and other people listening. His swearing, too, was second nature to him and he was too old to change now, although there were times when he caught himself in time, just a slight hitch in his speech before he plunged on regardless.

When introducing him, Forbes had explained that Jack had been with the *Scottish Daily Tribune* from the late fifties and stayed with the paper for the remainder of his career. He began as a copy boy but moved into reporting in 1962, eventually becoming the title's chief crime reporter and then a columnist. After he left the paper, he worked as a freelance, commenting on TV and radio about crime matters and writing a weekly column for the *Sunday Tribune*, all done in a down-to-earth way. Elspeth had known who he was as soon as he walked in, but he had retired well before Rebecca's time.

'They used to call me Judge Dredden,' he said with that rough little laugh. 'After the comic, you know? Judge Dredd? Course that was in the late seventies, early eighties, when I was established.'

'Who called you that?' Elspeth asked.

'The crooks, mostly. They knew if I was on their arse then it wouldn't be long before that arse was banged up in the Bar-L, one way or the other.'

'What do you mean, "one way or the other"?' Rebecca asked.

That laugh again. 'Hook or by crook, know what I mean? Police back then weren't too choosy about their evidence. This was in the days before DNA and all the forensic shite they have now. Back then it was real police work that snared the bad guys, and sometimes they had to be a wee bit creative in the establishing of proof, if you know what I mean. A bend of the truth here, an outright lie there, all to ensure the bad folk ended up where they belonged.'

He winked, as if the fact that police had been known to fabricate evidence or to lie was a great secret. Unfortunately, it wasn't. Rebecca knew of one senior police officer who admitted that officers had to commit what he called 'pious perjury' in order to strengthen cases.

Jack continued his own explanation. 'So, if I identified some bloke as a wrong 'un, then sometimes the evidence would be found that could put the bastard away, excuse me. S'not the same now – like the newspaper industry, the police have changed. Sometimes it's like they don't want to put bad guys away. Too many do-gooders, too many politicians soft on crime, too many degrees in fucking sociology and that shit, and fucking liberal lawyers picking holes in testimony and getting the bastards off.'

He didn't ask to be excused. Perhaps he felt he didn't need to. Rebecca thought Stephen might have something to say about this rant. In fact, Rebecca had something to say about it, but she held her tongue. Not only did she not have the time to debate with this dinosaur, she was professional enough to know that they needed to pick his brain, so taking him to task over his views on justice was not the way to get him to speak. She decided to remain silent and let Elspeth handle this one.

He sipped his water and grimaced, as if he regretted it not being something stronger, even after all these years. 'Aye, time was, the police and people like me would be out boozing, picking up birds.' He fixed his eye on Rebecca. 'Sorry, hen, don't mean to offend, but back then we would do what blokes do and not feel the need to apologise for it, know what I mean?'

Rebecca had a firm idea what he meant and hoped he didn't feel the need to expand on it for her benefit.

He set his glass down again. 'Now they're all fucking university graduates or something, excuse me. Every one of them sober as a judge, though I've known a judge or two who could drink Richard Burton under the table. There was one, Lord—'

Forbes clearly felt it was time to halt Jack's flow. 'Sorry to interrupt, Jack, but I wonder if we could address the matter in hand?'

Jack held up one bony hand. 'Sorry, ladies, it's a sign of old age, so it is, just talking about the old days as if everyone's interested. Also, I feel the need to get it all out 'cause at my age you're never certain you'll get to finish the sentence.'

The laugh that followed was mechanical, albeit one that needed a little oil, as if he had said that line many times before.

'Well, it's the old days we want to talk to you about, Jack,' Elspeth said.

'The Hollow Mountain, right?'

'Yes.'

'Never covered it myself. I was only a junior reporter at that time.'

'But you were aware of it?'

'Aye, couldn't help but be aware of it – it was a massive thing. Of course, after the initial stories about the work starting, it would have settled down because it wasn't news anymore, if you know what I mean, unless there was a disaster. People died howking that rock out of that mountain – bound to happen, given the scale of it and the number of guys involved. They took precautions obviously, but accidents will happen. Anyway, all that was reported, but nothing day to day.'

'It's a death we want to talk about.'

He nodded. 'Aye, Forbes said. A murder.' He paused, took a sip of his water. He didn't say anything for a few moments, as if he was gathering his thoughts. 'I think I'm here under false pretences, ladies, because I don't know anything about a murder. I've wracked my brain since Forbes phoned me, but I just can't remember anything like that. Accidents, sure. Fights, certainly, because some of they guys were as rough as a badger's bum. And there were arguments between upper class toffs on one side, who didn't like their hunting, shooting and fishing interrupted, and other upper-class toffs on the other side, who probably made a bundle out of the project. That didn't

75

turn into anything physical, though, no fisticuffs, no Marquess of Queensberry.'

He laughed again. Rebecca didn't know how rough a badger's bum was, but Jack's voice seemed to fit the bill.

The laugh subsided and he swallowed another mouthful of water. 'But I don't remember anything about an actual murder. Sorry.'

The murder that never was, Rebecca thought.

Elspeth pressed. 'No suspicious deaths?'

The pause that followed her question was slight, but it was there. 'No, not that I recall. Why you asking, anyway?'

'We've been told there was.'

'Who by?'

Forbes butted in. 'That's confidential for now, Jack, I'm sure you understand. Sources.'

Jack studied Forbes for a moment or two, then said, 'Oh, aye. Always protect sources, right. Rule numero uno.' He sipped his water again. 'I'll take a flyer then and say it's yon cousin of yours, Alice Larkin.'

Forbes kept his face straight but couldn't deny it.

Jack's smile was self-satisfied. 'Aye, thought as much. I know she'd been hudgering around up there. Worked on the local weekly at the time, didn't she, before her dad brought her into the *Tribune*. Never hurts to have a rich daddy, eh? Especially if he owns the fucking paper, excuse me.' He raised a hand as if to pacify Forbes, who hadn't reacted in any way that Rebecca had noticed. 'Sorry, Forbes, I know you never used that family connection to get on, but Alice wasn't averse to wielding her influence when she could. I'm going to be frank here, so don't take any offence, but she was never that hot as a reporter. Too conscious of her looks, you know? She was a good-looking lassie and she knew it, so I wasn't surprised when she moved to telly. Reading the news was more her style than actually finding it and writing it. Too flighty, she was. Looked down on the rest of us working hacks because she knew she didn't need to prove herself.'

Elspeth cleared her throat. 'I'm sorry, Jack, but you're being hard on her. Alice Larkin broke a number of stories in print and was responsible for some fine news reports on screen. Her exposé of the rise in right-wing groups in Scotland back in the mid-seventies was groundbreaking stuff.'

Something seemed to amuse Jack as he gazed at Elspeth. 'Aye, maybe. She was always seeing right-wing phantoms everywhere, that lassie. And maybe she was a better reporter than I remember. I never liked her – sorry, Forbes, but that's the way of it. She was a posh bird with connections, and she looked down on the rest of us working hacks.'

Forbes shrugged. Rebecca had the impression that he was used to hearing it.

Jack took another drink. 'Anyway, I don't think I can help you. I don't remember anything about a murder.' His gaze flicked to Rebecca, then to the notebook on the table in which she had made notes. 'I think you ladies have been given a bum steer, you know? Alice is almost as old as me, remember, and she could be misremembering. I mean, you could go up to the Mitchell Library and go through the papers – they've got them all there – but I'll bet you don't find a single word about a murder connected to Cruachan. Honestly, see, if there had been, I think I'd've known about it. I was young but I was keen, you know? And if there'd been a whisper of murder, or even a suspicious death, I'd've been all over it like shit on a shovel, you know? It's not something I would have forgotten. And if I hadn't been, then old Charlie Woodhead would have. You mind Charlie, Forbes?'

Forbes nodded. 'I met him once, when I was starting out.'

'Best crime hack this city has ever seen, taught me everything I know. If he didn't report it, it didn't happen. And I can guarantee that he didn't report on any murder up there.'

He smiled. He sounded certain. His words carried the authority of someone who had been there and done that, a confidence that his memory was not failing him on this matter.

Rebecca didn't believe a word of it.

78

7

Alice had never liked the man standing in her bedroom. He was too smooth, too oily, like a cabinet minister promoting a policy that should be examined but ensuring a reporter's questions slide away. Dennis had never had much time for him, either. When this man had been a working lawyer, her husband had worked with him on a couple of cases. Dennis had always said there was something unpleasant about him – no matter how well coiffed he was, no matter how elegantly dressed, no matter how politely he spoke.

He had arrived unannounced, but Alice had told Orla to show him up. Orla was hesitant. She knew who he was and didn't hide her disdain when she said his name but, when she ushered him into Alice's room, she politely offered him tea or coffee, or something stronger. Only Alice knew the offer was grudging, but the laws of civility demanded that she at least ask. Alice had cut in, saying the gentleman wouldn't be staying long enough for refreshments. The laws of civility no longer applied to her. He had merely smiled that easy smile of his and thanked Orla, saying that it was, in fact, a flying visit. Orla left, giving Alice a quick look that darted to the button on the side table, her way of telling her that she wouldn't be far away.

'It's good to see you, Alice,' said Finbar Dalgliesh. 'It's been quite some time.'

He was lying, of course. He didn't think it was good to see her, unless he enjoyed the sight of the toll her advancing years

79

had taken on her body and the fact she was stuck in this damned bed unless Orla lifted her out and into the wheelchair.

She didn't return the sentiment. 'What brings you to my door, Finbar?'

She knew why he was here. She had expected him to be here. And here he was, although it was sooner than she expected. When she suggested Forbes steer Jack Dredden in the direction of Elspeth and Rebecca, she had hoped that word would reach Dalgliesh, she'd banked on it, but the speed of it was remarkable. Dredden had always been a lickspittle to men like Dalgliesh. And there had been many men like Dalgliesh over the years.

'Dennis was a good friend of mine,' he said, taking a seat on the couch under the window, even though she had not invited him to do so. That was his way, though.

'That's a lie, Finbar,' she said, not feeling any need to be polite. 'Dennis did not look on you as a friend.'

He smiled. It seemed bashful, as if he knew he had been caught with his fingers in the sugar bowl and was using his charm to cover it up. 'That's a fact, but I would have liked it to be different.'

'That may or may not be true, but there was never any suggestion that you and he could be friends. He disagreed with everything you came to stand for.'

'A lot of people disagree with my views, but some remain friends.'

She let that sit between them for a moment, debating with herself whether she should pick it up and run with it. She had wanted to flush him out, but now all she wanted was for him to say what he had come to say and leave. In the end, she couldn't help herself.

'But they're not your views, are they? You merely adopted them because it suited your ambitions. That was one of the things that irritated Dennis. He could accept people's views, would argue with them, but he knew you were not what you said you were. You simply saw it as a means to further yourself.'

Finbar Dalgliesh had been a successful lawyer and still occasionally practised for certain clients. But in the early 2000s he moved away from the law and took an interest in politics, becoming a leading light of the SG, Spioraid nan Gáidtheal, ostensibly a nationalist party but not one that mainstream nationalists would have anything to do with. In fact, the Scottish National Party had publicly disowned any connection to them, and its leaders never missed the chance to declare the SG right-wing thugs and nutters, with Dalgliesh himself dismissed as little more than a mob lawyer turned rabble-rouser.

Nevertheless, the party had drawn a number of people into its embrace, riding the tide of the independence referendum with its extreme view of a Scotland devoid of any blood but Celtic, with a hard 'K' sound, for the football team had its roots in Roman Catholicism and the SG weren't too keen on that either, hence Orla's reaction to his presence. Judaism wasn't acceptable either. The Brexit debate also strengthened their position among those who believed that anyone with an accent who did not originate on these shores, or even those who did speak with Scots tones but whose colour suggested roots elsewhere, should be treated with at best suspicion, at worst outright hostility. Alice had heard that Dalgliesh was actively forging bonds with groups in England holding similar views, with the aim of creating what they might have called a British National Party, if that title was not already toxic. She felt sure that Dalgliesh would come up with something suitably Britonic, just as Spioraid nan Gáidtheal was Gaelic for 'Spirit of the Gael', even though the spirit on display was, to Alice's way of thinking, slightly more Germany in the 1930s than Scotland in the 2020s.

Dalgliesh was not insulted by Alice's statement, no doubt because others had inferred, and indeed stated openly, a lot worse. 'Dennis never understood my motivations properly.'

'I understand you, though.'

He seemed to find that amusing. 'Do you really?'

'I understand you very well, Finbar. I've been around people like you all my life.'

He smiled. 'Yes, you have, haven't you? And I also understand you.'

They understood each other in silence for a few moments.

Eventually Alice spoke again. 'So, to what do I owe this visit? I hesitate to use the word "pleasure".'

'The feeling is reciprocated, as I'm sure you know.'

She smiled. 'We know where we stand, then.'

'Alice, dear, we always did.'

Another silence. Another acknowledgement that each was fully aware of the other's faults and motives.

'So,' Alice said, 'now that we've established that this is not a social call, why are you here?'

He sat back on the couch, spread his arms wide on the back and casually positioned his right ankle on his left knee. He had the knack of making himself look very relaxed wherever he was and whatever company in which he found himself. It was that ability, and his undoubted charm (although that was lost on Alice, for she did, indeed, understand him too well) that had smoothed his way into politics, onto appearances on *Newsnight* and from there to right-wing news channels to spout his particular brand of silky bile.

'I think you know why I'm here,' he said.

She didn't reply. She wanted to hear him say it.

He took a deep breath and placed his foot back on the floor. 'You're turning over old stones, Alice.'

'Stones that should have been turned over years ago.'

'What happened is ancient history.'

82

'So is slavery, and we shouldn't forget about that. And in case you've forgotten, you're the man who completely misrepresented Culloden as a Scots-versus-English battle. You're not above manipulating history for your own ends.'

'Is that your intention? To manipulate history?'

'It is my intention to resurrect a history that has been suppressed.'

'In your opinion.'

'Of the two opinions in this room, mine carries the most weight. I was there, you were not.'

He had to concede that. 'You'll achieve nothing with this. It's all in the past. Let it lie.'

'I can't. I should have done something before now.'

'Why did you not?'

She felt shame then. 'I was scared.'

He nodded sagely, understanding. 'And you're scared no longer?'

'Dennis is gone, my father is gone. There is no one left for you and your people to hurt.'

'My people?'

'You know who I'm talking about.'

'I really don't.'

She sighed. 'New Dawn and their like.'

They were the real bully boys of their movement and had reputedly been behind minor acts of terror and major acts of criminality, like serious assault, extortion and gun running.

'I have no connection to them,' he said.

'You've defended them in court.'

'Dennis defended drug dealers in court – does that mean he was himself a drug dealer?'

She had no reply to that.

'I'm here as a friend, Alice,' he said.

'Take an "r" out of that word and you're closer to the truth.'

He blinked a few times, then laughed through his nose and shook his head. 'You've not lost your sharp tongue.'

'I intend to ensure that it continues to cut long after I'm gone.'

'Which will not be long, I fear.'

'Is that a threat?'

His smile now was almost sad. 'No, an observation.' He stood up, waved one hand around the room. 'This tells me that you are reaching the end of your days.' He walked to the bedside table and picked up a bottle of pills, read the label. 'That's why you're no longer fearful of turning over these stones. How long do you have?'

She held his gaze. 'Long enough, I assure you.'

He replaced the bottle on the table. 'I don't think so, Alice. I think you'll be dead before the story breaks, if it ever breaks.'

She already knew this, had come to terms with it. 'It will break.'

'Not if there is no story. And sixty years is a long time. Very few people remember it. And those who do, don't want to talk about it.'

'Nevertheless, I'll turn those stones over and stir up the mud. Some of it might stick.'

'But you're not turning the stones, are you? You're getting someone else to do your dirty work.'

So, Jack Dredden had told him about Elspeth and Rebecca. He really didn't waste any time and must have contacted Dalgliesh as soon as Forbes had arranged the meeting. 'They're very adept at it.'

'I know that. Ms Connolly and I have encountered one another before.'

Alice was aware of that. 'Then you know how determined she can be.'

'I do, and that is why I urge you to call them off, tell them you were mistaken, tell them you have changed your mind.'

'Why would I do that? I've already told you that you can't scare me.'

'I'm alerting you to a very real danger, Alice.'

'I don't care about that, I told—'

'Not you.' He glanced at the door, as if he thought Orla might be on the other side listening – which she very likely was – before speaking again, this time lowering his voice to little more than a whisper. 'You've brought Ms Connolly and the McTaggart woman into this, even your cousin.' He leaned forward, and she thought – no, was certain – she saw the shadow of something that might have been genuine concern in his expression. 'The danger lies in them turning over one stone too many.'

8

Someone was watching her.

Rebecca had experienced that sensation before, that prickling at the back of her neck, that flutter in her stomach. At the time she had put it down to paranoia but, as the line went, that didn't mean they weren't out to get her. On that occasion, it turned out she was being followed, so when she felt it again as she walked from the city centre hotel towards the restaurant where she was to meet her mum and her boyfriend – God, that sounded strange – she stopped suddenly to pay greater attention to what was going on around her.

The restaurant was on Bath Street, and she was on Hope Street, passing the hulking mass of Glasgow Central station to her right. People hurried towards the station after a day of working or shopping. Others sauntered from the station's Gordon Street exit, ready for a night out. A middle-aged man and woman passed her by, hand-in-hand, but didn't even look in her direction. She watched them go. The people who had been following her before had been such a middle-aged couple. Pat and Mike. They looked ordinary, seemed even affable, but they were far from ordinary, for they were professional killers and very efficient ones she assumed, although she had no real evidence of it. They were still out there, somewhere, probably still killing people and being affable.

The station had been constructed in the Victorian era, when Glasgow was expanding to engulf surrounding towns and villages. One such village was Grahamston, which disappeared under the burgeoning transport system. She'd been told the remains of the main street could still be seen in the bowels of the building, although she'd never taken the tour. Perhaps it was the ghosts of those long-gone residents who were watching her. She smiled at the thought of the spirits of those who had once lived in Glasgow still existing on some level, watching the city transform, the buildings they had lived in, loved in, laughed in, being flattened and rising as something new, only to be flattened again and then rising once more.

She checked her surroundings again but saw nobody paying her undue attention.

Dear God, Becks, you're getting jittery. What's that all about?

As she headed up the hill once more, she wondered if perhaps the reason for her unease lay in the interview in the hotel bar.

A lot about the man they called Judge Dredden had bothered her, and she knew why. It wasn't his misogyny – she was mature enough to know that he was a product of his time and arguing that particular point would have been pointless. The main thing that bothered her was the lies he told, and Rebecca didn't like being lied to. It had begun, like the sense of unseen eyes on her, as little more than a feeling, but the more he denied knowing anything, the more it grew into an absolute certainty. He seemed very open, sharing his views on the industry and reminiscing about the way things were in the good old, bad old days, but that was all smoke and mirrors, she thought. He knew what they wanted to know, and he was diverting them with what seemed like idle chit-chat, the absent ramblings of an old man yearning for an era that was dead and buried. But he wasn't some old codger living in the past – his eyes were too sharp, and his view on the superiority of those old days was the only truthful thing that had passed his lips. Her father used to say that lies could be detected not in what was said but in the way they were said. The way Dredden sat; the way his eyes flicked away suddenly, just a little; the strong note of pride in his voice as he'd told them his nickname. This was a man who was used to his words being taken as gospel, and he might have been convincing if they were in print – but in person she found him far from it. Something had occurred back in 1964 at Cruachan, and whether or not he had been a part of it she couldn't say, but he certainly knew about it.

When Forbes and the old reporter left, Rebecca had waited a few minutes with Elspeth and told her she thought the man was hiding something. Elspeth didn't dismiss it out of hand as she had worked long enough with Rebecca to take her gut feelings seriously.

'What, though? He seemed confident we wouldn't find any news reports about a murder. There's nothing online, we know that.'

'I'll double check that tomorrow at the Mitchell. I'm meeting Chaz and Alan at the station first thing, so we can go up there for an hour or two before they're due to be interviewed.'

Elspeth nodded her agreement and raised the A4 brown envelope Forbes had handed each of them before he left. It contained the next instalment of Alice's story. Jack had looked at the envelopes with interest but had not asked anything. Either he knew what was in there or he didn't want to appear too curious. That look had bothered Rebecca, too.

'I'll order room service and have a read of these,' Elspeth said.

'I'll read them later, after this bloody dinner,' Rebecca said, finishing her Coke.

'Be nice, Rebecca,' Elspeth warned. 'Give the man a chance.'

'I'm always nice.'

'And what about giving this guy a chance?'

Rebecca smiled. 'I'm always nice.'

She had been joking, of course. She fully intended to give James Wilton a chance, if only for her mother's sake, but now as she walked, ignoring that nagging feeling she was not alone, she wondered if her foreboding about this dinner had caused the continuing unease. That she had been dreading this all day she couldn't deny, so was it still playing its part by tingling her mind?

She turned left into Bath Street and found the Italian restaurant, which was situated in the basement of a building built in Victorian times as a townhouse but now separated into offices. Her father had told her that the street was so named because a series of public bath houses had once stood there, way back in the early eighteenth century. John Connolly had been full of such nuggets of information because he read widely and possessed a retentive memory. Anyone who came up against him in a game of Trivial Pursuit walked away feeling like a dunce.

Her mother and James Wilton were already waiting for her at the table. Rebecca instinctively checked her watch and was relieved that she wasn't late. She took a deep breath as she was led to them by the hostess who had greeted her at the door. Rebecca hoped the smile she had adopted appeared natural. The unease she had felt in the street had given way to nervousness. What if she hated this man? What would she do?

He stood up as she approached, his hand held out. 'Rebecca, I'm James. I've heard so much about you.'

For some reason she was surprised to see that he was of average height but a bit overweight, which made him look a little smaller. His hair was thick and grey and long. Her father had been a tall man who had kept not just his body but his hair trim. Rebecca didn't know what she had expected, but for some reason she had assumed her mother had a type, and James Wilton didn't fit that preconceived notion. His smile was easy and his handshake firm and dry, which was something. She hoped her own palm hadn't been slimy with nervous sweat.

'I've heard a little about you, too,' she said, about to sit down, but he pulled her chair out for her. Okay, mate, calm yourself down, she thought.

He gave her mother a quick smile as he took his own seat again. 'The food here's superb,' he said, handing her a menu. He seemed a little over-eager to please, she thought. Was he nervous? If so, that made two of them. She glanced at her mother and detected a slight tension in her jaw. Okay, that made three of them. Three nervous people sitting at a table, all smiling and pretending they weren't nervous. This was weird.

'I hope you like Italian?' he said. 'I didn't think to ask your mum before I booked the table, so I hope it's okay.'

Yeah, maybe you should have asked my mum first, she thought, then instantly felt guilty. The guy was trying to be nice here, stop being a brat. 'Yes, I like Italian,' she said, smiling. 'And I'm starved, it's been a long day.'

Her mother asked, 'How did it go?'

Rebecca studied the menu. 'All fine. A lot of sitting around, then a lot of talking. It's amazing how exhausting that can be.'

'Nerves, perhaps,' Sandra said, 'they can take it out of you. That and the unreality of it all. Cameras, lights, that sort of thing.'

'Your mum has told me about the documentary,' said James. 'It's for Netflix, right?'

'That's right,' said Rebecca, still reading the menu.

'When will it be on?'

'Not a clue. They've only just begun filming and it's a feature-length documentary, so they won't be finished for ages yet. Probably some time next year.'

'We'll need to make sure we watch it,' he said, resting his hand on Sandra's as it lay on the tabletop. Over the menu,

90

Rebecca marked the physical contact, then looked away. Her mother hadn't removed her hand. In fact, she had turned it upwards so she could entwine her fingers with his. The only other person she had seen her do that with had been her dad. This didn't seem real. This didn't seem right. This was weird.

Stop it, Rebecca. Stop being such a brat. This *is* real, this *is* right. Get used to it.

She cleared her throat. 'I think I'll go for the lasagne, what about you guys?'

The hands disentangled to grasp menus. 'Chicken cacciatore for me,' Sandra said. 'James?'

He smiled, laid his menu down. 'Sounds good, I'll have the same.'

Don't be a sook, James.

He waved a hand and caught the waiter's attention. 'Anyone for a drink? Wine? Or shall we be daring on a school night and hit the hard stuff?'

Rebecca was sorely tempted to order a whisky, if only to see the reaction on her mum's face, but she opted for a soft drink instead, explaining that she was working the next day and needed a clear head, which was actually true. Sandra opted for water and James grinned. 'Temperance meeting, we have here. Okay, I'm not much of a drinker anyway.'

He ordered a bottle of sparkling water for the table then the waiter asked if they were ready to order their meals. They did so, James changing his mind at the last moment and going for rigatoni al tartufo and pronouncing it expertly to Rebecca's ear. Good for you, Jimmy boy. Be your own man.

'Good choice,' said the waiter, who took the menus and left.

'I'll bet he says that no matter what you order,' James said, his face crinkled with good humour. Sandra laughed and Rebecca smiled dutifully. He seemed okay, so far. But it still felt weird.

'Your mum's been telling me about your exploits, Rebecca,' he said.

Exploits. She didn't know she'd had exploits – she simply thought of it as work.

'Got to say, it all seems kind of exciting to someone like me.'

He sounded genuinely impressed. Or maybe he was a good actor.

'It's not as exciting as it sounds,' she said. 'A lot of talking and knocking on doors and making telephone calls and a lot more talking.'

And, sometimes, someone is following you and you can't see them. She didn't say that, though. Her mum would have a canary if she thought she was in any danger.

'I've read those books by your boss, Elspeth . . .' His voice trailed away.

'McTaggart,' she filled in.

'Yes. It seems you lead a fascinating life.'

Fascinating. Sometimes it was so fascinating she almost died. Just as she didn't think of the stories as exploits, she didn't think she had a fascinating life. She did what she did, that was all.

'Not really,' she said. 'It's all pretty much routine. As I said, lots of talking.'

'I'm a surveyor, remember,' he said. 'The closest I get to excitement is not being able to work my theodolite properly.' His smile turned a little wicked. 'But then I'm an old man and that's quite common.'

Sandra spluttered out a laugh. 'James!' She hit his arm with the back of her hand.

He gave Rebecca a shrug and a smile, and she laughed. It was a genuine laugh. A waiter appeared with the bottle of water and Rebecca's Coke. They waited while he poured out three glasses, James and her mum stealing little glances and sharing smiles, those fingers intertwining again. Still weird.

When the waiter left, James asked, 'So, what are you working on at the moment, or are you not allowed to say? Is there a journalistic code of secrecy? I mean, apart from the TV thing.'

'Something has come up since Rebecca's been here,' Sandra said.

James found this interesting, maybe even fascinating. 'You only arrived yesterday.'

'There's always something coming up with Rebecca,' Sandra said, her voice just a little on the sharp side. 'She never stops working.'

'Yes, I was the same at your age,' said James. 'Drove my first wife crazy. Mind you, that was a short journey.'

He smiled again. Rebecca smiled back. Sandra laughed. Weird.

'So, can you say what you're working on?' he asked.

'It's something that came out of the blue,' she said.

'Does that happen often?'

'Sometimes. Usually it's routine – a commission from a newspaper or a magazine, or some court reporting, or a bit of research for TV people. All those things are the agency's bread and butter. But now and again something comes up that's out of the ordinary.'

'And is this story out of the ordinary?'

'So far, yes, although it may prove to be nothing. Early days yet.'

'What's it about?'

She took a deep breath. She didn't really like discussing stories ahead of time, but she felt that avoiding the question would be deemed impolite by her mother. Even so, she couldn't go into too much detail at this stage. 'It's hard to say, really, but it concerns a huge engineering project in Argyll back in the fifties and sixties—'

James interjected, 'The Hollow Mountain?'

'Yes, you know about it?'

93

'Oh yeah, I've visited the power station a couple of times. Incredible piece of engineering. My uncle helped build it.'

And with these few words, Rebecca saw him in a new light. 'Is he still around?'

'He's getting on, but, yes, he's still around. A bit wandered, but he's doing well.'

Suddenly things were no longer weird. It's funny how things work out.

9

Excerpt from Murder on the Mountain:
The Personal Testimony of Alice Larkin

I first met Gerry Rawlings in a pub in Oban. It was a Friday night and the boys had been paid so were ready for a weekend of play. I knew that some of them patronised that particular bar, but it wasn't somewhere I'd normally choose to frequent, it being on the lower end of the social life scale in the town. I knew approaching the company behind the project would not bring me anything but the usual press release and the official line, and that didn't interest me. I wasn't looking for facts, figures or statistics or how momentous this project was. What I wanted was to find out what it was like to be involved in such an undertaking at the ground level, or rather, the underground level. I wanted to speak to the tunnel tigers, the men who risked their lives to hollow that mountain out, some of whom had worked elsewhere to create the hydro industry in the Highlands because Cruachan was only a part – a major part, to be sure – of an overall project to harness the water that Scotland has in abundance. And I'd been told I would find such men in this pub.

Let's just be clear – what I was doing was not only frowned upon by society, it was damned risky. A young woman in those days didn't even go to the cinema alone, let alone walk into a place like that. Anybody who did was seen as little more than a whore, but I was willing to do it in order to somehow find a story. If Nellie Bly could risk her sanity by infiltrating a mental institution in the nineteenth century, I could risk my reputation in the twentieth by going for a drink.

If my father had known my intention, he would have locked me away in a dungeon, but I always worked under the mantra that what he didn't know couldn't hurt me. Not that he would ever physically abuse me, not his princess. But that, I suppose, was the issue; I believed then and I believe now that he saw me as a winsome, fey little flower who needed to be protected and married off at the earliest opportunity, preferably to someone like Lance, who might be comparatively penniless but at least came from a good family. It was 1964, for God's sake, and that kind of thing died out with bustles. My father never fully understood my desire to be a success in the media, that I wanted to make something of myself other than as a wife and mother. As far as he was concerned, he had worked hard so that I didn't have to. And, don't get me wrong, I was happy to avail myself of his largesse. I was independently minded but not stupid. And, as you already know, he indulged me. But if he had known I was walking into that pub alone, with all the arrogance of youth, wearing my tight drainpipe jeans and black turtle-neck sweater that was just clingy enough to show off my figure, my hair coiled on my head like Medusa's snakes sleeping off a large meal, he would have blown a gasket there and then and unlocked that dungeon. But I believed I could handle myself.

I was wrong.

The pub had two entrances, one for the 'public bar', the other to what was called the 'lounge', which was slightly more up-market because it was swept occasionally, spitting was discouraged and they stocked Babycham. I wasn't allowed to go into the former. Women had won the vote thirty-odd years before, but we still weren't free to walk into a bar. I entered the lounge and found it to be filled almost exclusively with men, perhaps overflowing from the bar on the other side of the wooden partition. All eyes turned in my direction and conversation seemed to still, with only the sound of male voices from beyond the partition and The Dave Clark Five thundering 'Glad All Over' from the jukebox in the corner. That had been an event a few years before, the arrival of that jukebox, and I remember wishing I could go and see it, but I was too young and not male enough. Now I could see it and hear it, but I had other things on my mind. I should have taken the stunned reaction of the patrons as a sign and simply turned and left, but I didn't. I strutted to the small bar where a man whose face I recognised, but to which I could not attach a name, watched me approach with something akin to horror.

'Miss Larkin,' he whispered, swallowing hard. 'You cannae be in here.'

'Why not?'

He licked his lips and glanced at the faces watching us as though this was a drama on television. 'It's no right, neither it is. This isnae a place for ladies like you.'

I looked around again and said, 'I see some ladies here.'

He lowered his voice further. 'No like you.'

I heard one of the women mutter 'cheeky sod', then laugh.

'I'm only here for a quiet drink.' As if by magic, his name popped into my head, so I added, 'Bobby.'

He shook his head emphatically. 'I cannae serve you, Miss Larkin. We don't serve women drinks here, no if they're unattended.'

'Unattended,' I repeated, suddenly finding this amusing. I should have been outraged but I suppose deep inside I'd known this would happen. Perhaps I thought my family connection would have smoothed the way, but it was a further

97

hindrance. Bobby knew that if he served me then it would inevitably reach my father's ears and there would be hell to pay.

'Aye, unattended,' he said, drawing himself erect, or as erect as he could, given he was not a tall man and somewhat round-shouldered. 'I'm sorry, but I'll have to ask you to leave. This is a respectable establishment and we cannae have unattended ladies in here. It's no right, neither it is.' His voice dropped again. 'And your faither would have my job if he found out I'd served you.'

I was about to ask what my father had to do with his employment but stopped short as understanding dawned. My father owned the place. I knew he had interests in many things, but I didn't see him as being a publican. No, not a publican, I reasoned – he owned the building and leased it to the licence holder. That had to be it.

'I'll buy her a drink.'

The voice came from behind me, and I turned to see a handsome young man around my own age, an almost empty glass of whisky in one hand, a pint of beer in the other. His thick black hair was slick with Brylcreem, and his blue eyes reminded me of the actor Paul Newman. I hadn't known he had blue eyes until I saw him in the film *Exodus*, having only seen him in black and white before then.

'That's very kind of you,' I said.

He smiled. 'My pleasure, hen. What'll you have?'

'A Coca-Cola will be fine, thank you.'

'Nothing stronger?'

I would have much preferred something stronger, for my nerves were working on me, but I was at least wise enough to understand that I needed my wits about me.

He accepted that and repeated it to Bobby, who hesitated. 'Miss Larkin, you really shouldnae be in here. What will your faither think?'

'What my father thinks is immaterial, Bobby. I'm over twenty-one and I'm thirsty.'

'You heard the lassie, mate,' said the black-haired man. 'So, how about you walking over there and fetching her a Coca-Cola.' He drained the whisky. 'And give me another one of these while you're at it.'

Bobby seemed intent on arguing the point, but the young man set the empty glass down and leaned in closer. 'Mate, a Coca-Cola for the lady and a whisky for me. I'll no ask a third time.'

I don't know what he saw in that man's eyes, but Bobby lost all trace of his former authority. He seemed to search for something on the bar top and then stepped meekly away to fetch the drinks.

'Thank you,' I said.

'No bother,' he said. 'I'm Danny, by the way.'

He held out his hand. I took it. His grip was dry and fleeting. 'Alice,' I said, immediately wondering if I should have given him a false name, but then he must have heard Bobby calling me Miss Larkin, so there was no point.

His gaze slipped beyond me to the watching faces, as if challenging them to hold it. Eyes dropped, turned away, just as Bobby's had, and conversation began to build again. Dave Clark changed to The Searchers singing 'Needles and Pins'. Danny turned back to me and smiled. 'Folk need to mind their own business, right?'

I didn't reply. He'd helped me, certainly, and there was every chance that he was working on the project, but in that moment I knew that I didn't want to have anything further to do with him. I didn't know why then, and I can't even say for certain now, although my misgiving would shortly be proved correct, but all I knew was that this young man wore around his shoulders an air of menace like some people wear a coat. The problem was how to extricate myself now that he had bought me a drink.

Bobby returned with a bottle of Coca-Cola, a glass cupped over the neck, and a whisky. Danny paid him and gestured to the corner where a small, round table had just been vacated. The lounge wasn't that large and it was dull and dingy, but these small tables and chairs helped set it apart from the bar next door, along with the lack of male expectoration and the retailing of sparkling water.

I took the chair facing into the room, caught some curious looks in my direction, while Danny spun the one opposite round and faced me, legs splayed. He probably saw it in a film, and I think it was supposed to be alluring.

'Don't see many burds like you in places like this,' he observed. 'Bobby there seems to know you, so you're from around here, right?'

I nodded, unsettled by the way I'd felt his gaze on me during the short walk across the floor.

'I'm frae Glasgow,' he volunteered, but I'd already guessed that from his accent. 'I'm up here to work on the hydro.'

This should have been ideal. I'd wanted to speak to someone like him. Like him, but not him, but I felt I needed to say something. 'What do you do?'

'A wee bit of labourin'. You sure you don't want nothin' stronger than that?' He nodded to the glass of Coca-Cola.

'No, thank you, this is all I want.' The Searchers stopped complaining about needles and pins. 'I'm waiting for someone,' I said.

He didn't take any notice. The song changed to Dusty Springfield and 'I Only Want To Be With You'. A little smile played on Danny's lips as he sang along quietly.

I took a sip of my drink, glanced at my watch. This had been a mistake, I knew it then. What the hell had I been thinking, coming here alone? Coming here at all?

'Your boyfriend late?' he asked.

'I'm not . . .' I revised my reply. 'Yes, I'll kill him when I see him.'

He squinted a little at my hesitation. 'No a good look, is it? A bloke gettin' a posh burd like you to meet him in a shithole like this and then no even showing up. Maybe you should reassess your relationship, know what I mean?'

Reassess your relationship, I thought. Where did a man like him come up with a phrase like that? Was he showing off because he knew I was what he called posh? 'I'm sure he'll have a good reason.'

'But you'll still tear a right strip off him, eh?'

'Yes, I will.'

He smiled. Threw back his whisky. 'Bet you're dead good at tearing things off, eh?'

He might have meant that as a joke, but I suspected not. Sometimes you know a person is not someone with whom you would wish to associate, and with him it began with the look in his eyes and now in the way he spoke. I was in danger from this man called Danny and I knew it.

I stood up, I thought a little too sharply, but he didn't seem to be at all fazed by it. 'I'll go home, I think.'

He sat back in his chair, his pint glass in his hand. 'You just got here, hen.'

I picked up my handbag. 'My boyfriend is obviously not coming.'

'Maybe I can take his place.'

I forced a smile but even I could tell it was tremulous. 'Thank you, but I'm happy with him.'

'Even though he doesnae turn up and leaves you in the lurch in a dump like this? That's no a boy that deserves you, darlin'.'

'He may have a good reason.'

'There is no reason good enough for jilting a piece like you.'

101

He hadn't reached out to touch me, but for some reason the way his eyes roamed over me felt like hands, stroking, fondling, probing. I stepped out from behind the table.

'You've no finished your drink,' he said.

'You finish it,' I said and took a step away, but he suddenly reached out with his free hand and grabbed my wrist.

'You know what? I bought you that drink – you said you wanted it, and I bought it. Now I think you should sit down and finish it.'

'I don't want it now.' His fingers were tightly wrapped round my wrist, but I reached into the pocket of my jeans with my free hand and found a pound note, dropped it on the table. 'That should cover it and your drink and one or two more, I should imagine.'

'It's no your money I want, darlin',' he said without even looking at me. 'As the song says, I only want to be with you. It's your company I want.'

I gestured towards the pound note crumpled on the table-top. 'You can have one but not the other.'

He looked up at me then. He was smiling, but there was no humour. 'Sit down and finish your drink.'

'No,' I said, then added, 'thank you.'

'Polite, aren't you?'

'I try to be.'

'So, what are you? Some rich bitch out for a bit of rough? I can be rough. I can be as rough as you like.'

'I am rich, and some will say I'm a bitch, but I'm not looking for anything, rough or otherwise. Now, will you let me go, or do I have to scream for help?'

'No need for that, miss,' said a voice, and Danny craned round to look at another young man, his body muscled, his hair fair, his face pleasing, his accent Irish. 'Danny here was just having a laugh, weren't you, Danny boy?'

'Stay out of this, mick, this is between me and her. We're talking.'

'It doesn't look like talking to me. It looks like pawing, and that's not very civilised, even for a Glasgow boy like yourself.'

Once again conversation had dulled as all eyes turned to them. I saw some knowing smiles and heard whispers but couldn't catch any words. Danny exhaled through his nose and freed my wrist.

'That's the lad,' the newcomer said, then touched a finger to his forehead as if he was wearing a cap. 'Sorry about Danny boy here, miss. He gets carried away with himself sometimes and steps over a line. And sometimes, when he steps over that line, he has to be carried away, that right, Danny boy?'

Danny stared straight ahead but didn't reply. However, the coldness in his eyes had been replaced by anger, and his jaw had tensed. I had the distinct impression that these two were not friends, despite the newcomer's relaxed manner. I didn't care about their history, though. All I wanted now was to get out.

'Thank you,' I said and walked as quickly as I could to the door without actually breaking into a run. That would have been unseemly, and I'd already made a spectacle of myself, one that would no doubt make its way back to my father, now that I knew he owned this damned place. I felt everyone's eyes on me once more, but not out of shock or curiosity as they had been before. They mocked me now, I knew it. I was being looked at not with pity but with contempt. I was a single girl who had entered this world and I deserved everything I got. I felt shame then. I had been stupid. I had been headstrong.

I rushed into the street, where the cool air coming off the Firth of Lorne hit me like a cold compress. The sun had gone down, but its ghost still lingered in the sky, and I stopped for a moment to breathe in the fresh air, looking to where the island of Kerrera lay low in the water and, rising behind it, the dark peaks of Mull. The street was deserted, the only signs of life being the occasional car passing on the esplanade, lights shining in windows and the sound of that damned jukebox, Big Dee Irwin now swinging on a star with Little Eva. I heard laughter from the men, perhaps at my expense, which made my face burn again. Would you rather be an ass, the lyrics went, and I had been.

I started to walk, the click of my high heels echoing from the walls like the ticking of a clock that I was trying to beat, a clock that I would dearly have loved to turn back, only an hour, to before I left my flat. I was embarrassed and angry and ashamed all at the same time, and my head was filled with self-doubt. I couldn't believe how ridiculous my idea had been. To walk into a place like that, alone! Perhaps my father was correct in his assessment that I should stick to lifestyle articles. Perhaps I didn't have what it took to follow in the footsteps of Nellie Bly and the others. Perhaps . . .

I was dimly aware of the music suddenly rising behind me, then falling again, as if someone had opened and closed the pub door, but my senses sharpened when I heard another sound. Someone else's footsteps. A man's. And walking quickly after me.

I shot a quick look, saw a figure but couldn't make out who it was in the twilight.

I began to increase my pace, my entire being lurching when he did the same. I searched for someone who might come to my aid, but there was still nobody in sight. It was that fallow time between people arriving at pubs and restaurants and leaving them. Everyone else was already in their home and watching *The Defenders* on TV.

My car was in sight but unless I broke into a run, I wouldn't make it before he reached me. And I wasn't about to run in these heels. I thought about taking them off but that would cost me time. My breathing fluctuated as fear took hold. Danny was following me, it had to be him. I cursed myself for letting him buy me that drink, that was a bad move. I should have politely refused and left there and then.

But I hadn't. I'd let him buy it. And here we were in a quiet street with the red streaks in the sky slowly dying and he wasn't far behind me, with God knew what on his mind and nobody around to whom I could call out.

As I hurried, I opened my bag and fished around inside, looking for something I could use as a weapon, anything, but all I had in there was a purse with some loose change, a compact, a handkerchief, some lipstick, my car key and a plastic comb.

And then I felt a hand on my arm, and I whirled round, that comb raised.

The Irishman raised his hands and took a step back. 'Sorry, miss, I didn't mean to scare you. When you looked back, I thought you knew it was me.'

I took two paces back from him. 'I didn't. All I saw was someone following me.'

'And you thought it was Danny boy?'

'Yes.'

He nodded towards the comb still held in my raised hand. 'And what were you going to do if it was him? Part his hair?'

I looked at the comb and felt a laugh bubble, but I believe it was nerves. 'I don't really know. Rake it down his face probably.'

'Well, that'd be smart, no doubt about it, but I don't think it would stop old Danny McCall. He's a terrible man with the drink in him. When sober, he thinks he's a hard man, and he is, but he's learned that there's always someone harder.' I knew then that this fellow in front of me was someone who was harder. At some point in the past, he and Danny McCall had come to blows. 'If it's any consolation, I don't think you were in any real danger from him. I've never seen him with a girl. He's got a wife and a little one back in Glasgow, I hear tell, and he remains faithful, to an extent anyway. Maybe a kiss and a cuddle up a lane somewhere, but no more than that, I don't think. But there's a bad bit in him when he's had a couple that sometimes likes to frighten people, especially young women. Gives him a jolly, it does.'

'Well, I'm glad I was there to provide him with some entertainment.'

Power, I realised. He was a man who liked to give the impression that he had power over a woman, and even though this man said I'd been in no danger, I still saw the look in those blue eyes. Danny McCall was a man who would some day do more than just frighten a girl.

'So, if he's so harmless, what made you come after me?'

He tilted his head sideways. 'What makes you think I was coming after you? Do you think you're worth coming after?'

'You sped up when I sped up, and you grabbed me. Why else would you do that? But yes, I do think I'm worth coming after.'

He laughed. He laughed easily, I learned. 'Aye, I was coming after you but only to make sure you were all right, not to see if you wanted to go somewhere a little classier for a drink, if that's what you're thinking. After what happened in there, I don't think that would be appropriate.'

For some reason, I felt disappointed by that. 'I'm fine, thank you. That was kind and thoughtful of you.'

'Well, I can be a kind and thoughtful fella,' he said. 'I'm Gerry Rawlings, by the way.'

'Alice Larkin.'

'Pleased to meet you, Alice Larkin.'

'Pleased to meet you, Gerry Rawlings.'

We grinned at each other for a moment.

'So, what about finding that somewhere classy for a drink?' he asked.

'I thought you weren't going to ask me that? I thought it wasn't appropriate?'

'The world moves on,' he said, with a little shrug. 'And if we don't move with it, we get left behind. There's a hotel down by the water that's so classy they not only clean the glasses but also put maraschino cherries and those little paper umbrellas in your drinks. I've often wanted to see if it's true.'

'It's all true. I've been in it before.'

'Rich girl, are you?'

'Filthy,' I said with a smile.

The word came out before I realised he might have thought I was flirting. Then I realised I *was* flirting. If he caught the double entendre, he didn't respond to it. 'Well, Alice Larkin, rich girl, what do you say you take me there and show this country boy how the other half live?'

'Are you picking me up, Gerry Rawlings?'

'Heaven forbid! Just looking after you following your encounter with Danny boy back there. If it makes you feel any better, you can pay.'

I laughed and we began to walk towards the esplanade.

And that was how I met Gerry Rawlings. Had I known the effect of that meeting on both our lives, I would have run in the opposite direction, high heels or no high heels.

10

Rebecca borrowed her mother's car to pick up Chaz and Alan from Queen Street station. They were going to stay overnight in the spare room, but neither of them was familiar enough with the city to make their way around. Chaz had been brought up on the island of Stoirm, off the west coast of Scotland, while Alan was originally from the south of England. Rebecca had met them while following a story on the island and a friendship had developed, although both now lived in Inverness. Chaz was a freelance photographer, which often proved fortuitous in her work, while Alan did something vague and – his words – incredibly dull in the administration of the University of the Highlands and Islands.

She used Google Maps to guide her to the station. She hadn't driven through Glasgow for some time but knew she would have to deal with so many one-way streets, roads that were open only to buses and taxis and the dreaded emission zone, closing the city centre to vehicles of a certain vintage on pain of a hefty fine. Her mother's car was not new, but she was certain its year of manufacture was recent enough to avoid punishment. Well, relatively certain. She was confident that the app was sufficiently up to date to guide her through the streets without incident. Well, relatively confident. In the end, it wasn't so easy. Welcome to Glasgow in the twenty-first century.

She stood on the concourse and spotted Chaz's blond head among the crowds and then the smaller, dark-haired Alan, as ever impeccably, though casually, dressed. Chaz, as usual, was simply gorgeous, and Alan's tutoring in how to dress well without being flashy made him even more so. They smiled at her as they exited the platforms through the barrier, Alan wheeling a small suitcase, Chaz carrying his travel bag.

'How was the journey?' she asked after the obligatory hug for Alan. Chaz knew she was uncomfortable with such tactility, even with close friends, and was in agreement with her that hugging was just not British. Alan half-agreed but did it anyway because he knew it made her feel awkward.

'It was good,' Chaz said.

'It was *complete* and *utter* hell,' Alan said, his southern English accent giving additional emphasis to his words.

'It wasn't that bad,' Chaz said.

'It *was* that bad. It was *excruciating.*'

She indicated the exit onto George Square. 'So, why was it excruciating?'

Chaz mock-groaned. 'You had to ask, didn't you? It really wasn't that bad.'

'How can you say that? We had a horde of children running around.'

'There were two children occasionally running up the aisle, hardly a horde.'

'They made enough noise to be a horde. And one on the seat opposite threw a toy car at me.'

Chaz grinned. He always treated Alan's tirades with good humour. 'He didn't throw it. He was playing with it and when he let it go, it rolled across the table and landed on your lap.'

'It was a deliberate attempt to do me harm. Had I not reacted with my usual cat-like grace . . .' He shot Chaz a glare when he erupted with a laugh. 'You may guffaw.'

'I think I just did.'

'But that toy was solid metal and had it landed on my delicate parts it would have been uncomfortable, to say the least.'

'It was an accident.'

'He had an evil look in his eyes, that child.'

'He was three or four years old.'

'He was the Devil's spawn.' Alan had a flair for the dramatic, which he enjoyed displaying. 'If we could have shaved his head, we would have found the number 666 on his scalp.'

Chaz laughed again and Rebecca visualised a scene in which Alan held down a struggling child while wielding a barber's razor. They were outside now, where it was another beautiful day, and heading across George Square to where Rebecca had left the car near the City Halls. Alan, however, was not finished.

'And then there were those damned sandwiches.'

'What was wrong with your sandwiches?' she asked.

'We didn't have sandwiches,' Chaz replied.

'No,' said Alan, 'But the mother and Damien opposite had sandwiches. Tuna and cheese sandwiches.' He paused for effect. Alan often paused for effect. Flair for the dramatic. 'With onion.'

'You like tuna sandwiches,' she pointed out.

'I like eating tuna sandwiches. Occasionally with cheese, I agree, but never – I repeat, *never* – with onion. The combination is an olfactory assault that also has a half-life afterwards. I do not appreciate sitting opposite a woman and her Devil spawn while they're devouring them and polluting the atmosphere. Did I mention they also had cheese and onion crisps? If I had been lactose intolerant, the smell alone would have had me rushing for the comfort station.' They were now out of the square and walking along Cochrane Street alongside the City Chambers, the heat bouncing from the stonework like a sun lamp. Alan suddenly changed the subject: 'How long are we going to be trekking through this concrete jungle?'

'We've been walking for five minutes,' Chaz pointed out. 'I don't think we've been trekking.'

'Thank you for the time check, darling, but I wanted to know how much further we are expected to go?'

'Just to the car park at Ingram Street,' Rebecca said.

'Because all this talk of food is making me hungry.'

'You've just been moaning about food,' Chaz said.

'Yes, and it has made me hungry, although I may never face tuna again. And I never moan.'

That made both Chaz and Rebecca burst into laughter. Alan glared at them both in turn.

'It's only a couple of minutes away,' she said.

'Good, because I hope your mother has been baking. I'm looking forward to one of her scones.'

'She has been, but you'll have to wait a little bit longer,' Rebecca said. 'We have a call to make first. We can get coffee and something on the way.'

'I know that tone of voice,' Chaz said. 'There's a story, isn't there?'

'There's a story,' she confirmed.

Alan perked up. 'What's the quest this time?'

'I'll tell you in the car.'

Alice Larkin sipped at her tea, doing her best to hide her exhaustion. Forbes might not notice, but Orla would. The little tremor as the mug was lifted to her lips. The dullness of her eyes. The slowness of her speech. Orla knew her well, knew her moods and her faults. She should do, for she spent practically every waking moment with her, apart from when she managed a day or two off. Alice had offered to engage a temporary nurse so she could take a holiday somewhere, but Orla was devoted to her. She would spot the tell-tale signs of her energy sagging but wouldn't comment on them, not in front of Forbes. Once he was gone, she would nag her about it, tell her she should be taking things easy, but Alice would fob her off. It was too late for that. Taking things easy wouldn't buy her any extra time, wouldn't make up for her errors of the past, wouldn't make up for the cowardice she had admitted to Dalgliesh. Orla knew that also. But it still wouldn't prevent her from delivering a lecture.

'They have the new pages?' Alice asked Forbes, who was sitting on the couch, two fresh envelopes on his lap to be delivered later that evening.

'Yes.'

'And that little sneak Jack Dredden told them nothing, as expected?'

'You said he'd fob them off and he did. How did you know?'

She tutted. 'I've known Jack Dredden a long time. He was so willing to spout the police line that they called him Detective Constable Dredden. He could have been part Force Information for all the real news he reported.'

'He said they called him Judge Dredden.'

'The only person who called Jack Dredden that was Jack Dredden.' She sipped her tea. 'Did they believe him?'

'I studied them carefully while they spoke to him. I think Rebecca suspected he was being something less than truthful.'

That pleased Alice. That was why she had thrown Dredden at them. They wouldn't like being lied to. 'Smart girl. Reminds me of what I was like at her age.'

Orla said, 'Headstrong and with poor judgement?'

'Smart and resourceful,' Alice corrected. 'Fearless.'

'I typed those pages, remember. There was nothing smart in what you did, and you were pretty fearful with that Danny fella.'

Alice ignored her. It was the truth, but the only time she ignored the truth was when it concerned her. No, that itself wasn't the truth, otherwise she would not be doing what she

112

was doing. Now she was facing up to truths that she had ignored too long.

'I had a visitor yesterday,' she said to Forbes.

'Who?'

'Finbar Dalgliesh.'

The news didn't surprise Forbes. 'That was quick.'

'Jack Dredden was extremely efficient.'

'And what did he say?'

'As expected.'

'Threats?'

'Naturally.'

Alice had already discussed with Forbes the possibility that someone would wish to block the story and that she wanted to flush them out. She thought it would be Dalgliesh, but he was merely a front. She knew there were others behind him and always had been. She wanted them to feel a little of the fear she had felt for years over this secret. Both Forbes and Orla were aware that there might be threats involved and had accepted it. Forbes had been the editor of what was once an influential daily newspaper and was well used to powerful, dangerous people doing what they could to intimidate him. Orla had lived through the Troubles as a child, had watched her father being gunned down in the street, had as a teenager spoken out against the violence and had also been threatened as a result. Neither of them had baulked at the prospect of being further menaced.

'Don't you think you should tell Elspeth and Rebecca about Dalgliesh?' Forbes suggested.

She had already considered that. 'I think they will find him for themselves.'

'How did you know Dredden would get in touch with Dalgliesh?'

'I told you, I know Jack. He was a police mouthpiece but also had other connections, some might call it a fellowship.

He was in awe of authority and sucked up to it whenever he could. He was an annoying, egotistical little shit with an eye for the main chance, but I didn't know it would be Dalgliesh per se, although I suppose I should have known those two would be drawn together and cling to each other like Velcro. Dalgliesh would be a conduit to those people in the shadows who impressed Jack and, in return, Jack would keep them informed of any police interest and also help manipulate the group's public image.'

'The group being SG?'

Alice paused. 'And perhaps others.'

'And the possibility that he might now threaten Elspeth and Rebecca doesn't concern you?'

Alice's smile was thin. 'I'm banking on it. I think it will make them dig all the further.'

Rebecca related the story in fits and starts as she manoeuvred through the city. Eventually though, she said she would tell them properly over coffee and cake in the Mitchell Library's café, her lack of familiarity with the city in which she had been born forcing her to focus more on the traffic. Road-works, diversions and the inevitable snarl-ups meant it took longer than she had expected to reach the impressive, domed building, yet another monument to the city's prosperous past, standing above the canyon of the M8 as it roared below Char-ing Cross. She found a space on Kent Road, bought and attached a parking ticket to the windscreen, and led them through the Granville Street entrance into the main vestibule, which housed the information desk, the stairway to the Mitchell Theatre and also the café. They found a table beside the large windows looking onto Kent Road and Rebecca bought the coffees and cakes – a fruit scone, as promised, for Alan. Sunlight bathed them through the windows as she ran over the main points of the Cruachan story and then finally told them about James and his uncle, who had worked on the various hydro projects.

Alan let out a groan. 'If I read that in a book, I wouldn't believe it.'

'Sometimes it happens like that,' Rebecca said. 'You meet someone who knows someone else, and they might know someone else. Life is funny.'

'Yes,' Alan said thoughtfully, as he absently rolled an empty sugar sachet into a ball, 'truth is stranger than fiction.'

'Wow,' said Chaz.

'Wow what?' Alan asked.

'Truth is stranger than fiction.'

'What about it?'

'Did you just think that up, right off the top of your head?'

Alan's eyes narrowed slightly. 'What's your point?'

Chaz maintained a straight face and feigned being impressed. 'I mean, it's so profound. Or something you'd get in a trailer for a film.' He lowered his voice to a rumble and adopted an American accent. 'Truth . . . is stranger . . . than fiction.'

Alan flicked the ball of paper in Chaz's direction but missed.

Chaz giggled as he stooped to retrieve it from the floor. 'Seriously, you should get that printed on a T-shirt.'

Rebecca held back a laugh, but Alan glared at her. 'You better not be laughing.'

'Not me,' she said, the laugh succeeding in breaking through.

'You just encourage him,' Alan said in feigned disgust, his lips twitching as he tried to suppress his own amusement. That was Chaz and Alan all over. Always sniping, never missing a chance to poke fun at each other, and yet theirs was the strongest relationship Rebecca had ever known.

'So, what are you looking for in these hallowed halls?' Alan asked.

'I want to see what was reported about the Cruachan project in 1964,' she said. 'If there was a death, then surely it will have been recorded somewhere. That reporter Jack Dredden was adamant that I wouldn't find a report on a murder, but something has to have happened.'

'So, what are you going to do?' Chaz asked. 'Go through all the newspapers for 1964?'

'We might not need to do that. There's a series of indexes in book form for the *Glasgow Herald*, stretching from 1906 to the early 1980s. We can go through the one for '64, searching for Cruachan, hydro, death, murder, accident, whatever. That will give us the issue date, the page and even the column number. If something happened, then it will be in there, and we can check not just the *Herald* but also the other titles for that day and beyond.'

'Simples,' said Alan.

Chaz looked at his watch. 'And perhaps time-consuming. I'm supposed to be at that studio in an hour.'

Rebecca looked at her own watch. She had lost track completely. 'Damn it,' she said. She also had to complete her interview. 'I hadn't realised we'd lost so much time getting here.'

Alan patted her hand. 'Fear not, oh forgetful one, you have a glamorous assistant who can step in and save the day. Again.'

'Elspeth is busy, though,' she said.

Alan's face creased. 'Very funny. As you know, I live for poring through old books and files.'

'That's because he remembers when those old books came out,' said Chaz.

Alan adopted a patient expression. 'Really? Back to the age thing again? I'm not that much older than you, remember?'

'Those few years make all the difference, though.'

Alan sighed and addressed Rebecca. 'I don't know why I stay with him, I really don't.'

Chaz said, 'Because I make you feel young again.'

After an elaborate eye-roll, Alan said, 'Look, I'm not needed this afternoon. I'd just be standing around like some sort of groupie while pretty boy here makes love to the camera.'

'When do they want to interview you?' Rebecca asked Alan.

'Not till tomorrow.' He lowered his voice. 'I think they said they'd need extra time this afternoon to fill in the lines on his face with make-up. I suggested they attach a plasterer to the crew.'

'Every one of these lines tells a story,' Chaz said, 'and they all begin, "Once upon a time there was a man called Alan . . ."'

'Yeah, yeah, yeah,' Alan said. 'Becks, write down what you need me to look for, tell me where I'm going and leave me to it. Take boy wonder here to his date with obscurity and come get me later.'

Rebecca took her notebook from her bag and began to write down a list of subjects for Alan to search for in the index, adding the names Gerry Rawlings and, recalling the pages she had read the night before, Danny McCall.

'Oh,' Alan said as he watched her write, 'and phone your mum. Tell her to keep those scones warm.'

11

After Rebecca's short second interview with the film crew, Chaz asked her not to hang around and watch his own star turn because he said it would make him self-conscious in front of the camera. Rebecca understood. She'd asked Elspeth to leave the makeshift studio the day before for the same reason. This was Leo Cross's world and he was relaxed on camera, but neither Rebecca nor Chaz were used to it. He, as a photographer, was more accustomed to being behind the lens while she just didn't like that sort of attention. She had already resolved not to watch the documentary when it was completed.

She'd decided to find somewhere quiet and with Wi-Fi access to do some further online research of her own, so she asked a young production assistant if she knew of anywhere. The young woman pointed her to a place called WiFidelity, a new café/deli on Byres Road that not only had decent Wi-Fi but also made an absolutely cracking tofu burger. Rebecca doubted anything that conflated burger with tofu was cracking, either absolutely or even slightly, but she thought she might give it a try. She was hungry – that cake in the Mitchell seemed so long ago – so she hoped the café served more than coagulated soy milk.

Luckily, they did, so she ordered a common-or-garden cheeseburger and a coffee and took a table by the window. She looked out at the busy street for a few minutes, watching the shoppers hurry by. She was not a native of the West End but this street had been a haunt in her student days, notably Tennent's, which she could see on the corner opposite, and the Curlers Rest further up the road, beside the subway station.

It was to the former that she had fled after her father died, seeking solace, if not answers, in gin. She recalled an older man had taken a seat beside her and instigated a conversation. She couldn't remember how he did it, what he said exactly, but she knew he was chatting her up. She didn't really care. She needed to talk to someone, but it had to be a stranger, and he had nominated himself for the job. He was just a guy out for a shag and what he got was an outpouring of grief. Drunk as she was, she could still remember the look of horror on his face and the speed with which he beetled off, probably in search of some other poor woman who might be more of a laugh. Rebecca's friends had been alerted by her mum – dealing with her own grief, but the mothering instincts always active – and they had found her at that corner table in the small lounge and prised her away, walking her round the streets of the West End until she was sufficiently sober to go home, where she and her mother wept in each other's arms, mourning the loss of the man who had been their world.

And now her mum had found James. And Rebecca had Stephen. The world turned, time passed, memories faded. Life went on.

She sighed, opened her laptop and logged onto the net. She stared at the search engine page for a few moments – her mind still half in the present and half in that tearful, drunken past – when she became aware of a face peering at her from the street. The man was big and broad and wearing a leather jacket that probably took a whole cow to create. His hair was black and slightly too long, and the eyes that regarded her seemed sleepy. She stared back at him, and he didn't seem at all ashamed. They held each other's gaze for a moment or two before he broke the connection and walked away. She watched his broad back until it vanished out of her sightline, wondering who the hell he was and what that was all about.

Her burger arrived and she bit into it, squirting relish from the side. She swore softly and reached for a napkin in a metal dispenser on the table. She pulled two free and dabbed at the sauce on her hand, then pushed her chair back to check her trousers in case she had managed to dribble some down herself. She saw a blob on her thigh and wiped it away, leaving a dark stain. She swore again and licked at the edge of the fresh napkin then rubbed at the offending spot.

The man reappeared in the street but this time he wasn't alone. Finbar Dalgliesh was motioning him to stay where he was and he didn't like it, but he remained outside, his dead stare fixed on Rebecca.

She hadn't seen Dalgliesh for a couple of years, but he was still as exquisitely tailored and expertly coiffed as ever. She would lay odds he smelled good, too, but she had no intention of getting that close. She hid her surprise but damn it, she thought, of all the cafés in the world, he had to walk into mine.

'Ms Connolly,' said Finbar Dalgliesh as he stood beside her table. He nodded to the stain on her jeans. 'Have an accident?'

'No, thanks, just had one,' she said, dropping the napkin on the table and spinning her legs back out of sight, her cheeks burning at being caught by him in such a pose.

He indicated the only other chair at the table. 'May I?'

'Would it matter if I said no?'

He smiled and sat down. 'Not really.'

'Then be my guest,' she said. If it was a done deal, she might as well be gracious. Anyway, she was curious as to why he was in this trendy little café on Byres Road.

He smoothed his jacket down and sat back, his elbows on the arms of the chair and his fingers intertwined in front of him. He was the kind of man who could appear to be comfortable anywhere, even a trendy little café on Byres Road.

'It's been some time, Ms Connolly.'

'Not long enough.' She jerked a thumb towards the burly man on the pavement, his gaze still intent on her. Pedestrians walked around him as if he was a roundabout. She expected some of them to indicate. 'Is the Big Arnie wannabe with you?'

'His name is Julian, and yes, he is my assistant today.'

'Julian? He doesn't look like a Julian.'

'What does a Julian look like?'

She gave the man another glance. 'Not like that. He's not a Julian. He's more an Olaf. Or a Chuck. Not a Julian.' She continued to study the man, giving him a little wave. He didn't wave back. His face remained immobile. 'Come to think of it, he doesn't look much like an assistant, either.'

'What does he look like?'

'A thug whose brains are in his fists.' She looked back at Dalgliesh. 'A prerequisite for membership of SG.'

Dalgliesh's eyes hardened. 'Are you trying to antagonise me, Ms Connolly?'

'Heaven forbid,' she said, her attention drifting back to the man in the street, giving him another wave. 'No, maybe he's more a Rip, something like that.'

Dalgliesh found his smile. 'You haven't lost your deluded belief that you are funny, Ms Connolly.'

Knowing she wasn't going to draw a reaction from Julian, she looked back at Dalgliesh. 'I'm not being funny, Mr Dalgliesh. I don't think there's anything funny when we have these little chats.' She was about to reach for her burger again but thought better of it. She wasn't going to eat in front of this man. 'So, to what do I owe the pleasure this time?'

Dalgliesh's eyes flicked around the small café. 'I wonder if we might talk somewhere more discreet.'

There was no way she was going anywhere with this guy, not to mention Julian. 'I'm happy here, thanks.'

'What I have to discuss with you isn't for others.'

'I didn't know I had anything to discuss with you.'

He unclasped his hands, laid one forearm on the tabletop, the tips of his forefinger and thumb rubbing together as if he was feeling the quality of the air. He watched a staff member clearing a table behind Rebecca and didn't speak again until she had moved away.

'Alice Larkin,' he said.

Rebecca forced herself not to react but inside she felt something tingle. 'Who?'

'Let's not play games, Ms Connolly. I know you and Ms McTaggart have been speaking with her.'

Okay, so her feeling she was being followed the night before was probably accurate. Dalgliesh didn't merely come upon her in this trendy little café in Byres Road. She had been followed, not by Julian, who would stand out, but by someone adept at not being seen. That thought made her shiver.

'If we had been speaking with her, why would I discuss it with you?'

'Because it would be in your best interests not to have anything to do with her.'

'My best interests in what way?'

He slipped a look at Julian.

Rebecca understood. 'You're threatening me, right?'

'I'm offering you advice.'

'And why should I take this advice?'

'Because it is well meant.'

She laughed. 'Mr Dalgliesh, why do I find that hard to believe?'

'Because you don't want to. You've made it clear in the past that you don't like me or my politics.'

She couldn't deny that. 'Anyone with half a brain wouldn't like your politics.'

He was used to hearing that, especially from her. 'Nonethe-less, I urge caution.'

'Why?'

'Alice Larkin is not well.'

He fell silent, as if that was all he needed to say.

'Okay,' she conceded, 'I saw that myself.'

'She's a dying woman raging at the approaching dark.'

'Very poetic.'

His lips compressed with what she hoped was impatience with her. She did so enjoy pissing this man off. 'I'm serious, Rebecca.'

'You always are, and it's "Ms Connolly". We're not chummy enough to be on first-name terms.'

That impatience was displayed again. 'I'm trying to be friendly.'

'Mr Dalgliesh, being friendly with you is not something on my to-do list. So, say what you've come here to say and let me eat my burger because the longer I'm in your company, the more chance there is that I'm going to need a packet of Rennies.'

His jaws clamped together and he breathed in deeply through his nose. That forefinger and thumb were rotating so fiercely they might kindle a spark.

'Alice Larkin is a delusional old woman,' he said, his voice tight.

'Old, yes; woman, yes; delusional, not so much.'

'She is a conspiracy theorist.'

She almost laughed. 'Takes one to know one,' she said, recalling one of his diatribes on TV. 'Tell me again how homo-sexuals and transexuals have banded together to undermine society and, how was it you put it, "corrupt the minds and bodies of our young"?'

He breathed long and hard again. 'If you follow this story, it will take you down a dangerous path, Ms Connolly.'

'You are threatening me.'

'As I said, advising caution.'

'And who or what should I be cautious about, Mr Dalgliesh?'

He didn't reply.

'You?' she pressed. 'Julian out there? Whoever you had following me last night?'

He blinked and she thought she saw a flicker of surprise. 'Oh yeah, I knew I had someone following me.'

'I don't know what you're talking about.'

'Of course you don't. So, who should I be afraid of?'

He stared at her, obviously unwilling to name names. She was about to press him further, but the waitress arrived at their side. 'Sorry,' she said, 'is there anything I can get you?'

'No, thanks, the gentleman is just leaving,' Rebecca said. She gave Dalgliesh a pointed look. 'Aren't you?'

It wasn't clear if the waitress had sensed a tension in the air but she hung around for a moment, then moved away, shooting a look back at the window table. Dalgliesh didn't even glance in her direction but made no move to stand. However, he did eventually rise slowly but remained standing over Rebecca for a moment, ostensibly smoothing wrinkles from his suit jacket. She discerned a surreptitious glance towards the waitress as he checked she was out of earshot, then fixed a smile that would appear friendly.

'The road Alice Larkin is leading you down is long and dusty and best forgotten.'

'I like to take the road less travelled. There's not as much traffic and no chance of a bus lane.'

His patience finally snapped, though he didn't raise his voice. That would have been unseemly for a public figure. 'Ms Connolly, why do you insist on acting as if you are some character in a trashy novel? I'm trying to make you understand that if you pursue this course then there will be repercussions.'

'I like trashy novels, and if I sound like a character from one then that's because you're also acting like one. You've had me followed, you pop up when I'm having my lunch – which is getting cold, by the way – and then deliver a warning so opaque that I need Windolene to see it. So, here's a thought, stop pissing about and tell me why the hell I should drop the story and then off you pop to planet fuck.'

She deliberately swore and was gratified to see him wince a little. Dalgliesh was many things, but he was also old-fashioned, and ladies did not use that sort of language in front of him. He exhaled hard again and glanced at Julian, still standing out there like a big, brawny statue. If he waited any longer, someone would put a traffic cone on his head.

'There are reputations and legacies that could be tarnished by these delusions.'

'Whose reputations and legacies?'

She could tell by his frozen expression that he had been as precise as he intended to be.

'Take heed, Ms Connolly,' he said. 'I would hate to hear of anything befalling you.'

'Now who sounds like a character in a trashy novel?'

He gave her a final stare that seemed tinged with sadness. 'You're being stubborn, Ms Connolly, and I'm sorry for that. My urging is sincere, even though you don't accept that. I mean you no harm. I never have.'

God bless him, he sounded as if he meant it – but he was a politician.

'So, who does? If not you, then who is it? Julian? New Dawn? The Coalition of Chaos? Who?'

He sighed, shook his head. 'Who, it doesn't matter. What matters is that if you pursue this investigation then there will be repercussions, and I would regret that. Being John Connolly's daughter only goes so far.'

That made her bristle. 'What's my father got to do with this?'

His self-satisfied little smile annoyed her but not as much as the suggestion that he knew her father.

'Dalgliesh,' she said, her voice hard, 'what has my father got to do with this?'

He didn't reply. He blinked a few times then shook his head – sadly, she thought – then turned and left the café. She stared after him as he shook his head again, said something to Julian and began to walk up Byres Road. Julian gave her a long, hard stare then took a mobile phone from his inside pocket, pressed a button, put it to his ear and followed his boss like a walking steroid.

Rebecca realised her fists had clenched, her nails digging into her palms, so she forced her fingers to relax and her breathing to slow. What the hell did Finbar Dalgliesh have to do with her father?

Her phone vibrated on the tabletop and she glanced at the screen, seeing a group text message from Forbes asking both she and Elspeth to visit Alice Larkin that evening. She glanced at her burger, now cold, but she was no longer hungry anyway. To hell with tonight, she thought, there's no time like the present.

Orla wouldn't let Rebecca in the house. Instead, she moved onto the step, half-closing the door behind her, and folded her arms. She was a sentinel and no one would pass.

'Her ladyship is sleeping right now,' she said, her voice low. 'She's not expecting you till this evening.'

'Can you wake her up?' Rebecca said. 'I need to speak to her.'

A flinty look took the place of Orla's previous good humour. 'That won't be happening. That poor woman sleeps little enough as it is, and I'm not about to go disturbing her when she does manage to go over.'

'This is important.'

'It can wait, I'm sure.'

126

Rebecca breathed deeply. It could wait, but she wasn't sure she wanted to. 'Orla, what do you know about this story?'

'I'm sure you know I input it all into the computer, apart from the final pages. But if you're going to ask me for spoilers then don't waste your breath. Her ladyship wants this done a certain way, and that's the way it will be.' Her eyes softened a little. 'You look flustered, pet.'

Flustered, Rebecca thought, was a soft word for the way her guts churned. 'I really need to speak to Alice.'

'Tonight,' Orla said, and Rebecca knew by the firmness of her tone that there was no way in hell she was getting over that threshold.

She took another approach. 'Have you heard of a man called Finbar Dalgliesh?'

Something flickered in Orla's face at the name. 'Aye, I know that devil.'

'Does Alice?'

Orla struggled with how to reply. 'Aye, she knows him, and she doesn't think much of him, I can tell you that. Why do you ask?'

'I've just had a conversation with him.'

That news didn't seem as surprising as Rebecca might have thought. 'That must have been a delight for you.'

'That's why I must speak to Alice.'

'And you will, pet, but tonight.'

'He made threats.'

That didn't surprise her, either. 'Aye, he's good at that, is Finbar Dalgliesh. But it's mostly bluster.'

'How do you know?'

'If there was action to be taken then there wouldn't be threats. Believe me.'

'How can you be certain?'

A rueful little smile tugged at Orla's lips. 'I've not been with her ladyship all my life. I've met men like Dalgliesh

127

before, and they're all talk. It's the quiet ones you have to look out for, the ones who stand on the sidelines and say nothing. If there's damage to be done, then they're the ones who will do it.'

Rebecca pictured Julian's impassive face as he watched them through the window then, as he left, making a call. She turned to study the gardens. When making the short drive from Byres Road to Hyndland, she had kept her eye on the rearview as much as she could but had not seen anybody following, not that she was trained in spotting such things. She hadn't re-experienced the feeling of the evening before, but that didn't mean there wasn't somebody there. She saw nothing untoward now, no men in cars parked nearby, nobody loitering or paying any kind of attention to her. In fact, there was nobody in sight. The sun was shining, the birds were singing in the trees behind her, but all that faded, and she felt a chill on her neck as if something large and malevolent was breathing on it.

She had to warn Elspeth, so she muttered a hasty thanks to Orla – who was only doing her job, after all – and reached into her pocket for her mobile as she walked down the steps to the pavement.

12

Rebecca waited in the car in the small car park outside the studio. She didn't want to go inside, didn't want to have to share small talk with Leo. She had sent Chaz a text to tell him that she was waiting, and he had replied that he wouldn't be long. She was calmer now – the shock of Dalgliesh's mention of her father had worn off. Now all that was left was curiosity, though Orla's statement regarding the quiet men who stand and watch remained planted in her mind. However, she knew Elspeth was safe in her hotel room because that's where she was when she had phoned as she walked back to her car on Westbourne Gardens.

'So, what does he have to do with it all?' Elspeth asked, after Rebecca told her about Dalgliesh.

'I don't know,' Rebecca replied, eyes darting around her, on the alert for any attack. 'He couldn't have had anything personally to do with whatever happened back then, he's too young. Reputations and legacies, he said.'

'Yes, but whose reputation and legacy?'

'I asked him, but he didn't answer.'

'He does that a lot, the bastard, or like most politicians answering without actually answering. So, what did your father have to do with him?'

'That's what I want to know. I went to see Alice. I thought she might have an idea.'

'What did she say?'

'I didn't get over the door. Orla barred the way.'

'I wouldn't like to tangle with that woman.'

Rebecca had heard the click of Elspeth's lighter. 'Are you smoking in your room?'

'I've opened a window.'

'Still not allowed.'

'They'll never know.'

Despite everything, Rebecca smiled. Elspeth was a force of nature.

'Right,' Elspeth said after Rebecca heard her exhale some smoke, 'let's look at this calmly. Well, I'll look at it calmly, you can just listen and be enraged.'

'What makes you think I'm enraged?'

'I know you, Becks. That bastard mentioned your father and that will piss you off. Threats are one thing, but make some kind of disparaging comment about John Connolly and you're ready to rip someone's heart out with a nail file. So, Dalgliesh knows about the story and isn't pleased, whether on his own or someone else's behalf is difficult to say. He was a lawyer, after all, both criminal and civil. He had clients that were crooks and politicians, and some of them were both. He mentions reputations and legacies, then drops your dad into the mix. Have you considered that he might simply be trying to rattle you?'

Rebecca had considered it and shook her head even though Elspeth couldn't see her. 'No, I had the impression he knew my dad.'

'Well, he might well have. Your dad felt the collars of a few villains in his day.'

Rebecca laughed. It felt good, as if something she had been keeping at bay had been released. Elspeth had used the phrase purposely to lighten the moment and draw a response. She didn't disappoint her. 'Felt the collars of a few villains? Did he slap the darbies on them, too, and did they say, "It's a fair cop, guv'nor"?'

'Just a figure of speech, no need for mockery. Anyway, the chances are him and your dad would have gone head-to-head somewhere down the line – in court, I mean, not in a fisticuffs sort of way.'

'But why say that my father's name would only go so far in protecting me?'

Elspeth made a dismissive noise. 'Dalgliesh will say anything to throw people off balance. He's good at it, too. On the other hand, maybe he respected your dad, could be as simple as that.'

Rebecca considered this. 'Could be.'

'You're convinced that you were being followed?'

Rebecca, now back in her car, automatically checked her rearview and her wing mirrors. Still nobody around. 'Yeah. Dalgliesh didn't just happen by that café and see me in the window. Someone told him where I was, so that means they followed me there.'

'That guy Julian?'

'Maybe, or someone else.'

'How the hell did he know we're on this story, anyway?'

Rebecca had been thinking about that, too. 'Either Alice told him . . .'

'Can't see that.'

'Neither can I. Or it was the only other person we've spoken to who dropped a dime on us.'

Elspeth snorted. 'Dropped a dime on us?'

'Hey, you said "felt the collars of a few villains".'

'At least mine was of British vintage, while yours is something foul and American. You think Jack Dredden told him?'

'Who else? Wouldn't be Forbes.'

'No.'

'Or Orla – believe me, she's devoted to Alice.'

'So, Jack it is. Why?'

'Beats the hell out of me. Think we should ask him?'

Elspeth didn't reply at first, and Rebecca visualised her sitting at the window of her hotel room, looking down on the street below and drawing on her cigarette. 'No, he'll just deny it.' Elspeth paused again. 'I don't like being told to back off from a story, Becks.'

'Neither do I.'

'I don't like being threatened by scum like Finbar Dalgliesh.'

'Neither do I.'

'I'm not planning to walk away.'

'Neither am I.'

'Good.'

They agreed to meet up that evening and go to Alice's together. Elspeth said she would wait outside her hotel and Rebecca could drive them.

Now, back at the filming location, Chaz emerged from the old warehouse doorway, nodded farewell to Tris and looked around the car park for Rebecca. She stuck her hand out of the open driver's side window and waved. He acknowledged her and weaved through the parked cars towards her, climbed in.

'If that guy's jeans were any tighter, they'd be back to front,' he said.

She laughed. Again, it felt good. 'How did it go?'

He puffed out his cheeks. 'It's nerve-wracking. I mean, there's no audience, just the crew, but when those lenses are on you, it's as if they're seeing into your soul. I sweated through one shirt with nerves and had to change it. Thank God I had my overnight bag with me. Don't tell Alan about that, though.'

'Your secret's safe with me.'

He gave her a look that suggested he found that highly suspect, and she had to agree. It would be trotted out at a propitious moment. That's the way their friendship was.

'Alan's waiting for us in the café at the library,' she said.

'Yeah, I saw the group text when I switched my phone back on. He didn't say if he found anything, though.'

She turned the ignition and began to back out of the space. 'Let's go find out.'

'What did you do with yourself this afternoon?'

She shifted gear into first, steered towards the exit. 'You'll never guess who I ran into ...'

Alan had found nothing about murder directly related to Cruachan, which didn't surprise Rebecca. After all, it couldn't be a 'murder that never was' if it was reported in the press. Rebecca listened to him as she drove, her irritation growing over the way Alice was guiding this narrative. Initially she had been happy with it, enjoying its uniqueness, but with the involvement of Dalgliesh, SG and possibly New Dawn, she now found the process annoying, and she intended to tell the woman that when she saw her later.

'So,' Alan said, 'having been abandoned for an entire afternoon—'

'You weren't abandoned,' Chaz said, 'you volunteered.'

'I was left alone in a strange place with nothing but a packet of Polo Mints for sustenance, I'd call that abandoned.'

'With a café a lift ride away,' Rebecca pointed out.

Alan grunted, something he had learned from Elspeth. 'Anyway, having been left to my own devices – I hope that better pleases you – I decided to extend the range of my search from 1964. That index really is a marvellous resource, by the way. Once you become used to how the compiler's mind worked regarding subject matter and headings, it is absolutely superb. It's a shame it only goes up to 1982. Anyway, I widened the timescale and went back to when work began on Cruachan, bearing in mind that your friend whatshername—'

'She's not my friend,' Rebecca said. 'She's a source.'

'Okay, bearing in mind your *source* whatshername—'

'Alice, her name is Alice.'

A slight sigh from the back seat. 'Fine, bearing in mind your source *Alice* hasn't specified when this incident took place, I thought I would check further on.'

Alan stopped talking. Rebecca glanced in the rearview and saw him gazing out of the window. 'Well?' She asked. 'What did you find?'

He met her eyes in the mirror, as if startled. 'I was building the suspense.'

Chaz groaned. 'Such an arse, just get on with it.'

'It's called storytelling, darling, and someone who deals only in the visual image can't begin to understand it.'

'Alan,' Rebecca said, doing her best not to sound irritable, even though she was, 'can you tell us what you found, please?'

'See?' Alan said to the back of Chaz's head. 'That's how you ask a person to move on. Courtesy, Charles Wymark, costs you nothing.'

'Yeah, yeah,' Chaz said, shooting an apologetic glance towards Rebecca, which she shrugged away to let him know it didn't matter. This was Alan's way, and she knew it. Her irritation was not with him. 'Just get on with it, you arse.'

Rebecca shot another glance at the rearview. 'So, what did you find, Alan?'

'Absolutely nothing about murder. There were accidents at the hydro works, of course, and some caused loss of life, but no murders, either solved or unsolved.'

'Okay,' Rebecca said, a little deflated, even though it was as she had expected.

'I did eventually find something about a killing, though.'
She perked up. 'Really?'

'Yes. I had to go through a number of years, however.'
'Years?'

'Yes, all the way to 1977, in fact. It involved one of the names you gave me, Danny McCall.'

'He was murdered?'

'No, it seems he was the murderer. He killed his wife and very nearly did for his teenage son.'

'Was he arrested?'

'No, he was never caught as far as I could tell. I checked right up to 1982, but there was no further mention of him, either an arrest or a court appearance.'

Rebecca frowned. That couldn't be what Alice was referring to, could it? 'What about the son, any further mention?'

'Not a thing.'

'What was his name?'

'David. He was fifteen at the time.'

In Alice's memoir, that man Gerry Rawlings had said that Danny McCall had a wife and child back in Glasgow. The boy would have been around two when his father worked at Cruachan. Was this connected to Alice's story somehow?

'There was also one accidental death in 1964 that you might be interested in,' Alan said.

She flicked her eyes to the mirror again, saw Alan grinning at her. He had found something and was, as usual, making a big deal out of it. She waited for him to continue.

'It was a fall from the dam up on the mountainside. Nobody saw it happen, but witnesses said that earlier the man had been seen drunk and it was believed he had gone up there alone and pitched over the rail.'

'Who was it?'

Alan paused. 'His name was Gerry Rawlings.'

13

Alice saw the face of Gerry Rawlings. He was smiling. He was always smiling. And then, suddenly, he was gone. A scream echoed and echoed in darkness and when her eyes opened, she was in her room, sunlight edging through a gap in the curtains. She thought that perhaps that scream had been hers. Her heart was beating, and her mouth was dry, and her fingers trembled more than usual as she reached out for the glass of water that Orla always ensured was on the bedside table. Her hand hovered over her pills but she realised it wasn't time to take them. Orla would have a fit if she knew she had taken them early. She plucked the glass from the table and took a long drink, being careful not to spill any on the bedclothes.

She lay back, the after-image of Gerry's face still haunting her. He had been a charmer and he hadn't deserved what happened to him. She had to make things right.

The door opened and Orla's face peered round it. 'You're awake,' she said.

'Thank you for letting me know,' Alice said, forcing the image of a man dead these past sixty years deeper into the dark recesses of her mind, where he now lived. 'I wouldn't have known otherwise.'

Orla came fully into the room. 'I love it when you're sarky after your nap. Makes me feel all warm inside.'

She helped Alice sit up, leaned her forward a little before padding and adjusting her pillows around and behind her.

Alice loved the way Orla did this – it was like a cocoon of softness around her, both supportive and comforting. During sleepless nights, of which there were many, she had tried to replicate this structure herself but had never succeeded.

'You were dreaming again,' Orla said as she eased her back against the pillows. Alice almost sighed with pleasure, but she refused to let the nurse know she had provided any sort of gratification. It was not their way.

'I know,' Alice replied, 'I was there.'

Orla grimaced. 'Sarky.' Satisfying herself that the pillow positioning and punching had met her own high standards, she stepped back and stared at Alice as if waiting for her to outline her dream. But she had no intention of doing that. Orla knew when she was beaten and moved away from the bed to adjust the curtains. She must have closed them while Alice had been sleeping. 'That girl Rebecca came by.'

Alice squinted as the afternoon light flooded in. 'They were to come this evening.'

'I told her that, but she was quite insistent.' Orla turned back. 'And with good reason. That creature Finbar Dalgliesh spoke to her.'

'He didn't waste any time, did he? What did he say?'

'She didn't tell me, and why should she? But whatever he said had upset her. He did threaten her, though.'

'Of course he did, that's his modus operandi. What did you tell her?'

'I tried to reassure her.'

'Good. Did you succeed?'

'Hard to say, but I imagine it will come up again tonight.'

'I'm sure it will. I must say, Finbar has been very quick off the mark.'

Orla moved back to the bedside. 'I think you should tell them the full story now.'

137

Alice shook her head. 'No, they need to receive it as I planned. That way they will make their own inquiries, draw their own conclusions. I'm a source, not the story. They need to act independently, take my account and follow the trail themselves.'

'Even if it puts them in danger?'

Alice gave her a sharp look. 'Was the girl intimidated by Dalgliesh?'

Orla thought about that. 'No,' she said eventually, 'she was annoyed, and I can't blame her. But something had put her on edge – she kept looking around, and she sat on the phone for a time in her car after she left me – although I didn't get the feeling she was planning to throw in the towel, if that's what worries you.'

Alice's smile was satisfied. She had chosen well. 'These women are resourceful and focused. Once they are hooked on a story, they will not give up.'

'Just like you.'

'Just like me.'

But Alice knew that wasn't the complete truth.

After a lovely meal prepared by Sandra Connolly, Chaz managed to usher Alan upstairs to the spare room. Alan would have sat all night gossiping and telling Sandra stories about her daughter, very few of them completely true. Sandra knew this and had reciprocated with stories of her own from Rebecca's childhood. It was all good-natured, but Chaz was aware it was not the night for such conversations, so he made every effort to prise his husband away from the dining table. Alan eventually sensed something in the air and relented. He did take two scones with him, though.

Rebecca and her mother began to clear the dishes from the table, scraped the residue into a grey recycling bin on the kitchen worktop, and stacked them in the washer.

'Mum,' Rebecca began as she rinsed some gravy from a plate before handing it to Sandra at the open dishwasher, 'have you heard of Finbar Dalgliesh?'

Sandra stooped to put the dish into the rack. 'Of course I have, dear. I watch the news.'

'You know I've had dealings with him, right?'

'I've also read Elspeth's books.' Sandra smiled. Dalgliesh featured in two of them. 'Where's this leading?'

Rebecca dried her hands on a towel as she leaned the small of her back against the sink. 'Did Dad know him?'

Sandra frowned. 'Why do you ask that?'

Rebecca told her about Dalgliesh tracking her down to the café and mentioning John Connolly. She said nothing about being threatened or Julian swelling like an abscess in the street. 'I got the impression he knew Dad.'

Sandra turned away to place condiments in the overhead cupboards. Rebecca wondered if it was a move to avoid her revealing a slight flare in her eyes. But Rebecca had caught it – just a glimpse, but it was enough.

'It's always possible, I suppose. Dalgliesh is – was – a lawyer.'

'That's what Elspeth says.'

'Then that's probably it.' Her tone was confident, but it sounded forced. 'I wouldn't worry about it. Your dad came into contact with a lot of people, and the worlds of the police and the legal profession may be linked, but they aren't as large as you might think. It's easy to brush up against people you might not want to.' She turned back, adopting a reassuring smile. 'Pop the kettle on, would you? I could do with a cup of tea.'

She left the kitchen to continue clearing the dining room table and leaving Rebecca to consider that fleeting look. She had been brushed off many times in her career, had been told that something she thought might be important was not. She knew the look of someone avoiding a truth when she

139

saw it. And that was the second time she'd seen it in her mother's eyes.

Elspeth lay on her bed, staring at the ceiling. The TV was on, a young newsreader talking about a new scandal in the Scottish government, with spokespeople from opposition parties calling it a disgrace, irrespective of the fact that the national news had carried stories about both of their parties also being mired in controversy. Politics, she thought, was a mean and dirty business that attracted mean and dirty people. Not that there weren't politicians who were caring, competent and principled, but lately she had come to believe that they were the exception. Or, in her opinion, they didn't achieve high office in any party.

It brought her mind round to Finbar Dalgliesh. She had met him a few times, both professionally and socially. He had been a highly proficient lawyer. He had, she assumed, once believed in justice, but he had ditched whatever ideals he had to pursue political power and would say anything to achieve it. She wondered what went through his mind when he made some of his more outlandish statements. Did he know he was spouting bullshit, or had he genuinely come to believe them?

One thing was for certain, he was no great believer in Scottish independence. SG had been around for years, mumbling about true Scots and attaching itself to home rule, but the men and women of the party prior to him didn't really believe in breaking up the union. It was Dalgliesh who had carried the party, for want of a better word, into the mainstream, riding the back of various referenda, jumping on the anti-migrant bandwagon, tapping into an undercurrent of unease and, yes, hatred, that bubbled below the surface. There was a market for his nonsense, on social and mainstream media, and that was the disturbing thing. Elspeth believed people to be generally level-headed and, with a few exceptions, welcoming and open-minded, but when SG managed to have two candidates elected to the Scottish Parliament and another to the European Parliament, plus seats on various councils, she feared she was overly generous in her judgement. She believed that at their core, all people were the same, whether Scots, English, Welsh, Irish, French, American, whatever. Men, women, no matter their race, colour, sexual or gender preference. All the same. The same mix of humanity and venality, as capable of nurturing, loving and showing compassion as they were of stealing, maiming and killing.

But was Dalgliesh capable of it? Talking was one thing, even issuing a warning, but would he really have someone hurt?

She recalled Rebecca telling her about the time she caught him in Inverness on the way to catch a train. She thought he had been couching his words in a way that would please the two bruisers who accompanied him. It had never been proved that he had forged links with New Dawn – a group that nobody actually admitted existed, least of all Dalgliesh and SG – but he had defended suspected members in court. That bunch was more than capable of dishing out some bruises when they felt like it, as well as bomb threats against mosques and synagogues, having suspicious parcels delivered through the post to Muslim clerics and Scottish government ministers sympathetic to any cause in which New Dawn did not believe – and there were many of them – and, if rumours were true, engaging in robberies and drug-dealing to finance their activities.

She sighed and hauled herself upright to swing her legs over the side of the bed, using the bedside table set into the headboard as a lever. Her hip ached. Her knee ached. Julie had told her she should get them fixed. Rebecca had told her she should get them fixed. She had told herself she should get them fixed. But to get them fixed she would have to place herself into the hands of someone she had never met, and she wasn't keen on that.

Elspeth had never suffered a day's serious illness in her life. In her youth she had been athletic, even svelte, and had enjoyed being both, was proud of being both, but time has a habit of adding more than lines to the face. A fondness for food and drink, and a job that saw her spending long hours at a desk, had wrapped her former svelteness in a layer of flesh that her younger self would find shocking. Julie said it merely meant there was more of her to love, which was kind of her.

She smiled at the thought of Julie. That woman had changed her life, and she loved her for it. It was she who had convinced her to step back from the agency and bring Rebecca in to do the day-to-day labour, and that had been a godsend. Elspeth had grown tired of the grind. She liked writing, but she didn't like having to undertake the increasingly tedious toil of attending court, arranging interviews and following up the human interest stories that weekly magazines loved so much but Elspeth herself hated. She liked the meaty stories, the ones that she had written the books about. Julie had made her realise that they could afford to take it a little bit easier, and she was right. The bookshop-cum-café in Drumnadrochit on the shore of Loch Ness was ticking over nicely. They'd had some lean times, certainly, but they had weathered them. The agency itself was doing well enough, largely thanks to Rebecca. And the books had been well received. She wasn't topping the bestseller lists like Ian Rankin and that guy whose name she could never remember who wrote about Kintyre, but they were doing well, and the money from the TV people was decent.

Her gaze fell on the new pages Forbes had delivered. Rebecca had told her what Alan had discovered and though Alice's account hadn't reached Rawlings' death, she had a

142

suspicion it would. Was that the murder that never was? She knew she should do some net surfing – she couldn't leave it all to Rebecca and her friends – but her laptop was at home because she hadn't expected to be working on this trip; and she hated using her phone, which was so old and cantankerous it thought the web was something Spiderman slung. Anyway, Rebecca was going to pick her up in forty-five minutes to take her to the West End. And she had a call to make.

She reached out for that old and cantankerous phone, found the name she wanted in her contacts. She waited only a few moments before it was answered.

'How's Glasgow?' Bill Sawyer asked.

'Big and noisy.'

'You'll fit right in, then.'

'Cheeky bastard,' she said, laughing. 'You're not too big that you can't get a skelp.'

'Many have tried, and many have failed. So, why the call? You missing me?'

She took a deep breath, for a moment considering whether this was necessary. But she'd phoned now and Bill was sharp. He might have retired from the police service but he still didn't let much get past him. Apart from his wife, who left him a few years back. To hell with it, she thought, better safe than sorry.

'How do you fancy a few days in the big city?'

14

I don't know why I agreed to go for a drink with Gerry Rawlings. Perhaps it was gratitude for him stepping in when he did. More likely it was because he was handsome and charming and funny, and I liked handsome and charming and funny men. He had a way with him, did Gerry, I sensed that within minutes of talking with him in the street. More importantly, he worked on the project, and that made him exactly what I was looking for. The fact that he was handsome and charming and funny was only a fringe benefit. Also, anyone who had obviously annoyed a man like McCall couldn't be all bad.

I soon discovered that Gerry Rawlings had a penchant for annoying people.

We had that drink. I had a gin cocktail, complete with maraschino cherry and paper umbrella, which pleased him. He had something soft. I thought he was trying to impress me. I did indeed pay, and it led to another. This time he paid. He asked me what I did, and I told him the truth, which didn't seem to bother him in the slightest. He told me he was a tunnel tiger, which was exactly what I wanted to hear. He had worked on hydro construction across Scotland but had decided this would be his last project. He was well paid and had some money put by. Unlike other workers, he didn't blow all his wages on whisky and women, he told me.

Two drinks, that was all we had. In my book, one drink with a man you have only just met is polite, two shows you're interested, three and you might as well stop your grinnin' and drop your linen there and then. I was no prude, and I hadn't been a virgin for many years – unknown to my father, of course. I'd surrendered that particular prize at the age of eighteen to a young man whose name I no longer recall, which is shocking really. It's not that I've had many sexual partners – if there's an average number then I feel I'll have hit it, though I won't bother you with all the names – but for some reason his is the one I can't dredge up. I do remember the experience was as remarkably unmemorable as his name, my fault as well as his. Thank God sex grew better with the years, or I grew better at it.

Anyway, after those two drinks in the hotel bar Gerry walked me back to my car. It was one of those lovely early summer nights. The sun had vanished behind the hills of Mull, but it was reasonably warm, the breeze from the water soft and pleasant, or perhaps that was because the two drinks had heated my blood. Or something had. Gerry, of course, was fine. I know I shouldn't have been driving but I had an incredible capacity for liquor and, anyway, things weren't as stringent back then. We didn't even wear seatbelts. That didn't become law until around twenty years later, when that dreadful man Jimmy Savile exhorted us to 'clunk-click, every trip'. My God, if we had known what sort of creature he was, we might have ignored what is most sage advice. In fact, thinking back, I'm not even sure my car had seatbelts fitted. Gerry was the perfect gentleman. He held my door open, closed it behind me, then he leaned down – I thought at first for a kiss, but it wasn't. He seemed almost sheepish.

'Maybe I'm stepping over a mark here,' he said, 'but I'd really like to see you again.'

I kept my face straight. It was a struggle because I really did want to see him again but not, I guessed, for the same reasons as he wished to see me. At least, that's what I told myself.

'I'd like that,' I said.

He perceptibly relaxed, as if he had been tensing himself during the walk from the hotel. 'That's grand,' he said. 'So, can I have your phone number? Obviously, living in the camp I don't have a line to myself, but there's a phone box down the road I can use.'

I was well aware of the potential distances between phone boxes in that part of Scotland. 'How far down the road?'

He gave me that almost-but-not-quite shy grin again. 'About two miles, but I'm willing to tackle the hike if it means talking to you again.'

I swear I felt my face flush. I was used to men chatting me up, as we used to say – or perhaps young people still do, I don't know – but something about him had reached me. To hide it, I made a fuss of reaching into my bag, found my notebook and pen and scribbled my number down. I handed the ripped-off page to him, our fingers touching, just barely, but the slight tingle I felt was enough for me to know that my interest in him wasn't solely journalistic. Handsome and charming and funny, remember?

He looked at it, folded it and placed it in his pocket. 'I'll give you a call, Alice Larkin.'

And he did. He waited the customary two days, for to call the next day would have been too eager, and to wait three would have been simply rude. The call came and he asked me out to dinner the following Saturday. I agreed and he said he'd book a table in the restaurant of the same hotel in which we'd had drinks. I said I'd meet him there, as there was no way that I could have him collect me. The chances were, given my father's connections in the area, that he would hear about me having dinner with a strange man, and I didn't want to compound the felony by having said strange man come to my flat in the town. I think by now you will have realised that my youthful rebellion was more targeted than wide-ranging. In other words, I pushed back on some things but not anything that might endanger my life of comfort and security. I admit to being very calculating at times, in that regard. My father had already been informed of my encounter in the pub and had expressed his dissatisfaction with me in the strongest possible terms, so I had agreed never to darken the door of that or any other similar establishment again. It didn't matter. I had my source now. I just had to draw him out.

Again, that was how I rationalised it.

I took my time over my outfit, and I think I hit the right note of 'this is business but, hey, it might go somewhere else'. My black skirt was a decent length, my shoes were high-heeled but not enough to give me a nose bleed if I stood up too quickly, my white blouse buttoned to the neck. My make-up was carefully applied, my hair loose and around my shoulders. I thought myself the epitome of the modern, professional woman.

He was already at the table when I reached the hotel, a gin cocktail waiting for me. He stood up – as I said, a gentleman – took my coat and handed it to the waiter to hang up somewhere. Gerry was wearing a blue suit, white shirt, blue tie. His black shoes were polished, his hair combed and his chin scraped clean. He looked, frankly, stunning. But then, so did I.

I suppose we made small talk during the meal, but I also learned about his life. He was thirty years of age and had been in the army, where he'd learned how to use explosives, a skill that had stood him in good stead as a tunnel tiger. He was from Londonderry but called it Derry, and both his mother and father were dead, lost in a house fire that almost claimed him and his little sister as well. He said he still had a burn scar on his chest where he was hit by a piece of falling debris. Although the fire was an accident, there was the minor suspicion that some gentlemen of an Orange persuasion, with whom his father had fallen foul, might have been responsible, but Gerry was certain they were not. It had been a stupid argument in a pub, he said, one of hundreds of similarly stupid arguments in hundreds of similar pubs, and it meant nothing. Faulty wiring caused the fire, not faulty thinking. Of course, four or five years after he and I met, sectarianism flared into what became known as the Troubles. Gerry was born a Roman Catholic, although he wasn't practising, and he told me that even him calling the city in which he was born Derry could cause an argument with Loyalists. He didn't agree with the hatred on either side and said he'd been glad to get away from it.

I saw him look across the room towards the entrance at that point and his eyes hardened. 'Of course,' he said, 'I didn't get away from it, did I? There's all kinds of hatred.'

I followed his gaze towards a tall man with black hair slicked back in a duck tail with enough Brylcreem to grease a tank. He must have thought he was Tony Curtis, but he didn't have the dark good looks to go with it. There was something unpleasant in the set of his mouth, the look in his eye – I think now it was an inner ugliness showing itself. Or at least, that's how I came to see it. He must have been in his early forties at that time and he was a powerfully built man. When he saw us looking, he turned to face us directly, his back straight, his shoulders back, his head held high as if he owned the place. I learned he gave that impression wherever he went.

Approaching us, he said, 'Mr Rawlings,' his accent Scottish but not Glasgow or Edinburgh, nor Highland or Lowland. Rather it was an amalgam of them all, as if he was trying to be all things to all men. 'I didn't think this was the sort of place someone like you would frequent.'

There was a curious emphasis to the words *someone like you*, and not a complimentary one. Gerry didn't reply and the man's eyes turned to take me in. The glint in his eye wasn't sexual – it was judgemental, as if he was wondering what a nice girl like me was doing with a man like this.

'The name's John Lane,' he said, holding out his hand. I was brought up to be a lady so I took it, briefly, the way I would touch a dead fish if I wasn't wearing waterproofs and waders, but I didn't volunteer my name. He hesitated slightly before he said, 'Some call me Bronco, though.' It was as if he was prompting me to return the favour, but all I did was shoot him a slim smile and then glance at Gerry, who seemed to be holding himself very tense. Finally, the newcomer asked, 'And who might you be?'

I might have been someone whose first impulse was to tell him to fuck off, but breeding will out. I adopted my sweetest smile. 'I'm someone who, had I wished you to know my name, would have given it to you.'

I don't know whether he was more surprised by what I said or the way I said it, in my perfectly modulated, expensively honed diction, but it seemed to shock him into a moment's silence. Only for a moment, though, for John Lane was very quick to adapt himself to circumstance. Even so, the little laugh he gave sounded forced to me.

'She's a cheeky one,' he said to Gerry. 'You're going up in the world, aren't you, son? Punching well above your weight here.'

Gerry refused to look at him. 'You've said hello, Bronco. Now, off you trot.'

'That's not very sociable.'

Gerry finally looked up at him. 'I'm choosy who I socialise with.'

149

Bronco nodded as if he was deep in thought. 'Aye, but maybe not that choosy, eh? At least in the past.' He looked at me once again, another assessment made. 'This one's a step up for you, right enough. I can tell from her gear and her speech and the way she's looking at me – as if I'm some under-footman who's dared to catch her eye – that she's slumming, and she knows it.' He addressed Gerry once more. 'This place is posh, and she fits. But you, Rawlings, don't fit anywhere but in some stinking bog in the old country pulling potatoes or such like. Not here with decent folk.'

I had the impression, as I had in the pub the previous week-end when Gerry had faced down Danny McCall, that there was history between these two men. That night Gerry had never lost his good humour, but this time it was different. He was holding himself in, as if there would be an explosion should he let himself go. His right hand had grasped a butter knife so tightly that he seemed to be trying to melt it with the heat of his anger. I don't believe he considered using it as a weapon, it was just something into which he could squeeze his fury. He may have disliked Danny McCall, but he hated this man, whoever he was.

Lane smiled, but there was nothing pleasant about it. 'How is your mate old Howie, by the way? Terrible thing to happen to him.'

Gerry's knuckles turned even whiter as they gripped the little knife. 'Fuck off, Lane. This isn't the time or the place.'

That amused Lane. 'Not very nice language to use in front of a lady.' He addressed me once again, even gave me a little bow. 'I apologise, miss, he's no gentleman. You can take the trotter out of the bog but not the bog out of the trotter.'

I thought Gerry was about to rise to that. 'That's okay, I've heard the word before,' I said. 'I've even used it once or twice myself. In fact, I'm thinking of using it now.'

Lane blinked at me, his eyes hardening a little, because this time I didn't soften my words with a smile. 'Well, we wouldn't want that now, would we? Ladies shouldn't sully their lips with such language.'

'Sometimes sullying ourselves is the only way to rid us of pests,' I said.

His smile grew forced, then he placed a hand on the table-top and leaned in closer towards Gerry. 'While I've got you, here's a word or two of advice. You've been talking out of turn, Rawlings, and I'd suggest you keep your Taig mouth buttoned. Loose lips sink ships, and all that, you catch my drift?'

'You don't frighten me, Lane. Maybe the others you can bully, but not me. I sorted your man McCall out a wee while ago, and he's the best you've got.'

'Danny's a good man. Patriotic, loyal, steadfast. You're none of these things.'

'I seriously doubt he's any of those things, but he still ended up on his patriotic, loyal and steadfast arse. Your threats don't frighten me.'

Bronco straightened again. 'No threats, just friendly advice is all. One worker to another. Stop spreading lies about me and we'll be fine and dandy.'

He let his words lie there for a moment, then after another long look at me, as if he still expected me to introduce myself, he sauntered across the dining room to where two men waited for him. I had seen them before somewhere but didn't at that time place them.

'Who is he?' I asked.

'John Lane,' Gerry said, his voice tight.

'Yes, he said that, also known as Bronco. But who is he?'

'He's a supervisor on the project. And an absolute bastard.'

'That I worked out for myself,' I said. 'So, what's the trouble between you two?'

He exhaled sharply, the tension beginning to leave his body. His fingers loosened on the knife. 'It doesn't matter.'

'But he threatened you.'

'You heard him: friendly advice.'

'Gerry, I know a threat when I hear one. You should report him to your employers.'

He managed to crack a smile. It wasn't his usual easy, charming one, but it was at least a smile designed to reassure me. 'Ah, no. Believe me, there was nothing there that can be taken seriously. He likes the sound of his own voice, does John Lane. Fancies himself as a politician, so he opens his mouth and lets his gums flap at any opportunity.'

'A politician? For what party? Is he a shop steward or something?'

'No, he's no fan of us union members.'

'So, he's what, a working-class Tory?'

'No, he's not a Tory, either, although I think he has friends, and those friends have friends in all parties.'

'Then what is he? Liberal?'

'No, he's not aligned with any of the main parties. None of them would have the likes of him.'

'You're being very mysterious.'

He laughed. 'I don't want to talk about him, is all it is, Alice Larkin. He's cast enough of a shadow over our evening as it is.'

It was clear he wasn't going to tell me anything about him. 'One more question, though.'

'Shoot,' he said, but I thought I heard a touch of exasperation in that single word.

'Why is he called Bronco?'

He seemed relieved by the nature of my query. 'After the telly programme.'

'What telly programme?'

He saw I was mystified, and he was, in turn, surprised. 'You've never heard of *Bronco*? Western programme with Ty

Hardin? Plays a character called Bronco Layne.' He started to sing: '*Born down around the old panhandle, Texas is where he grew to fame—*'

I decided to interrupt before he started whistling and cracking whips. 'I don't watch a lot of television and certainly not some dismal cowboy effort. And what sort of name is Ty?'

He laughed. The original Gerry had returned, the tension vanished. But now and then I saw him shoot looks across the room to John Lane and his two companions and something dark crept into his eyes for a moment, then he smiled at me and it was gone.

15

Rebecca raced through the pages, knowing that Alice – and Elspeth – would expect her to have read them. As she changed into a fresh shirt and jeans, she tried to discern what they told her. That Alice had been attracted to this man Rawlings was clear, and she hadn't tried to disguise the fact. Yes, she wanted to use him as a conduit to the life of the workers on the project, but she'd obviously found him pretty charismatic. Handsome, funny and charming, she'd said.

The real point of interest was John Lane. A supervisor, Gerry had said, and a would-be politician, although not with any of the main parties. In the early sixties it was Conservative, Labour, Liberal or Communist, and apart from fringe candidates, that was it. Rebecca recalled from a lecture on Scottish political history she had attended that although the Scottish National Party had been formed thirty years before, it wouldn't be until 1967 – another three years – that they won their second Westminster seat, when Winnie Ewing took the former Labour-held Hamilton constituency. So, if none of the main parties, who was Lane with?

She could make a guess but, glancing at her watch, she realised there was no time to do an internet search. She had half an hour to drive into the city centre, and she knew Elspeth would be on time and waiting outside her hotel. Elspeth had many faults, but she was obsessively punctual and deplored the lack of it in others, so if Rebecca kept her waiting for even five minutes, she would receive a lecture. Rebecca was not in the mood for a lecture. Dalgliesh's appearance still disturbed her, while his suggestion of some kind of link to her father niggled. She tried to reason that John Connolly would never have anything to do with a man like Dalgliesh, no matter how charming he could be, but that look her mother had tried and failed to hide spoke volumes. There was something there, she knew it.

She picked up the pages and her notebook, thrust them in her bag, and left her bedroom. She poked her head into the spare room as she went by and told Chaz and Alan to be good.

'I'm always good,' Alan said. 'I can't say the same for young Lochinvar here.'

Chaz feigned a frown. 'Young Lochinvar?'

Alan sighed and looked up from the crime novel he was reading, the cover that of a swimming pool with what looked like currency floating in the water. 'I've told you before, read more books and fewer Twitty posts. I beg you, broaden your mind, not your prejudices.'

As much as she enjoyed their feigned bickering, she was in a rush. 'I'm running late. I'm not sure when I'll be back, so don't wait up.'

'I had no intentions of waiting up for you, I'm not your guardian,' said Alan. 'It's been a long day. First catching the train at oh-my-god o'clock in Inverness, followed by that hyperactive thug-in-training throwing toy cars at me and finally I was incarcerated in that library for hours doing your work for you—'

'You volunteered,' Chaz pointed out.

'Don't bother me with details. The fact is, I am, not to put too fine a point on it, well and truly cream crackered.'

A laugh burst from Chaz. 'Cream crackered? Where the hell did you pick that up?'

'We're in Glasgow,' Alan said, smiling, his eyes dropping to the pages of the book once again. 'The natives do like their rhyming slang, I understand.'

Chaz shook his head and said to Rebecca, 'You sure you're okay driving? I'm happy to do it.'

'No,' she said, 'you stay here. I'll be fine.'

'But what about Dalgliesh's threats?'

She waved a hand. 'We've been threatened before. Elspeth always says that if we aren't threatened, cajoled, sidetracked or lied to at least once when following a story then it's not worth doing. The news is something that someone somewhere doesn't want printed, remember.'

'So, you don't think there's any real danger?'

She made sure she didn't pause. 'Nah. All sound and fury, signifying nothing.'

'Ooh,' Alan said, 'Shakespeare, get you!'

Rebecca was already leaving the room. 'I do occasionally look up from Twitty, you know.'

Elspeth was out of cigarettes. She hated being out of cigarettes, not just because as soon as she discovered she had none, she developed an overwhelming urge to smoke. Mind you, that occurred even when she had a full pack. No, it irritated her that she had been so disorganised in the first place that she had run out. She was chaotic in many ways – not least in her mode of dress and her hair, which tended to stick out as though it was giving directions and couldn't make up its mind. It was only in her work that she come anything close to being orderly. However, when she took the lift to reception, she found her packet of John Player Specials contained no more than the foil wrapping and some flakes of tobacco at the bottom. It was a sorry sight, and she must have muttered a curse too loudly, for the man standing in front of her turned around.

'You can't smoke in here,' he said, his accent posh, his gaze towards the packet in her hand disdainful.

'I realise that,' she said, 'especially as the bloody thing is empty.'

She held the pack up to let him see. He grunted something she didn't quite catch then added, 'Perhaps you should take that as a sign to stop it.'

She crumpled the cardboard box in her hand and dropped it in her bag, then gave him her sweetest smile. 'I take it as a sign that I need to get more, but thank you for your concern.'

The lift dinged to announce they had reached the foyer and the man tutted, then strode out as if he was on some parade ground. Elspeth hobbled towards the main door, knowing she wouldn't get through the evening without a nicotine hit while also being fully aware that she couldn't call Rebecca and ask her to pick up a pack. For one thing, she'd already be on her way and, not being in a car with hands-free connectivity, wouldn't answer the call. For another, she'd refuse to buy them. Rebecca recognised her boss's right to smoke if she wanted, but she wouldn't help her do it. She, too, thought it was a filthy habit, and often she and Julie banded together to convince Elspeth to stop.

The thing was, Elspeth wanted to stop. She had tried to stop. She had even managed to stop a few times, but it didn't last more than a few months and then she'd be back, puffing on the tobacco like a steam train. She knew she was a strong person in most ways, but she didn't have the internal or mental fortitude to keep the craving at bay for long. She'd tried the patches, the gum, hypnotism (an exercise that was singularly unsuccessful as she giggled throughout), kicking it cold turkey, but nothing worked. She'd even given vaping a go but, as an old pal once said, using those things was like sucking Doctor Who's sonic screwdriver.

She reached the hotel's wide entranceway and stepped outside, lingering on the top step of the short flight to street level

157

and staring across the Broomielaw towards the Clyde, still blue and almost inviting in the evening sunshine. A glance at her watch told her she had five minutes before Rebecca was due to pick her up. There was a newsagent not far away, and she tried to calculate whether she could get there and back in time. Perhaps in her younger days but not now, which was annoying. She had to get her knee and hip fixed. Then lose weight. And give up smoking. But not tonight, Josephine. She found her mobile in her bag and thumbed Rebecca's number. As she expected, the call went to voicemail.

'I'm heading round to the shop to buy fags,' she said. 'If I'm not back in time, come find me.'

She mentioned where the newsagent was, rung off and eased herself down the three steps to the pavement, then turned to her right. The shop was on Argyle Street – not far and the exercise would do her good, she thought.

As she clicked around the corner, she considered what she had read in Alice's account. John Lane's name resonated, but she wasn't sure from where. She should have had a look, but she'd thought what the hell, she'd just ask Alice later. This whole 'make your own inquiries' business was annoying, but she understood it. Too many journalists now wanted their stories handed to them on a plate: a press release rewritten, a couple of calls for some quotes and, bing-bang-bosh, that's the story done. She didn't blame the journalists – she blamed the bean counters who'd seen to it that staff levels were so decimated that fewer people ended up doing more work than they could handle. However, she reasoned that asking Alice about John Lane *was* making her own inquiry. If she refused to answer, which was always possible, then she'd find out another way. Or Rebecca would. Or Alan would, given he seemed to have become the unofficial researcher.

She was on a side street, a city canyon with a mixture of modern and older buildings looming high on either side, blocking the evening sun and making the sound of her sticks hitting the concrete echo like someone typing very slowly. The street was deserted apart from a man walking towards her, one hand gesturing as though he were conducting an invisible orchestra. She hoped he wasn't some weirdo, or drunkard, or addict, who would ask her for money. He seemed to be respectably dressed but that didn't mean anything.

The office blocks were closed for the night but light still flooded the glass-fronted vestibules and glinted in windows above them, even though the workers had likely headed home. She didn't miss the day-to-day grind of office work. She hated being tied to a desk, phone and computer. She much preferred her life now, writing a little in the morning, helping Rebecca when she needed it, although that was growing increasingly unnecessary. The girl was doing well. She had shown promise the first time Elspeth met her when she arrived at the *Highland Chronicle* for her interview, fresh out of university, sporting a degree in journalism. She'd done her research and so her questions about the job, the paper and the area proved she was bright and eager and sharp. But despite that, Elspeth saw the darkness in her, shadows that hid behind her eyes. Eventually she learned about her father, who had been taken too soon. The girl had loved – still loved – him, and even though Sandra Connolly was a fine woman, it was he who'd been the major influence on Rebecca's life. Elspeth was certain that Finbar Dalgliesh had dropped that line about John Connolly on purpose, simply to destabilise Rebecca and perhaps send her off on some wild goose chase.

The buildings she passed now dated from the late nineteenth century, former warehouses with the one on the far side of the road converted into offices but still carrying the austere look of a Victorian warehouse. The solid stone wall alongside which she hobbled had been reduced to nothing more than a frontage for a more modern building. At least they had retained that, she thought. It showed some kind of respect for Glasgow's past.

The man approaching her was walking very slowly, and she could now make out the Bluetooth device clamped to his ear. Elspeth felt a mild rush of envy. With her reliance now on two sticks to get around – and she did very well, it had to be said – she couldn't walk and talk on her mobile at the same time. To take a call while on a street she had to step to the side and lean against a building. Again, Julie had often urged her to upgrade her old and cantankerous device so she could have Bluetooth connectivity, but Elspeth resisted because she thought there was plenty of life left in that phone and she hated discarding something that was still operational. Anyway, she didn't fancy wearing those devices on her ear, or ear buds. Of course, as soon as she said that, Julie jumped in by pointing out to her that if she had the surgery she could walk and talk at the same time. Such simple pleasures were denied to her thanks to her fear of the knife and her resistance – a quite irrational insistence, she admitted to herself but never to Julie – to putting her trust in the hands of someone she didn't know. Julie told her to get over herself, to have the procedure done and to claw back some sort of life without the need of artificial support. She was neither a young woman nor was she old, Julie would say. She still had years ahead of her, Julie would say. Get the knees sorted, lose weight, stop smoking, have some fun in life, Julie would say. We live in one of the most beautiful countries in the world, if you discount the plagues of midges in the summer, and you can only see it through the window of a car, Julie would say.

She and the man were almost level now and, perhaps a little too late, Elspeth thought of Dalgliesh's warning. She looked around, but apart from a car that had turned into the street from Argyle Street and pulled into the kerb, and a young couple just rounding the corner at the bottom of the street, there was no other sign of life. It was that kind of street. During the day it would be busy with cars, delivery vans, bikes and pedestrians, perhaps not as many as there would be on the main shopping thoroughfares, but there would be life. But at this time of the evening, the dead period between commerce and entertainment, it was deserted.

She looked back to the man. Though still talking, he seemed to be watching her very intently as he approached. Her hands tightened on her canes. Was she being paranoid? It wasn't beyond the realms of imagination that Dalgliesh was simply playing mind games, throwing out a vague threat in the hope that they'd be so preoccupied with looking over their shoulders that they wouldn't do their jobs properly, or that they would even walk away from the story – but if he believed that then he really didn't know them very well. She should cross the road now, the left turn onto Argyle Street was up ahead, but if this guy did mean her harm, then she was damned if she would let him see any fear. Forewarned is forearmed, as they say, and she had two weapons already in her hand. Nevertheless, she moved a little towards the edge of the pavement. The man was only a couple of feet away, still talking, still gesturing, still looking at her, and she braced herself to swing the stick in her right hand if he so much as twitched a finger in her direction.

He smiled and walked on past, and she heard him say something about tickets to a concert.

The tension flooded from her muscles as she stood on the kerb, feeling a laugh building over her foolishness. She had been threatened before, more than once and by experts in the game, and nothing had ever happened, so why should it be any different this time? Dalgliesh was a blowhard – a bawbag, as they say in Glasgow.

She stepped off the pavement and began to cross the road, shaking her head at her own skittishness. Bloody fool, she thought. What would Julie say?

161

She didn't hear the car at first, so lost was she in her own self-chastisement. She was halfway across the road before she became aware of it hurtling towards her, the headlights blazing even though it was still light. As quickly as she could, she moved to the side, but the car swerved, the shriek of the engine like a scream. Or perhaps she screamed, or the young woman and her boyfriend screamed, she couldn't tell. All she knew was that it rammed into her, throwing her onto the bonnet, where she hit the windscreen so hard that she heard its hot crack – or perhaps it was part of her that cracked. Then the vehicle's forward momentum carried her onto the roof and she was rolling, rolling, tumbling over the rear and onto the road, her head striking the cobbled road. She didn't feel pain after that initial impact. She didn't feel anything, even when she hit the concrete. She heard the car screech away, its tyres squealing and fading as it righted itself and spun around the corner. And then there was silence.

She lay on the cobbles, staring up at the blue sky, a little cloud ambling across her vision. It was almost peaceful, but she knew she should move. She couldn't, however, so she lay still, staring at the streak of blue above the buildings and that puffy, white cloud sailing away. She would have loved to have been like that cloud: not a care, just floating above the world.

All she could think of was what Julie would say when she heard. She would be furious.

Then she saw Rebecca's face above her then looking away, speaking to someone, but Elspeth couldn't hear what she said. Rebecca had her phone in her hand and then looked back at Elspeth, tears erupting.

Don't cry, Becks, Elspeth said. *I'll be fine in a minute. It just took the wind out of me, is all.*

Rebecca didn't reply, speaking into her phone now, her breath coming in huge gulps. Elspeth couldn't hear it, but she could see it.

Don't fuss, Becks. I said I'm fine. I don't feel any pain. It's just shock.

When Rebecca still made no reply, Elspeth realised that she hadn't been speaking at all. Hadn't uttered a single word, even though she had heard herself say it. Okay, what's that about?

And then that little cloud floated downwards to wrap itself around her, and it wasn't wet but warm and cosy and comforting, and Elspeth decided that the best thing to do was to relax into it.

16

The hospital waiting room was empty, apart from a woman with bleached blonde hair and tired, careworn eyes. She wore a large, shapeless blue dressing gown and moccasin slippers, as if she had been teleported to the infirmary while sitting in front of the TV. Those worried eyes flicked to the hallway leading to the treatment rooms in the Accident and Emergency Department every time a young man's screams pierced the air. He didn't seem to be in pain, but he was distressed and complaining loudly, his protests punctuated at intervals by the steady voices of the medical staff. The receptionist behind the glass panels, her gaze fixed on the computer screen in front of her as she punched something into the keyboard, seemed not to notice, but then she would be used to all sorts of drama here. After all, this was at one time – and perhaps still was – the largest, maybe even the busiest, facility of its kind in Europe, Glasgow being what it was. A quiet period like this must be unusual, Rebecca thought, but she was glad of it. It meant Elspeth could have the best possible care without distractions, without other emergencies.

Rebecca inadvertently caught the woman's gaze, and they shared an embarrassed smile. The woman pulled her dressing gown together and looked down at her feet, as if noticing for the first time that she was dressed more for sleeping than waiting.

'I came just as I was,' she said, feeling the need to explain her appearance. 'In the ambulance.' She jerked her head towards the sound of the young man. 'That's my boy. He's taken some-thing, so he has. Don't know what, the daft bugger.' She stopped as the yelling became a howl, shifted her feet as if she was about to rise but thought better of it and sank back again. 'They wouldnae let me stay in there. I suppose they don't need someone's mammy fluttering around them when they're doing their stuff.'

The howl faded, to be replaced by sobbing and a faint cry for his mum. The woman's chin trembled, and she reached into the pocket of her dressing gown to produce a green packet of paper hankies. They were impregnated with balsam, Rebecca noted but didn't know why. It was such a tiny, stupid little detail to notice. The woman peeled one of the tissues free but didn't do anything with it, just sat with it in her hand as she stared almost absently towards the corridor.

'His dad'll kill him when he finds out,' she said, then faced Rebecca to explain. 'He's polis, doing a late shift, doesn't finish till midnight, but they've sent him word and I'm sure he'll be here soon.' She glanced at the corridor again. 'He'll murder him, so he will. Bloody murder him.'

'I'm sure your son will be fine,' Rebecca said, feeling the need to be reassuring. 'He's in the right place.'

'Aye,' she said and then blinked away tears. 'He's a stupid bloody fool, so he is. God knows what he's taken. We've telt him and telt him, don't be touching they drugs. But he's in with a bad crowd, you know? Bunch of wee neds and they'll have led him on. I've said to him since he was a wee boy not to be a sheep, not to follow, but he doesnae listen, neither he does.' She was silent for a moment, the tissue finally being utilised to blow her nose, before she repeated, 'Doesnae listen.'

Rebecca didn't know what else to say, so she didn't say any-thing. The woman stared at the corridor. Her son's sobbing continued, the only sound apart from the traffic on Castle

Street outside and the occasional unseen movement in the hospital – a door closing, the squeak of a shoe on the floor tiles, the rattle of a trolley, a voice, a laugh. Rebecca sat back and closed her eyes, concentrated on her breathing. She had to relax, she had to be calm, she couldn't help.

'What about you, hen?'

The woman's voice interrupted Rebecca's attempt at composure. She opened her eyes again, frowned because she didn't understand the question.

'You got somebody through there, too?'

The woman obviously needed to speak to someone, perhaps to take her mind off her son experiencing what sounded like a meltdown.

'A friend,' Rebecca replied. 'She was hit by a car.'

'Sorry, love.' The woman looked at the blood still visible on Rebecca's hands and her clothes. There had been a lot of blood. Too much blood. 'Were you there?'

Rebecca nodded. She had picked up Elspeth's voicemail when she arrived at the hotel so had driven round the one-way system to find her.

'Who was the driver?'

'Don't know,' she said. The car had been speeding away towards the Broomielaw as Rebecca turned into the narrow street from Argyle Street, thinking Elspeth might be on her way back to the hotel. She closed her eyes against the image of her friend and mentor lying broken on the cobbled surface, but it clung to her lids like a tattoo.

'Hit and run, that's terrible.'

Terrible, Rebecca thought. Yes, that's what it was. She had screamed at a young couple on the pavement to call an ambulance, but they seemed frozen in shock. An older man further down the road looked back but kept moving, not wishing to be involved. Or was he involved?

'Are the polis on the case?'

'Yes.'

She had spoken to two uniforms at the scene and then two detectives. They had been very caring, very professional. *Do you know the victim? Why was she here? What did you see?*

'I hope they get the bastard,' the woman said.

Rebecca couldn't tell the police officers much. She didn't have a registration number, couldn't even identify the make of the car.

'I mean, why would he no stop?'

He had steered straight for her, according to the young couple. It was as if he meant to hit her.

'I don't know,' Rebecca said.

But she did know. She knew who was behind this. She had told the police about Finbar Dalgliesh and his threat, even though she knew it had been vague and no one could corroborate it.

'Does she have family?'

Julie was the only family she had, and Rebecca had already made that call. She would get down as fast as she could, which from Drumnadrochit on the shores of Loch Ness would not be all that speedy.

'She has a wife,' Rebecca said, expecting at least a raised eyebrow. Even in the twenty-first century there were people who couldn't quite comprehend same-sex marriage, but the woman accepted it with a nod.

'Well,' she said, repeating Rebecca's own words, 'your friend's in the right place.'

Rebecca nodded her agreement, but she didn't mean it. Elspeth wasn't in the right place. This was the wrong place because she shouldn't be here at all. She should be out there smoking and swearing and laughing and eating and bitching about her knee. She shouldn't be along that corridor, lying on a gurney with wires poking out of her, and saline and blood being pumped into her, and nurses and doctors tending to her.

This was the wrong place. This was the wrong time. It was not Elspeth's time.

She made a decision. She couldn't simply sit there and hope. Chaz and Alan were on their way, she knew that, and they would wait for news. They were good friends.

It wasn't Elspeth's time, but it was time for Rebecca to do something.

Elspeth thought she really should do something, but it was so restful here.

The cloud remained wrapped around her, comforting her, its wispy fingers stroking her cheek and her forehead, soothing her. She still felt no pain at all, which surprised her because she was aware she had somehow taken one hell of a thump. All she felt was warmth and, yes, love. The cloud loved her. Not the way Julie loved her, and not the way Rebecca and her friends loved her. The cloud's love was something far deeper even than that. Elspeth was not a spiritual person, and she told people that she was a faithful atheist, agnostics being mere ditherers lacking the deliberation to make their mind up one way or the other. But as she felt herself being lifted from that street – and she *was* lifted, for she could see through the gossamer veil below her, to where Rebecca knelt beside her body – she suddenly felt the presence of something other than herself. She still didn't believe in God, some old white man with a long beard passing judgement on those below, but she sensed . . . *something*, was the only way she could look at it.

Despite that, she remained connected to her body as it lay back there on the roadway. She felt the pressure of the cobbles under her body, saw the faces of the various people now crowded around her. She watched as a young female police officer eased Rebecca away. She was crying – she'd never seen Rebecca cry. She still couldn't hear what was being said, but she knew the PC would be asking the name of the victim.

168

That's me, she thought, I'm the victim.

Elspeth didn't know how she ended up on that street. Apart from knowing that she had experienced something debilitating, she remembered little of what had occurred immediately before the cloud had descended. Even though she was hovering above them, she saw the faces of the paramedics as they tended to her. She felt their hands on her as they gingerly examined her wounds. She felt something burning her eyes as one flashed a small pencil light in them. Slowly, gradually, sound began to penetrate. It was muffled, as if someone had placed a pillow over her face, but she heard her name spoken softly, yet she couldn't reply. She tried to speak but couldn't make them hear, so she gave up and drifted away again on her soft, secure, warm bed of mist.

Now she was in a little room somewhere else, still snugly ensconced in her warm little cloud. There were different hands on her, different voices, and she heard strange noises. Bleeps. Hisses. Drips. There was no sign of Rebecca, and though she didn't know who these persons clustered around her were, she guessed they were doctors and nurses. White coats and blue uniforms were the giveaways, well done, Elspeth. You might not be certain where you are or how you got here, but you've not lost your deductive powers.

She heard them talk to her, asking if she could hear them. A doctor flashed one of those lights again and, again, it pierced her brain. She tried to tell them that she didn't much like that but couldn't find the words. She felt a slight nip at her arm as something was inserted. As before, even though she was floating above them – look up, for God's sake, and you'll see me – she could still feel what they were doing. She heard them talk about fractures and contusions. She heard them mention her spleen, her ribs and lungs, her skull and her brain. She heard the word 'surgery' and talk of a possible transfer to the Queen Elizabeth, and she tried to object but couldn't. Couldn't they tell she was fine? She felt good. No pain, not even a twinge, apart from that bloody light in her eyes and the pressure on her arm where they had stuck that damned needle in.

She gave up trying to make contact and settled once more into the warm folds of the cloud.

I'll sleep here for a wee while, she thought. Let them get on with things. I'll sink into the cloud and sleep and when I wake up, everything will be fine. Yes, a wee sleep.

Maybe a long one.

17

In the end, Chaz insisted on accompanying Rebecca. Alan had a book with him, although he said he doubted he would read much. He liked Elspeth, and Rebecca saw the worry cutting deep lines on his face. The waiting room had begun to fill up, and Alan, sensing her concern for him, tried to lighten matters by saying this meant he could people-watch, which, along with playing detective, was one of his favourite pastimes. He rested his fingers on the back of her hand.

'I'll stay here as long as is needed, Becks.' His voice was gentle. 'I'll phone if there's any news. And if Elspeth needs anything, I'll make sure she gets it.'

She laid her other hand on his and he tightened his fingers. His eyes were filled with tenderness. Chaz stood over them and nodded reassuringly. She felt tears sting her eyes. She had good friends whom she really didn't deserve.

She was still jittery – the adrenaline, she supposed – so Chaz drove. They headed for the M8, leaving it again very soon at the Kelvingrove off-ramp to hit Charing Cross and then Woodlands Road, heading west. On the way, Rebecca filled him in more fully on what she had seen.

Chaz's fingers clenched the steering wheel as he watched the road ahead. 'You think it was deliberate, don't you?'

'Witnesses said the car had been idling on the roadway until she crossed, then the driver steered straight at her.'

Chaz was silent but his face was set in tight lines. Rebecca didn't think she'd ever seen him like this. There was a time, back in Inverness, when he had sped across town to warn her of impending danger, but when he'd found her on the banks of the Caledonian Canal, that danger had already found her. So, on that occasion he had been worried and, yes, scared. The year before, when they heard a shotgun blast in the night, he had raced ahead of her, fearing for Alan's safety. Even then, he had been concerned rather than filled with rage. Chaz Wymark was not a man generally filled with rage, but he was this night, and it was evident in the whitening of his knuckles as he gripped the wheel and the way his jaw clenched and unclenched.

'Your mum said I was to bring you home,' he said, his voice as tight as his cheek muscles.

'Later,' she said.

He shot a quick glance at her hands and her jeans. 'You want to see this woman like that?'

She looked down at the dried blood. 'I want her to see what she has caused.'

He let it go. She knew he would. He was only raising it because he had promised Sandra. Chaz would want to see the woman who had caused Elspeth's accident.

Chaz asked, 'Have you called Stephen to let him know?'

Shit, she thought, it hadn't even occurred to her. She didn't deserve him, either.

'I'll phone him later,' she said and that prompted another sideways glance from Chaz, but he didn't comment further. They were turning off Hyndland Road into Westbourne Road by that time, the Gardens lying before them. They found a parking space, and Rebecca led Chaz to Alice's door. She rang the bell and breathed deeply, centring herself. She intended to be forceful.

172

Orla opened the door, her welcoming smile fading when she saw the blood. 'What happ—'

'Is she awake?' Rebecca brushed past her without waiting for an invitation. Chaz was more courteous and lingered on the doorstep until Orla gestured for him to enter.

'Of course she is, pet. She's been expecting you – and you're late. Her ladyship doesn't like to be . . .'

Rebecca didn't much care what her ladyship liked or didn't like. She rushed up the stairs.

'Rebecca, you can't just run up there,' Orla protested.

'Watch me,' she said as she took the steps two at a time.

'What's happened?' Orla shouted, but Rebecca let Chaz reply.

'Elspeth is in hospital,' he explained as Rebecca rounded the banister at the top of the stairs, heading towards Alice's bedroom door. She burst in without knocking to find the old woman propped up in her bed, a complex array of pillows surrounding her like castle walls.

Alice glanced at her watch, her lips thinned in preparation of delivering a reprimand for being late. But then she noticed Rebecca's expression and the stains on her clothing.

'It's Elspeth's blood, Alice,' Rebecca said.

That shocked her. 'Elspeth's . . . ? What?'

'She was hit by a car.'

'An accident?'

'No accident.'

Rebecca moved to the window, which was open to let in air, and looked out onto the Gardens. Although darkness was gathering, a mother sat on one of the benches while two children chased each other with water pistols. Life carried on. But not for everyone. The image of Elspeth lying in the infirmary rippled through her mind on the back of the children's laughter, and she turned to pace back and forth like a boxer desperate for the fight to begin.

Alice asked, 'Are you suggesting it was deliberate?'

Orla and Chaz appeared in the doorway. Rebecca gave them little more than a glance. 'Not suggesting, Alice, I'm stating it as a fact.'

Even though she was stalking to and fro at the foot of the bed, Rebecca didn't take her eyes from Alice. She saw the woman's mind working as she held her gaze.

'You think Finbar Dalgliesh did this?' Alice asked.

'I know it.'

'You have evidence?'

Anger rose, but Rebecca kept it under control. 'Alice, who the hell else would it be?'

Something in Alice's eyes told her that there might be somebody else who might be responsible.

'What aren't you telling me, Alice?'

She didn't reply, but her eyes didn't waver.

'What has all this to do with the death of Gerry Rawlings?'

Alice still made no effort to reply.

'We know he died, fell from the dam. Is that the murder that never was?'

Alice studied Chaz. 'Who is this young man?'

'A friend.' Rebecca stopped pacing to lean over and grip the bed's baseboard. 'No more games, Alice. It was fun at first, but Elspeth is lying in a hospital bed right now and she might not make it. What the hell don't we know?'

Alice shook her head. 'It's not for me to say. You have to find out for yourself. I can't influence you.'

'Fuck!' Rebecca pushed herself off the baseboard, whirled away and stared onto the Gardens again, watching the children, the sound of their play distant, even though they were only a few yards away. She struggled to control her fury, but it wasn't easy. This woman was stubborn. Even now, after what had happened, she wanted it done her way.

'Are you dropping the story?'

It was Rebecca's turn not to respond, nor did she turn from the window.

'Rebecca,' Alice said, 'are you dropping the story?'

She had considered it. No story in the world was worth losing Elspeth. But giving up would not save her and, if she did lose her, neither would it bring her back. Also, she'd be damned if she would let the likes of Finbar Dalgliesh scare her off.

She took her time turning to face Alice, delaying her reply, hoping that somehow it would cause the woman some anxiety. 'No.'

Alice was relieved.

Rebecca added, 'But the rules are changing.'

'In what way?'

'I want the rest of your pages, right now, not in dribs and drabs. I want to know what the fuck is going on here.'

Alice began to shake her head.

'This isn't a request, Alice, it's a demand. A dealbreaker. You either give me the full story, right now, or I walk, and you can find someone else to do your donkey work. I'm sure Forbes can find you some eager young journo willing to dance to your tune.'

'This story will make your name if you do it correctly.'

'I've already got a name. And Elspeth has a name, which was why you wanted to use us in the first place. And what fucking good has her having a name done her?'

Alice said nothing for a few moments, then she sighed and said, 'You may have most of them. The final few I will keep until you have completed whatever inquiries you want to make.'

'That's not good enough,' Rebecca objected.

'Perhaps not, but it's the way it has to be.'

She gestured to Orla, who opened a drawer in the bedside table and pulled out a sheaf of paper.

'As you can see, it's not a long account,' Alice said, 'but as I explained, it is purely subjective, and I need you to bring the objectivity.'

'Then why hold back the final pages?'

'You'll understand when you read them. Do you agree with my terms?'

'Alice, I said no more games!'

'I'm not playing ga—'

'You're fucking around.'

Alice's eyes closed as if she was in pain. 'Please, Rebecca, don't curse.'

Rebecca didn't buy it. 'Don't give me the ladylike posturing, Alice. You were in the media for decades and swearing flows like bad coffee there.'

The eyes opened again to reveal flinty resolve. 'Very well, let me be frank, then. I am sorry for what happened to Elspeth, and I fervently hope she makes a full recovery. But I must retain a measure of control. Those final few pages, while important, do not impact on the work you have to do in putting this together. Objectivity is vital if this is to be taken seriously. It's your decision, Rebecca. You can walk out of here right now – and, given the circumstances, that would be understandable – or you can stick with this story and perhaps do some good. It's your choice.'

She was calling her bluff, although Rebecca hadn't realised she was bluffing until a few moments before. She thought she had meant it when she said she would walk, and perhaps she did, but now she knew she wouldn't – couldn't – let this go. She owed it to Elspeth to follow it through. Alice sensed this because she flicked a finger for Orla to hand them to Rebecca, which she did, along with a look of warning, whether over proceeding further or continuing to upset her employer, Rebecca couldn't tell. Rebecca looked at the top page, saw a now familiar name.

'Who is John Lane?' she asked.

'A dangerous man.'

'Did he kill Gerry Rawlings? Was it made to look like an accident, or covered up somehow? Is that the murder that never was?'

Alice shook her head. 'Read the pages, make your inquiries, do your research. Do your damned job, Rebecca. I chose you and poor Ms McTaggart for a reason, as you said, and that reason is that neither of you are easily led. I make the point again: you must read and make up your own mind if there is merit in the story. I think you will find there is, but it must be your decision.'

Rebecca had already resolved to continue. 'I want to see Dalgliesh again. Can Forbes perhaps find out where he'll be over the next day or two?'

She knew she could dig around herself but hoped the former editor would have contacts that would save her some time.

'I'm sure he could,' Alice said, her voice a little guarded but then softening. 'But my advice right now, Rebecca, is that you go home and get some rest. You look done in.'

Rebecca felt herself wilt a little. Thus far she had been buoyed by her anger, but that had dissipated and now exhaustion washed over her muscles and bones and thoughts. The words on the page blurred and she knew that Alice was correct. She needed to decompress. A gin, a lie down on her old bed at home. Sleep, if she could.

But she knew she wouldn't. She knew she couldn't.

Orla showed them out but touched Rebecca's shoulder at the door. Rebecca turned and saw that warning look again. She waited for the nurse-cum-assistant to berate her, but the woman's voice was gentle when she spoke.

'You take care of yourself now, pet.' She jerked her head towards the stairway behind her. 'Her ladyship is a stubborn old bat and has been fixated on this for years. This thing has eaten away at her, and she didn't really know that until her husband died. She had time to think then, and now that she's weakened, she's had more time to dwell on the past.'

'What is wrong with her?'

'Nothing but old age and a body that is gradually calling it quits. Her mind is all there, I think you know that, but it's housed in a shell that's well out of warranty.' She paused, looked back up the stairs again, then lowered her voice. 'She's also out of the firing line, so to speak. You're not.'

Rebecca ignored the reference to potential danger and looked at Alice's pages again, aware that Chaz was leaning in to see them. She knew she should ask further questions, but she didn't have the energy.

'You take care of her, young man,' Orla said to him.

'I'll do my best.'

She looked him up and down. 'No offence, love, but that might not be good enough.'

Rebecca thought of a question. 'What is it you know, Orla?'

'Only what's in those pages, I give you my word, pet. And one other thing, though it's more of an impression than a knowledge of fact. Her ladyship is driven – has been all her life, I'd say. You had to be back then, being a woman in what was largely a man's world. You had to be driven and you had to be strong-willed, and she still is, despite the betrayal of her body.' She stopped, took a breath, perhaps wondering if she should proceed. 'But there's something else going on there. In her youth, it was ambition; when she was established, it was professionalism, but now . . . ?' She paused again, as if trying to gather her thoughts. 'Now I think it's more than that.'

'More in what way?'

Orla didn't reply at first. For the third time she craned round and stared up to the second floor, as if the answer stood at the head of the stairs. 'I don't know.' She turned back. 'But whatever happened back then, she let someone down. And I think what she's feeling is guilt.'

18

Excerpt from Murder on the Mountain:
The Personal Testimony of Alice Larkin

Over the next few weeks I saw Gerry Rawlings every weekend. I had an ulterior motive, of course, and that was to find out how the men lived and worked – the highs, the lows, the problems of having thousands of differing personalities thrown together in close proximity. When I mentioned that to him, he smiled and pointed out that was what *all* life was: millions of people rubbing shoulders on a small rock hurtling through space. And all that rubbing caused friction some-times, and that friction sometimes created a spark, and that spark could become a blaze.

That made me return to John Lane and the root of the conflict between them, but he refused to be drawn on that, even though during our evenings together we ran into the man three times – even now Oban isn't that big a town, so crossing paths with him was not easy to avoid. Although they exchanged no further barbs, the looks they shot each other were sufficiently hot that I was surprised they didn't set off fire alarms. Each time, Lane eyed me with that mix of curios-ity and contempt, as if he was judging me for being seen with Gerry. I didn't care. I was on the job and Gerry was a source, and a damned good one.

At least, that's what I told myself, but I knew in my soul that I was seeing him for other reasons.

The fact is, I had fallen for this man. Handsome, charming, etc, etc. I'll add another adjective. He was sexy. Despite rumours to the contrary, we didn't invent sex in the sixties, but we did more to bring it out into the open than at any other period during the twentieth century. It was no longer something to hide but to proclaim loudly, especially if you were female. Miniskirts, of course, showed off acres of thigh. Later we had hot pants, see-through blouses, the Pill more widely available. Naturists had been parading around their camps for years, but topless beaches started to spread to mainstream locations in the south of France and beyond. We weren't ashamed to be sexually attractive to others or attracted to others. In fact, we positively revelled in it. As I've said before, that's not to say that I was promiscuous; despite his many attempts I had never gone beyond what we used to call heavy petting with Lance, much to his great disappointment, partly because, handsome though he was, I simply wasn't that into him. Deep down, though, while my conscious brain was telling me that Gerry was nothing more than a means of fleshing out a story that I hadn't even begun to write, I knew that it was going to be different with him. Sooner or later, as the phrase later went, we'd get it on.

Even so, I didn't consummate the relationship, to coin another phrase, until I was told not to see him. I'm not saying the diktat influenced my decision, but I was then, and am now, thrawn in the extreme, and so I remain unsure whether it was instigated by love, lust or sheer bloody-mindedness.

It was my father who issued the ultimatum. He arrived unexpectedly in the newspaper office one lunchtime, causing the editor and advertisement manager to fluster. They fawned in their usual manner, but he wasn't there to talk to them – he was there for me. He announced he was taking me to lunch and, naturally, that was perfectly fine with the editor, even though it was deadline day. When the owner says he's taking his daughter for a bite to eat, it is the editor's job to say, *Yes, sir, of course, sir, do you want my luncheon vouchers, sir*?

My father's Bentley S2, one of the last from the production line in 1962, waited outside and when I climbed into the passenger seat, I found Lance in the back seat. I hadn't seen him for a few weeks, and he was tanned, which meant he'd been in the south of France. Lance loved the place and jetted off there whenever he could to top up his tan and show off his toned muscles on the beach. On seeing him, I realised I had been ambushed.

Lance leaned forward to deliver a kiss, but I managed to avert my face by pretending to position my handbag at my feet while my father climbed into the driver's seat. He always spurned the use of a driver, much preferring to have control of the vehicle himself, but he didn't make any move to start the engine. He twisted in the plush seating to face me, and I could tell from the set of his jaw that I was in for a lecture. I was well-acquainted with his *I'm about to give you a talking to, my girl* face.

'So, lunch is off, then?' I observed.

'I've heard something disquieting about you, Alice,' he said. His voice was soft and measured – he seldom shouted, for sometimes a quiet word from him was sufficient. At least with other people, not with me. Even so, I struggled to remember him ever raising his voice to me.

I gave him a smile. 'Only one disquieting thing, Daddy? I must be slipping.'

'This isn't funny, Al,' Lance said. He always called me Al. I later came to hate the Paul Simon song for that very reason.

'Not funny at all,' my father emphasised.

I decided that, at this juncture, silence was my best course of action as I had no idea what I had done, so I waited until they enlightened me on the nature of my disquieting behaviour. I didn't have long to wait.

'Do you know a man called Rawlings?' my father asked.

I saw no reason to lie. 'I do.'

'What is the nature of your relationship?'

'The nature of my relationship?'

'Yes.'

'I'm not sure we have a relationship, as such. Certainly not in the way you are suggesting.'

At that moment I did see a reason to lie. As plush and elegant as the Bentley was, there was something decidedly uncomfortable in the air.

'That's not what we hear,' Lance put in.

I looked towards him over the cream leather upholstery. 'What have you heard?'

'That you've been seen often in his company.'

I wondered who had been talking and decided it could be anyone. Thanks to my father treating the town like a Monopoly board and my work with the paper, I was well known around these streets. 'That is true,' I said.

'Then I ask you again, Alice,' my father said. 'What is the nature of your relationship with this man?'

'He's a source.'

'A source for what?'

'A story.'

I knew I was annoying him because that was my intention. His lips thinned in frustration. 'What sort of story?'

'I told you about it, Daddy. The one about Cruachan and the hydro scheme.'

I saw recollection gleam in his eyes. 'You haven't filed any copy. I thought you'd given up on it.'

'I'm taking my time in gathering material. It's not time-sensitive.' I smiled again. 'I may even write a book about it. I have some fascinating stuff and—'

183

'You will stop seeing him,' Lance butted in.

When I regarded him again, I made sure that my movements were slow and deliberate. 'That's not your decision to make, Lance.'

'No, but it's mine,' said my father. 'And I want you to stop seeing him.'

I was about to point out that I was over twenty-one and this was 1964, not 1864, but I was more interested in finding out the reason behind this prohibition. 'And why would I do that?'

'Because I'm telling you.'

'That's not a good reason.'

He inhaled deeply before he spoke again. 'He's not someone with whom I wish you to associate.'

'Why not?'

'He's not your type of person.'

'He's not *your* type of person, you mean.'

My father stared at me, his eyes lidded. I knew that look well, too. It meant he was being serious. Sometimes he would tell me not to do a thing but really didn't care whether I did or not, he was merely fulfilling his fatherly duty. But this time he meant what he said. He didn't want me to see Gerry Rawlings. Now I was really interested.

'And if I don't agree to your request?'

'It's not a request, Alice.'

'Your demand, then. What happens? Will you cut me off without a penny? Sack me? How will that look, that you fired your only daughter because she was doing her job?'

I saw that I had him. He meant what he said, but I knew he wouldn't take any action against me. I was his Achilles heel, and we both knew it.

'I won't have you associating with him,' Lance said.

I levelled my gaze at him again, mirroring my father's hooded eyes. '*You* won't, Lance?'

'I won't.'

'And if I refuse to accede to my father's order, what makes you think I'll listen to you?'

His mouth opened and closed a couple of times before he said, 'We have an arrangement, you and I.'

I looked again at my father, but he looked away. 'That's news to me,' I said.

'Everyone knows it,' Lance said.

'Everyone but me, it seems.'

There was a silence, then. People walked by the car, some admiring it as they passed. I looked at the dashboard clock. I had a story to write before deadline, and if the editor wouldn't stand up for professionalism then I would. I estimated how long it would take me to write it and for it to be typeset. Another few minutes wouldn't hurt. I had questions for my father.

'What's this really about?'

'It's not seemly for you to be seen with this man,' my father said.

'Seemly?' I laughed. 'Have we jumped into the Tardis and gone back a few decades?'

My father held my gaze once again. 'He's not what he seems.'

'None of us are,' I countered.

'Stop debating this, Al,' Lance said. 'Just do as we say.'

'Oh, shut up, Lance.'

That really annoyed him. 'Don't you tell me to shut up, you jumped-up little tart.'

He lunged forward as though to strike me, but my father moved quickly, his left arm darting out to act as a barrier. 'Sit back, Lance, and leave this to me.'

Even with his tan, Lance was red in the face. 'That girl needs discipline.'

'But she won't get it from you,' said my father, his soft voice rasped by a growl, his forceful gaze a silent shove that sent

185

Lance sinking back again. My father stared at him for a moment, then faced me again.

'Are you involved with this man?'

'Involved in what way?'

'Don't be obtuse, girl, you know what I'm asking.'

I was being obtuse but deliberately. 'No,' I said, truthfully.

'And you will not stop seeing him?'

'Daddy, what do you think?'

He sighed. 'You are an obstinate girl, Alice.'

'And from whom do I get that from, I wonder?' I laid my hand on the door handle. 'Now, if we're done here, I have a story to write.'

Without waiting for confirmation that the interview was over, I retrieved my bag from the foot well, opened the door, climbed out and walked around the bonnet to the pavement. The rear window rolled down.

'You'll regret this, Al,' Lance said.

'I don't think so, Lance.'

'I won't have you shaming us like this with some ... Irishman. See sense, before it's too late.'

I fixed me eyes on him for a long time before I said, 'And if I don't see sense?'

He returned my stare, then rolled the window up without any further reply. I looked at my father, but he stared straight ahead. The Bentley pulled away.

That was a Thursday. The next night, Gerry Rawlings was in my bed.

19

The city streets gave way to green fields, the sunlight flickering between branches, but Rebecca, her face tilted towards the passenger window as she leaned against the headrest of the Land Rover Discovery, paid it little heed. James, her mum's boyfriend – still a weird thing to even think – was driving, for which she was grateful, and they were heading to Largs, on the Firth of Clyde, to see the uncle he had mentioned. Chaz was at the hospital, having picked Julie up from the station.

There was no change in Elspeth's condition. She was in a coma, a deep one, and Rebecca had considered calling this interview off, but everyone – her mother, Chaz, Alan, even Julie – agreed that doing so would serve no purpose. She could sit around a hospital waiting room drinking coffee from a machine, or she could be out there doing what she did best. Elspeth would want her to get on with it, Julie had said. She would want her to carry on with the story.

Rebecca thought of it another way. Elspeth would want her to get the bastards.

James was considerate enough to remain silent as they drove westward out of the city, apart from repeating that though his uncle Duncan could be a little wandered in his thinking and may sometimes take the long way round, he always got there in the end.

'Just let him ramble a bit,' he'd said, 'and if I think he's gone seriously off track, I'll edge him back, is that okay?'

She said that was fine, then thanked him for taking the time to do this. He must have work to do.

'I took the day off,' he said. 'I'm the boss, I can do these things.'

'It's good of you, though.'

'I'm happy to do it. Your mum didn't want you to be alone.'

As far as her mother was concerned, Elspeth's accident was a hit and run. She hadn't told her about Dalgliesh's threat. 'I'm not in any danger,' she said to James.

'No, but your friend is seriously injured. I get it that you want to work, to keep busy, I really do, but you're best not to be alone.'

She understood he was doing this more for her mother's benefit, which was understandable. 'Still, it's kind of you to take time off.'

He shrugged it away. 'We have to do things for people in this life. The business is ticking along nicely and doesn't need me there every day.' He stopped, took a breath, as if he was considering whether to say his next words. 'I'm going to take more of a back seat from now on, anyway.'

Rebecca asked why, even though she had already guessed the answer.

When he spoke, there was a hint of embarrassment in his voice. 'For too long I put my work ahead of my life, if you understand what I mean, and that was wrong. Work to live, not live to work, right? My marriage was a nightmare. We married too young – neither of us were ready – and we stayed together far too long, but I suppose it made concentrating on the business that much easier. I don't want to do that now. I've got a second chance here and I don't want to screw it up.'

That second chance was her mother. As he spoke, she thought of Stephen. She'd finally remembered to contact him the night before to tell him about Elspeth. She'd texted first, around 10 p.m., thinking he might be asleep, but he called back right away.

'What the hell happened, Becks? Do you need me to come down?'

She told him what she knew, which wasn't enough. As with her mother, she left out the part about Dalgliesh. If she had told him about that, he'd be on the first train to Glasgow, and she didn't want that.

'Jesus,' he said, his voice a mere breath. 'How is she?'

'In a coma,' she said. 'It's not looking good, Stephen.'

Her voice broke a little and she swallowed back something hard and bitter. A tear burst free, and she wiped it away with her hand. She was glad he couldn't see her like this.

'And the police are on it?'

'Yes. Not sure what they can do, though, unless they pull some CCTV from somewhere.'

'Is it connected to the story, maybe?'

Stephen wasn't stupid, but she lied anyway. 'I don't see how.'

There was a silence on the line, just a brief one, but enough to tell her that he wasn't convinced. Then, 'Okay, but are you sure you don't want me to come down?'

'Positive. What good would us all sitting in a hospital do? Julie will be here tomorrow morning.'

'Yeah,' he conceded. 'Look, I'll understand if you don't make it to the dinner on Saturday.'

'No, I—'

'Becks, don't stress about it. You need to stay there, I get that.'

She felt she should argue the point but didn't have the energy. 'We'll see how things are by then.'

He agreed and they said their goodbyes. He told her he loved her. She said she loved him. He said to let him know if there was anything he could do. She said she would. She went to sleep feeling guilt over the relief she'd felt when he said she didn't need to get back for the dinner. She felt that guilt again as James drove on in silence. What was wrong with her?

Forbes sounded half-awake when he answered his phone.

'Did I wake you?' Alice asked.

'What time is it?' His groggy voice was all the answer she needed.

'Time you were up and about.'

She heard him groan as if he was hauling himself upright. 'I am up.'

'Yes, but not out of bed. Where were you last night? I tried to reach you.'

'I was out.'

'With one of your lady friends?'

Forbes had never settled down with one woman, much preferring a string of relationships of varying timespans ranging from days to months, but never more than a year. It was the one facet of his nature that Alice could never accept. There came a time when you had to settle down with one person. That person for her had been Dennis, although for a few months in the summer of 1964 she thought it might have been someone else.

Forbes chose not to answer, without doubt knowing her views and fearing a lecture. Not that it would have stopped her from delivering one anyway, but she had other matters to attend to.

'Elspeth McTaggart was involved in a hit and run last evening on her way here,' she said.

He swore softly down the line. 'Is she badly hurt?'

'Apparently.'

'Is this connected to—'

'I would say almost definitely,' Alice said, her voice curt. She felt guilt over the turn of events, but she couldn't let it divert her from her purpose. Time was short, she could feel it. The dreams were becoming more frequent. Faces, voices, incidents. The feel of Gerry Rawlings' body against hers. His smile. John Lane's scowl. Her father's understated fury when she refused his demand. Lance's face suffused with rage. Danny McCall's cold look.

Blood.

Screams.

'Rebecca wishes to speak again to Finbar Dalgliesh,' she said. The girl had made the request before she left the previous evening.

'Is that wise? Perhaps the matter is best dropped now before—'

'I gave her the option. She declined.'

Alice had been proud of the girl when she said she would continue. She showed spine.

'I want you to find out where he'll be this evening.'

'What makes you think I can do that?'

Alice laughed. 'Forbes, you and I share genes. If I was able to myself, I would find him, so I know you can, too. Track him down, Forbes. And then, perhaps, you might take a holiday until all this is over.'

'You really think that is necessary?'

'Necessary? No. Advisable, yes. I am in this for the duration, Orla too. She's faced worse individuals in her life.'

'And Rebecca?'

'Rebecca has made her choice. She knows the risks, if there are any. But I believe that is why she wishes to confront Dalgliesh. I like that in her. She goes for it.'

'As long as he doesn't go for her.'

Her laugh was short but dry. 'Not Finbar. He doesn't get his hands dirty.'

'No,' said Forbes, 'he lets others do it for him.'

*

Bill Sawyer listened to the ringing tone as he drove down the A9, the shrill little beep pulsing from the hands-free speaker clipped to his visor. He had already tried to reach Elspeth three times, but it kept going straight to voicemail. He'd left messages but hadn't heard from her. That wasn't like her.

He kept an eye on his rearview, in case any traffic cops loomed behind him. If they thought he was using a hands-free, they could pull him over, and he wasn't in the mood to talk himself out of being reported. It wasn't technically illegal, but they could still prosecute – all it would take was one little waver in his steering. Being a former police officer only went so far, and hardly anywhere at all with traffic.

He had just about given up, believing the call would connect to the answering service again, when he heard a voice say, 'Hello?'

A woman's voice he didn't recognise. 'Who is this?'

'My name is Angela, I'm a critical care nurse in Glasgow Royal Infirmary.'

Critical care, he thought, that can't be good. He felt the car wobble a bit with the shock, and he instinctively checked his mirror. The road was empty, thank God. 'Where's Elspeth?'

'Are you family?'

He considered telling the truth but then opted for a lie. If he didn't claim any blood connection, they might not tell him anything. Medical staff rival the police for being tight-lipped. 'I'm a cousin. My name's Bill Sawyer.'

'I see.' He couldn't tell whether he'd been believed, but she continued nonetheless. 'Well, I'm sorry to have to tell you this but your cousin has been in an accident.'

'What happened?'

'She was hit by a car. The driver didn't stop.'

'Is she badly hurt?'

'She's in the ICU, Mr Sawyer. I'm sorry to tell you that she's in a coma.'

192

Sawyer felt his initial shock give way to anger. A fucking hit and run. An accident, the nurse had called it, but something in his gut told him it was no accident. Elspeth had called him in because she was rattled, and that wasn't like her. Finbar Dalgliesh had made veiled threats to Rebecca. If he was behind this, he'd pay. Hell, maybe he'd give him a kicking anyway, just for the hell of it. 'Will she be okay?'

A slight pause. 'We're doing everything we can. She's getting the best possible care. We have some very good medical staff here.'

As a police officer, Sawyer had delivered such news many times and knew it was difficult to appear both caring and optimistic without making it sound in any way forced, but this nurse managed to land on the compassionate side of mechanical.

'Is there anybody with her?'

'Her friends are here and her partner.'

Julie was there. That was good, even though Sawyer was still a little uncomfortable with the idea of same-sex relationships. He was old-school and still struggled a little to come to terms with it, but he knew the world had changed and he was trying.

'Is there a Rebecca Connolly there?'

'I don't . . .'

'Young woman, reddish hair?' He almost said 'attractive' but he didn't want to appear to be some kind of dirty old man.

'I'm sorry, I don't know. I've seen only Ms McTaggart's partner and two young men, that's all.'

The two young men had to be Chaz and Alan. Where the hell was Rebecca, though? She should be there too. He frowned as he thanked the nurse and rung off. He scrolled through the phone attached to a magnetic holder on his air vent until he found her number, all the while checking behind him for the tell-tale blue lights. He hit *Call* but was bounced straight through to voicemail. Bugger it, Becks, what are you doing? He cut the connection, gripped the wheel with both hands. He was on the Perth bypass and the Broxden Junction was up ahead. He'd planned to stop there for a coffee and a sandwich, but if he pushed on, he'd be in Glasgow in ninety minutes or so. Sooner if he broke a speed limit or two.

Screw the traffic boys.

He put his foot down.

20

James still called Duncan Saunders 'Unkie Duncie'. Ordinarily Rebecca would have found this amusing, appealing even, but she wasn't in the mood for amusing or appealing. He had probably been strapping in his day, but age had withered him slightly. Even though he was of similar age to Alice, he was in far better condition, physically at least. His body remained strong and relatively fit, as Rebecca witnessed when he walked ahead of them towards a table at the far end of the lawn fronting the care home, but James had suggested that his mind sometimes became fuzzy, even though Rebecca was yet to see any evidence of it. Alice was the opposite. Her mind remained as sharp as a knife, but her body had betrayed her.

Duncan gazed over a hedge towards the road that clung to the coast towards Gourock and Greenock. Beyond it was a stretch of grassland and then the sun shimmering on the water, haze ghosting the opposite bank, although it might have been the Isle of Bute she could see. That and Great Cumbrae, the low-lying island to the left, were just two of the forty or so islands of varying sizes in the Firth of Clyde, although she could think of only four that were inhabited, the largest being Arran, which was off to the west of where she was now. A small yacht glided across the sparkling surface and, for a moment, Rebecca wished she was aboard with nothing but the breeze in her hair and the sun on her face and no need to worry about Elspeth or murders that never were or Dalgliesh.

Duncan followed her gaze and smiled. 'Looks brilliant out there, eh, hen? Do you sail?'

She forced a smile. 'I don't know a spinnaker from a halyard, but my boyfriend does, and he's taken me out a couple of times on his father's boat.'

'Rich bugger, is he?'

'He's a lawyer.'

Duncan laughed. 'He'll be worth a bob or two, right enough. Never met a poor lawyer yet.'

Rebecca had but she wasn't here to discuss the vagaries of income among members of the legal profession. 'Thank you very much for seeing me, Mr Saunders.'

'Call me Duncie, everyone does. I'm gonnae take them to court, you know.'

Rebecca was puzzled. 'Take who to court?'

'They doughnut people, for using my name.'

It took a second or two before Rebecca made the connection. 'Dunkin' Donuts?'

'Aye, that's the fellas. I'm gonnae sue them for leaving me open to mockery, or something. The number of people that call me Duncie Donuts drives me up the wall. I don't even like the bloody things. Too sugary. Folk eat too much sugar these days. Me, I never touched it, nor much salt, either. Sprinkle it on my chips a wee bit – salt, I mean – but never add it otherwise. That's just me, though, I'm no lecturing. Don't care what people do, me, live and let live, but they sufferin' donut people have really got my goat, so they have.'

This was the second time in recent days that she had listened to an elderly man ramble. With Jack Dredden it was, she believed, a means of diversion, but not with Duncie Saunders. His delivery was deadpan, and she couldn't decide whether he was joking. Was this part of the wandered mind James had warned her about?

Then Duncie laughed. 'I'm pulling your leg, hen.'

Rebecca cracked a smile, made it as wide as she could. She didn't feel like smiling, but it seemed the thing to do.

His expression grew dour again. 'I'm gonnae have a serious word with they folk at that fried chicken place, though. Sufferin' bastards need to take my name off that Colonel bloke.'

She laughed, felt herself brightening, but then images flashed in her mind like slides on a screen . . .

Flash. A cobbled street.

Flash. Blood sticking to her fingers.

Flash. The screech of a car's wheels.

Stop it, Becks. That doesn't help anyone, not Elspeth, not you. Focus on the job, that's the only thing to do.

She flicked a glance at James, who smiled now but watched her intently. Her mum had probably told him to keep an eye on her. James gave her an encouraging nod, so she flipped open her notebook and placed her digital recorder on the table between them.

'Do you mind if I record our chat?'

Duncie shrugged his permission. 'Been recorded a lot, so I have. People wanting to know about the same stuff as you. Others wanting to know about life in the sixties, but you know what they say about that: if you can remember the sixties, you weren't really there.' His brow furrowed. 'I don't mind much about them, so I must've been there, right enough.' He glanced at his nephew and leaned forward across the table. 'I'll bet he's told you I'm a wee bit gaga, right?'

Rebecca didn't know what to say and looked to James for assistance.

'No, Unkie Duncie,' he said. 'I told her you were off your rocker.'

Duncie grinned. 'Cheeky bastard. He always needed a good clip around the ear, and he thinks he's too big and I'm too feeble to give him one. But wait till he's no looking, hen. I'll make his head spin, so I will.'

Rebecca responded with another smile, and he watched as she pressed record on the small device, then picked up her pen.

'You record and take notes, hen?'

'Yes, it's so I can be as accurate as I can.'

'And you're doing this for what? Newspaper, magazine?'

'I don't know yet. It's speculative.'

'Speculative. Good word. I'll mind that for Scrabble. We have a wee tourney every Saturday night, keeps us auld yins' brains from fogging too much. That and Wordle, but I never took to that.' He paused, then said, 'So, what do you want to know?'

'You were part of the workforce at Cruachan, right?'

'The Hollow Mountain, aye, that and other projects in the hydro scheme right across the sufferin' Highlands, all through the fifties and sixties.'

'You were a tunnel tiger?'

'Aye, tigers in the dark, we were. The elite, you know? 'Cause it was so dangerous, down there in the guts of the earth, drilling, blasting, hacking our way through rock and muck and mud. Got paid good money, we did. You know what they say: where's there's muck, there's brass. We got three, four times the going rate for the work, but we got danger money, too. I mean, handling gelignite was dicey enough but doing it in a bloody tunnel that could collapse on you at any moment was sodding hairy, if you know what I mean, so we earned every shilling.'

'Were you ever involved in any accidents?'

Flash. Brake lights, flickering.

'Aye, caught in a cave-in once. Nothing too bad, as it turned out, else I might no be here to tell you about it, hen, but it wasn't pleasant being buried in a ton or so of earth. I thought my last breath would be some Argyll muck, but my mates hauled me out by my feet. I'm glad that's the only way I was hauled out feet first, if you catch my drift. Others weren't so lucky.'

'So, was health and safety lax?'

'Lax? Another good word, hen. A good ten-pointer in the old Scrabble, more if I can get it placed over a double or triple pointer. No, it wasn't particularly lax, it was just that things were different in they days. We took risks without knowing they were risks – they were just the job. I mean, now they'd have planning meetings and crisis management meetings and, what do you call them, risk assessment meetings, all sorts of bloody meetings, before you could switch on a sodding lamp and wield a sufferin' shovel, but back then we just got on with the job in hand. There were safety measures, and we took precautions, but accidents happened and blokes, good blokes, died. At Cruachan I mind there was some guys perished when the lorry they were driving backed into the loch. That's all it was, nothing dangerous, just an accident and three men were gone, just like that. Still down there in that Loch . . . whatsitcalled?'

'Loch Awe?'

'Aye, that's the one. Loch Awe. I don't think they ever recovered, they poor sods, or the lorry. Another guy was buried in a sandpit. Just an accident, that's all. And then there was dust – it was like being caught in a desert sandstorm, if you catch my drift. We covered our mouths, of course we did, but I think I must've breathed in half that mountain in the few years I was there. It's a wonder I haven't got silicosis, or some sort of cosis or other, from all that sufferin' dust. And the fumes – jeez! Between the explosives and the diesel trucks and the dust, yon air must've been toxic. Wouldn't be allowed these days, not without specialist equipment.' He stopped talking, looked away, and Rebecca swore she saw a tear in his eye. 'I've lost mates through lung disease. I swear it was working there that did it. But I've been lucky, so I have. I'm still healthy. I'm still here. Lucky . . .'

He gazed across the hedge again, his eyes on some teenagers performing gymnastics on the grass, their laughter tinkling as they challenged each other to cartwheels and hand-walking. Rebecca waited for him to speak again but when he didn't, she looked at James.

'Uncie Duncie,' he said.

Duncie looked up. 'Aye, I'm still here, no gone wandering, if that's what you're worried about, son.'

Rebecca knew he had, but not through any form of age-related dementia, and neither had he been taking note of the youngsters. Duncan Saunders had briefly been transported back in time to recall the faces of those men he had befriended decades before and now lived on only in memory. In those few moments he would have relived conversations and experiences, flitting through his mind at high speed. Rebecca had done the same herself many times.

Flash. Elspeth, eyes open, mouth working as if trying to speak.

Flash. Tyres screeching, a car spins round a corner out of sight.

She decided to bring focus to the conversation, if only for her own benefit. 'Did you know a man called Gerry Rawlings?'

His eyes narrowed as he searched among those faces still alive in the time capsule of memory. 'Irish fella?'

'Yes.'

'Didn't know him, not personally. I saw him around, of course.'

'At Cruachan?'

'Aye. You have to remember, there were maybe twelve or thirteen hundred of us blokes blowing the guts out of they hills up there during that time. I had my mates, and my mates had mates, and Gerry Rawlings was mates with one of them, so I

200

met him. That Rawlings guy was a dab hand at the cards, so he was. Like *Maverick*, you know *Maverick*?'

Rebecca nodded. She'd come across the old TV show when she was looking into the source of John Lane's nickname. That brought her to the next question.

'And what about John Lane? Bronco Lane?'

Duncie's face darkened. 'That bastard! Aye, I knew him, no well, mind you, but well enough to know I didn't like him.'

'Why not?'

'Why not? He was a bully and a shitehawk, that's why not. He was always pushing people around, acting the big man. Thought he was something, said he was going places. The only place I wanted him to go was a long walk off a short pier.'

'Did he push you around?'

Duncie's laugh was sharp and dismissive. 'Nah, I was a big lad. Might no look it now, hen, but I was.'

'You still look fit, Mister Saunders.'

'It's Duncie, for God's sake, and thanks for that.' He beamed, enjoying the compliment. 'Aye, Bronco was a bully, and they don't pick on the big lads. He had his mates, of course, and they ganged up on a few boys.'

'Did you know anyone who they picked on?'

'I knew them but couldn't give you their names now.' He jerked his head towards James. 'Mind's gone, you see?'

'So, none of your immediate mates suffered?'

'No, we were a tough bunch, us tunnel tigers and we stuck together. Lane and his boys, they picked on them that were outsiders, if you like. Like a bunch of hyenas, they were, picking out the weak ones in the herd.'

'Were they ever reported?'

'They were too clever. They never did nothing where there were witnesses. Anyone else, if there was a row, it would be a square-go right there and then, a few punches and then down the pub for a drink. But no that sod Lane and his cronies.

They were always careful, waited until after dark and then jumped whatever poor bugger they didn't like.' He looked over the water again. 'That bastard Bronco Lane. Haven't thought about him for a long time. He was sleekit and he was as yellow as a Fyffes banana, but no anywhere near as tasty.' He looked back at Rebecca. 'Course, you'll know what he did later, right?'

She nodded. Her late-night online trawling had revealed who John Lane was and raised a suspicion as to why Dalgliesh had become involved. Reputations, he'd said. But not his. She saw Lane's face in a newspaper photograph now. The dark hair, the hooded eyes, a look that seemed somehow familiar to her, but that she couldn't quite place.

'And how often did these beatings take place?'

'It wasn't a weekly thing or anything like that. But there were three, maybe four, that I know of over the years. That was enough.'

'So, there were never any charges?'

'Charges? Listen, hen, this was like the Wild West, you know? It was a man's world and there were fights and fall-outs all over the place. But we all knew what they were about so gave them a wide berth. Your man Rawlings didn't, though. He got in Lane's face at every opportunity.'

'Do you know why?'

'Never found out. Maybe they just didn't get on.'

'Do you know how Gerry Rawlings died?'

Duncan searched his memory again. 'No, can't say I do. Was it recent?'

'No, the late summer of 1964. At Cruachan.'

''64? I was away from hydro work by then. Left in '62 'cause I'd had enough of it. I'd met a lassie and we moved back to Glasgow where I set up my business. Building. Did well, too. Well enough to pay for this place in my dotage. So, was Gerry involved in an accident?'

'He fell from the dam.'

Duncan's brow furrowed. 'The dam? What was he doing up there?'

'Nobody knows.'

'I mean, why would he go away up there?'

'The suggestion was that he was drunk and lost his footing, went over the side.'

'Gerry Rawlings, you sure?'

'Yes, it was reported in the papers.'

'I never saw that. Late summer? 1964? Maybe I was away on my honeymoon, Benidorm. That was something in they days, believe me, going to Spain, but I could afford it, so we went. My Sadie fair enjoyed that holiday. She'd never been any further than Rothesay before.'

He drifted again, transported to blue seas and balmy breezes and walking hand-in-hand with his new wife through a twilight heady with the aromas of the Mediterranean.

'Duncie?' Rebecca prodded.

He came back to the present. 'Aye, I'm here, hen, don't worry. You say Gerry was rat-arsed?'

'The report said it, not me.'

He shook his head. 'Don't see that, not the Gerry Rawlings I knew.'

'Why?'

'He was tee-total. He went out with the lads but never had anything stronger than a lemonade shandy. I can't see him getting so drunk that he'd pitch over the barrier. No way.'

21

Of all the people Rebecca expected to see in her mother's kitchen when she and James returned, Bill Sawyer was at the bottom of the list, but there he was, drinking tea and finishing off a home-baked scone. He stood up, wiping the crumbs from his lips with a paper napkin – Sandra Connolly insisted on napkins, even if you were having a digestive biscuit, not that there were many such delights on offer as she didn't approve of processed foods.

'Bill, what are you doing here?'

Rebecca's words came out a touch sharper than she meant them, but he didn't seem to notice. His gaze flitted to her mother briefly before he said, 'I was down here to see an old pal.'

Rebecca caught a careful note in his words, and his eyes seemed to bore into her, and she understood he wasn't here by chance.

'Bill heard about Elspeth,' Sandra said.

'I came here to find out what happened,' Bill said, 'and Sandra here was good enough to give me a meal and one of her delicious scones.'

Bill. Sandra. They were getting cosy. 'How did you find out where my mum lived?'

'I went to the infirmary and spoke to Chaz. Julie was in with Elspeth.'

'Did you see Elspeth? Has she woken up?'

She saw something quiver in his cheek. As much as Bill Sawyer liked anyone, he liked Elspeth. He also liked Rebecca, she knew that because of things he had done for her in the past, which was amazing given that they met when she was looking into a murder case in which he may have fabricated evidence when he was still a police officer. He was retired now but kept himself fit and trim. That had come in useful in the past, too.

'She's still in a coma,' he said, then blinked something away. 'Anyway, Chaz gave me your mum's address and I came here to see you.' He looked at James and held out his hand. 'Hi, I'm Bill Sawyer. I'm a friend of Becks from Inverness.'

James and he shook hands. 'Pleased to meet you,' James said. 'I'm James Wilton.'

'Aye, Sandra's partner, she told me you were off with Becks here doing an interview.'

There it was, Sandra's partner. Rebecca would have to get used to that.

When Bill looked at her again, she saw some sort of accusation in his eyes. 'We need to talk, Becks.'

Sandra sensed a need for discretion. 'Of course, why not go into the sitting room? James can help me in here while you two catch up.'

Bill nodded his thanks. 'Thanks, Sandra. I appreciate that. Nice to meet you, James.'

'You too, Bill,' said James.

Rebecca navigated Bill away from this sea of courtesy and into the sitting room, where she got right down to it. 'Why are you really here?'

'Aye, and it's good to see you, too, Becks,' Bill said as he sat down in her father's favourite armchair. She was about to object but caught herself in time. She was being ridiculous about this. It was a bloody chair, and her father was long gone.

She wasn't in the mood for Bill's usual patter. 'Elspeth phoned you, didn't she?'

'Aye.'

'She was worried about Finbar Dalgliesh, right?'

'With good reason, as it turns out.'

Rebecca couldn't argue with that.

'So, you're here as a bodyguard.'

'I'm here as a concerned mate.'

For some reason, coming from Bill Sawyer, that hit home. She felt tears well up and her lips trembled. He must have seen it because he said, 'Don't get all emotional on me, Becks. You'll have me greetin', too.'

This struck her as funnier than it should, and she laughed as she wiped the moisture from her cheeks with her fingers. 'Where are you staying?'

'Elspeth booked me a room in the same hotel as her.'

Elspeth had shelled out cash on this. Bill had proved he was a pal, but he was also on the books. 'She took Dalgliesh seriously, didn't she?'

'As I said, with good reason. I take it you've not given up on this story?'

'No.'

'Why not?'

'You know why not.'

'Tell me anyway.'

'Why?'

'I like the sound of your voice, even if it does get a bit whiny now and then.'

'I never get whiny.'

'She said in her whiny voice.'

She laughed again. She and this man held differing views on so many things, but he could make her laugh. He was also doing it on purpose. 'Elspeth would want me to carry on with it.'

'Don't let the bastards have their way, right?' He smiled as he took a deep breath. 'You and Elspeth are the same, like tigers when you get your teeth into something. You never bloody let go.'

Elspeth had often made similar statements, the bastards being whoever had a vested interest in not seeing something in print or broadcast – politicians, businesspeople, the nobility, the government and even police officers like Bill. The news being something that someone somewhere doesn't want printed. The question was, who were the bastards here? Dalgliesh? Or someone else?

Bill settled further into the chair. 'So, bring me up to speed.'

'What do you know already?'

'Pretend I know bugger-all.'

She took a deep breath and began to tell him everything she knew. She told him about Alice Larkin summoning them to her house in Westbourne Gardens . . .

'Alice Larkin,' he said wistfully. 'I remember her from the telly. I used to fancy her rotten when I was in my teens.'

She told him about the Cruachan project and Gerry Rawlings and how Alice Larkin met him . . .

'Ah, the meet-cute,' he said.

'Where did you hear that expression?'

'It's from rom-coms and it's how the lovers first meet.'

'I know what it means, I just wondered where you'd heard it.'

'God knows. I'm surprised I even used it myself. Carry on.'

She told him about John Lane, known as Bronco, after the TV show . . .

'Never heard of it,' he said.

'Neither had I until Alice mentioned it and then I googled it.'

'I'm surprised you had to do that. I thought you were an expert in these old TV shows.'

'Why did you think that?'

'I mind you mentioned *Gunsmoke* once.'

'That's because it's been rerun on satellite, and I caught it once or twice and my dad used to mention it. He never mentioned *Bronco*.'

She told him about the animosity between Gerry Rawlings and John Lane. She told him what Duncie had said about the man. She told him that Gerry Rawlings died after falling from a dam . . .

'Did he fall, or was he pushed?'

'That is the question, Horatio. Was it murder made to look like an accident? Alice mentioned a murder that never was, and I suppose that would fit the bill.'

'Unless he really was pissed and took the tumble.'

'Duncie said he was tee-total.'

'Maybe something happened, and he decided it was time to hit the bottle.'

That was a possibility. Rebecca was aware that there was a lot she didn't know. Duncie had described the tunnel workers as tigers in the dark. Bill had said she and Elspeth were like tigers – and they, too, were in the dark: Elspeth, somewhere in her own mind; Rebecca feeling her way round a world in which only Alice Larkin had the means to switch on a light.

Bill asked, 'So, you think this John Lane character was responsible?'

'Maybe.'

'Or it could simply be what it seems to be, an accident?'

Flash. Elspeth, lips moving. And the blood.

'I don't believe there are any accidents in this case, Bill.'

That caused him to fall silent for a moment and he turned thoughtful. She had no clue what he was thinking, but she knew what was going through her own mind.

Flash. The girl on the pavement, screaming.

Flash. The tyres, screeching.

'So, what's the next step?' Bill asked.

She hadn't been sure where she was going to go next – until she'd received a text from Forbes on the way back from Largs. 'First, I'm going to have something to eat. I'm not hungry, but there's no way mum will let me go anywhere without food. Then I want to read a few more pages of Alice's manuscript.'

'And then?'

She smiled, but it was more like gritting teeth. 'And then tonight I'm going to pay Finbar Dalgliesh a wee visit.'

'No, you're not,' Bill said emphatically.

She steeled herself for an argument. 'Why not?'

'Because *we're* going to pay Finbar Dalgliesh a wee visit.'

This time her smile was more natural than it had been all day.

Elspeth was walking through a meadow. The sun was gentle but warm – a lovely warm, not stifling, sweat-inducing, knickers-crawling-up-your-backside hot. The grass was long and soft and stroked her legs as she moved, as if welcoming her. Yellow bloomed through the green – she didn't know the names of the flowers, but they were wild. Around her was the pulsing chirp of grasshoppers, a sound she had always associated with happiness as a child. She had played in a meadow such as this and would lie down in the cool, long grass and listen to the insects. She never saw one, though. They were always just out there, somewhere, making their curious little noise. At the far end of this meadow was a copse, and birds sang from the branches. It looked enchanting in there. Cool. Peaceful. Even more peaceful than it was in this meadow. She glanced over her shoulder to her little cloud. She knew it was waiting but she didn't know for what.

She walked towards the trees, enjoying the caress of the blades of grass on her skin. The breeze breathing through them, the chorus of grasshoppers and the birdsong combined into a symphony of peace.

But that wasn't the truly incredible part of this walk.

She didn't have her sticks. She didn't need them now, not here. It had been years since she'd been able to walk without them, and the feeling of freedom, not to mention the lack of pain, was . . .

She searched for the word . . .

Sublime. Yes, that was it. This was sublime.

She wasn't sure how she got here, apart from knowing that somehow the cloud had brought her. The last thing she remembered was snuggling down, then the next moment she was walking in this beautiful field with the sun on her face and no sticks in her hands. She could still hear voices, but they were muted even further, as if someone had turned down the volume to almost a minimum. She couldn't make out what they were saying – they were just a buzz in the background, like insects weaving between the flowers.

She kept walking, enjoying the sensation.

The trees were closer now, and she saw figures moving between the boughs. No, they weren't just moving, they were floating. She was still too far away to make them out clearly, but yes, they were definitely floating.

How cool was that?

She wondered if she'd float, too, when she reached them.

22

Excerpt from Murder on the Mountain:
The Personal Testimony of Alice Larkin

It was a week or two later that I finally managed to prise some information out of Gerry about John Lane. I refused to call him Bronco because to use someone's nickname suggests affection, and I was far from enthralled by this man, and not simply because of the friction between him and Gerry. No, there was something deeply unlikeable about him and I've met a few men like him since, those who affect a blokey, man-of-the-people approach and proclaim love of country, but you know that they are, at heart, unspeakable, self-serving and deeply untrustworthy little shits.

After that first sexual encounter with Gerry there were further bouts of such activity, because once that wall was broken down, I found myself unable to keep from climbing over it again. And climb over it I did, figuratively and literally. I apologise if this embarrasses anyone, but it's important to understand how quickly and deeply I fell for this man. The lovemaking was wonderful, obviously, but I confess to being no neophyte myself. Without going into any further detail, for this is no *Fifty Shades* memoir, you can take my word that it was as satisfying for him as it was for me.

However, what made it all the more exciting was the emotional connection we made. I say that I fell in love with him, and I believed he felt the same. We would lie on my bed and talk for hours about life and literature and music and art and the cinema and the theatre. Lane had called him a bog-trotter, but Gerry was far more than that. He read widely and was able to converse on a number of subjects. And on those subjects he knew nothing about he was keen to learn more. He was, as I've already noted *ad nauseam*, handsome and charming and funny, but he was also smart and tender.

It was after a particularly enthusiastic round of pleasure that we lay in my bed – his cot in the workers' accommodation not being particularly suitable for such pursuits. Wanton I may have been, but I was no exhibitionist. He was on his back, and I lay with my head on his shoulder. He was smoking, a habit that never hooked me, but I didn't mind someone else firing up, which was just as well because in those days nearly everyone smoked. It seems curious now, when watching films or TV shows from decades past how a burning cigarette seems to grow from the fingers of everyone involved.

We were relaxed. We were happy. We were, not to put too fine a point on it, sated and I thought it was precisely the time to broach the subject of John Lane.

Gerry didn't reply for some time. He lay there, staring at the ceiling, his only movement to place the cigarette between his lips and then remove it again, occasionally flicking ash into an ashtray perched on his chest. Streetlight shone behind the thin summer curtains at my bedroom window. A ship's horn blew somewhere out on the Sound. The occasional car passed on the street below my flat.

Then, finally, a lungful of smoke was expelled on a sigh. 'John Lane is not someone I like to talk about, Ally,' he said.

He had started to call me Ally, another contraction of my name, but unlike Lance's Al, I didn't mind it on his lips. I didn't mind anything on his lips.

'Why not? Why do you two hate each other so much?'

'He's a bastard but he's also a dangerous man, and I wouldn't want you to be anywhere near him.'

'I don't intend to be.'

Gerry moved the ashtray, set it on the bedside table and stubbed his cigarette out. Then he propped himself up on one elbow and reached out with his free hand to stroke my hair and face. I loved it when he did that. 'I know you, Ally,' he said softly. 'Your curiosity is piqued and you won't stop until it's been satisfied.'

I smiled, took his hand and kissed his palm. 'You've satisfied everything else, Gerry, now you can satisfy that.'

He was very still, staring into my eyes as he reached his decision. 'Okay, I'll tell you, but this stays between us. Don't you go off being Nancy Drew.'

Now he really had my attention. I promised him that whatever he said would stay with me.

'No stories, no questions, no getting your dad involved – don't even mention it to him.'

Mention of my father confused me, but I nodded my agreement and placed my hand on my chest. 'I give you my word of honour.'

'Okay,' he said and then lay back down again. When he didn't say anything further for a full minute, I began to wonder if he'd changed his mind. I didn't want to nag him, so I waited.

Finally . . .

'You know I worked other projects in the hydro scheme, I told you that.'

'Yes.'

'So has Lane, so we've crossed paths a few times before this.'

213

'Okay.'

'I had a mate, another tunnel tiger. His name was Howard Rose – Howie, we called him – and he was from London. He was older than me, had seen action in the war, involved in liberating one of the camps there. You know what camps I mean?'

I knew what he meant. The concentration camps. 'Which one?'

'Bergen-Belsen in April '45. He didn't talk much about it, hardly said anything at all really, apart from telling me that it was the most horrific thing he had ever seen in his life. I was down in London on a break later and I went to the library to look it up. I knew about the camps but I really didn't know the extent of the horror. When the British forces moved in, they found bodies piled around the place, mounds of rags with skin and bone underneath them. And the living weren't much better. Men in striped clothing stumbling about, their skin pale, their bodies shrivelled against their bones, their eyes hollowed out by inhumanity and lack of hope. There were reports of the stench rising from the place like a fog. I couldn't imagine how Howie felt when he saw that. He was a Jew, you know? It must have hit him hard, knowing that if he'd been born in Poland or Germany or anywhere that the Nazis took over, he could have ended up there. No wonder he couldn't, or wouldn't, talk about it. Neither would I. I wasn't there and I find it hard to even repeat.'

I'd known about the camps, of course, but that knowledge was gained at a distance and from the perspective of fiction, namely *Exodus*, by Leon Uris. To read it was upsetting enough, but to have actually been there and seen the people left behind after the Nazis were overcome would be something that would live with a person for the rest of their lives. I wondered what this had to do with John Lane, but I didn't want to interrupt Gerry for fear of breaking the flow. I'd only just got him talking about it.

'The war had been bad enough for Howie, I think, but seeing that, in that camp, was worse,' Gerry continued. 'Still, despite all the horror, despite the slaughter, despite the inhumanity, he really believed that the war itself had been a necessary one. You can't say that about all wars. He thought that the cause was just and that, amid all the blood and death and sacrifice, some good had been done. Fascism was evil, any kind of extremism was evil, he believed. He even disapproved of the bombings in Palestine by Jewish groups, didn't think that was the way to win independence from the British. But when he came back home, he found that fascism was still alive and active here in Britain.'

He asked me if I knew who Sir Oswald Mosley was and I did. I had actually met him, albeit briefly, at a party my father threw in 1959 in his London flat. I remember this tall, handsome, dark-haired man with a slight limp – the result of a flying accident. He had been living in Ireland for a few years but was back to stand in the general election for Kensington North. Until then I'd no idea who he was so I asked my mother – this was the year before she died. She told me that he was a man who could have been great but who took the wrong path, and she left it at that. I didn't understand what she meant but I subsequently learned that he had first been a Conservative MP, then crossed the floor to Labour, and he had economic ideas that were well ahead of their time. However, he became dissatisfied with mainstream parties and set up his own, which eventually became the British Union of Fascists thanks to his admiration of Benito Mussolini.

Gerry seemed pleased that I knew these things. 'The BUF gained some traction, thanks to Mosley and his gift for oratory. But they were fiercely anti-Semitic, and the strong-arm wing, the Blackshirts, were a bunch of thugs. It was their brutality that saw the party lose much of their support, especially after a rally in London in '34 that turned nasty. Then a couple of years later came Cable Street, do you know about that?'

Again, I did, as it had come up when I did my poking around after meeting Mosley at that party. He and his Blackshirts had marched through a predominantly Jewish area of East London.

'Howie was there,' Gerry said. 'He and his friends joined the locals who banded together to stop the Blackshirts coming through. There were others, thousands of them, who wanted to see the march stopped – trade unionists, communists, even Irishmen like me – but a petition was dismissed by the Home Secretary. There were various flashpoints along the route, but Howie was at Cable Street, manning the barricades. The police escorting the marchers tried to break those barriers, and there was fighting, missiles thrown, people injured. But the marchers – supported by the police, remember – couldn't break through. The route as planned was later abandoned, though the Blackshirts were allowed to march through the West End of London.'

'What has this all to do with John Lane?'

'I'll get to him. Howie was eighteen when he was at Cable Street. He said it had just been a lark to him and his mates. But when he saw those blokes in their black shirts being supported by police officers, and when he read some elements of the press praising them, he realised that there was something at work that he could only describe as evil. He was Jewish and he became a Communist, too, though by the time he and I met he'd seen through that particular mirage. He could have gone to Spain to join the International Brigade and take on the fascists, but he felt it more important he get an education. When war broke out in '39, however, he didn't wait to be called up, he volunteered. He was twenty by that time and he was ready, he said. But he wasn't ready, not for what he saw, and he came back in '46 a changed man. He was in his late

216

twenties but he'd aged, he said. But still he thought they had fought to make the world a better place, that the millions who had been killed in battle or murdered in the camps hadn't died in vain.'

Gerry reached out to pull a cigarette from the pack on the bedside table and lit it. He sucked in the smoke, the tip flaring in the dim light, before exhaling deeply. 'But some things hadn't changed. Mosley was back to his old tricks, stirring up hate, claiming the Holocaust had been exaggerated, that the camps were necessary, that the burning of bodies was to combat disease, that the malnutrition was the result of Allied bombing cutting off the supply chain. He also used the resistance in Palestine against British rule as an example of Jewish ingratitude. He pointed at Jewish refugees and blamed them for everything, from the black market to crime to housing shortages. He demanded that they be sent home.' He drew on his cigarette again. 'Have you heard of the 43 Group?'

I shook my head.

'For want of a better term it was a Jewish resistance, right here in Britain.'

'Why were they called the 43 Group?'

'Because there were forty-three members at first, but more flocked to the cause. Many of them were ex-military like Howie, medal winners, bona fide heroes, and they had come back thinking they'd fought the good fight but discovered that the enemy was still here and always had been. Mosley and his boys continued to stir up hatred, and though they couldn't wear their black shirts – paramilitary gear had been banned by law after Cable Street – they were still Blackshirts at heart.'

'So, what did the 43 Group do?'

'They organised themselves into a force to break up fascist meetings whenever they could. They had spies in the Mosley camp and would infiltrate and disrupt gatherings.'

'Violently?'

'If need be. The fascist cause evaporated around 1950, largely thanks to what they did. Some of the fascists drifted into the mainstream, but they still held their extreme views.'

I began to have an inkling where this was leading. 'John Lane was one of them, right?'

He nodded. 'He wasn't John Lane then. He was Jim McNair.' He emitted a small laugh. 'Howie recognised him from some of the meetings he helped break up – Lane had spoken at them – and thought he might even have swapped punches with him at Cable Street but was never certain. But when he saw him at the Errochty Dam project, he knew him immediately. In his Blackshirt days, Lane, when he was McNair, had blond hair like a true Aryan, but he dyes it now.'

'He does a good job, I wouldn't have known,' I observed.

'Aye, it'll be a pricey job, right enough. Though Howie was sure it was him, he wasn't *sure*-sure, if you know what I mean? That wasn't until he realised that Lane was giving Jewish workers the shittiest jobs he could find. We had workers from all over, even Poland. Howie was a tunnel tiger, like me, so Lane had no hold over us. We're a breed apart, I suppose, and his influence only extended to the other workers. Also, he gathered around him a bunch of thugs who would have looked good in black shirts. Knuckle-draggers, the lot of them, and maybe some of them were with the old BUF, too.'

'Is Danny McCall one of them?'

'Danny boy is a hanger-on, nothing more. Sure, Lane uses him when he feels like it, but Danny doesn't have any political ideals. He's a Glasgow thug, smarter than some maybe, but still just a thug.'

'So, why did you tangle with him?'

He glanced at me. 'You know about that?'

'I sensed a history.'

'That was nothing, a difference of opinion over my skill with the cards and Danny's lack of it.'

'He thought you were cheating, right?'

A short laugh. 'That's about the size of it. I disabused him of that notion.'

I recalled Lane asking Gerry how 'old Howie' was. 'What happened with Howie?'

Gerry swallowed, the humour over his disabusing Danny McCall of his notion gone as he took another draw of his cigarette, then stubbed it out, even though it was only half-smoked. I'd seen him do this before and knew he would smoke the remainder, the 'dout', later. He was doing all this to delay his answer because what was to come was painful for him. I didn't press my question. He would respond eventually. He'd come this far.

'Howie confronted Lane one night. He couldn't help himself. His old 43 Group sensibilities dictated that he face up to this guy.'

'Were you there?'

A brief nod. 'It wasn't dramatic, there were no raised voices, no flying fists. It was in a pub in Pitlochry, and Howie had been drinking. I tried to stop him, tried to explain to him that it wouldn't do any good, and anyway, he had no firm evidence. But the drink had made him sure-sure. McNair and Lane were one and the same, he was certain. He spoke to him at the bar, told him he knew who he was. Lane looked him up and down and said he was drunk and to sit his arse back down. Howie refused. He mentioned a rally in London, at a place called Ridley Road, and he said he'd helped break it up, just like they had at Cable Street. I saw something change in Lane then. Outwardly he was still smiling, you know the way he does, but it was kind of stiff, you know? Like he was struggling to hold it in place, not let it become a scowl or a snarl. And there was contempt in his eyes as he stared Howie down, like Howie was some piece of shit that had stuck to his shoe. He told him he was imagining things – he'd never even heard of a Ridley Road – then he turned away. But Howie grabbed him by the arm, told him not to turn his back. Howie shouldn't have done that, but he was drunk, like I said. Lane jerked his arm free and whirled back – his smile was gone now and the snarl had broken free, and he might have laid one on Howie if I hadn't stepped in between them. Howie was drunk but he was strong. Lane was big and powerful, but he didn't have Howie's military training. I think Howie might have killed him if anything had kicked off, and I couldn't have that. I told them both to cool down and Lane sneered at me, told me to get my pal out of there if I knew what was good for him. I dragged Howie away, but not before Howie said, almost in a whisper, "I know who you are. I know what you did. And I won't be silent anymore. I'll tell everyone I can, the bosses, the papers, anyone. I'll bring you into the light, McNair, and watch you burn."'

'I'll bet that went down well.'

'Lane didn't respond. He laughed, shrugged it off and got back to his drinking. I got Howie out of there.'

'And did he follow through on his promise?'

'When he sobered up, he thought about it – but he had no proof, so who would listen to him? He wrote to his family and friends back in London, asking them if they could find any photographs from Ridley Road or Cable Street, to see if there was one of McNair, or Lane, whatever you want to call the bastard.'

'And did they?'

Gerry fell silent again for a moment. His voice was sombre when he spoke again. 'I don't know. The weekend after that scene in the pub, Howie was walking back to the camp alone, drunk again, because Howie had to drown his memories somehow, and he was hit by a car. It ran right over him. They

220

say he might've stumbled in the dark, taken a fall and the driver didn't see him until it was too late.'

'What did the driver say?'

Gerry looked straight at me then. 'Whoever it was didn't say anything. He didn't stop. They found the car later, burned out in a field in the middle of nowhere. Turned out it had been stolen in Perth and police think the driver panicked and legged it.' Gerry turned his head away again. 'Howie isn't dead, but he might as well be. He was in a coma for weeks and when he came out of it, he was in what they call a persistent vegetative state, thanks to extensive brain damage. He's alive but can't speak, can't communicate at all. He eats, he sleeps, he breathes. Maybe he thinks, I don't know. But he's not Howie. Howie died on the dark little road in Perthshire that night.'

'You don't think it was an accident, do you?'

'It was murder, pure and simple, but nobody called it that.'

'And you think Lane did it?'

'Not personally, but he had it done. He's a bastard, Ally, and one day I'll prove it.'

I lay back then and wondered how he would prove a murder that never was.

23

Rebecca read Alice's pages before she and Bill left after dinner, and she filled him in on their contents as he drove towards the city centre.

'Another hit and run,' Bill observed. 'Seems there's a pattern.'

Flash. Elspeth, her eyes vacant. Blood . . .

'And at the heart of it is this guy John Lane, or Jim McNair.'

'You think this Howie bloke was right? That John Lane was a former Blackshirt?'

'Given what I now know of him, I'd say there was every chance of it.'

She'd already told Bill what she'd gleaned about John Lane and was braced to raise it with Dalgliesh when she saw him. She had a look online herself for pictures from Cable Street and Ridley Road, where the post-war British Union of Fascists, by that time renamed the British Union, had held rallies but found no images that bore any resemblance to the pictures she'd seen of John Lane, either with black or blond hair. She also discovered that the road had become the focus in 1962 for a resurgence in anti-Semitism, leading to the creation of a new anti-fascist group, the 62 Group. Ridley Road had witnessed yet more hate, more violence. For some the war never ended, lessons were not learned and old hatred still echoed.

'Where's Lane now?' Bill asked.

'He died in 1982 of a massive stroke.'

'How do you know?'

'There's this thing called the internet, maybe you've heard of it.'

'Oh good, I thought maybe you'd use something less dependable.'

'Some sites are dependable, and this is genuine. I read his obituary in the *Herald*. Also one in the *Telegraph*.'

That satisfied him. 'So, we have three, eh, "accidents" here – this guy Howie, what was his second name again?'

'Rose.'

'Aye, so him, then Rawlings taking a tumble and now Elspeth.'

Flash. Rebecca holding her hand.

Flash. Blue lights bouncing from the walls.

'That's right,' she said, pushing the images from her mind.

Bill pulled the car to a halt at a red light. He stared at it, as if willing it to change, his forefinger tapping on the steering wheel. 'Maybe you should drop this,' he said.

'No,' she replied.

'Is it worth it?'

'What do you think, Bill? Elspeth lying up there in the infirmary, still out of it, God knows what damage this will do to her. I mean, look at what happened to Howie.'

'Medicine has moved on a bit since the sixties.'

'My point is, what do you think Elspeth would say if you suggested she drop it?'

He thought about this as he pushed the car into gear and set off when the light turned green. 'She'd have a lot to say and there would be swearing involved.'

'There would. I'm not going to let this drop, Bill, not going to happen.'

'Even though you know it could be dangerous?'

'I don't think it is, not now. And I'll point that out to Dalgliesh when I see him.'

'And if he doesn't listen?'

'He'll listen. He probably knows it already. He's not stupid.'

'Still—'

'Still nothing, Bill. I'm not giving this up. It's personal now and I'm not stopping. I'm surprised you even suggest it. Elspeth is your friend, too.'

The hint of a smile tweaked his lips as he drove. 'Just doing my due diligence, Becks, being the grown-up in the car and giving you the option.'

'Out of interest, if I'd said yes, what would you have done?'

This time he did smile. 'What do you think?'

She sat back, smiling herself. She knew what he would have done. He would have carried on, she had no doubt about it.

Alice was having doubts. She didn't often have doubts and she didn't like the feeling. She was alone in her room, Orla downstairs doing whatever she did when she wasn't tending to her. As usual the TV was on and, as usual, Alice was paying no attention to it. Some drama or other in which people were being very angry with one another. They spoke in harsh tones, their faces contorted, spitting out their lines as if they were bullets. Anger was something that needed to be controlled and channelled, Alice believed. She had managed to do that with her own rage for decades, keeping it in check until the day came when she could expunge it by sending it out into the world. That day was almost dawning, the first glow could be seen, but now she wondered if she was doing the right thing.

Alice Larkin wasn't one for self-doubt, the benefit of being privileged and cossetted throughout her life, first by her father and then by her husband. She'd had her moments, of course, had her wobbles of indecision, but had never really known what it was to analyse her own actions, to be wracked with uncertainty, or to worry about the future. She'd never experienced money worries or fears of unemployment. She was, and she knew this herself, over-confident to the point of arrogance.

That's not to say that she didn't have empathy for those who were less fortunate, because she did. She understood that not everyone enjoyed her advantages, and over the years she had done what she could to help those in need. She donated to a list of charities. When she was ambulatory, she dropped coins in the collections plates of those unfortunates begging in the streets. Yes, she had heard the stories about them being organised, but she didn't care. She had the change, she could afford it, so she gave it. She helped young journalists find their voices. She would see them come into newsrooms, some of them wide-eyed and out of their depth, armed with a degree in journalism but precious little experience of the actual job. She told them that confidence was everything, that questions had to be asked with authority and to never back down, to keep going, even if they had to ask the same question time and time again until they got the answer. Posing a simple yes-or-no question was always good, even though the interviewee would never commit themselves to such a simple reply. But the secret was for the journalist to never doubt that he or she was there on behalf of the readers or viewers or listeners. They were there to pose the questions that the audience could not.

But that confidence wavered as Alice lay on her bed, the TV drama rising, wishing she had asked Orla to slot in one of her husband's old *Mission: Impossible* DVDs. She didn't like the programme, but it might help her feel closer to him. He always had the ability to calm her down when she was angry, or to help her reason out any difficulties she was having.

Of course, she could never share what happened back in 1964 with him. She'd had to deal with that herself over the years, the guilt, the rage. She had honed both, sharpened them in her mind, weaponised them, and waited until she could unleash them. Now that time had come, more by dint of her failing body than anything else.

But was it the right thing? Would it make any difference after all these years? The guilty men were all gone, and what good would it do to reveal the secrets held for sixty years?

Although she hadn't shown it, she had been disturbed by what had befallen Elspeth McTaggart. The act itself, and the means by which it was carried out, were both a warning and a reminder of what had happened to Howard Rose. She had never met him, but she had been moved by Gerry's account of his fate. Later, she tried to track him down, or his family, but had never succeeded. Now she wondered if she had tried hard enough.

Damn it, pull yourself together, Alice. The die is cast, the game's afoot, the ball's in play. Choose any metaphor you like, but you can't stop this now. Rebecca Connolly is a very capable young woman – she proved that with her previous stories. She can look after herself.

She forced her attention onto the screen, where the anger had subsided, and tried to follow the storyline. God knows what the programme was about. Something to do with infidelity. Something to do with a breaking of a trust.

Her lips thinned. She knew all about that.

24

The slight hitch in his step and the tiny frown as he crossed the foyer told Rebecca that Finbar Dalgliesh was surprised to see them waiting for him. He'd been at a charity show in the City Halls, a somewhat posh affair judging by his sharp blue suit and dazzling white shirt. Julian was there, too, which did not surprise her one little bit. He was also smartly dressed, but his suit jacket looked a size too small, and the trousers were somewhat snug around the thighs, or perhaps they didn't make an SS size for steroid swollen.

She and Bill remained in the street, watching them through the glass doors. The sky had darkened considerably but it remained warm. Footsteps clicked on the pavements around the old fruit market, and from Bell Street laughter and music trickled from the various bars and restaurants that now peppered what had once been the produce heart of Glasgow. Tables and chairs in the outside areas were filled with the young and the beautiful doing what the young and the beautiful did. Rebecca was young and she had been told, by Stephen anyway, that she was beautiful, even though she didn't see it, but she had no idea what these people did with their leisure. She was never one for sitting in or outside bars because she couldn't settle and, anyway, she didn't often drink to excess. She had no interest in being seen in those places in which it was good to be seen because, frankly, she didn't see the point. She and Stephen went out, of course, for meals, to the cinema, to the theatre if there was something good on at Inverness's Eden Court. Otherwise, she worked.

You're a boring young fart, Elspeth used to say. Rebecca closed her eyes briefly to stem the flashing images, forced her mind to insist that she would still say it. *You owe it to yourself to live a little. Life is for living because you don't know what can happen in a week, a day or even a minute . . .*

She felt something burning behind her eyes as she glared through the glass doors towards Dalgliesh, who had banished the little frown in favour of a smile that might have appeared natural if she didn't know him so well. He edged towards them, shaking hands with the great and the good as he went, but darted an occasional sideways glance in their direction, either to confirm they were still there or because he was curious as to the reason behind their presence.

We're still here, you bastard, Rebecca thought, *and you should have known I'd be here, that sooner or later I'd be in your face after what you've done.*

Some of those to whom he spoke were given little more than a quick press of the flesh, others were granted the full double-handed shake. She had no idea who these people were, but she assumed the recipients of the latter would be the ones who were fully on his side or who might be able to further his interests. Dalgliesh had managed to temper his views to fit into the mainstream, albeit a little uncomfortably in some areas, and some members of the city's glitterati were happy to be seen with him. There were others, though, who hurried away, lest they be contaminated. Unfortunately, she didn't have that luxury.

'Who's the Hulk wannabe?' Bill whispered as they watched Dalgliesh work the room, Julian trailing behind him, his hands clasped in front of him. He was alert, not just regarding those clustered around and participating in Dalgliesh's glad-handing, but seemed also to be listening carefully to what his boss had to say. No, not listening, she thought, there was something about his body language that suggested he was monitoring.

'His name's Julian,' she said.

Bill's eyebrows shot up. 'No way.'

'Yes way.'

'Julian? Really?'

As if he had heard them, the man in question scowled in their direction while Finbar detached himself from his final lickspittle. As he pushed the door open to let his employer pass, Julian's eyes flicked expertly over Bill, assessing his threat level.

'Ms Connolly,' Dalgliesh said as he stepped into the street. 'Is this mere kismet, or are you stalking me?'

'Hunting you is perhaps the correct word, Dalgliesh,' she said.

'Well, aren't I the lucky one.' He stepped away from the doorway to let other patrons leave, exchanging a nod or a goodbye here and there, then turned his attention to Bill as if noticing him for the first time. 'And you are?'

'With her,' Bill replied.

'Do you have a name?'

'We all have names. Some are given to us, others are earned.'

Dalgliesh seemed amused. 'And what is your given name?'

'Bill Sawyer. Former Detective Sergeant.'

'Ah.' Dalgliesh didn't expand on that. He'd either heard of Bill, which was possible, or he saw Bill as Rebecca's version of Julian. He held out his hand. 'I'm Finbar Dalgliesh.'

Bill barely even looked at the proffered hand. 'I know your name, the one you were given and the various epithets you've earned.'

'Epithets,' Dalgliesh repeated, outwardly displaying no offence as he let his hand drop away. 'Not a word I would have expected from a man like you.'

Bill also didn't take umbrage because he, too, was accustomed to it. He merely shrugged and said, 'I've read a book or two.'

'Really?' Dalgliesh was amused. 'Your lips must be very tired.'

Finbar had been offended, then, thought Rebecca. Good for you, Bill.

Dalgliesh's expression grew sombre as he turned to Rebecca. 'I was very sorry to hear of Ms McTaggart's accident.'

He knew why she was there and was seeking to control the conversation by jumping right in.

'It wasn't an accident, and you know it.'

'I know nothing of the sort, although I was visited earlier this evening by two of Glasgow's finest who seemed to suggest that perhaps I and/or my associates had something to do with the unfortunate incident. I take it you dropped my name.'

'I didn't drop it. I threw it with considerable force.'

He affected curiosity. 'And why would you do that?'

Rebecca couldn't believe he was pretending innocence. 'Why? You threatened us earlier today.'

'I didn't threaten you in any way, Ms Connolly.' The lie slipped so easily from his lips that it must have been oiled. 'I told the two detectives as much and they accepted my word. You really should curb that imagination of yours, my dear.'

Despite her desire to remain calm and professional, Rebecca felt her anger about to boil over. It was the *my dear* that did it. 'You might have been able to smooth-talk the cops, Dalgliesh, but I was there. I know what you said. And now Elspeth is seriously injured.'

His expression turned grave, and he angled his head slightly towards Julian. 'I'm truly pained to hear that. It's a tragedy and not something I would've wished to happen.' Despite herself, Rebecca detected an element of sincerity there, although he ruined it by following up with a lie. 'I hope they catch the individual concerned. Someone drunk or a junkie, no doubt. There are many people in this country who really should not be here, so perhaps it was someone not used to our roads and laws.'

He couldn't help himself. Always blame a foreigner. 'If it pains you so much, why did you order it?'

He paused, another quick flick of the eye in his body-guard's direction accompanied by an almost imperceptible shift of his feet. Rebecca perceived it, though. She had seen that look from him before, years ago, when she had approached him unannounced outside Inverness railway station. Now that she thought about it, there had been similar furtive glances in the café towards Julian standing in the street. She considered the brief conversation she had witnessed between them as he had left the café, the tension in Dalgliesh's shoulders as he walked away and then Julian making a call. There was a dynamic here that Rebecca wasn't quite grasping. And now, despite his casual manner, Dalgliesh was still tense. The man was uncomfortable, and she'd never seen him like that.

Bill had spotted Dalgliesh's body language, too, for he craned past him to stare at Julian. 'Does he talk, or just stand there and bulge?'

Julian had been focused on Rebecca, his face blank, but his eyes slid towards Bill.

'Julian talks,' Dalgliesh said, 'when he has something to say.'

'Strong silent type, eh?'

Julian showed how strong he was by remaining silent. His eyes, though, seemed to be telling Bill to back off.

'You didn't answer, Dalgliesh,' Rebecca prompted. 'Why did you order the attack on Elspeth?'

That slight shift of his feet again, that little glance towards Julian. Was he trying to tell her something?

231

'I didn't order it,' he said. 'And you can't prove otherwise.'

'I don't need to prove it, I *know* it.'

He smirked a little. 'I thought you were an honourable journalist who worked solely on fact.'

'There's fact and there's the truth, and sometimes they aren't the same thing. You know that, being a lawyer. What can be proved in court isn't necessarily the way it was.'

He accepted that with an inclination of the head. 'Nevertheless, I had nothing to do with what befell Ms McTaggart. It is a most regrettable turn of events, and my thoughts and prayers are with her and her loved ones.'

Thoughts and prayers, Jesus. 'You're not writing a press release, Dalgliesh, so save the phoney sympathy,' Rebecca sneered. 'And let me make this quite clear, if you or any of your' – Rebecca jutted her chin towards Julian – '*associates* come after me then it will not go well for you. Another accident won't look good, especially now that the police know about your threat.'

Dalgliesh ruminated on that. 'As far as I'm concerned, you're quite safe, Ms Connolly, you have my word. I truly wish you no ill will.'

He might have been saying that for Bill's benefit, him being a witness, but again there was a sincerity behind it; she noted something different in Julian's eyes. Dalgliesh's word was far from this man's bond.

'However, please let me repeat my friendly advice from today.'

Rebecca's attention returned to Dalgliesh. 'Your threat, you mean?'

'No threat, I assure you. Just some wise counsel, which I hope you will take.'

'And what is it?'

'This fairy story that Alice Larkin is spinning is baseless, I hope you realise that?'

232

She was glad he had brought the conversation round to this. 'I don't think it is.' She gave it a beat. 'I know about John Lane.' She gave it a further beat, just for the drama. 'Or rather, I know about Jim McNair.'

Despite her attempt at drama, he remained unfazed. 'I don't know what you're talking about.'

Rebecca scoffed. 'Come on, Dalgliesh! John Lane was the founder of SG, the very party you now lead, so please don't pretend you don't know the name. But as Jim McNair he was part of another movement altogether, wasn't he? He was one of Oswald Mosley's Blackshirts. He was a thug and an anti-Semite and a racist. He wasn't so much interested in home rule for Scotland as he was in getting rid of anyone that wasn't white and Christian. I'll bet he wasn't overly keen on women being allowed to vote, either.'

'This is absurd.'

'Is it? Is it really? He was almost exposed back in the day but was saved by two very convenient accidents, one of which was incredibly similar to what happened to Elspeth.'

She didn't know how close Lane had come to being outed back then, but it was worth taking a flyer, she thought, just for the look in Dalgliesh's eye. He wasn't exactly panicking but he was rattled. Still, he kept up the pretence of nonchalance.

'This is all supposition.'

'I have photographs of him,' she said, hoping Bill wouldn't startle at the lie and give the game away, but he didn't even take so much as a sharp breath. 'Shots of him in his black shirt at Cable Street in London. You do know about the battle of Cable Street, right?' She didn't wait for Dalgliesh to reply. 'Also at rallies in Ridley Street in London, after the war. Fascist rallies, Dalgliesh. A true Aryan bastard with his blond hair.' She saw his eyes widen at that. 'Oh yes, I know he dyed his hair later, lost some weight, might even have had a nose job, though it's difficult to tell with these old pics.' She was freestyling now, but hoping she wasn't over-egging this pudding. 'And, of course, changed his name. I believe it was pretty easy to do back then, create a new persona. Change your name, change your appearance, get some documents by stealing a dead child's name and details. The full *Day of the Jackal* thing. He was helped later by nobody in the media digging into his background – or maybe they did, and the story was spiked. Not so simple now, with social media and all, credit scores and the like. We all have a digital footprint these days, but not then.'

She waited for him to respond but he simply stared at her. Julian was focused on her fully now, his lidded eyes unblinking. That was creepy as hell, she thought, but she forced herself to ignore him.

'So, here's my thinking, Finbar,' she said, using his Christian name purposely. 'When you spoke about reputations in the café, it wasn't yours you were thinking about, not directly anyway, or even mine or Elspeth's or Alice's, it was your party's. God knows anyone with a brain rejects what it stands for but, amazingly, there are a number of people who don't reject it. I'm talking backers, I'm talking those disaffected politicians you've wooed over to your side, I'm talking some elements of the media. You spout bile and half-truths, and you dress it up with a good suit and a decent shirt and what passes for charm, but it's still bile and half-truths. But these people buy it, God knows why. Maybe you speak to their personal grievances and prejudices, maybe they see some benefit to themselves, maybe they're just bitter and vile.'

Rebecca paused, priming her metaphorical weapon. 'But here's the thing, Finbar' – she did it again – 'how many of them would turn away if they found out that the man who formed this party of yours, this standard-bearer of Scottish and British values, the party of God and country, which stands for all that is right as long as it's white, was nothing more than a cheap little anti-Semitic thug in a black shirt mentored by a disgraced politician almost forgotten by history. Lane went to a lot of trouble, even then, to whitewash his past – and yes, I used that word purposely – and how will that look when this story breaks? And yes, it's *when*, not *if*. I reckon you'll see at least some of your donors, the public ones and perhaps even the private ones I'm sure exist, turn their back on you. You'll have questions to answer, and you'll use your oily charm to smooth them over, but they won't go away. Despite popular opinion, there are still decent journalists out there and they'll pick it up and run with it. And if they don't, I'm working with a TV production company who are always on the look-out for material, and you and SG and the likes of Julian here will find themselves as stars on Netflix or the BBC or Channel 4.'

Dalgliesh tutted, his head shaking a little. 'I think you're overstating the importance of this story, even if it were true. Not to mention the power of the press.'

'I don't think I am. This country may have drifted to the right in recent years but it's still not ready to fully embrace the teachings of Oswald Mosley and McNair, or Lane, or whatever the hell he would have preferred. But even if the mainstream media don't pick it up, there's social media and it can be powerful. And you can say what you like there, more or less, especially if you're canny enough to cover your digital tracks. There are a lot of "facts" floating around in the ether, and all it takes is a little bit of manipulation to make them go viral.' She paused, once again for effect. 'But I've not mentioned the most disgusting thing about Lane yet. SG was bad enough, a party of independence that really had no interest in independence but only in spreading hatred and dissent. But Lane went further than that, didn't he?'

Dalgliesh knew where she was leading – she could tell, even though he tried to dismiss it. 'I don't know what you're talking about.'

'I think you do. I think you know exactly what I'm talking about.'

'I don't,' Bill interjected.

'I'm talking about New Dawn, Bill,' Rebecca explained.

'What? The terrorist nutters who attack mosques and synagogues with paint and the like and pose in black ski masks?'

'Worse than that. They firebombed a mosque. They've physically attacked Muslims and Jews. They sent anthrax through the mail to the First Minister and the Prime Minister. They've threatened and beaten and burned and disrupted meetings. Remember when we first met, Finbar? In Inverness? The protest in Inchferry over plans to move a convicted paedophile into the area? You were there, hijacking the issue to promote your views. And there were people planted among the crowd primed to stir it up the first chance they got.'

'That's nonsense.'

'No, not really. They were strangers to Inchferry, those men and women, and they picked on a friend of mine to spark the trouble. They started a riot, then were aided by local youngsters who seized the chance of a spot of vandalism. Or, now that I think of it, perhaps they were paid to run amok.'

'Pure speculation with not an ounce of foundation in fact.'

'Remember what I said about truth and fact? Anyway, John Lane founded SG, not alone certainly, but he was in there right up to his black shirt. And he also set up New Dawn.'

She was bluffing again but she thought, what the hell . . .

'New Dawn doesn't exist.'

'Yes, you've said that before, but it does, doesn't it? It's like the military arm of SG, the modern-day equivalent of the Blackshirts. Back in the thirties they could be out in the open, but now they're more discreet. No rallies, no marching in the street, no Nazi salutes to their leader, no pictures in the press unless they have those ski masks on. Well, not unless the more idiotic among them get pissed. And like SG, they're not really interested in independence. It's all about disruption for them.'

'Fantasy, Ms Connolly.'

'Is it? Is it really?' She stepped closer to him, darting a quick look towards Julian, who also stepped forward.

'Easy, big boy,' Bill said, easing between them. 'I don't think the lassie is much of a threat to your boss, do you?'

Rebecca ignored the sexist remark and addressed Dalgliesh. 'I know what you're thinking, Finbar.'

'Enlighten me,' he said, managing a small smile, but she knew he was worried. If not about what she was about to say, then about something else.

'You're thinking about Alice Larkin and what she has that's finally made her want to get this out there.'

'Alice Larkin is thinking only of Alice Larkin. After all, why break the habits of a lifetime? Even if that lifetime is reaching its natural conclusion.'

'Well, you're very much alike in being self-obsessed, but you don't know what she might have, though, not for certain. She's been sitting on this for years, after all, and who knows what she's uncovered in that time?'

In that moment, his manner changed, as if he was back on firmer ground. 'And that raises a question, does it not? Why didn't she come forward before now?'

It was Rebecca's turn to fail to respond because she had been wondering that herself.

'Let's just for a moment say that what you claim is true—'

'It is true,' she insisted.

He held up a hand. 'Indulge me. If this was all true, then what is it Alice herself has to hide?'

Rebecca's thoughts turned to the final pages of the memoir, which Alice had still not released.

Dalgliesh knew he had hit some kind of mark. 'I see. You've been considering that yourself, haven't you? Of course you have, you're not stupid. You're John Connolly's daughter, after all.'

'That's the second time you've mentioned my father. I want to know why.'

'He was my friend.'

'I doubt that.'

'Doubt it all you wish but it remains the truth.'

'Why would my dad be a friend of yours? He would have despised everything you stood for.'

'Would he, indeed? I have many friends in the police service' – he glanced towards Bill – 'but you are correct, he didn't agree with my views. However, opposites attract, as the saying goes.'

'He wouldn't have had anything to do with you.'

'But he did. He asked me to perform a small service for him, and I obliged.'

'What service?'

'It's not for me to breach your father's confidentiality. Let's just say that had I not stepped in, his memory would not be quite as untarnished as it is.'

'You're a liar.'

'I'm a politician, it comes with the territory. I also exaggerate, obfuscate and embellish.' He flicked another look towards Bill. 'I've read a book, too, Mr Sawyer. But on this occasion, I'm doing none of these things.'

'What did you do for him?'

His smile annoyed her. 'Why don't you ask your mother? I'm sure she knows. In fact, I'm certain of it. Ask her about Brian Hancock.' He let the name sit between them for a beat. 'But, delightful as this has been, Ms Connolly, I have another appointment this evening so I must take my leave. Please take note of my counsel, my dear. I really am very fond of you.'

She felt her skin crawl at the thought, and Dalgleish began to walk away. Julian lingered for a moment, giving her the stare.

'Move on, big boy,' Bill said, 'nothing to see here.'

After a slithered gaze in Bill's direction, Julian followed his employer. If he was his employer, which Rebecca was beginning to question. But she knew she couldn't leave it that way. Dalgliesh had undermined her attack with his barb concerning her father, and there was no way he could have the final word.

'Dalgliesh,' she shouted, ignoring the turning heads of those people still exiting the venue. He stopped, turned back. 'I don't care what you say about my father,' she lied. 'But I want you to know this. I won't let this rest. I won't stop. I don't care what shit you throw or how many thugs you send. I'll keep going until I know everything. You've had an easy ride with the media up till now, and I'm going to do everything I can to bring that to an end.'

He took that in and then tapped his forehead with his forefinger in a mock salute. 'I would expect nothing less.'

He gave her that little salute again, then turned and walked down the street. Again, Julian hung back, this time smiling, the first expression she had seen him adopt. It was mocking. It was threatening.

'I'd listen to him if I were you,' he said, his accent indeterminate. He could be polite Scottish, he could be English, he could be from bloody Mars, as far as she could tell.

'He does speak!' Bill exclaimed. 'Wonders will never cease.'

Julian gave him that half-lidded gaze again. 'You're a funny man, mate.'

'Thank you, I'm here all week.'

Julian pondered that for a moment. 'That remains to be seen, doesn't it?'

And then he followed Dalgliesh towards Bell Street.

'Nice fella,' Bill said. 'Very warm.'

They turned to walk back to the car park on Ingram Street. She heard Bill chuckle. '"I won't stop. I won't rest,"' he echoed.

239

Rebecca couldn't withhold an embarrassed smile. 'I was angry. I didn't know what I was saying.'

'Rebecca Connolly IS the Terminator.' He laughed again. 'How much of the rest was bluff?'

'Him or me?'

'Both.'

'Quite a bit from me, I've got to admit.'

'And that stuff about your dad? What's that about?'

'I don't know. He could be bluffing, too.'

But he wasn't. Something in her gut told her that he wasn't. Who the hell was Brian Hancock?

Bill said, 'But your mum knows.'

'Yes,' she said.

'You going to ask her?'

She gave him a grim smile as she repeated his earlier words. 'What do you think?'

Something above their heads caught her attention. A big, white gull, its underside illuminated by the streetlights, its wings not moving as it coasted on the currents and thermals of the city. She had seen such a gull before, back in Inverness, curiously on the night she first met Finbar Dalgliesh. As she'd said, there had been violence in the street that night. Later, there was death. The sight now made her think of birds as portents of calamity. And here was another, floating above them like a soft cloud.

They *were* floating. Not far, certainly, but their feet were not touching the ground. How the holy fuck were they doing that? Elspeth instantly regretted swearing, even if she hadn't said it out loud, because she sensed this was not the place for profanity. She vowed to temper her language in the future. But they were floating, for fu— goodness sake. That's not something you see every day, and she wanted to find out how they did it.

Elspeth picked up her pace through the long grass, still wondering at the sensation of walking unaided. This was incredible. She felt slimmer, too, the way she was when she was in her twenties, which was also pretty cool, as the young folk say. The voices behind her had faded further. Even the one she thought was Julie, saying her name, urging her to come back. She stopped, turned, looked back to the white cloud. Was it watching her progress, or waiting for her to return? Both, she decided. She gazed towards the little stand of trees again, saw a couple of the figures gesturing, encouraging her to join them.

Come back to me. Julie's voice. *We need you here.*

'Stay with us.' Another voice, one she hadn't heard for many years.

She turned fully away from the cloud and peered at the copse. It couldn't be. Could it? She's been dead for thirty years.

But then she heard the voice, far clearer, and this time she was certain.

'Hurry up, Elspeth. We're waiting for you.'

Mum?

25

Bill returned to the hotel after dropping Rebecca off at home. Chaz and Alan were in the kitchen, drinking hot chocolate. Julie was still at the hospital, even though a nurse had told her there was nothing she could do and promised to let her know as soon as there was any change.

'That wasn't good enough for Julie, though,' said Alan.

'She said she would stay by Elspeth's bed,' Chaz said. 'She wanted to hold her hand and speak to her.'

'Do they think Elspeth can hear?' Rebecca asked, feeling guilt over not being beside her mentor and friend.

'They don't know,' said Chaz.

'But Julie is sitting there, talking away to her, asking her to come back to her, to us,' said Alan, and she was certain she could hear something break in his voice, perhaps recalling the time he spent beside Chaz's bed following a near fatal road incident on the isle of Stoirm, when they had been forced onto some rocks by a bunch of drunken yobs.

They were all silent for a moment, each lost in their own thoughts.

Finally, she said, 'Bill Sawyer's here.'

'Your mum told us,' Chaz said.

'Where is Mum?'

'In the sitting room, I think. She waited up for you.'

'James seems nice,' said Alan.

Rebecca looked at the clock, saw how late it was. 'He's still here?'

'No, he was leaving as we arrived back. As I said, he seems nice.'

'He does,' she agreed. She meant it, but she couldn't shake off this automatic resistance to her mother being in a relationship. The thought that he might still be here – could, in fact, be staying the night – had momentarily appalled her. She couldn't fully explain why.

'I need to chat with her about something, okay?' In other words, she was urging them to stay where they were.

Chaz said, 'Okay,' then added, 'Stephen phoned me.'

'Why?'

'He hadn't heard from you. He was concerned.'

She should have called him, but it had been a busy few hours. 'I'll phone him later.'

She thought she saw something in Chaz's eyes but then he nodded and lifted his mug of hot chocolate. 'Yeah, you should.'

As she left the kitchen, she was certain a look passed between the two of them, but she wasn't inclined to probe further. She found her mum in the sitting room, an old black-and-white film on the telly, the sound low, the flickering shadows of people long dead merely something to stare at, not to follow. The chances were that Sandra, a big movie fan, had seen it many times anyway. When Rebecca entered, she clicked the screen off with the remote.

'How did it go?' she asked.

She had known where Rebecca was off to, of course, and had voiced concerns over her essentially doorstepping Dalgliesh. Rebecca had said it was something she had to do and, anyway, it wouldn't be the first time. They'd be in the street and quite safe, she'd said, and Bill would be with her. That went a long way towards mollifying her mother.

'He said he had nothing to with what happened to Elspeth.'

'Does that surprise you?'

'No. I hit him with what I know, or have guessed, about John Lane, but he didn't seem all that worried.'

'Perhaps you're wrong.'

Rebecca had considered that and rejected it. 'No, John Lane was this McNair guy, of that I'm sure, and somehow I'll prove it, unless Alice Larkin has something concrete up her sleeve.'

Rebecca hoped she did, even though her testimony was personal. She was keen to get back to her room to read further, but first she had a thorny subject of her own to raise.

'He mentioned Dad again,' she said.

Sandra merely nodded, her expression betraying no surprise. Instead, there was weary resignation.

'You knew he would, didn't you?'

'I knew he wouldn't let it lie. A man like Dalgliesh uses everything to get what he wants, and he knows that your father is your weak spot.'

'My Achilles heel,' Rebecca said, thinking of how Elspeth had made the same point earlier.

'Yes,' said Sandra.

Rebecca waited, but when she realised her mother would say nothing further without prompting, she said, 'So?'

Sandra sighed. 'What did he tell you?'

'He said they were friends.'

'They weren't friends.'

'I didn't believe him about that. He mentioned a Brian Hancock.' Still no look of surprise. Sandra Connolly had been expecting this. 'He said he performed a small service for Dad.'

A bitter, breathy laugh from Sandra. 'I suppose that's one way of looking at it.'

'He said that if details of that small service were revealed it would tarnish Dad's reputation.'

Sandra said nothing but she blinked.

Rebecca realised she was standing over her, so she sat down beside her. 'Mum? You need to tell me.'

Sandra angled her head away, but Rebecca had already seen tears forming. She hadn't seen her mother cry since her dad's funeral. She had always been so strong – she'd had to be through his illness as he wasted away and became a living, breathing, walking ghost of the man they had both loved. She had cried when he died, and she'd cried when they cremated him, and then she had cried no more, not in front of her. Sometimes, when Rebecca was still living at home, she would hear weeping in the darkness and she knew it was her mother in the bedroom, in the bed she had once shared with the man she loved.

Rebecca took her mother's hand. 'What did Dalgliesh do for Dad? Who was Brian Hancock?'

Sandra smiled, her free hand wiping the moisture from her cheeks. 'It was a bad time.'

'Why?' Rebecca searched for what might be a bad time for them. 'Was it to do with money? Did he take some sort of bribe from this man?'

'No, nothing like that. Your dad, he . . . well, he made a mistake.'

'What kind of mistake?'

Sandra squeezed Rebecca's fingers as she looked down at their hands entwined. 'You were a child, we kept it from you.'

'Kept what from me?'

Her mother gathered her words together. 'There was a case, a young boy sexually assaulted. I won't go into details, but it was quite horrible. Your dad knew who did it, but there was no evidence that would stand up.'

'Brian Hancock.'

'Yes.'

She stopped and Rebecca filled the void. 'Did Dad manufacture evidence, is that it?'

A shake of the head, very tiny, a tightening of the lips. 'No.'

'What, then?'

A deep breath. 'Your dad went to see him, to confront him. He saw him alone. And . . . he lost his temper over the man's smug attitude. Your dad had seen this boy, had spoken to him, had sat and watched as his mother wept – she was a single parent, had nobody. And there was this . . . creature . . . sneering at him. He thought of the little boy and his mother, he thought how he would feel if it had been you. And Hancock denying it but at the same time so dismissive of what he had done, as if he had merely dropped litter, so contemptuous that the law could not do anything about it. It got to your father, Becks, it really got to him, and he lost it.'

'He hit him?'

'He beat him, Becks. He told me it was as if he had been possessed by something. He thought that, had he not stopped himself in time, he would have killed the man.' She cast her eye towards her husband's favourite armchair. 'He sat there and wept, Becks. I've never seen him so . . . broken. He sat there with the man's blood still on his knuckles and he wept in my arms.'

Rebecca recalled once hearing voices and creeping downstairs to see her father in that chair, her mother perched on the arm, holding him as he sobbed. She remembered seeing what she thought was blood.

'So, Hancock reported him?'

Another shake of the head. 'He didn't get the chance. Your father thought he would and took some confidential legal advice.'

'Finbar Dalgliesh.'

'Yes.'

'Why him?'

'Because although your father didn't like him, he knew him to be tenacious and fearless when he chose to be. We may

246

disagree with his politics now, but back then he was an outspoken critic of the establishment and he fought hard for his clients.'

'So, what do you mean when you say Hancock didn't get the chance to report it?'

Sandra raised her eyes to her. 'Dalgliesh sorted it.'

'Sorted it?'

'I understand that it was explained to Hancock that it wasn't in his best interests to report the assault.'

'So, by "sorted", you mean "threatened"?'

A blink. 'We assumed as much, anyway. Even then, Dalgliesh surrounded himself with dubious characters. But he denied all knowledge when your father asked him. He said that obviously the man had decided that there was no point in taking it further as it could cast a light on the original crime.'

'But that put Dad in his debt in some way?'

'That's what he thought, but Dalgliesh didn't collect, never mentioned it again. All those years, life went on, and your father rose in the ranks. He always expected Dalgliesh to come back with a quid pro quo, but he didn't mention it again.'

'And what happened to Hancock?'

Sandra licked her lips slightly before she answered. 'Two years later someone beat him to death and his body was found in a back court in Shettleston.'

'But two years later, it couldn't be connected to Dalgliesh, and certainly not Dad.'

'That's what reason tells us, but guilt is the shadow that haunts reason, isn't it? The entire episode tormented your father forever after that. He hid it from you, even from me, but only to an extent. I knew it preyed on his mind from time to time, whenever Dalgliesh's name appeared on the news, or if he faced him in court. I swear the stress of it partly contributed to the growth of the cancer.'

'But why would Dalgliesh do it for no gain to himself? He doesn't strike me as the public-spirited type.'

'That's what haunted your father. He couldn't understand why he did it – if he did do anything, of course.'

But he did do something, Rebecca knew it. Dalgliesh had admitted performing a small service for her father. Or was he using that in his attempts to wean her away from the story? With a man like him, you never knew.

26

Excerpt from Murder on the Mountain:
The Personal Testimony of Alice Larkin

I should have known Lance wouldn't let the subject of Gerry lie. Lance was very competitive, in sport and in life. He didn't like to lose, and he must have believed he was losing me, even though he never actually had me in the first place. Don't get me wrong, I'd had some fun times with him and perhaps, on reflection, it could be argued that I was leading him on, but I didn't make any pledges. Little had passed between us other than a kiss and some heavy petting, as I said before, but I suppose a kiss can mean nothing to one person and everything to the other. I understand that now, whereas I didn't realise it then. I was young, headstrong. I remain the latter but am no longer the former.

Anyway, over the following few weekends I became aware of him hanging around my flat and a couple of times caught a glimpse of him following us. However, he didn't approach us and didn't make any further contact with me, so I did my best to ignore it and didn't say anything to Gerry, although I did mention it to my father.

'Lance believes there is an understanding between you,' he said, somewhat irritably, I was sure not at Lance but at my continuing to defy his entreaty to sever contact with Gerry. 'I thought there was, too.'

'I've never said such a thing,' I said.

'It was an unspoken arrangement.'

'Between you and him perhaps, but not him and me.'

'You are a good match.'

'Not from where I sit.'

I could tell he was far from pleased, but he agreed to have a quiet word with Lance. I hoped that would be sufficient, but part of me knew that it wouldn't.

The following day I had another encounter. With my father I had an element of control, but with John Lane I had no such advantage.

He accosted me as I left the office at the end of the day. It was a Thursday evening, and I had a doctor's appointment to attend. Gerry was away for a couple of weeks, in London visiting the family of his friend Howie. Lane had just left the newsagent beside the entrance to the *Sentinel*'s office and the meeting was made to appear very casual and random, but I knew in my heart that it had been engineered.

'Miss Larkin,' he said, looking up from the newspaper he had apparently just bought. He removed the cigarette that burned between his lips, flicked it away into the gutter. 'Nice to see you.'

I noted that he now knew my name, which was no surprise as a few questions around the town would have revealed it. His tone was courteous, but I didn't match it as I kept walking. 'I wish I could say the same, Mr Lane.'

He kept pace with me. 'No need to be like that. I know we got off on the wrong foot, but—'

'We didn't get off at all.'

He laughed. 'I heard you were quick with that tongue of yours. I like a girl who can speak up for herself.'

'I'm gratified to hear that. Now, I'm in a hurry, so if you don't mind . . .'

'Just a minute of your time is all I ask.'

I knew then for certain this meeting was not a twist of fate but planned. I could guess why he wanted to talk, but I was curious as to what he wanted to say. To his credit he got right down to it.

'I wanted to warn you about Rawlings.'

'I don't think I need any warnings from you, Mr Lane.'

'He's not what you think, darling.'

'There are two things wrong with that sentence. One, you don't know what I think; and two, I am not your darling.'

Despite my obvious hostility, he remained civil. 'He's a charmer, no doubt about it, and he's got all the blarney of his race. Handsome bugger, too. But I've seen him do this sort of thing before. He picks up a local lass, strings her along, then drops her when he's had enough of her.'

'He's not like that,' I said, feeling the need to defend him against what I firmly believed was a lie. 'But that aside, what makes you think I have any interest in your views?'

He laid a hand on my arm. He didn't grip it, didn't pull me back, so to bystanders it would appear to be only a friendly pat, but it was enough to have me stop and glare at him.

He removed his hand. 'He's dangerous, darling. He's got an agenda and he wants to spread lies about me. I don't know what he's told you, but don't believe a single word of it.'

'It's funny, he said the same thing about you.'

He gave me a stare for a few seconds then took a half-step back and reached into his jacket pocket to produce a pack of Benson & Hedges. 'You're not going to listen to me, are you?'

'Why should I?'

He tapped a cigarette out. 'Because I'm here as a friend, darling.'

I took that half-step, too, but towards him. 'Let me make something quite plain. You are not now, nor will you ever be, my friend. I know what you are, Mr Lane or Mr McNair or

251

whatever you may wish to call yourself, and frankly I find you and your kind repulsive.'

An eyebrow flicked when I used his real name, but he didn't make any move to deny it. I decided I'd said enough and turned away, before throwing over my shoulder, 'And I am still not your darling.'

I heard the scratch of a match. 'You should heed your father, Miss Larkin. Stop seeing Rawlings.'

I faced him again. I was surprised, I must admit. 'How did . . . ?' I stopped myself, realising that he would enjoy my reaction. But his almost casual mention of my father was like a punch to the stomach. How could this man know that my father had urged me to cut myself off from Gerry?

He put the flame to the cigarette and waved the match to extinguish it. He dropped it into the gutter, took a deep draw and smiled, knowing he had thrown my thoughts into disarray. 'Listen to him. Go back to that posh lad, get married, have more posh kids.' He took the cigarette from between his lips, held it between his middle and fore fingers as he pointed at me. 'Stay away from Rawlings. He'll regret pissing us off, and I wouldn't want you to get hurt, darling.'

He didn't wait for me to remind him that I wasn't his darling. He placed the cigarette back in his mouth and swaggered off down the road, the newspaper tucked under his arm.

27

Rebecca dropped the pages on her bed and leaned back against her pillows, reflecting on the many parallels between Alice's story and the present. The similar accidents that befell Howard Rose and Elspeth. The involvement of extremist groups. The suggestion that their respective fathers were involved. The more things change, the more they stay the same.

She closed her eyes. It had been a long day. She had kept busy, purposely, because if she took time to breathe, like now, she would think of Elspeth ...

Flash. Tyres screeching ... and how helpless she had felt in that road.

Flash. Blood from Elspeth's head, nose, ears.

She recalled Dalgliesh's face as he expressed his regret and thought again that she had seen a flicker of sincerity. He was involved but perhaps not responsible. She detested Dalgliesh and everything he stood for, but she was convinced that the threat didn't come from him – it came from Julian, whoever the hell he was. He may look like little more than muscle on legs, but she was certain there was more to him than the occasional scowl and ability to crack walnuts with his thighs. She wished she had his surname because then she could run a check. She wished she'd had the presence of mind to snatch a shot with her phone, but on the occasions their paths had crossed she had been too preoccupied with Dalgliesh. Which was exactly the way the likes of Julian wanted it. They were the men who stood in the wings, letting the performers garner all the attention while they pulled strings.

But who was he? He was SG, obviously, but was he also New Dawn? And who stood in the shadows behind him, pulling his strings?

She thought of Alice's testimony. She had now read everything she had given her and had a feel for where this was going. The murder that never was, Alice had said. At first, she had thought that referred to Gerry's death – and given the amount of hostility directed towards him, it may yet be – but now it seemed it may be what happened to Howard Rose. Tomorrow she would visit Alice and get from her the final pages and, hopefully, at last understand what was going on. There was still work to be done before anything could be printed or even pitched to Leo Cross, but Rebecca was absolutely convinced that there was a story to tell. And when Elspeth awoke, she might find she had another book to write.

Flash. Her legs, twisted.

She should phone Stephen, she knew that, but thinking of Elspeth sent her in another direction. On her laptop, she found the file of old photographs Elspeth had asked her to have digitised the year before. They were pictures of Elspeth's childhood, a few with her husband but very few shots of her in later years. Rebecca clicked open one of the JPEG files at random. It showed Elspeth at the age of six or seven, a slim little girl with brown hair and brown eyes, standing beside her mother, who had been quite a beauty. Her mother couldn't accept Elspeth's sexual orientation and that meant in later years their relationship was fraught. Elspeth used to say that the old bisom was too pig-headed and obstinate to see that the world had changed, that the old values were being uprooted. In many ways, Elspeth was just like her mother, because she was pretty well planted in her own prejudices. In the old photograph they looked happy to be together. Mother and daughter, not so alike in looks, Elspeth having perhaps inherited her father's features, but so very alike in temperament, the camera lens looking across the years, the colour dying with time.

Her mum looked beautiful, Elspeth thought. She was the way she remembered her as a child, not the way she became when age and the disappointments of life had left their marks on her body and soul. Her mother had not had an easy life. Two husbands, both absolute bastards, and a daughter whose lifestyle she never fully understood. When Elspeth had been married to a man, albeit unhappily, that was something she recognised, that was *normal,* but living with a woman had been beyond the reach of her understanding. The way she spoke about it, sitting in her favourite chair in her flat, her cat Jasper on her lap, it was as if her only daughter had somehow invented same-sex attraction in order to shame her personally. She only had to bear what she'd termed her 'deep shame' for a year or two before she passed, still never accepting the fact that her daughter was a lesbian.

But here she was, in this sunlit copse in the middle of wherever the hell they were, smiling at her. And young. And, oh yeah, floating.

'I've been waiting for you, Ellie,' she said.

Ellie. She was the only one who had ever called her that. Not her husband, not her deadbeat father who pissed off when she was five, not even Julie. Only her mum, who was standing in front of her, once again young and beautiful.

'Mum, you're not old anymore.'

She smiled. 'We're not old here,' she said, nodding towards her daughter. 'Can't you see that?'

Elspeth looked down at her legs again, slim and shapely, the way they used to be. She didn't need a mirror to know that somehow she had shed the pounds and the years and looked the

255

way she had in her twenties. She hadn't been in the same class as her mum but she'd been relatively attractive back then, before those pounds piled on and too much gin and too many cigarettes and too many pain-in-the-arse people had taken their toll.

'Where are we?' Elspeth asked.

Another smile from her mother. God, how she missed that smile. It used to shine brightly but it was turned off by life. This was a different woman from the bitter, acid-tongued and – yes – wizened creature that had spat insults at her over her sexuality.

'Don't you know?'

'I'm dreaming, right?'

'Something like that, Ellie. But it's a dream that you never need to wake up from.'

Elspeth . . .

The voice was like an echo, faint and distant, and Elspeth wasn't sure she'd heard it at first.

Elspeth . . .

It was as soft as a summer breeze. It drifted towards her, swirled around her, then faded. It was familiar, she knew who it was, but couldn't quite put a name to it. She'd known who it was just a few moments ago, but now that knowledge had been picked up by the breeze and carried away. She looked around hoping for a face she might know but saw nobody she recognised. In fact, the features of all the floating people were blurred, as if someone had smeared a drawing with a thumb. As she studied them, she became aware of other faint figures emerging from the grasslands behind her, some walking, some running – others, like her, adrift, as though they were lost and looking for a landmark they knew. Most of them were met by one of the floating figures. There were embraces, there were conversations, and then they accompanied them into the trees where they merged with the sunbeams slanting through the branches.

She looked back. The cloud, her cloud, was still there, as if idling at a kerb, and she knew she could walk back to it any time and leave this place.

'There's nothing for you there, Ellie,' her mother said.

'I have a life there.' She wasn't sure what that life was, but she knew something – someone – waited for her there.

There was sadness in the way her mother shook her head. 'That life is over.'

Elspeth refused to accept that. 'Not if I don't want it to be.'

'That's true, but you may not want what lies back there for you,' her mother said. 'Do you remember what happened to you?'

There were gaps in her memory. She could instantly recall her childhood and teenage years, right up into her twenties. There were patches after that, good memories, fun memories. She could recall laughter but not tears, not pain, apart from her mother's insults, and even they were already fading. She could recall nothing from immediately before waking up in that cloud and then finding herself here.

'Let me remind you,' her mother said.

And then Elspeth felt sharp, jagged pain in her head, legs, back. She felt a solid impact, then the impression of falling, falling, falling before jarring to a halt against something hard and unforgiving. And she remembered.

'There was a car.'

'Yes.'

'It hit me.'

'Yes.'

'I was hurt.'

'Yes.'

Elspeth felt tears burn. It felt wrong. There should be no tears here. 'Am I dead?'

'No. You're still alive, in a way.'

'In a way?'

257

'Your body is there,' her mother said, waving her hand towards the cloud. It was a slow, graceful movement that left a trail, like a photograph taken at slow shutter speed. 'But your consciousness is here, with me. The longer you stay here, the more you will forget all the hurt and pain.'

Elspeth followed the gesture to stare at the cloud again. The sudden pain in her head she had experienced remained with her. 'I should go back.'

'You will return to a world of agony.'

Elspeth, come back to me . . .

The voice again, louder this time, and a name returned with the pain. Julie. Her partner. Her lover. Her life, though she had never told her. She should have told her. Why didn't she tell her?

'Because that wasn't you, Ellie,' said her mother. 'You can't be something you were not in life. You were never demonstrative, never particularly loving, not in an open way. But here you can be whatever you want to be and also something you used to be. Young, fit, happy.'

The pain was growing. 'I was happy there, with Julie.'

'No, you weren't. You lived, you were content. You settled. But you didn't look after yourself. Smoking, drinking, refusing to take care of the vessel in which you existed.'

The vessel in which she existed, like she was the *Starship Enterprise*.

'You kept your sense of humour, though,' her mother said, obviously hearing her thoughts. But then, Elspeth was beginning to glimpse a glimmer of understanding of what was happening here. 'That was the one thing from your previous life that you kept. You needed it, didn't you?'

Elspeth, please come back . . .

Louder now, and when she looked, she thought the cloud had come closer, too. Or she had moved towards it. And the headache was building towards excruciating. Her mother was

258

a little further away than before, yet she had no memory of taking a single step. She *was* moving, though, slowly being drawn away from the copse of trees and the floating figures and the people they were meeting and the sun that shimmered and shifted among the branches that waved so invitingly.

'Ellie, choose wisely. Only you can decide whether to go or to stay here. If you go back, you will never again be as you were before the accident, I think you know that.'

The pain in her head was almost unbearable and she recognised that there was damage to her brain, serious damage. She was midway between the copse and the cloud, but she finally understood where she was. This wasn't Heaven, it wasn't Hell, it was a mixture of both, and both were inside her own mind.

I can't be without you . . .

Julie was calling to her from the cloud. Elspeth could hear the anguish in her voice, and she felt her heart break.

'Ellie, I know you understand what is happening,' said her mother. 'I know you love her.'

Despite her awareness that she was arguing with her own subconscious, Elspeth hit back. 'You never understood that I could love a woman.'

'I do now. I recognise my faults – it's something you come to terms with here, the mistakes you made back there.'

There is no back there, Mum, Elspeth thought. There is no here. This is all me.

'Yes, there is,' countered her mother. 'And if you go back, the pain you feel now will be with you for the rest of your life. You won't be the same. You won't walk or talk or even feed yourself. You'll be dependent on Julie for even the most basic of functions. Is that what you want? Is that the life you want her to lead?'

She didn't want that.

'It's your choice, darling,' her mother said, and Elspeth felt her cool fingers brush her hair, even though she seemed to be many yards distant. 'Only you can make it.'

The cloud waited.

Her mother floated.

She looked from one to the other.

The breeze whispered its soft song in the grass. The birds sang. The grasshoppers chirped.

Insects.

Rebecca could hear insects buzzing around her, buzzing, buzzing. No, not insects, it was too rhythmic, too precise.

She woke with a start and the buzzing continued. She was still propped up on the headboard, slumped against the pillows with her head dangling, and she realised her neck ached. Her laptop lay open, half on her lap and half on the duvet, its screen sleeping, Alice's pages strewn at her side and on the floor. She'd fallen asleep rereading her testimony and looking at Elspeth's photographs.

It wasn't an insect buzzing, it was one of her phones vibrating on the bedside table, rumbling on the veneer top of the table as if it was angry. She didn't think the hospital would call her, but Julie most certainly would if there was any change in Elspeth's condition, and that was her first thought. Her second thought was that she wouldn't call this device, the agency phone. As she reached for the offending mobile, she automatically checked the time on her alarm clock – God, it's 2.35 in the bleeding a.m. The caller's number was withheld, and Rebecca gritted her teeth. Probably some bloody scammer, so she cut the connection, dropped the phone back on the table, began to punch and manipulate her pillows to a horizontal position and prepared to settle down.

Almost immediately it began to rumble again.

Damn it, I should switch the bloody thing off. Who is going to call me at this time of night with a story? But something told her she should answer it. She didn't know what that something was, just a little voice in her head. She swiped to accept the call. If it was a scammer or a sales call then the words she was prepared to summon would be powerful enough to blister the caller's ear.

It wasn't a scammer and it wasn't a sales call.

'Rebecca, it's Finbar Dalgliesh.'

She didn't reply. He was talking very quietly and sounded tense. And using her first name, too. Frankly, she was surprised at the familiarity. She wondered if this was a nightmare.

'I'm sorry to call at this hour.'

She still didn't reply. She rotated her neck to ease those cramped muscles and tendons.

'Are you there?'

She licked her lips, her tongue feeling sluggish. 'Yes, I'm here.' God, even she could hear the sleep in her voice.

'I'm sorry to wake you,' he said.

'Why did you, Dalgliesh?'

He might be acting all chummy, using her Christian name, but there was no way in hell she was going to reciprocate.

A sigh down the line. 'I don't know, I really don't.'

His voice trembled a little, as if he was cold, but it was a warm night. She pulled herself more erect, sensing something in the ether.

'I suppose it's because I trust you,' he said.

Okay, maybe she was dreaming. Why would Finbar Dalgliesh, who in her eyes was only a white cat short of being a Bond villain, profess trust in her?

'Thank you.' Her voice raised a little at the end, as if she was posing a question, unsure that being trusted by him was something she would put on her CV. 'Now, what do you want?'

'Can we meet?'

She looked at the time again. 2.37. 'What, now?'

'No, tomorrow, if that's convenient.'

'What's this about, Dalgliesh?'

'You know what it's about, Rebecca.'

Of course she did. Stupid question. Her brain was as torpid as her tongue. 'Where do you want to meet?'

'Not in the city. I need to get away for a while.'

She wanted to ask why but didn't. She feared posing too many questions might spook him even further. And he was spooked, she could tell that from the wavering whisper.

'Where, then?'

'Do you know Kilchurn Castle on Loch Awe?'

She did: a ruin on the edge of the water in the shadow of Ben Cruachan. Despite herself, she smiled. Even when he was ruffled, he hadn't lost his flair for the dramatic. He would get on well with Alan, if the latter had a lobotomy.

'Why there?'

'Why not? It has a synchronicity about it, doesn't it?'

'Are you going on the record, Mr Dalgliesh?'

A pause as he thought about the question, even though he must surely have known she would ask. 'In a way.'

She felt the familiar tingle of anticipation when she knew she was onto something, but it dissipated when he spoke again.

'But you have to come alone.'

He had to be kidding, but she chose not to argue the point. 'Why should I trust you, Dalgliesh?'

'I assume you've spoken to your mother about what I did for your father.'

'Yes.'

'Does that not gain me some form of trust?'

Jesus, she thought, after all these years he was looking for her father's debt to be honoured. 'I don't know why you did what you did back then, but I feel sure you got something out of it.'

'I helped one of the few police officers who I respected out of a situation in which any one of us could have found ourselves. Hancock was a monster, and I was happy to do it.'

'You'll forgive me if I take that with a trunk full of salt. You're a politician. You don't do anything unless there's benefit for you.'

'I'm not the villain here, Rebecca.'

She almost laughed. 'I'll reserve judgement on that. So, why the sudden desire to spill the beans? Another attack of public spirit?'

'It's not sudden,' he said. 'But I won't speak about it on the phone. Tomorrow.'

Paranoid much?

'I'll see you there at 2 p.m., Rebecca.'

'And will *you* be alone?'

He hesitated for a moment. 'Yes,' he said and then rung off.

She stared at the screen for a few moments, still a bit numb from the unexpected nature of the call. Then she thought of phoning Bill immediately but decided against it. He needed his beauty sleep. Not so long ago she would have called Elspeth right away, but she couldn't do that now. She set the phone down, rested her head on her pillows and stared at the ceiling. She heard what might have been a fox barking somewhere in the distance and then someone's car alarm. She didn't think the two sounds were in any way connected.

But that call and the slight changes in body language she'd seen in Dalgliesh were connected, of that she was convinced. The man was going to drop some sort of bombshell, she could feel it.

She was nearing the endgame.

263

28

Alice Larkin looked like death. Her face was even more drawn than before, the circles under her eyes had deepened and darkened, the eyes themselves seemed to have shrunk into her sockets, and as she held out a sealed brown A4 envelope containing the final pages, her hand trembled. Orla had told Rebecca that her ladyship had experienced a bad night, but she didn't expand in any way. The nurse, assistant, secretary, companion, bodyguard, friend – for Rebecca sensed the woman was all of these – stood by the door, her manner professional, calm, competent, but there was the shadow of concern in her eyes as she looked at Alice.

The woman in the bed didn't notice it, or if she did, didn't acknowledge it. As Rebecca reached out to take the envelope, Alice gripped the edge as if unwilling to relinquish her hold or having second thoughts regarding whatever revelations they held. Finally she let go, but her eyes never left the envelope as Rebecca transferred it into her bag, which was then placed beside the couch under the window. Once it was out of sight, for the first time in their short acquaintanceship, Alice looked lost. In parting with that envelope, she had given up something that was part of her. A page was being turned and she had no idea what the new chapter promised.

Or perhaps she did.

'What's Elspeth's condition?' Alice asked, her voice weak.

Rebecca had spoken to Julie before she left. 'No change.'

Orla had handed Alice a glass of water and she sipped it, then gave it back with an appreciative nod. 'She remains in a coma?'

'Yes, though the doctors say there is some brain activity present, so I think that's hopeful. And Julie, her partner, was certain she heard her murmur something in the night.'

Mum. Julie was sure she heard her say *mum.* Even in our subconscious we call out for our parents, she said.

Alice's gaze dropped to the bedspread. Weariness or guilt, Rebecca couldn't decide which.

'When will you read those pages?'

'As soon as I can. I'm heading up to Loch Awe, so I'll read them in the car.'

The eyes rose. 'You're going to Cruachan?'

'Not to the power station. I see no point in that because this story really isn't about that, is it?'

The familiar steel hardened Alice's eyes. 'No, it's not. So, why are you going?'

'I'm going to meet with Finbar Dalgliesh.'

That surprised her. 'Why?'

Rebecca told her about challenging him the evening before and her gut feeling that he had something to say in connection with Alice's story, something he couldn't say in Julian's hearing.

'I'm sure he does have something to say,' Alice said. 'You're not going alone, are you?'

'No, I'm taking a friend.'

'That young man who was here the other day?'

'No, someone else.'

She had called Bill first thing that morning, knowing that he would be up and about, and she was right. He was actually at breakfast.

'This other friend, is he capable?'

Rebecca knew instantly what Alice meant. 'Yes, he's more than capable.'

She had first seen how capable Bill was when he chased a man who had threatened people at a funeral with a shotgun. She then saw him wield an extendable baton in a cramped little house in Inverness when they were both under the barrel of another man with a gun. Men with guns, she thought, she had seen too many of them.

Alice gave a small, satisfied nod. 'Good, because you can't trust Dalgliesh, you do know that?'

She knew it and Bill knew it, but she was determined to see this through. He had strongly advised against going but had grudgingly agreed. He was waiting in the car in the Gardens now. She hoped he had his baton.

Bill dipped his fingers into the pocket of the car door and felt the reassuring sturdiness of the extendable baton. It had served him well, especially doing work for, and on behalf of, Rebecca and Elspeth. He'd once fended off three neds in an Inverness pub while their boss watched from her table. It was a handy piece of kit, not just for such situations, but also when beating down weeds in the garden. He had hacked a swathe through entire patches of nettles with it.

While he waited for Rebecca to return, he tapped Loch Awe into Google Maps on his phone and checked the time. It was almost 11 a.m. but he wanted to get to the castle early and it would take at least a couple of hours to get there from Glasgow's West End, depending on traffic on the A82 at Dumbarton and then on Loch Lomondside. He twisted round to look at the fancy terraced house Rebecca had entered, but there was still no sign of her.

He was pretty damn sure that this whole 'meet me at a remote castle' thing was a trap. He'd brushed up against all types when he was on the job and had developed a pretty jaded view of humanity. He believed that even though individuals were capable of great compassion and selflessness, the

266

majority were, to varying degrees, venal and corrupt and self-ish. He didn't trust easily, but when he did, it was complete, and heaven help anyone who broke that trust. He trusted Elspeth and he trusted Rebecca. Not only that, although he would deny it with his dying breath, he liked those women, and that was why he was here. Rebecca had a talent for getting herself into trouble. He did not trust that bastard Dalgliesh as far as he could throw him, and he would love to throw him a very long distance. That would be after he gave his pal Julian the old heave-ho, too.

In the rearview he saw Rebecca trotting down the short flight of steps to the pavement. He started the car, gave the baton another glance. It was always good to have a back-up plan.

After the Connolly girl left, Alice asked for a cup of tea and perhaps some toast with jam. She hadn't been eating much at all, and so the request pleased Orla, even though it meant she had to go to the shop on Hyndland Road for the jam. Alice knew that because Orla had mentioned it the day before. She didn't want a cup of tea, let alone toast. She just needed some time alone to do what she had to do.

Those pages with which Rebecca had left were her final testimony, the truth of what happened sixty years before, a truth she had told nobody, a truth she had even ignored herself. It had felt good to get it out when she typed it, but now that it was out of her hands she felt somehow deflated. She had anticipated this moment for many months, had decided on it following the death of her husband, but now that it was here it seemed strangely anti-climactic. Of course, the story was not fully told, but that was a task for others. She had completed what she had set out to do. She had revealed her part in what happened and the aftermath. Rebecca had apparently flushed out SG, through Dalgliesh. She would continue with the story. She would tell it.

After . . .

She heard the front door close and Orla descend the steps to the street. Alice hauled herself onto her side and withdrew from the drawer beside the bed a white envelope with *Orla and Forbes* handwritten on the front. She propped it up against the lamp then reached back into the drawer for the full bottle of pills. She'd had a devil of a job hiding these from Orla over the past few weeks, pretending she had been taking them then slipping them into this bottle. It had meant she had suffered more pain and sleepless nights than she would have otherwise, but that was a price she had to pay. In a way, the pain was deserved.

She poured a glass of water from the carafe, her trembling hands making her spill a little. She didn't know how quickly the pills would take effect. She hoped very quickly. She hoped there would be no unseemly vomiting. She just wanted to sit back and fall asleep, never to awaken. She was heading in that direction anyway, albeit slowly, so all she was doing was speeding up the journey.

It was time.

29

Gerry didn't return until midway through the following week, so I was eager to see him again. I couldn't believe, let alone understand, how much I had missed him while he was down south. I wasn't a silly young girl – I was well aware that love could bloom then die with time, emotions being fickle and transient – but I had deep feelings for this man, my bit of rough, as he once called himself. All I knew was that, finally, I had found someone with whom I wanted to make a future, for however much time we had together. I didn't know then how short a time it would be.

He had telephoned me from Glasgow, saying he was catching the next train. He said he had something to tell me, but I also had something to tell him.

He suggested that I meet him at Loch Awe station. I would have preferred him to stay on board till Oban, so we could go back to my flat and make love, but he wanted to enjoy our fine West Highland air after almost two weeks in London. It was late summer, and I could feel the cool beckon of autumn in the air. The light was soft and pleasant, and I was the only one on the platform awaiting the train from Glasgow. Birds

269

trilled in the trees and a gentle breeze swirled around me. I was excited and daunted in equal measure. I was looking forward to seeing him but apprehensive over what I was about to tell him.

I was pregnant. The doctor had confirmed it at the appointment I had been eager to get to when John Lane approached me in the street. These were the days before the Pill, you see, and birth control was either by using a condom, the rhythm method, hoping for the best or abstinence. Gerry and I had been careful – yes, we had used a condom. Well, mostly. There had been two or three occasions when we had been carried away by passion, and it seemed that some of his little soldiers had managed to march to their destination and make camp. I was exhilarated, and I was dreading it. I was a mass of conflicting emotions, but the one thing of which I was certain was that Gerry would be shocked at first but he would stand by me, because I had come to love his decency and his sense of honour. As I said, the permissive society had not quite reached the West Highlands, so I was not yet ready to face the world as a single parent.

The Glasgow train pulled in and he was the only passenger to alight, his duffel bag over his shoulder and a big, warm, stupid grin on his face. I admit I ran along the platform to him, rather like a heroine in some awful romantic film. We hugged, we kissed, we each said we had missed the other. I told him I loved him. He held me tighter. I'd never told him that before, not even in the throes of passion.

I broke away from him, aware that he had not reciprocated and trying not to blurt it out like a silly schoolgirl. As I said, emotions in an uproar. I made a bid to cover up what might have been a blunder, although if he thought that was a bombshell, in the words of Al Jolson, he hadn't heard nothin' yet. As it turned out, it was me who was about to be stunned.

'What was it you had to tell me?' I asked as we walked hand in hand from the platform to the small car park.

His fingers tightened on mine. 'I've got the bastard, Ally. I've really got him.'

I knew to whom he referred, of course. 'What did you find?'

'I'll show you in the car, then we can go for a stroll up the hillside, get some air and decide what the next step will be.'

We reached my car, and he unfastened his duffel bag and pulled out a large manila envelope before he climbed into the passenger seat. Once I'd settled behind the wheel, he passed the envelope to me. I had intended to tell him my news, but he seemed so excited about this, so I delayed my announcement. We had the whole afternoon and the evening together. I had plenty of time to tell him.

'I sat for three days going through old newspapers in the Smoke,' he said. 'But I finally found him.'

I opened the envelope and withdrew a series of photographic prints, all black and white, of course. They were grainy and showed groups of men in black shirts, some giving the Nazi salute to Sir Oswald Mosley, younger in these shots, but I recognised him immediately. Others in the bundle had been snatched during what looked like street fighting.

Gerry handed me a small pocket magnifying glass that flipped open. 'Second from the far right, which is kind of fitting.'

I took the glass and studied the face he'd specified. 'You think this is Lane?'

'I'm certain of it.'

I peered at the image. 'Could be.'

'It is.' He took the photographs from me and flipped through them. 'Look at this one. This was taken by someone at Cable Street. Look almost direct centre, the fella just about to punch another fella.'

271

I studied the snarling face as he held a much smaller, and older, man by the lapel with his left hand while his right was raised and clenched. I remained unsure.

'You could take these to one of the Sundays, right?' Gerry said, his voice eager. 'You must have contacts.'

'And say what?'

He smiled. 'You mean they wouldn't be interested in a Nazi sympathiser, a Blackshirt thug, working on the country's biggest civil engineering project under an assumed name? And with political ambitions of his own? That's not a story?'

I studied the face again. There was some familiarity in the features. 'I don't know, Gerry. The quality of these prints isn't great. It could be him but . . .'

The smile slid away, and Gerry's jaw tightened. 'It is him, believe me.'

'But what if it's—'

He took the photographs back. 'It is him, and I'm going to show these to anyone I can.'

'Let's say it is—'

'It is,' he insisted, thrusting the pictures back in the envelope before turning his head away to stare towards the station.

'Okay,' I said, realising that he was taking my caution as something negative, which I absolutely did not intend. 'It's just . . . if you're going to reveal this, there can be absolutely no wiggle room. You cannot give someone like Lane the opportunity to fudge it. Can the shots be cleaned up somehow? Blown up so that they're clearer?'

He faced me again. 'You don't think this is him, do you?'

'All I'm asking is if there's some way we can be sure. Can we find someone who was at one of these meetings who could positively identify him?'

'And how do we do that?'

'What about that group you mentioned, the one Howie was part of?'

'The 43 Group is long broken up.'

'Then let's look at Lane himself, the name he used. Trace the origins of that.'

'How?'

'I don't know. Hire a private detective maybe.'

'Do you realise how much it would cost to get a good one?'

'You have money, Gerry, so have I. Between us . . .'

He looked away again. 'I'm going to confront the bastard with this. I'll know from his reaction if this is him.'

'And then what?'

He tapped the envelope but still didn't look at me. 'Then I'll know for certain. And then I'll use this somehow, with or without your help.'

That stung. He thought I wasn't being supportive, but I really was. 'Of course I'll help. I believe you, Gerry, and I believe Lane should be exposed, without a doubt. I just don't want you to plunge headlong into some rash confrontation that he could easily shake off.'

He remained silent. I sensed he knew that I was right. He was excited by this because it was confirmation of what his friend Howie had told him, and he would have been bursting with enthusiasm to tell me. I regretted being so pragmatic so quickly. I should have matched his enthusiasm then slowly brought him down to earth to forge a more effective way forward. But I had been my usual self, headstrong, so sure of my own opinion. But then, was it not better that I was upfront about my misgivings, rather than pander to him?

Nevertheless, I felt I had to make some form of consoling move, so I reached out and took the hand that rested on the envelope. 'I'm sorry, Gerry, I didn't mean to sound as if I didn't support you.'

Thankfully, his fingers tightened on mine, and he looked back, gave me a weak smile. 'No, it's my fault. All the way up from London I was visualising that bastard's face when I shoved these into it. I got carried away with it, I suppose, swept up in the fantasy.' He threw the envelope into the back with his bag. He nodded to the steering wheel. 'Come on, then, let's get the old bus fired up and get up to the mountain. I need to purge my lungs of that foul city air.'

His old light tone had returned, and I was glad. I still had to tell him my news, but I would delay that until I was certain he was in a good enough mood to receive it. I steered out of the small car park and turned left, heading for a spot near the Falls of Cruachan where I could park. The trail up into the hills towards the dam was a favourite stroll of ours and I had brought my hiking boots because I knew the path was rough and, thanks to some rain the week before, might be muddy.

He talked about his trip, how much he both hated and loved London; hated it for its vastness and noise and press of humanity; but loved it for its vibrancy – because if the sixties did swing, the King's Road and Carnaby Street were where it was at its swingiest. He expressed delight at meeting Howie's family, but sadness at seeing his friend in the care home, a ghost made flesh and bone, his eyes open but still sleeping a sleep that would never end. Those were Gerry's words, a sleep that would never end, and, as I type this, desperately ignoring the pain that is my constant bed companion now, I long for such release myself.

It was as if the temper and pique had never happened. This was the Gerry I loved. This was the Gerry with whom I wanted to move forward. This was the Gerry I wanted to marry, to hell with my father and Lance, and John Lane.

We met no one during our walk, which was unusual, but I was glad of it. I let Gerry natter on, enjoying the lilt of his voice but waiting for the opportunity to tell him that he was going to be a father. We stopped here and there to take in the view, at one point looking towards the loch over and between trees still green but beginning to show some autumn gold, the water blue, the sky broken by only a few puffs of cloud. His arm snaked around my waist to pull me in front of him, his face resting on top of my head, his hands cupping my belly and the baby we had created together. I wrapped both of my arms over his and leaned into him. Now was the time, I told myself. Do it now.

I wondered if he could feel the nerves in my stomach as I plucked up the courage. I didn't know then exactly why I felt such trepidation. After all, this was a good thing – a child, born of both our bodies, would bring us even closer together.

I took a deep breath. 'Gerry, there's something I need to tell you.'

'If it's that I am the most wonderful man that ever set foot upon this Earth, then it's fine, darling, I already know that.'

I patted his hand. 'Yes, darling, you keep telling yourself that. Although you are to me.'

He turned me round so he could look into my face, one hand caressing my cheek. 'Then that's all that matters.'

He kissed me. It was a long kiss. It was the kind of kiss that told me his anger had dissipated. It told me it was definitely time to tell him. But still, I hesitated. This was big news, this was life-changing, and I couldn't do what I normally do and simply barge in. I rested my face on his chest and he kissed the top of my head.

'So, what is it you have to tell me?'

I took another breath, then raised my face to stare into his. 'I hope that this will make you very happy.'

He smiled. 'Well, unless you come out with it, we'll never know.'

My smile in return, I knew, was more of a flutter of my lips because the nerves that had taken hold wouldn't let a real smile loose. I berated myself for being such a ninny. Tell him, Alice, I told myself. Just bloody well tell him. So, I did.

'We're going to have a baby,' I said.

Right away I knew that it was unwelcome news. His smile drooped, a frown began to line his forehead. 'You're kidding, right?'

I eased myself from his arms and stepped away from him. 'No, why would I kid about something like that? I'm pregnant, Gerry.'

He blinked a few times in rapid succession, the smile drooping further. 'And it's mine.'

That made me angry. 'Of course it's yours. What do you think, that I sleep around? That I'm some sort of chippy?'

He didn't reply. He didn't need to. I saw it on his face and the way he turned away from me. This was not good news. He moved to the edge of the path, the thumb and middle finger of his left hand stroking the corners of his mouth and down to his chin. I'd seen him do that when he was considering something, and he was considering this.

'Gerry,' I said, cursing the fact that my voice broke a little. I could feel the tears coming, and I cursed them, too. I willed myself not to cry, to be strong, to talk this out with him.

'You'll be keeping it, I suppose?'

'The baby, Gerry. I'm having a baby, not an "it". And of course I'll be keeping the baby. It's part of us, you and me.'

I had never considered having children prior to this, always thought they would get in the way of my ambitions, but once I found out I was carrying a child, that view changed. Perhaps it was the hormones and the chemicals that a pregnancy releases, I don't know, but I was actually looking forward to being a mother. The concept of carrying my child, our child, his child, to term did not daunt me in the slightest. I wanted this.

He looked down at the path, scuffed at the dirt with his shoe, thrust his hands into his pockets. The good humour had vanished again and in its place was an uneasy tension.

I was decidedly irritated. 'I've got to say, this is not the reception that I expected from you.'

'What did you expect, then?'

I wasn't actually sure, to be honest. 'I don't know. Surprise, yes, but followed by some kind of joy.'

'Well, you got the surprise.'

'But not the joy?'

He kicked a pebble across the path. 'No, not the joy.'

The tears of pain, of anger, burned but I forced myself to keep them at bay. I would not be an emotional female, and even though my emotions were running wild, I kept a lid on them. I was very good at that. 'Why not?'

He didn't answer. He had found another pebble and was pushing it around with his toe.

'Damn it, Gerry, will you turn around and tell me why you are not happy with this? I realise it's a shock, I realise we hadn't planned it, but in case you're desperately trying to apportion blame here, just remember it takes two to tango and—'

'I'm married, Alice.'

He said it quietly, but it reached me like a slap, bringing my speech to an abrupt halt. I think I stood there open-mouthed as he finally looked back at me and gave a little, shrugging jerk of the head.

'She's back home, in Ireland,' he said. 'That's where I send most of my wages, back to her. The money I splash around here is what I win at the cards. I told you I'm very good at the cards.'

I didn't know what to say. All I could think of was John Lane's words. *He's not what he seems.* This was what he meant by that.

'I'm sorry,' he said.

'Fuck being sorry,' I said. I was shaking, I felt sick, but I had to defend myself against them both, and the best form of defence is attack.

'Don't be like that.'

277

'Don't be like what, Gerry? Hm? I mean, is that really your name? Gerry?'

'Of course it is.'

'Well, you kept your marital status from me, perhaps even your real name.'

'Don't be stupid, Ally.'

'Stupid, am I? Yes, I suppose I am, stupid enough to fall for you.'

'We can work this out, you and me.'

I butted in. 'Are there children?'

He looked away again. I had my answer.

'How many?'

'Two, both girls.'

'Two girls,' I said. 'I hope their mother brings them up to beware of smooth-talking Irishmen.'

'I'm sorry, Ally.'

'Yes, you said that. Saying it a second time doesn't make me feel any better.'

The tears had died stillborn now. All I felt by that time was an icy calm.

'God, I've been such a fool,' I said.

He took a step towards me, reached out. 'No, you haven't, darling, I—'

I stepped back and held up a hand, my forefinger stabbing at him. 'No, you don't touch me, you don't touch me ever again and you don't call me darling. You lied to me.'

'I didn't lie.'

'You sure as hell didn't tell the truth. How could you lead me on like that? How could you have sex with me knowing that you have a wife and family back home?'

And then it hit me. Again, Lane had told me.

'Christ,' I said, 'You've done this before, haven't you? In other parts of Scotland where you've been working, found some local girl, slept with her, had your fun and moved on.'

'No.'

My laugh was short and bitter. 'Yeah, like I'll believe you. John Lane told me I shouldn't trust you, and now I know why.'

That roused him. 'When did you speak to him?'

'Does that really matter?'

'I can't believe you were talking to Lane behind my back.'

'This isn't about him and you, this is about you and me. This is about the child, your child, the one I'm carrying. This is about me finding out that the man I loved – yes, Gerry, I loved you – has lied to me. My God, Lance is a better man than you, if only because he never lied to me.'

He was angry now. 'Well, maybe I'm seeing you in a different light, too. Getting chummy with Lane. So, what was it? Daddy put you two together?'

'What has he got—'

'Come on, darling, don't do this now, don't try to pretend you don't know your father is involved with Lane, and Mosley before him. Him and his friends, the ones with the money and the influence. Lane's been cultivating them all for months.'

I recalled the two men I'd seen Lane with that first night in the hotel, and suddenly I knew where I'd seen them. I'd only met them once, at the same party I'd met Mosley, but they were part of that group of quiet men who wield influence and money behind the scenes, leaving the spotlight to men like Mosley. And my father. And Lane?

A triumphant gleam grew in Gerry's eyes. 'Aye, that's right, darling. Your old dad is in bed with Lane, or rather McNair – because let's not tarnish further the memory of whatever poor dead child whose name he stole.'

'Is that why you—' I stopped, unsure of what to say, my anger now becoming muddied, confused. God, was my father a fascist?

'No,' he said. 'I fancied you, is all. I never intended to hurt you, I never intended to use you to get at your father.'

'But it would have been a nice bonus, right?'

That little shrug again. It was extremely annoying.

'You're a bastard, you do know that, don't you?'

He had found his confidence again. 'And so will that child be, if you have it.'

Even though I now knew him to be an utter shit, I didn't expect that from him. I was left mute, first with shock at his callous tone, and then by the anger that slowly bled through it. He regretted his words immediately, I'll give him that, but it was too late, the damage had been done. He looked as if he was going to apologise but then thought better of it. He cast his eyes down again, his tongue moistening his lips. He seemed to be looking for inspiration on the ground but gave up when he found nothing, looked back at me and shook his head. I thought he might say something, anything, to make this right but he didn't. Instead, he stared at me for a second or two, then brushed past me to head back down the path. I watched him go, willing him to stop, face me again, talk about this, but he kept walking.

That was when I broke.

I don't remember picking up the rock. I only barely remember rushing after him. I heard the echoes of a high-pitched scream that I believe emanated from me. What I do remember most vividly is Gerry spinning round, the shock on his face turning to horror before he attempted to dodge out of the way, but not quite fast enough to avoid the blow. The first blow. The rock swung against his temple. It was as if someone else's hand was responsible. He pivoted on his heel, a little grunt escaping from his lips, staggered back, blood bursting through his skin, his expression quizzical, as if he was trying to place me and not quite doing so.

I hit him again. This time I knew it was me.

He stumbled, dropped to his hands and knees. Raised a hand as if in supplication.

The third blow crashed against the back of his head. I swear I actually heard the skull split. I still hear it in my dreams. A thud, a crunch, a groan. The arm supporting him gave way and he pitched forward face-first, his feet kicking against the dirt as if trying to right himself but not making any purchase. He made a curious little noise, like a baby talking. That made me even angrier, and I raised the rock in both hands, let it hang there for a moment, watching him scrambling at my feet but getting nowhere. And then I let it fall on his head. His legs and arms twitched a little and then stilled.

I don't know how long I stood there, staring down at the body of a man I had loved. Now realising that it had all been a mirage.

He's not the man you think he is.

I dropped the rock beside the body, stepped over it and walked back down the path. I didn't know if he was still alive. I didn't know if he was in pain. I didn't know and I didn't care. It had all been a dream, a bad dream, and I was walking away from it.

I didn't meet anyone on the way down. Once back in the car I had the presence of mind to check myself for blood. There were a few spots on my boots, and I spat on the corner of my handkerchief and tried to rub them away but didn't succeed. There were further traces on my jacket, which I took off and threw in the back seat beside his duffle bag and the envelope. I would have to deal with that, too.

I remember being strangely calm. A man had just died in front of me. I'd heard his skull shatter. I'd seen the blood. I'd watched as his nerves ceased to function. And yet there I was, in my car, contemplating disposing of evidence without losing a breath. What did that indicate about me? Was I some sort of psychopath?

Of course, my lack of reaction was a reaction in itself. I had managed to somehow dissociate myself from the act – my mind had removed me from any wrongdoing. It didn't last, of course, it couldn't. I had reached Taynuilt when the enormity of it kicked in.

I had killed a man. I had taken up a heavy rock and killed him with it.

My body trembled uncontrollably, I sucked in deep, whooping breaths. My fingers tightened like claws on the steering wheel, but I managed to pull over. I didn't know it, but I was having a full-blown anxiety attack. I was hyper ventilating and that caused my hands and fingers to lock. Carpopedal spasm, it's called. But, of course, I'd never heard of such a thing then.

Whether by accident or design, I had pulled up beside a public telephone box, the familiar red colour strangely comforting. I found some pennies in my purse – it was difficult with my hands contracting as they were, but I did it. I sat for a minute or two, forcing my breathing to slow. I couldn't make this call like this. I didn't think I could even get out of the car, let alone speak. I had to control myself.

It took a few minutes but I succeeded in bringing my limbs under some form of control, well enough to get me from the car and into the phone box. I dialled my father's private number, praying as it rang that he was in his office in Glasgow. It rang and rang and I was beginning to despair, could feel the panic rising again, when I heard his voice. I pressed the button with my knuckle to make the pennies drop and connect the call.

'Daddy,' was all I got out before I broke down into tears.

'Alice?' I could hear the concern in his voice. 'What's happened?'

My reply was faltering but I told him. He listened, asking a question here and there.

He was very calm. 'Are you sure he's dead?'

In my mind's eye I saw the body. The blood. Saw again the spasmodic jerking of the legs and hands slowing and stilling. 'Yes.'

He breathed hard, asked for the exact location of the body then told me to go home, not to stop anywhere else, to go straight home and stay there until he or someone else arrived to take care of me.

'Don't talk to anyone. Don't do anything, do you understand?'

'Yes, Daddy.' I sniffed a few times. 'What are you going to do?'

'Never mind, it will be dealt with.'

God help me, I felt relief. My father was on the case. Everything would be fine. I was about to hang up when I thought of something else to say.

'Daddy?'

'What?'

'I'm sorry.'

Another harsh breath reached me from the city so far away. 'As am I, Alice, as am I.'

Whatever his reasons for warning me away from Gerry, in that moment I recognised that I should have listened. But the only perfect vision is hindsight, I suppose. We never spoke again about what measures he took to protect me, although given that the body was found at the foot of the dam, the assumption could be made that he had some people transport the body from where I had left it. I don't know who those people were – it may have been Lane himself, along with others. Perhaps even Danny McCall.

A man I didn't know, a quietly spoken, tall, sallow individual, turned up later that evening at my door, telling me he had been sent by my father, and asked to see what I had been wearing that day. He took my boots and clothes away in a

283

large canvas bag along with Gerry's duffel. He didn't give his name and I didn't ask for it. I never saw him again.

I was questioned by the police regarding the death. It was known that I was involved with Gerry, so naturally they came to see me. There were two detectives, both from Glasgow. The one who took the lead seemed to be an old-school policeman, brusque and suspicious.

He asked me about Gerry's mental state.

I told him I hadn't seen him since before he left for London.

His body had reeked of whisky, the Glasgow officer said. Was he a heavy drinker?

I had seen him hit the bottle quite enthusiastically, I lied.

We've spoken to others who say he never touched a drop.

In public – I lied again – but in private it was a different matter.

Why was that?

I said he told me he didn't like to lose control in front of other people.

So, why would he be up at the dam in the middle of the night, drunk as a skunk?

I said I had no idea. I said that the truth was, he and I had broken up. I said that it might be possible that he was drowning his sorrows. I said all this, and I hoped I was convincing. The officer smelled some sort of whisky-soaked rat and might have pursued me more rigorously, but his colleague steered him away. He was another man I had seen at my father's social functions.

I heard nothing further. Like any sudden or suspicious death in Scotland, it was reported to the Procurator Fiscal, but no further action was taken. Gerry's death was a tragic accident: a heartbroken man losing his footing and plunging to his death.

But I knew it wasn't an accident, and while I was relieved that no blame had attached to me, I knew then, as I know

now, that I should have come forward. But I didn't. I was scared, and I remained angry over Gerry's betrayal of my trust, over him not being the man I had thought he was. The stress of it all was unbearable, especially given I was carrying Gerry's child. When I told my father of my pregnancy, I expected him to finally snap and disown me, but he didn't. He remained very calm, very collected and he knew exactly what to do. He arranged everything. I was taken away for a few months, and my job was left open for me. The child was born in a private clinic on the continent and taken away from me immediately. An adoption was arranged. I wasn't even informed of the baby's sex. Nobody knew what had happened.

But I knew. And the guilt of my actions has been like a second shadow ever since.

I tried to make some sort of amends by taking on stories that nobody else would – rather like both of you, Ms McTaggart and Ms Connolly. I tried to use my position in the media and in society to make a difference.

Only once before did I consider making a clean breast of things. About Gerry. About the baby, who I never attempted to trace. My father, still around, still powerful, still as rich as Croesus, ordered me to remain silent, arguing that the fact that I'd had a child out of wedlock would have a detrimental effect on my career. I was adamant, however, that I had to purge myself.

And that was when I had my final encounter with the man known as John Lane. He came to my home one morning. It had been a few years since I'd seen him, but he hadn't changed a bit. He still had that supercilious sneer in his voice, still had coal-black hair. He had moved into the political arena by that time, forming SG, campaigning against any attempt to take Britain into what was then the Common Market, arguing against immigration, even speaking alongside Enoch Powell at political meetings. Like others of his kind, he had found a new target for his bile. He repeated my father's advice but in a way that left me under no illusions that, should I continue with my intention to go public, it would not be in my best interest. Reputations, he said, were at stake, including that of my father, who was backing him in his political aspirations. He did this in a quiet way, very understated, but I knew that it was not only our good names that he threatened, but our very lives.

I remained silent. Silent, but not idle. I worked quietly under the surface, beginning with the two men I'd seen with John Lane that first night.

My father is gone now, and Dennis is gone, and the dead care nothing for reputations, only the living. Even John Lane, or Jim McNair, has gone to whatever reward he deserved – if there is any justice, a fiery one. If there is such a place as Hell, then I feel sure I will join him there soon. He cannot be hurt with this story, but his legacy can be damaged. He was a man who proclaimed a love for Scotland, but he did not love Scotland. He was a man who said he spoke for decency, but he had none. He was a man who created a party that proclaimed solidarity with the Scottish people, but the only solidarity it had was with those men, like my father, who backed it.

I leave the attached documents to aid you. Perhaps with current technology the images can be enhanced sufficiently to be of some use and comparison made between McNair, as he was then, and Lane, as he became. Perhaps the list of names will also be of some assistance.

This may be too little, too late, but it is the best I can do. They say that our lives are made up of choices, both good and bad, and how we handle the outcome is what makes us what we are. I made poor choices sixty years ago and I stuck with them. Should this story ever reach the public then those choices will define me, no matter how many better ones I have made since.

So be it. I will go to my rest knowing that I finally did the right thing.

30

'He's not here yet,' Rebecca said as Bill pulled his car into the small car park off the A85.

'Unless he's parked somewhere else,' he said, ever suspicious.

'Is there somewhere else?'

He opened his door. 'There's always somewhere else if you want to be a sneaky bastard.'

He had rocketed up the A82 away from Glasgow and then along the Oban route because he had wanted to get to the meeting point ahead of the appointed time to ensure that nobody lay in wait. During the journey, Rebecca had ignored the scenery around Loch Lomond to race through Alice's final pages, the shock of Gerry's murder tingling her fingers, the sorrow mixed with rage at the cold and calm way Alice had handed over her child burning her gut. Rebecca had lost a baby through miscarriage. She had grieved. And yet Alice had given up her living, breathing baby without a qualm, without so much as a single thought as to what had happened to him or her. She couldn't bring herself to despise Alice Larkin because society looked on single mothers differently then, but she felt uneasy over the apparent lack of interest in how the child, her child, had turned out.

She had summarised the contents to Bill as he drove and, now parked, he ducked into the back seat and produced a long raincoat that had seemed better days.

'So, this murder that never was . . .' he began as he shouldered himself into it.

'Was one she committed,' Rebecca completed. 'But it was never investigated as a murder.'

He walked round the rear of the car, his right arm held a little stiffly as he thrust his hand into the coat pocket. With his other hand, he threw her an aerosol spray. 'Give your face and hands a spray with this. The midges will be out in force today.'

She sprayed the liquid onto one hand, rubbed her palms together and smeared it over her face, being careful not to get any in her eyes, then worked more into her hands before dropping the can in her pocket.

'So, all this is . . . what?' Bill continued as they walked towards the gate that would take them to the castle. 'Her way of purging herself of guilt?'

'Her way of finally making things right, perhaps,' Rebecca ventured. 'Of letting the world know the truth about a death that has been forgotten.'

'I'm sure Gerry Rawlings' kids haven't forgotten. They could still be around, after all, maybe even his wife.'

That had occurred to Rebecca, too. She would have to make efforts to trace them. 'They deserve to know what happened.'

'Or is it better that they think it was an accident rather than a killing that went unpunished?'

'You don't think they deserve to know the truth?'

'Sometimes knowing the truth isn't all it's cracked up to be.'

She fell silent. She knew the truth, or at least part of it, about her father and Dalgliesh. Was she the better for knowing it? That her father, who she had always thought was the most logical, reasonable, caring and just man she had ever met, had beaten someone so badly that he'd needed the help of a man like Dalgliesh to avoid prosecution? But Brian Hancock had been a child molester, so did that make a difference? The answer, she knew, was no. John Connolly used to tell her that there were rules to civilised behaviour which had to be followed even if you disagreed with them. He had broken those rules, even though his job was to enforce them. It didn't matter that he was wracked with guilt afterwards, or that he regretted it, or that he wept over his actions.

And yet . . .

The victim had been a monster. He had deserved the beating.

Hadn't he?

Rebecca didn't know the answer to that. She would never know the answer to that.

They walked under the bridge that carried the West Highland Line to Oban and emerged onto a grassy plain with a path leading to ruined Kilchurn Castle, standing at the edge of the grey, cheerless waters of the loch like an ancient warrior in threadbare armour. The fine weather had been left behind in Glasgow, Scotland's climate being mercurial, for here the clouds had closed in to obscure the bulk of Ben Cruachan and drape across the hilltops like a curtain. Somewhere in the heart of that mountain lay the cavern carved out by the likes of Gerry Rawlings and Duncan Saunders. Rebecca scanned the slopes for the dam but couldn't see it. A breeze swooped down the valley to ripple the water before lifting again to waft around them. She pulled her thin jacket tighter, wishing she had checked the weather before setting out. Bill's long overcoat may have been a bit worn, but it was thick enough to ward off the damp chill hanging in the air.

'Good, he's not here,' he said as they neared the castle and headed towards the entrance. 'You keep an eye open for him coming while I check inside.'

After Bill went in, Rebecca stood shivering and she pulled her jacket closer, holding her shoulder bag across her stomach as if she feared it would be blown away. She had been stunned by Alice's revelation and was still struggling to come to terms with it. This was a woman who had been a legend in the media. She had achieved what her idols had, beating men at their own game, but all the while had hidden the fact that she was a murderer. And had abandoned her child. Sandra had said that the guilt and fear over what he had done might have contributed to John Connolly's death. How much of her guilt and fear had also eaten away at Alice Larkin?

Bill emerged again. 'All clear.'

'You always take precautions, don't you?'

He gazed across the grassland. 'Always be prepared, that's the Boy Scout motto.' He noticed her shudder a little as she hunched into her jacket. 'Cold?'

'Yeah.'

'You should've worn a warmer coat.'

'I didn't know it was going to be cold here.'

His gaze remained fixed on the grassland and path that led from the car park. 'It's Scotland – you have to assume it's going to be cold. Or wet. Or both. And dress accordingly.'

'Come on, it was warm and sunny in Glasgow, and between there and here it changed. How did you know that would happen?'

'Us Highlanders have a feel for these things that you Low-landers don't have. We can smell it, feel it in the air and hear it on the breeze.' He sniffed and thrust his hands in his pockets. 'Also, I checked the weather app on my phone this morning.'

'If you were a gentleman, you'd give a lady your coat,' she said.

He let this sink in for a moment. 'You're right,' he conceded. 'But being a gentleman is not something anyone has ever accused me of.' He suddenly became more erect, and his left hand appeared again as he jutted his chin towards the path. 'He's coming.'

Rebecca turned to see Dalgliesh's tall figure striding across the grassland, the collar of a smart brown coat pulled up. He'd also known the weather was going to turn chilly. She hated that kind of foresight, especially when it hadn't occurred to her. Or perhaps she just hated him. She tightened her grip on her bag, knowing that the brown envelope nestled within it. She was going to enjoy this.

Bill met him about six feet from Rebecca, ensuring nobody was trailing behind or taking a wider route to reach them, his right hand still in his pocket. 'You're alone, right?'

Dalgliesh's stare towards Rebecca wasn't as accusatory as it might be, as if he had perhaps expected her to be accompanied. 'I said I would be. You promised me you would be, too, Rebecca.'

She felt no guilt as she shrugged his comment aside.

'We're all alone in our own way,' Bill said philosophically, then jerked his left forefinger upwards a couple of times. 'Arms out.'

Dalgliesh took a half-step away, but his eyes crinkled. 'You plan to search me?'

'I plan to search you,' Bill confirmed, then repeated, 'Arms out.'

'What do you think I may have? Some kind of weapon?'

'No idea, but I'm not taking the chance. Arms. Out.'

With a half-smile, Dalgliesh extended his arms, standing like Jesus on the cross while Bill checked under his coat and in his pockets, pulling out a high-end phone and inspecting it.

'You're a cautious man,' Dalgliesh said, his arms still outstretched.

'It's the Boy Scout in me. You can put your arms down now, you're not the Messiah type, despite your complex.'

Dalgliesh squinted at him as he accepted the return of his phone. 'And you don't seem to be the Boy Scout type. Bob a Job, good deeds, that sort of thing.'

'You'd be surprised. I'm a dab hand at helping old ladies across the road.' Bill stepped away, looked to Rebecca. 'He's all yours.'

She didn't particularly want him, but she took him anyway. 'So, what did you want to tell me, Dalgliesh?'

He thrust his hands into his coat pockets and hunched down a little, his insouciant manner deserting him on being reminded of the purpose of this meeting.

'What I have to say is for you alone. If your bodyguard here could step out of earshot, I'd be grateful.'

Bill was unconcerned. 'I'll be right over here. You try anything, Dalgliesh, and I'll kick your arse into that loch.'

'Somehow I think that's not an idle threat.' Dalgliesh watched Bill take about a dozen paces further away before he took a couple of paces of his own towards the water's edge. Rebecca followed and waited as he stared towards a wooden walkway jutting into the loch.

'This isn't easy for me,' he began.

Rebecca didn't care how difficult it was for him.

'I don't quite know where to begin.' A quick, shamed smile flickered. 'I can't find the words.'

Rebecca would have noted the day that Finbar Dalgliesh couldn't find words in her diary, if she kept a diary. She continued to maintain her silence, believing it was better to let him get to whatever his point was without her usual barbs. Then she would confront him with what was in her bag.

Dalgliesh glanced back at Bill, as if checking he wasn't listening, then took a deep breath. 'Very well, best to just get this out there.' He breathed deeply once. 'I must urge you again to drop this story, Rebecca.'

She tutted. 'Dear God, Dalgliesh, did you bring me all the way here just to say that again? If I didn't listen before, what makes you think I'll listen now?'

'Because I'm going to tell you why and I need you to listen. You are in this over your head, so far over your head that even your cautious friend over there can't protect you.' He jerked his thumb towards Bill, who was switching his gaze between them and scanning the area around them. 'Look what happened to Ms McTaggart.'

'You admit that you were responsible?'

'I wasn't responsible. I didn't want that. I never wanted that.'

'You expect me to believe you?'

'Whether you believe me or not, it's the truth.'

'Okay, let's assume you're telling the truth. So, if not you, who *was* responsible for Elspeth's accident?'

'You met him, in Byres Road and again outside the City Halls.'

Rebecca understood immediately. 'Julian? But he works for you.'

'No, he doesn't work for me. Not directly.'

'He's not your minder?'

Dalgliesh considered this for a moment. 'Yes, but not in the way you mean.'

Rebecca, recalling her impression the man had been monitoring everything Dalgliesh said, feigned surprise. 'So, who does he work for? Directly?'

Dalgliesh exhaled, shrugged his coat higher upon his neck, thrust his hands into his pockets. Rebecca had never seen him this uncomfortable. He had been telling the truth when he said this wasn't easy for him. His right hand reappeared, and he stared at it for a moment, as if expecting to see something there, before he looked to Bill. 'Your friend doesn't happen to smoke, does he?'

'No,' she replied.

Dalgliesh looked at his hand again, turning it over. 'I gave it up years ago but at times like this I wish I hadn't. A cigarette was often a comfort, even if only to give you something to do with your hands.'

'Dalgliesh, this isn't exactly what I would call just coming right out with it,' Rebecca said, barely keeping her impatience under control. 'Who does Julian work for, and why are they so intent on not letting this story out? Is Julian New Dawn?'

'New Dawn,' he said. 'My God, you really do think they're the bogeymen, don't you?'

This was new, Rebecca thought. 'So, you admit New Dawn exists? That's a first.'

'It's not the force you think it is, but yes, it exists.'

'And it's the enforcement arm of SG, right?'

'No, it's separate.'

'But still linked.'

He hesitated before answering. 'In a way. They will do things with which my party can have no connection. Spioraid nan Gáidtheal is a political party, Rebecca, not a terrorist organisation.'

She resisted the impulse to debate that, instead asking again, 'Who does Julian work for?'

His hand was thrust back in his pocket once more, his expression indecisive. In her experience of Dalgliesh, limited though it was, she had never seen him like this. He was always so sure of himself, but today his confidence had deserted him. He didn't say anything as he stared again out at the water.

'It's beautiful here when the sun shines, but I think I prefer it this way.' He nodded across the loch. 'There's a spot over there where you can take photographs of the castle and the mountain, did you know that? It's quite something.'

'For God's sake, Dalgliesh, will you get to the point? Who does Julian work for?'

He slumped a little, as if resigned to some kind of fate. He turned back. 'Perhaps this was a bad idea. I'm sorry.'

He turned to head back towards the path, but Rebecca stepped in front of him.

'Okay, if you won't tell me what you know, then let me tell you what I know,' she said, her hand already in her bag and withdrawing the manila envelope, to wave it like a fan. 'This is Alice Larkin's account of what happened back in 1964. It makes for interesting reading. It talks about John Lane, the artist previously known as Jim McNair. It talks about two deaths, both murders, although both declared accidents. There are a lot of accidents around this story.'

He gave her a dismissive shake of the head. 'That's a subjective account, purely personal. It carries little more weight than rumour.'

'No, it's more than that,' Rebecca said, slipping the copies of the photographs free from the envelope, finding the best of them, and holding it out before her like a shield. 'That's your man John Lane, the founder of SG. Or rather, that's Jim McNair, Blackshirt thug and enforcer for the British Union of Fascists.'

She had bluffed about this during their last meeting and was glad that it had paid off. Dalgliesh moved closer to study the photograph, but the impression she had was that his scrutiny was merely for show. He knew who John Lane had once been. 'They're not terribly clear.'

'Not yet, but modern technology can clean them up and then compare them with other photographs of John Lane.'

Dalgliesh straightened, shrugged, but he held himself stiffly, as if tensing himself.

'Okay, he's dead – and, frankly, good riddance – so it won't make a bit of difference to him,' she said. 'The dead have no need for reputations, right? But it would weaken SG's claim to be the patriotic, moral heart of Scotland, wouldn't it? Their founder being nothing more than a thug? And one perhaps responsible for at least one death?' She threw that in, even though she couldn't prove he had anything to do with what happened to Howie Rose. She slipped the list of names out from under the photographic sheets. 'But there's more. Alice has been busy over the years. She's been digging through the dark, just like the men who dug out that mountain over there, and like them she's sifted through a lot of dirt. These are the names of men who were connected to Lane in the early days. She started off with two men she saw him with, two men who knew her father. Backers, financiers. The men who hide behind the cheque books of shell companies and enable vile and vapid front men and women to spew bile in print and on TV and in parliament. Present company not excepted.'

Dalgliesh didn't make any effort to look at the names, probably because he already knew them.

'And there you hit upon the nub of the issue, Rebecca,' he said. 'That's why I'm here, talking to you now. Spioraid was never the threat, but that list could be.'

'Why? Most of them are probably dead.'

'But their progeny aren't, and those who followed them aren't. And they don't like any attention drawn to what they have done and continue to do.'

Rebecca understood now that this was what he had come to tell her, for whatever reason. 'And what do they do?'

He smiled with a little grunt. 'Put simply, they run the world.' He reconsidered. 'Or at least, do what they can to profit from those who run the world.'

Her laugh was short and dismissive. 'Yeah, right.'

'You can scoff if you wish, but there have always been groups of very powerful, very rich people who wish to manipulate governments for their own ends. The saying that money makes the world go round may not be entirely true, but it certainly gives it a push.'

Rebecca studied the names again. A laugh rippled her throat. 'What are you selling me here, Dalgliesh – Spectre?'

'That is exactly the reaction they want from people. Disbelief is their camouflage. Apathy is their weapon.'

'Okay, so why would men like this wish to back SG? It's not exactly ever going to get into power, is it? I mean, you've done a good job of making it slightly more palatable, I'll give you that, but let's be honest, you guys will never get the keys to Holyrood.'

She expected him to deny that, but he didn't.

'Spioraid was a means of achieving a certain instability. You have to remember, these people care nothing for politics or ideals. They only care about profit, and they support – you might say, infiltrate – all parties. The groundswell of support for independence, the backlash against immigration, even pulling out of long-established unions – these things can all be destabilising, upsetting the status quo. And such instability can be taken advantage of.'

'In what way?'

'There is money in chaos, in fear. A natural disaster, war, civil unrest, epidemic, pandemic, economic instability. All can be used to turn a coin, and these people have centuries of experience at turning coin. Also, there is money in power, and should my party have ever reached government, or even just gained enough seats to influence a ruling party, then we could have helped ensure that these men and women continue to reap the rewards by controlling policy.'

She studied the list again. They did appear to be rich men. Rich men hedging their bets by backing all and sundry on the off-chance that it might some day pay off. 'And their sons and daughters carry on that tradition?'

'And their grandchildren, because membership is inherited by those offspring who display the necessary acumen and ruthlessness. But there have been other recruits in recent years, men who are from the shadows beneath the shadows, if you like.'

'Like who?'

Dalgliesh hesitated, obviously considering how far he should go.

'You asked to see me, Dalgliesh,' Rebecca prompted, 'and I think this is what you wanted to tell me, so don't wimp out now.'

Dalgliesh reached a decision. 'Have you heard of the Nikoladze brothers?'

Something that might have been fear fluttered in Rebecca's stomach and she glanced towards Bill. They had both been living under the threat of reprisals following a story on the island of Stoirm some years before that had involved the brothers – who were on the face of it respectable businessmen, but under that face were crooks. It was only the fact that other people knew what they knew that had protected her and Bill then. But it hadn't helped the local landowner, Lord Henry Stuart, who had been working with them. He had died the previous year when his car's brakes failed on a country road in France. Another accident, she realised.

'They, and others like them, now dominate the group,' Dalgliesh said. 'That makes it infinitely more dangerous than ever before.'

Rebecca didn't want to let him know that she was concerned. 'Why are you telling me all this?'

'Because I've had enough. I want out.'

'You don't believe in your message now?'

'I do. I believe we have to stem the tide of immigration. I believe we have to purify our country. I believe society is in danger from too much political correctness and pandering to a sub-strata of minorities and deviants.'

Purify the country. Rebecca felt something bitter burn in the back of her throat. 'That really is bollocks.'

He shrugged it away. 'However, the fact is, I also believe in law and order, and I cannot in all good conscience continue with a cause that has been used by gangsters like the Nikoladzes for their own gain.'

'Rather than you using it for your gain, right?'

'Nevertheless, I intend to vanish. Right away, in fact. Which is why I wanted to meet here. I said I liked the symmetry, but really, I'm heading north. I have a friend whose boat is moored at Oban and I'm leaving the country. But I stress once more that you are best not to pursue this story any further.'

'And if I do, then these people will do what? Put out a contract on me?'

'These people have proved they will not hesitate to remove anyone they feel might endanger them, or embarrass them, or even just turn the weakest of spotlights onto them. They don't like any attention, which is why they hide behind pressure groups, focus groups, research groups, lobbying groups.'

'If they're so powerful then what are they afraid of? They can use their influence to get any story stopped.'

'You said it yourself, they can't control social media. All it takes is someone with an internet connection for reputations to be destroyed. A story can gain so much traction that the mainstream media simply cannot ignore it. And should they learn of that list of names, even at this remove of time, they might grow twitchy.' He paused again. 'But I don't believe they are the immediate threat. I don't believe they are fully aware of what's been going on. The attack on Ms McTaggart was sloppy – and, believe me, they don't do sloppy. I suspect that Julian has been acting without their knowledge.'

'Why?'

'He has a personal stake in this.'

'What sort of personal stake?'

'John Lane was his grandfather. I told you this group can be a family affair.'

In that moment she realised why the portrait shot of John Lane had seemed slightly familiar. He and his grandson shared certain features, not enough to make it immediately apparent, but enough to kindle faint recognition.

'He's very proud of his grandfather, and the actions he has taken were both a warning to you and an attempt to prevent those above him from seeing him as a weak link,' Dalgliesh said. 'They don't like weak links, and if they come to believe that his family connections could result in adverse publicity, even on social media, then there might be another accident.'

'So, Julian arranged what happened to Elspeth?'

'I believe he was actually in the car.'

The bastard, she thought.

'Dalgliesh, I'm not buying this conspiracy bollocks,' she said, 'but this is something I can get behind. You're saying Julian wanted to stop us from going further? That's what you meant about reputations and legacies?'

'That's about the size . . . of . . . it.'

Dalgliesh faltered as his attention focused on something over Rebecca's shoulder. She turned and saw Bill stiffening. She followed his gaze to the unmistakeable figure of Julian walking towards them, flanked by two other men of similar girth, one wearing an army camouflage jacket, the other a brown leather bomber jacket.

'You bastard,' Bill said as he strode quickly towards them.

Dalgliesh paled. 'I didn't tell them, I give you my word,'

'Then how did they know you—' Bill stopped. 'Your phone. They have a tracker on your phone.'

Dalgliesh reached into his pocket and pulled out his mobile. He stared at it as if he had just been told that it had cheated on him with another man's phone.

Bill glared at him for a moment, then returned his attention to the three men closing in. 'Becks, when I tell you, run like fuck for the castle.'

31

As he and his two friends came to a halt about ten feet away, Julian's eyes flicked over both Rebecca and Sawyer before settling on Dalgliesh. 'You better come with us, Finbar.'

Dalgliesh was nervous and took a step away from them, glancing anxiously over his shoulder towards the castle, as if Bill's advice also applied to him. Rebecca didn't know why she had been told to take refuge there, but she knew she wouldn't do it. She wouldn't leave him here alone with these three. She wasn't sure what she could do when push came to punch, but she could keep at least one of them busy. She tried to remember what she had been taught in her self-defence classes and prayed muscle memory would kick in.

'Maybe he doesn't want to go with you, *Julian*,' Bill said, pronouncing the name like some kind of insult.

The emphasis wasn't lost on Julian. 'And who's going to stop us, old man? You?'

'Aye,' said Bill, his lips thinning into a mirthless smile. 'I may be older than you, *Julian*, but I reckon I could take three shitehawks like you without losing breath.'

There it was again, that mocking tone. Bill was deliberately goading him, trying to provoke anger, because an angry man is a careless man and mistakes can be capitalised upon. Rebecca's father told her that, and she now knew his own anger had led to a mistake.

Despite the hard look in his eyes, Julian didn't appear to be angry, though his smile seemed rather fixed as he flicked a finger at the man in the camouflage jacket, who peeled the front back to reveal a gun tucked in his waistband. Rebecca was no armaments expert, but it looked like the kind of automatic she'd seen on TV and even if it wasn't, it didn't matter a damn because whether it was an automatic, a revolver or a bloody flintlock it could still put a hole in a person and, frankly, she didn't find that an appealing thought. She couldn't help herself; she took an involuntary step towards the small door to the castle, her heart hammering harder than ever before.

Bill Sawyer didn't even flinch. 'That supposed to scare me?'

Julian stepped closer, his head cocked as he scrutinised Bill's face. 'I think it's working, old man. You're hiding it well, I'll give you that, but you're scared. And you should be because we're not messing around here.'

One corner of Bill's mouth lifted. 'It's a bit direct for you, isn't it? I thought you and your mates preferred the accidentally-on-purpose approach.'

'You've no fucking idea what we are capable of, old man.' Julian turned towards Dalgliesh, who was edging away, as if he could escape round the side of the castle. 'Where you going, Finbar?'

Dalgliesh stopped but didn't reply.

'You really shouldn't have slipped away from me, Finbar. That sort of thing makes me suspicious, you know? Makes me think you've been talking out of turn with this pair, and that means you need to explain yourself to some people.' Julian gestured with one hand. 'So, let's go.'

'You think we're going to let you take him?' Rebecca said, grateful that her voice was even, despite her stomach flipping like a child on a trampoline.

Julian gave her a long look up and down. 'You do see the gun, right? I mean, you do know it doesn't shoot blanks?'

'You're not going to shoot us,' she said, with a confidence she really didn't feel.

That seemed to amuse Julian a great deal. 'We're not?'

'No, you're not. Accidents are one thing, but shooting someone is too direct. People like you don't come at things head-on like that, it's all oblique angles.'

Julian seemed on the verge of laughter and his two mates stared at Rebecca as if she had just declared that the Earth was flat, the moon landings were faked and the government practised mind control with gas in vapour trails. Actually, they probably believed all three anyway. The important thing was, their attention was on her, and Bill was taking small, slow steps towards them.

'As I said before,' Julian said, 'you have no fucking clue what we can or will do.'

He was obviously a well brought-up lad, because when he swore he pronounced the 'g'.

'I know that you're not very good at whatever it is you do.' Rebecca's words wavered a little. She swallowed hard, forced her voice to settle. 'First, you let Finbar here slip away from you – that's really shoddy work there, Julian – but you also messed up with Elspeth.' Curiosity narrowed his eyes slightly, so she added, 'You do know she's still alive and talking?'

He obviously didn't. 'So?'

'So, she saw who was driving that car and can identify him.'

He was totally focused on her now, trying to gauge whether she was bluffing. She swallowed again, hoping to dislodge the lump of fear forming in her throat. She kept her eyes away from Bill, who was still edging closer to Julian. Instead, she checked the other two men to ensure she had their attention, too. There was no reaction from Camouflage Jacket, whose fingers rested on the butt of the weapon. It was Bomber Jacket's expression that was interesting. His mouth had opened slightly, and he sported a frown. Dalgliesh had told her that

304

Julian had been in the car, but so had this guy, she suspected, and he was worried. Good, she thought, I hope it gives you stomach ulcers and that they start to bleed. She moved slightly to her right to draw their eyes even further away from Bill.

'And guess what?' she said, warming to her thought process but still deeply concerned by her proximity to that bloody gun. 'That description fits you and this guy here.' She jerked a finger towards Bomber Jacket, who immediately shot Julian a look that wasn't exactly panicked, but it wasn't far off. 'Mind you, it could have been either one because their sort is interchangeable, I find. They're like Tweedledum and Tweedledummer.'

It wouldn't do any harm to give them both a little scare. The main thing was that nobody paid attention to Bill.

'She couldn't have seen nothing,' said Bomber Jacket. 'That cow went down like a sack of spuds.'

'Shut up, dick,' said Julian from the corner of his mouth. Rebecca couldn't tell if that was his name.

'I'm telling you, Jules, there's no way she could have seen us, you saw it yourself. She didn't know what hit her.'

Julian whirled on him. 'For fuck's sake, shut your mouth. Can you not see she's bluffing?'

'Here's the way I see it, Julian,' said Rebecca, still inching to her right, bringing her closer to the man with the gun, which was not something she particularly relished but she managed to maintain a conversational tone – which might not have impressed them but it seriously impressed her. They had to believe she was totally in control, very sure of herself. There's nothing more compelling than confidence, even when your guts are broiling. Her rage at what these men had done to Elspeth fuelled her, however. 'You loved your dear, dead grandad, I get that, I really do. And when you learned that we were on the story, you didn't like it, so decided to put a stop to it. You had no idea how much we already knew, but you took action without the go-ahead from Dalgliesh—'

'I don't need his go-ahead.'

So, old Finbar had told the truth, in that regard at least. Wonders would never cease. 'But you needed someone's go-ahead, and you didn't bother getting it. You went ahead without permission. You would have come after me as well, eventually. Maybe Alice, too, but she's on the way out anyway.'

His lip curled. 'Yeah, that bitch, getting all holy. Bloody cheek, after what she's done. She killed a guy, covered it up. Abandoned her child. And she thinks she's better than us.'

'Your dear, dead grandad told you about that, right?'

'Yeah, he told me about that. He was the one who dragged that guy's body up that hill and pitched it over the side of the dam. He said he enjoyed listening to it hit the bottom.'

'I'm sure he did,' Rebecca said, covering her shudder by thrusting her hands into her jacket pockets as if to ward off the cold. She wasn't cold now, far from it. Sweat had broken out on her back and forehead. 'There was no love lost between Jim McNair and Gerry Rawlings. You do know your grandad's real name, right?'

'His name was John Lane,' Julian insisted. 'You're talking shite.'

So, either Grandad didn't tell his devoted grandson everything, or Julian was sticking to the legend. 'Maybe, but time and a few wee record checks will tell. Reputations and legacies. That's what this is all about, right? You know he was a fake.'

That brought a grim little tightening to Julian's lips. 'I don't give a fuck. You'll not be checking anything.'

She presented him with a smile she really didn't feel. 'My God, you really don't see the world as it actually is, do you? Do you think we've not already shared what we know with others?' That ploy had worked before, no reason why it shouldn't this time. The gun was still a worry, though. She forced herself not to look at it and kept her attention firmly

306

on Julian. 'And don't forget that Elspeth has fingered you. I'll bet even now the police are looking for you. I mean, I'm sure you were with Dalgliesh when he was interviewed, so they'll clock her description of the men in the car pretty smartish, and it's only a wee step to link you with your dear, dead grandad.'

'Stop calling him that.'

'What, dear, dead grandad? It's all true, isn't it? You hold him dear, he's your grandad and he's as dead as Dalgliesh's election hopes once all this comes out. And it's coming out, Julian, no matter what you do today.'

Julian's teeth worked at the inside of his mouth as he weighed up Rebecca's words.

'You've screwed up, Julian,' she pressed. 'You've over-stretched without thinking it through and what's more you've dropped this pair right in it, too. And Dalgliesh has told us all about your bosses.'

Julian shot a glance at Dalgliesh that was so sharp it didn't need a gun. Rebecca didn't care about Dalgliesh – she only cared about keeping them occupied while Bill edged closer, so carefully, so imperceptibly, it was like ultra-slow motion.

'From what he's told us, I don't think they'll be hyper chuffed with you Julian and, by extension, your mates here. You know them better than me, what do you think they'll do? A rap on the knuckles, or a wrap in a carpet and dropped off a high bridge?'

Julian simmered but Bomber Jacket was clearly suffering some internal distress. He hopped from one foot to the other.

'Julian, we need to think about this,' he said, his eyes darting around as if looking for the nearest convenience.

'She's bluffing,' Julian insisted, but this time doubt coloured his words.

'I don't know,' said Camouflage Guy, his accent Liverpudlian, his tone easy. 'She sounds as if she knows what she's talking about.'

307

'Then put a bullet in her, and you won't need to listen to her anymore.' When Camouflage Guy hesitated, Julian said, 'What you waiting for? Go on, it's not your first time.'

That wasn't what Rebecca wanted to hear. When the gunman's eyes turned to her, she saw the coldness that lived there. His fingers tapped the butt of the automatic. Shit, she thought, this guy is really considering it. She wondered if she'd have time to dive out of the way. She wondered if he might miss at that range. She wondered if that was only possible in films, like shooting out the tyres of a speeding car. She wondered a lot of things while he seemed to mull over the concept of putting a bullet into her.

It must only have been a second or two, but it seemed like an eternity as everything around her froze. The whisper of the breeze stilled, the grass no longer rustled, the faint lap of the water halted. Then his gaze flicked back to Julian.

'Nah,' he said, 'I came here to scare them, not to waste them.'

'Fuck it,' Julian snarled, reaching out for the gun. 'I'll do it, then.'

Camouflage Guy stepped away, twisting his body and the weapon away from Julian's hand. Julian swore. Bill seized his chance. The baton he'd concealed up his right sleeve slid free and extended with a practised flick of his wrist and then swung with a powerful, assured stroke against Julian's shoulder. Julian yelped. Bomber Jacket jumped forward. Bill whipped the baton back, cracked him across the nose. Bomber Jacket howled, staggered backwards, his hands to his face, blood streaming through the fingers. Julian whirled, reaching out for Bill, but squealed as the baton arced back again, slamming with such force on his wrist that Rebecca was sure she heard something snap, but it may merely have been the sound of steel striking flesh. Julian stumbled, his other hand instinctively cradling his injured arm.

Camouflage Guy was surprised by the sudden action, but Rebecca shot forward, the midge spray she'd grasped in her pocket now in her left hand. She shot a burst of the chemical directly into his face and he swore as his fingers clawed at his burning eyes. Rebecca didn't waste any time with idle chit-chat. She swung her right foot directly between his legs, delivering a kick that would have had them roaring at Murrayfield. That stopped him with a strangled groan, and he tried to say something as his knees gave way. She plucked the gun from his waistband and threw it towards the water, then edged around him as Bomber Jacket recovered sufficiently to take an uncertain step towards Bill. She spritzed him, too. He screamed, stumbled backwards, and she followed, pulling back her elbow to drive the heel of her right hand into his nose. She had done that before and it had worked and now she did the same again, putting every ounce of strength she had into it, all the rage and fear and tension she had felt in the past few days. Then she hit him again. She was sure she heard something crunching, and more blood immediately erupted from both nostrils. He swayed backwards then went down.

Julian hadn't given up. He launched himself at Bill, knocking the baton away with his uninjured forearm, and they both tumbled to the earth in a tangle of arms and legs. Julian was younger and perhaps fitter, but he was debilitated by the two baton strikes and Bill capitalised on that. He'd lost his weapon as they rolled on the grass, but he managed to deliver a punch to Julian's face then grab his already injured wrist with his other hand and bend it back. Julian screamed and tried to writhe away, but Bill held firm, rising to his knees and really putting everything he had into it. He leaned closer to Julian, who was crying out in pain and doing what he could to snatch his arm free.

'This is for Elspeth, you fucker,' Bill snarled, then gave the wrist a ferocious twist. This time Rebecca was certain she heard something snap.

Julian rolled free and Bill stood up, his chest heaving with exertion. He looked at Bomber Jacket and Camouflage Guy, both on their knees. 'You okay?' he asked Rebecca.

'I took down two of them to your one,' she said, her voice trembling, her hands shaking and her legs threatening to give way.

He grinned. 'Yes, you did.'

'Nicely done,' said a voice that Rebecca recognised. She looked towards the castle entrance to see Detective Chief Inspector Val Roach smiling at them, two uniformed officers already rushing past her. A stocky man with long, thinning blond hair was by her side. Rebecca had seen him somewhere before. More men and women galloped across the grassland towards them and along the bank of the loch from the far side of the castle.

'You took your time making an appearance,' said Bill.

'We wanted to hear them implicate themselves a bit more,' she said, moving towards them and standing over the still squirming Julian, now weeping with the pain. 'Anyway, you seemed to have it all in hand.' She noticed the puzzled expression on Rebecca's face. 'Bill gave me the heads-up about this at stupid o'clock this morning. He disturbed my beauty sleep, but I thought it best that I be here.' Roach jerked her head towards the blond man heading straight for Dalgliesh. 'DCS Lonsdale was already on the job, though.'

Rebecca remembered where she had seen him before: a press conference in Inverness with the wife of a man murdered on Culloden battlefield. He'd angrily demanded it be halted when Elspeth asked one question too many. He was with Specialist Crimes, she later learned.

'Specialist Crimes have been after Dalgliesh and New Dawn for some time, as you know,' Roach said. 'So, when this opportunity arose, they mounted a very swift operation. I've got to say, I'm impressed.'

This was an *operation*, Rebecca thought. She was part of an operation. She could have been shot during an operation.

It dawned on her: Bill hadn't been checking the castle for an ambush, he'd been ensuring that Val was there.

She pointed at Camouflage Guy. 'That bastard had a gun! He could've shot us, for God's sake.'

Val hid a smile. 'That wasn't likely to happen.'

Rebecca was about to argue but Bill gave her a head shake. There was something more here to which she wasn't privy, but she was still annoyed.

'So, you put us in danger? And how the hell did you hear everything from in there?'

Roach removed an earpiece then jerked her head towards Lonsdale, who was fishing a tiny device from Dalgliesh's coat pocket. 'We heard every word. Specialist Crimes have lots of lovely toys to play with.'

Bill hadn't merely been frisking Dalgliesh – he'd managed to slip that small transmitter into his pocket. Dalgliesh stared at it for a second, then shot Bill a weary glance.

'But what if they hadn't confessed at all?' Rebecca asked Val.

'If anyone could get these people to fess up, it was you, I knew that. Although, I think some pretty fancy footwork will be needed to cover up the excessive force, Bill.'

Bill defended himself. 'If you'd appeared earlier, then it wouldn't have been necessary.'

'Judgement call,' said Roach.

Rebecca watched the plainclothes cops swarm around Bomber Jacket and Camouflage Guy, clamping plastic cuffs on their wrists. Julian nursed his injured arm with two burly cops standing over him. She had no idea where they had all hidden themselves, but as Bill had said, sneaky bastards always found a way.

Rebecca gave Dalgliesh another glance. He was like a still photograph, his face pale as he listened while Lonsdale spoke to him. 'What about him?' she asked.

Roach followed her gaze. 'We'll take him in. He'll get bail, I would imagine, but he's in trouble.'

'And the Nikoladze brothers?'

'Ah yes, I've had a pointed exchange of views with one of them before, and I'm sure DCS Lonsdale and his colleagues will have some questions for them, thanks to this.' Val jerked a thumb towards Julian. 'What's his name again?'

'Julian.'

'Really?' She studied him more carefully. 'Well, I would never have believed it. His pal over there with the bloody nose will almost certainly flap his gums energetically, I've seen his type before.' She stooped and picked up Bill's baton. 'This is highly illegal, Sergeant Sawyer.'

'I use it to keep down pests growing in the garden.'

Val's smile was tight as she pointed the baton in Julian's direction. 'Very effective with pests, I see.' She telescoped the baton back down. 'You came prepared.'

'It's the Boy Scout in me,' Bill said, even making it sound as if he'd never said it before.

'Did you have a woggle?'

'Of course, you couldn't be a proper Scout without one.'

Val handed the baton back to him. 'I do like a man with a woggle.'

Good God, Rebecca thought, they're flirting. She was as disturbed by that as she would be if she caught her mum kissing James. To cover up her disquiet over the thought of older people flirting and locking lips, she watched Dalgliesh being led away, his hands pinned behind him with ziplock ties. She took a few swift steps and asked the blond senior detective if she could have a few words with the detainee.

'Mr Dalgliesh is under arrest, miss,' he said, his accent Yorkshire.

'I realise that but—'

312

'I think we owe Rebecca that, DCS Lonsdale,' Roach said.

He looked from one woman to the other and puffed out his cheeks. 'Two minutes, no more.'

He had the good grace to step away but even so, Rebecca led Dalgliesh towards the castle. He waited for her to speak, his eyes accepting that for him the game was up.

'My father,' she said.

He waited.

'What did you expect from him in return for what you did?'

His smile was weary. 'I expected nothing from him.'

'Then why help him?'

He took his time before answering, his eyes ranging to the loch, as if visualising a time when he was something more than he became. 'Because sometimes being a good man isn't enough. Sometimes even good men need the help of someone like me.'

'And what did you get from it?'

He turned his eyes back at her. The weariness had been replaced by something else. Sadness, perhaps. Longing. 'Because there are times when someone like me needs to help good men.'

She accepted that. 'And Brian Hancock? He died.'

'I know.'

'Did you have something to do with that?'

'I don't have people killed, Rebecca.'

'But they die all the same.'

'Rebecca, death is the only certainty in life.' He gazed back across the water again. 'And when it comes, we can only hope that whatever comes after is better than this.'

32

Elspeth seemed stuck in the no man's land between the trees and the cloud, where she could hear Julie's voice.

Come back to me, Elspeth, I need you . . .

'You have to choose.'

Her mother still hovered what seemed like yards away, but her voice sounded as if she was right beside her.

'How long have I been here?'

'You've always been here, dear. This is part of you, a part that has been lying in wait for this moment.'

The trees looked closer. She hadn't taken a single step, and yet she'd moved.

'You've decided,' her mother said.

'I haven't yet.'

'Yes, you have. Otherwise you wouldn't be moving.'

Elspeth studied the trees. Yes, they were closer. She glanced back to the cloud. Yes, it was diminishing.

'It will be fine, dear,' her mother assured her, now floating by her side. 'I'll be with you and, when her time comes, so will Julie.'

'Do you know when that will be?'

Her mother smiled. 'In no time, don't worry.'

Elspeth forced herself to come to a halt. 'Are you saying that she'll . . . ?'

'No, time is different here. It stretches and contracts and whirls around us. It has no meaning. Julie will live her life and then you will be reunited.'

They were moving again, almost at the edge of the trees. Her mother held out her hand.

'Take my hand, darling,' she said. 'There's nothing to be frightened of.'

For the first time in forty years, Elspeth took her mother's hand and was once again a little girl. She looked down at her legs, saw they no longer touched the grass. She took a last, long look behind her, but the cloud was already evaporating as if the sun was burning it away, and Julie's voice faded along with it until all that was left was the faint echo of her pleas on a wind that caressed the grass and hung on the branches.

She looked ahead again and let her mother guide her.

Together, they merged with the sunbeams.

33

The sun filtered through breaks in the cloud to dapple the waters of Loch Ness as they said their final goodbyes. It was a small gathering. Julie walked ahead, carrying the little box with Elspeth's ashes, Chaz and Alan behind her. Rebecca held Stephen's hand, followed by Bill Sawyer and Val Roach.

The main service had been held over a week before and had been well attended by other friends, acquaintances and Julie's relatives because Elspeth had none apart from her ex-husband, who was also there. There was also a scribble of journalists and ex-journalists – those who had worked with and for her, those who had learned from her, those with whom she had fought. The people she had helped, the people she had loved, the work she had done, all these were Elspeth's legacy. Elspeth had been respected. She would be missed.

Leo Cross made the trip up from London, which was good of him. He hadn't told Rebecca what he planned to do regarding the documentary. She assumed it would go ahead as too much money had already been spent and he had an interview with Elspeth in the can. Anything else he needed, Rebecca could provide, and she would do so willingly.

Alice's story was another matter. There was something there, and Rebecca would have to work on it. But Alice was dead. Any further questions would have to be answered in another way, and Rebecca wasn't sure how to go about it. But that was a problem for another day.

Val Roach had filled Rebecca in on what had occurred after the arrests at Loch Awe.

Julian and Bomber Jacket had been remanded in custody because they had previous, she explained.

Rebecca had asked about Camouflage Guy and Roach had smiled.

'You're not his favourite person,' she said. 'His eyes are still stinging, not to mention his voice being an octave or two higher.'

'My heart bleeds.'

'He's a police officer,' Roach said, making Rebecca's head jerk up. Roach shrugged. 'Undercover, on secondment from Liverpool. You know Specialist Crimes have had an eye on New Dawn for some time. This isn't the first time they've had someone with them, you'll remember.'

Rebecca remembered. That undercover had ended up dead. Others, too. That story was the subject of the documentary.

'So, Counter-Terrorism brought in a Detective Sergeant from Merseyside. I won't tell you his name, for obvious reasons. That's why he didn't shoot you and Bill, and also why it was comparatively easy to have the operation sanctioned when he tipped us off that Julian had skulduggery in mind. The possibility that we might lift Dalgliesh and have the means to break up New Dawn was too good to miss.'

She remembered the cold look in the man's eyes. 'The undercover guy played his part well.'

'That's his job,' said Roach.

Rebecca let that go. 'And what about Dalgliesh?'

'Bailed.'

'He's free?'

'For now. He'll go down for something, though, don't worry.'

'If he doesn't leg it.'

'That's his choice.'

317

'And what about his claim about the men pulling all the strings?'

Roach wrinkled her nose. 'I tend to think it's a fantasy, all a bit conspiracy theory. Julian's keeping his mouth shut, but his mate is singing us a three-act opera, not that he knows anything beyond Julian. New Dawn is toast, though. He can tell us about what they've been up to. Threats, assaults, bomb-making, extortion, even some drug-dealing. They've been very naughty boys.'

'And what about the Nikoladze brothers?'

'There's nothing at all linking them to any part of it. There never is with those guys. That's if they're involved in the first place. It's just Dalgliesh's word, and a good lawyer would argue that he was trying to save his own skin by offering up some bigger fish to fry.'

'So, they'll get away with it?'

Roach sighed. 'Looks like it.'

'Again.'

'Yeah. But that's the way of it with these guys. They have so many buffers between them and the actual wrongdoing that they're insulated. That and friends in high places.'

Rebecca replayed the conversation in her mind as they stood by the water's edge, her hand still in Stephen's. She was grateful for the tactility, but there was guilt there, too. She hadn't treated him at all well. She'd not called him nearly as often as she should have. She hadn't kept him in the loop because she didn't want him to rush to her side, which he would have done, all men seeing themselves as Sir Galahad. She hadn't attended his parents' dinner and he was all right with it, but she wasn't. Despite knowing that she shouldn't, despite vowing to do better only a few months before, she had put her work ahead of him. Yes, what had happened to Elspeth made it personal, but that was no excuse and she knew it. She thought of James, of how he was willing to step

318

back from his own business to be with her mother, how he cancelled his day in order to take her to see his uncle. That was a level of commitment she wasn't sure she possessed.

She eased her hand from Stephen's grip to step to Julie's side. She looked back at the faces before her. Elspeth's friends. Her friends.

'I think we all know Elspeth would have hated this,' she said, and there was a ripple of laughter. 'You know what she would have said: "Bloody well get on with it and stop faffing about." Well, Elspeth, if you're listening then I'm sorry, we're about to faff big time.'

Another laugh. Rebecca saw Chaz smile. They had discussed the tone of this little speech and decided that it should not be maudlin. She had checked with Julie, and she'd agreed. Elspeth didn't do maudlin.

'Elspeth was many things to those of us here. Partner' – she nodded to Julie, who managed a slight smile, but the tears weren't far away – 'boss, mentor, friend.' She looked at Chaz and Alan. 'And quite often a bloody pain in the backside.'

'Oh yeah,' Roach said, eliciting her own laugh.

'She did many things well. As a reporter, she was top of the range. As an editor, she was the best. As a boss, my boss, she was wise and supportive, but tough when she needed to be. As a partner, I'm sure Julie will agree, she was problematic. Stubborn, cantankerous, sometimes downright crabbit.'

She looked to Julie, whose tears had freed themselves and were trickling down her cheek.

'But she loved you, Julie. She loved us all, in her way – even you, Val, though you were often at odds.'

Roach tilted her head slightly and blinked. Good God, was she about to cry?

Rebecca moved on. 'Maybe not you, Bill.'

'Don't you kid yourself. If she didn't have Julie, she'd've been away with me in a flash,' he said, his smile fond.

Roach quickly wiped her cheek with the back of her hand. 'Now who's kidding himself.'

Rebecca and the others laughed along with them. This would be the tone Elspeth would want, even though they had never discussed it.

Rebecca let the laughs subside, her own smile sliding away. 'But she's gone now and there is a giant Elspeth-sized hole in our lives. It will never be filled. It will always be there. And now and again, we will do or say or see something and we'll think, Elspeth would have loved that. Or, more likely, Elspeth would have hated that.'

'True,' Alan said.

'And sometimes, maybe in a street or in a corridor that we once walked with her, we'll hear the tap of her cane and hear her laugh and complain.'

They fell silent, as if they were all listening for that tap, that laugh, that complaint. But all they heard was the wind in the trees and the birds in the branches and the slap of the water on pebbles.

'So, we'll say our final goodbye to the woman who was our friend, our boss, our partner. We'll say goodbye and let her rest in the waters of the loch she loved and hope that one day soon she manages to find the creature she insisted didn't exist, even though she would stand on this very spot watching for it.'

Julie began to unfold the top of the box, her hands shaking. Rebecca helped her, then stepped back.

'Goodbye, Elspeth. Thanks for everything.' Rebecca felt her voice break a little. She was going to lose it. 'We'll miss you so very much, but we know that wherever you are, whatever else you're doing, you're giving someone a hard time over not being allowed to smoke.'

She stepped back to let Julie move closer to the water. Julie stared into the box for a moment and mouthed a few words that Rebecca didn't catch, and she was glad because they weren't for her ears. Then she hefted the box to allow the ashes to be caught by the breeze and carried a little way over the water.

And in that moment, just as the dust that had once been her friend took flight, Rebecca heard, thought she heard, a voice. It was the merest of whispers, a trick of the wind, a figment of her imagination, a longing perhaps, but it was Elspeth's voice.

Be happy.

And then it was gone as the fragments fell away or were borne on the soft draught to somewhere beyond.

Epilogue

To the casual observer walking past the immaculate car parked in the neat, respectable street, they were just two people talking, with one beginning to unwrap a bag from a high street baker.

Mike looked at Pat. 'You know I don't like you eating in the motor.'

'I do know you don't like me eating in the motor. You've told me many times that you don't like me eating in the motor, but here I am, about to eat in the motor.'

Mike sighed. 'I've just had it valeted. You can eat off these floors, so you can.'

'It's okay,' Pat said, revealing the bridie, 'I'll eat it out the bag, thanks.'

'See, if you spread crumbs, I'll no be best pleased.'

'I'll no spread crumbs.'

'It's a bridie, how the hell you no gonna spread crumbs?'

'I'll eat it in the bag.'

'That doesnae work.'

'Don't worry, I'm a professional.'

Mike gave up trying to reason with his partner. He didn't know why he bothered anyway – they had been together for years, both professionally and personally, and in the myriad of similar conversations he had won few. One day, he'd make his argument and it would be accepted. The law of averages, he supposed. From the corner of his eye, he saw some flaky pastry drop off to land on Pat's lap, from where it was scraped off with one hand. And so it begins, Mike thought. He could vacuum them up himself later, he supposed, but that wasn't the point.

Deciding to change the subject because he knew he was onto a loser, Mike stared across the road at the door to the elegant flats. 'So, what's this, then? Straight-up removal, accident or what?'

Pat chewed on the meat pasty, sprayed particles when answering. 'It's not a straight-up removal.'

Mike tried hard to ignore the food spatter. 'How come we never get easy jobs anymore?'

'Because we're the best, and the best always get the most difficult jobs.'

'Mebbe, but now and again I'd like to have a straight removal. A bullet to the head and walk away. Jobs like this give me heartburn.'

'Quit moaning, that's why we get the big bucks. Helps you pay for all the car valeting.' A sizeable chunk of meat fell away to the floor. Mike watched it go, feeling his heart sink with it. Pat had the decency to look ashamed. 'Sorry.'

Mike gave his partner a long stare. There were people in this world who would have wilted under that stare, but not Pat, who simply gave him an apologetic smile, then bent over to find the offending morsel, spilling more crumbs in the process.

'Leave it, for God's sake. You're just making it worse.'

Pat straightened and glanced through the windscreen. 'Here we go.'

Mike forgot the food particles and watched their target exit the flats and climb into a waiting taxi. He turned the ignition. 'We got a timetable for this?'

'Next few days would be good.'

'So, we just follow and wait for our chance?'

Pat wrapped up the remains of the food and dropped it in the pocket of the door. 'Aye.'

The taxi pulled away, followed by Mike's car.

Finbar Dalgliesh had no idea his days were numbered.

Author's note and acknowledgements

Using the Cruachan (Hollow Mountain) project as a backdrop to some sort of storyline has been with me since I included a brief account of the hydro work in a little book comprised of stories and facts about Scotland. Once I began the Rebecca Connolly series I knew that at some point she'd be involved in something concerning the scheme. The difficulty was that the time period would necessitate a dual timeline, the early 1960s and the present day. It was author Denzil Meyrick who suggested looking at the earlier events through the eyes of a Rebecca counterpart, and I'm grateful to him because that allowed me to examine the project and the world as it was while also progressing Rebecca's own story in the present day. (Denzil will now be demanding a cut of my royalties, of course. I'll stick a postal order for £2.65 in the mail.)

There are many books and articles about the Cruachan Project and the wider Highland hydro scheme. I've only used this astonishing feat of engineering as a background, because this book is not about the scheme as such, so anyone interested in discovering more could do no better than turning to *Cruachan* by Marian Pallister (Birlinn, 2015).

Similarly, more information on the 43 Group can be found in *The 43 Group: Battling with Mosley's Blackshirts* by Morrison Beckman (The History Press, 2013). Both of these, and others, were my research tools. Naturally, any errors of fact are mine.

Also, let me stress that all characters, and in particular the murder described here, are figments of my imagination.

And now to the thank-yous, for no author achieves any kind of success on their own. If I forget anyone, please forgive me.

First to the readers, reviewers, librarians, booksellers and festival organisers who have supported the series from the outset. We need you all, more than ever in these tough times.

To Hugh Andrew of Polygon for greenlighting the series in the first place and to editors Alison Rae and Craig Hillsley for taking whatever state the text is in when I submit it and turning it into something readable. Also, the rest of the Polygon team for their hard work.

To Jo Bell, my agent, for always being in my corner and calming me down when I make something that is nowhere near a crisis into a drama.

To author buddies Caro Ramsay, Michael J. Malone, Gordon Brown, Mark Leggatt, Theresa Talbot and the aforementioned Mr Meyrick, who are always on hand for advice and help.

Many thanks to Jim McNair, who in the 2022 Children in Read appeal, successfully bid for a dedicated copy of one of my books. He also won the chance to have his name used as a character in this very book. I assure readers that he is nothing like the Jim McNair described here! Thank you, Jim, for your generosity.

Finally, to Sarah Frame.

Just because.